WHEN WE
WERE YOUNG

WHEN WE WERE YOUNG

JACLYN GOLDIS

FOREVER
New York   Boston

Copyright © 2021 by Jaclyn Goldis
Reading group guide copyright © 2021 by Jaclyn Goldis and Hachette Book Group, Inc.

Cover design by Daniela Medina. Cover photographs © Getty Images. Cover copyright © 2021 by Hachette Book Group, Inc.

Forever
Hachette Book Group
1290 Avenue of the Americas, New York, NY 10104
read-forever.com
twitter.com/readforeverpub

First Trade Paperback Edition: February 2021

Forever is an imprint of Grand Central Publishing. The Forever name and logo are trademarks of Hachette Book Group, Inc.

The publisher is not responsible for websites (or their content) that are not owned by the publisher.

The Hachette Speakers Bureau provides a wide range of authors for speaking events. To find out more, go to www.hachettespeakersbureau.com or call (866) 376-6591.

Library of Congress Control Number: 2020946453

ISBNs: 978-1-5387-1929-9 (trade paperback); 978-1-5387-1930-5 (ebook)

Printed in the United States of America

LSC-C

Printing 1, 2020

To my grandmothers, Libby Newman
and Khana Vinarskaya

All language is a longing for home.

—Rumi

WHEN WE WERE YOUNG

chapter one
Joey

corfu
2004

It was all because they went to the fancy Taverna Salto for the one-year anniversary of their first date.

They nearly opted for something more casual, a picnic in their meadow by the Old Fortress. Why didn't Joey just insist on the picnic?

But nope, she and Leo set off to celebrate at Taverna Salto, with its distant location from the apartment building by the sea where both their families lived. Corfu Town was awash with its rusty, evening glow when, about halfway to the taverna, Joey paused by an arched stone Venetian colonnade.

"My feet are killing me," she admitted, gazing down at her new espadrilles that were imprisoning her toes.

"Didn't someone tell you to wear comfy shoes?" Leo's green eyes had a laugh inside them.

"I wanted to wear my new ones. But you were right. Next anniversary, you pick my shoes."

"Just a little farther, Jonesey."

"FYI, another mile is not *just a little farther*. I think I'll go barefoot."

Leo's mouth feigned a pucker, like she'd said she was going to lick the floor of an airplane bathroom. He wore flip-flops even in nice hotel rooms. But he knew Joey hated wearing shoes, especially, somehow, on Corfu. Corfu was for flitting barefoot down cobblestone streets.

"If you must, I'll be on glass patrol."

"You're good to me, Winn."

Joey kicked off her espadrilles. She felt tipsy from their earlier aperitifs, and she also felt very happy, that sometimes elusive sense of finding a home in her own skin. She'd always felt that home-ness with Leo though, ever since they were ten and their families met in the stairwell of their common apartment building. Over successive summers vacationing on Corfu, their separate families had intertwined like one. Joey and Leo were nineteen now, but she'd loved him from the first moment they'd met.

Leo smiled at Joey, a smile that said *I like being good to you* and *I like all the weird things about you*.

At Taverna Salto, the maître d' greeted them each with a handshake. He led them to a table at the edge of a terrace bordered in lush trellises. Beneath a grass-green awning, a local string quartet was playing a set with emotive violin work. Leo pulled out Joey's chair. Joey felt very grown-up arranging her napkin on her lap as Leo circled the table to his seat—and that was when his eyes took on a strange, startled look.

"We have to go! *Now!*" Leo practically leaped back to Joey's side. He yanked on her arm, pulling her up with such force that it shot pain through her shoulder socket.

"Wha…huh?" Joey's feet tripped over each other to

balance. Her napkin slipped to the ground. She twisted to gaze back, but Leo whipped her around. "Leo? What the hell?"

On Leo's warpath toward the entrance, they nearly barreled into a waiter. He thrust his water pitcher over his head, sending some of it sloshing out onto Joey's shirt.

"Leo? *Leo!*"

The maître d' scurried after them, calling, "Sir? Madam?"

But Leo didn't speak, just kept his tight grip on Joey's arm, propelling her along. She glanced behind uncertainly at one point, only catching a blurred sliver of an awning before Leo jerked her forward. Joey's veins went Popsicle-cold. Her feet shuffled along robotically, the shock of it all churning in her head.

After Leo pulled them around a corner, Joey finally shook herself from his grip. Shook herself back to life. "Leo, seriously! What are you doing?"

Everything quieted, but it was a loud quiet—roaring in Joey's ears. Night had cloaked the island and sent most of its inhabitants to sleep, leaving behind the pristine aura of a deserted movie set. Leo rubbed his forehead, his eyes unreadable.

"Leo, talk to me. What was that?"

"Nothing." But his gaze bounced from the fuchsia bougainvillea adorning a balcony to a cat lolling at the mouth of a moonlit garden—anywhere but at her.

"Seriously, Leo?"

"I don't know!" he shouted, and she staggered back. He'd never yelled at her before. Never treated her with anything but care.

"I just didn't like the menu," he said, softer. "Leave it, okay, Joey?" He never called her Joey either. Only Jonesey or Jones or sometimes J.

"Leo, come on. Please tell me the truth. Don't invent something about the menu."

"I have a headache. That's all. You're blowing this out of proportion. Can we just be quiet for a bit? Go home?"

After some time, Joey heard herself say in a weird, foreign voice, "Okay." Then Leo took her hand, and Joey let him squeeze away her questions.

The next morning, he broke up with her. Broke her heart. Broke her.

And she never saw him again.

chapter two

Joey

florida

2019

"Thanks for coming, darling! The clickey thingie keeps getting lost." Joey's grandmother ushered her into her glacial foyer, a startling contrast to the thick heat endemic to August in South Florida.

"Joey, have a look at my new orchids. Can you believe they're fake? They look expensive, don't they?"

G walked toward the orchid pots, her rose chiffon dress twirling around her calves clad in pantyhose, her auburn wig laced with faint raspberry highlights in a fresh fluff around her tiny head.

"Wow, they really do." Joey glanced at her phone, half expecting to see a text from Leo saying *Just kidding, I'm not coming to Delray to see you after all.*

But nope. Only her David Hockney screensaver stared back at her. Joey's eyes blurred with the blues of the iconic swimming pool. So apparently Leo Winn was still coming to town. It was unbelievably surreal.

Mere minutes prior, Joey had been driving over to her

grandmother's condo along the highway that straddled the ocean, completely carefree, or as carefree as a bride can be twelve days before her wedding. Her phone had rung, identifying an unknown number. Joey never answered calls from unknown numbers—the introvert in her required time to prepare. But maybe it had been the wind whipping her hair, the contentment she'd felt. At thirty-four, life had finally slotted into place. She'd been happy, and apparently happy people answered unknown numbers. Joey had nearly swerved off A1A when she'd heard Leo's unmistakable voice.

Leo, who'd broken up with Joey out of the blue the morning after their botched one-year anniversary dinner on Corfu. They hadn't spoken to or seen each other in the fifteen years since. But now he'd heard about Joey's wedding from his parents, and he was flying over from Europe with something important to tell her beforehand that, no, he couldn't just say over the phone.

"You look beautiful, G. How was your birthday dinner with your friends?" Joey kissed G's cheek—soft, with wrinkles in a swirl like a cyclone.

"Oh, it was nice, darling. I had the salmon. It was a little dry, but they did it with some nice mushrooms, and Doris had dolphin. Can you imagine? Dolphin, they're serving now at the clubhouse."

"That can't be right. Dolphin's an endangered species."

"Do you think I'd make it up? Dolphin—right there on the plate."

"Of course I don't think you'd make it up. Dolphin! Who knew?"

The TV in the living room blared with an outburst from a Hallmark movie, the volume its usual senior-citizen high.

Joey was struck by a melancholic image of G in her house all alone, watching other people get saccharine happy endings. And somehow that made Joey think of herself, in the months after Leo broke up with her, sitting on that sad brown couch in her off-campus apartment, watching *Sex and the City* reruns. Leo's mom used to watch them on a loop in their Corfu apartment, and it had made Joey feel pathetically closer to him to adopt the habit.

While she'd watched, she'd eaten Cinnamon Toast Crunch from the sole bowl she owned, that received the tiniest rinse between cereal meals, meaning the same crusted-up pieces adhered eternally to its sides. She'd dyed her hair dark then, an almost blue-black that in hindsight only served to enhance her deepening under-eye circles. In the throes of her Dark Ages, Joey had hardly ever answered her phone. She'd certainly not gotten beneath anyone to get over Leo, as her girlfriends had advocated. She'd basically only left the apartment to go to an occasional class or to the supermarket, to stock up on her three essentials: cereal, milk, and cookie dough.

The memory vacuumed up Joey's breath. "I can't stay long, G, so let me help you with your mouse."

G frowned. "My mouse?"

"The clickey thingie. It's called a mouse. Remember?"

"I thought it was a moose."

"It's a mouse."

G pulled out her phone in its pink glitter case and jabbed at her screen. "I'll make a note of that. Okay, darling, let me just dash to the bathroom, and then you'll help me find that mouse. Maybe the darn thing will answer to cheese. I have cheddar."

As G laughed her melodious laugh and slipped into the

powder room, Joey's heart thumped in unison with the tock from the grandfather clock.

I need to see you, Jonesey.

That's not a good idea, Leo. I'm getting married in twelve days.

What he'd responded kept cycling around her head.

I know. That's why I'm coming. Please, Jonesey, you need to hear this. I have to tell you why I really broke up with you.

Taverna Salto. Leo's eyes shading over, like he'd seen something. But what? For years, Joey had relived the way he'd pulled her from the taverna, analyzing it so exhaustively that the CIA would have been impressed. She'd conjured secret lovers and fanciful conspiracies before shifting focus to herself, trying to figure out which part or parts of her hadn't been good enough to make Leo stay with her. Finally, Joey's best friend of twenty years, Siya, who'd occupied a front-row seat to Joey's breakdown, laid down some harsh truth. *Jo, you need to let go of the restaurant. Leo's a textbook commitment-phobe, and you deserve someone who sees your amazingness.*

Joey considered spilling all to Siya as soon as she left G's. But Siya had married her first boyfriend, whom she'd met at age thirteen. She'd never so much as poked a toe into twenty-first-century dating. And she adored Joey's fiancé; Siya had captained Team Grant from the start. Bottom line: If Joey were to call her best friend like she now longed to, there was little chance Siya would say, *Sure, meet Leo, it will be harmless closure.*

But Joey needed to confide in someone about Leo's call. She should tell Grant. Of course she should. But she couldn't yet fathom it. Not because she was about to embark on some affair or had lingering feelings for Leo—that was laughably off base. She adored Grant. Period, end of story. Only, Grant knew that Leo was her Big Ex, and Joey suspected he'd be more than a little wary at her agreeing to meet Leo right before their wedding.

It's just, wouldn't most people grab an ex-boyfriend's attempt at closure, however long after the relationship it came? Everyone stalked their exes a little. That was basically the whole point of social media.

Joey thumbed to her Facebook app, typed in *L*, and immediately the search box filled him in. Leo Winn. God, Leo fucking Winn. Joey clicked on his latest picture, from three years prior. She stared at the picture as if for the first time, although it was not her first look over the years, or second, or if she was being honest, even hundredth.

It was Leo sitting on a boat with an easy smile, like the world was his, like a natural magnet for good things. His hair still hovered between blond and brown but it had that hipster vibe, the top middle flicked up, the sides shorn. His biceps were bulkier, and his face had more freckles these days. Joey peered closer, trying to deduce things in his eyes. *Are you actually coming? Do I even want you to?*

Oh, to hell with the lies she liked to tell herself.

I want you to come. I only wish that I didn't.

⌣

"Okay, Joey, let's trap the mouse!"

Joey followed G to her office, past cupboards teeming with old doilies and handkerchiefs, items that meant various things to various people seventy or eighty years ago. G was from the Holocaust equivalent of the Depression era; all overflow got boxed up and relegated to a closet overrun with a lifetime of forgotten semi-treasures. The office was no different, tchotchkes on all surfaces, with an antique secretary's desk against the wall, framed by bay windows overlooking the neighboring condo. Tricycles and playhouses now littered its overgrown lawn, but once Joey's father had lived next door. There he'd fallen in love with Joey's then-teenage mother, who was always twirling in roller skates.

"See." G indicated the mouse on its pad. "Where did the clickey thingie go?"

The screen was on Facebook. How had her grandmother figured out Facebook? And why? But Joey didn't have the energy to pry. She jiggled the mouse. "The mouse is right here."

"But I want to find something on the Facebook. And every time I go to that box, the clickamajig disappears."

"You mean the arrow?" Joey hovered the arrow over the search box and clicked.

"That's all? You did it?"

"Sometimes the arrow drifts off screen so you can't see it. You just have to jiggle."

"Jiggle it. I see." Her grandmother wrote it in her notes. "You're just brilliant, darling. Oh, this has helped me out so much."

"Of course, G. I'm still really impressed you've joined the computer age." G wasn't just her grandmother but also one of Joey's main confidantes—the reason, in fact, why Joey had moved back to Florida. As she waded further into her as yet single, childless, career-floundering thirties, it was strangely harder to endure her grandmother's ascension through her nineties.

"It was time. Doris says there's far more to conquer. Something called Instaham. It turned her into a deer, I think. She said her skin never looked so luminous."

"Instagram." Joey smiled. "We'll do stories together, for sure, but can we save the lesson for next time? I need to sketch tonight." The lie filled her with guilt, but Joey had to get out of there. Go to her favorite beach. Dip in the sea. Get out of her head.

"Okay, dear. But have some strawberries first, how about it?"

"I wish I could stay for strawberries, but I can't today."

G cocked her head. She had a keen sixth sense for trouble, always trying to ferret out the illness she suspected you were keeping from her. Just earlier on the phone, Joey had coughed, and G had accused her of having bronchitis when really Joey had just choked a bit on her smoothie. "You aren't having those panic attacks again, are you, Joey?"

"I'm not." Joey swallowed hard. "I promise."

G's forehead released some of its ripples. "Thank God. We don't want to go back there, no siree! I'm so excited for your wedding, darling. My robe's all ready to go." G had gotten it specially made for when they'd be getting ready pre-ceremony, with GRANDMAMA OF THE BRIDE in Swarovski crystals on the back. "And Grant is just wonderful. Any new moles that pop up, he said I can call him. Any moles at all!"

Joey bit back a smile. G's name had been lighting up Grant's screen with increasing regularity. What Joey was to G's computer illiteracy, dermatologist Grant was now to G's rapid detection of new moles.

"He's the best," Joey said, and gripped the evil eye charm in her dress pocket.

Grant was the best. Really, really.

"Good luck on your sketching, love. I'm so proud of you." The lies were thick in Joey's stomach now, lodged there like cement. "And we'll do the miracle face masks again before the wedding?"

"Definitely."

For G's birthday present, Joey had splurged on a treatment that yielded baby-soft feet after sloughing off all the old skin, along with a Botox-in-a-jar face mask. Since leaving her legal career on the precipice of partnership, Joey hadn't so much as purchased a new eye shadow—a striking contrast with her ten years in Manhattan, where she'd frequented Barneys like others did bodegas. But G deserved a special present. They'd tried the face mask after G's birthday party, and G had pooh-poohed its actually working until after, when she'd exclaimed that she looked seventy again.

As Joey slipped on her nude studded sandals, G put an oval, cherry-red fingernail on the glass overlay of a picture of Joey's grandfather. "He was a beautiful boy, wasn't he, Grandfather?"

"Yeah. He was." Although unwritten, the photo's time line was plain: It was her grandfather BA. Before Auschwitz. He wore a little cap and a pensive stare. Joey had to look away. That picture only ever reminded her of the evil that had come for him after.

"'Night, G. I love you." Joey squeezed her grandmother's shoulders, but G was lost in the picture and didn't answer.

Joey opened the door to a tidal wave of heat. She had a thought: *I could tell Leo I'm not meeting him.* But it was a thought almost humorous in its futility.

Just by answering his call, Joey knew she'd pushed a boulder that was already rolling away from her, impossible to catch.

chapter three
Joey

florida

2019

The revolving door of Joey's high-rise blew her inside the white marbled lobby. The doorman's back was to the inky panorama of ocean that sprawled beyond A1A, his attention detained by an old man who took up far greater space in the world than his diminutive stance would suggest. As Joey recoiled at the blast of aircon on her post-sea skin, she caught snippets of conversation. She gleaned the following: A tree in a planter on a neighboring balcony had dangled its leaves against the armrest of the old man's chair; one of the leaves had dipped dangerously close to the old man's whiskey tumbler. *And who knows what kind of chemicals they feed that thing. I could have been poisoned!*

Joey hastened into the elevator. Her phone dinged with a call. She put a hand to her heart and slowly slid out her phone. But it was only her sister, Lily. Joey silenced the ringer.

She pressed the elevator button for the twelfth floor and rested against the elevator's citrine-lacquered side, imagining how Grant would laugh over the old man's latest tirade, the Episode of the Encroaching Tree. In their yearlong residency at Palmetto Towers, they'd witnessed a slew of poor doormen tasked with resolving various problems sparking the old man's outrage. There was the Episode of the Noisy Air, the Episode of the Boy Who Played Very Loud Video Games, and, Grant's favorite, the Episode of the Too-Gray New Hallway Carpet.

At the wedding invitation place, there'd been a pinch to Joey's knee. *But babe, is the wording too gray?*

But she didn't want to tell Grant about the Episode of the Encroaching Tree, not until she told him about Leo. She needed to tell him about Leo. Maybe she was making too big a deal of it. She'd already mentioned her boyfriend on Corfu, and Leo had contacted her wholly unprovoked. Grant would understand that Joey would need to see Leo and hear whatever he had to say that was apparently so important.

Wouldn't Grant understand?

The elevator dinged. Joey walked down the brightly lit hall atop the plush, too-gray carpet. She stood outside their apartment for some time, unable to force herself over the threshold.

In a spurt of courage, she swiveled her key and entered cold darkness. Flashes of moonlight illuminated the jumbled contents of the catchall on the entry hall table. It was intended to hold their keys—which Grant was constantly misplacing—but his were there, for once.

"Joey?" called Grant, light now trickling from beneath their bedroom door.

She popped into their bedroom. Grant glanced up from his phone with that light, glad look he always got just to see her.

"Hi, babe!" He was shirtless and wearing gray sweatshirt shorts, his dark hair doing something different from normal that she couldn't pinpoint. As he leaned over to kiss her, she could hear his favorite weatherman from the news app he favored, talking about South Florida's heat wave.

"Hi! I'll just shower, 'kay?"

"Sure."

She slipped into the bathroom, stripped, and stepped into the shower. Her hands roamed her skin, brushing sand as she went. It surprised her anew each return from the beach just how much sand managed to burrow into crevices. After Joey's shower, she toweled off, rough-dried her hair, and appraised herself in the mirror—her eyes sometimes light brown, sometimes hazel; her skin its late-summer caramel; her long chestnut hair with new pre-wedding ombré highlights; her lips with their little bow, her favorite feature; and on the unfortunate end, her ears that stuck out a little bit like Dumbo.

Leo's coming to town, she practiced, making her voice nonchalant. *It's not a big deal.*

Oh God, a giant arrow pointed to *it's a big freaking deal.*

Joey slipped into a purple lacy lingerie set Grant liked and crept to the bedroom. It was dark, the lamps now toggled off. She slid beneath the covers and felt his warmth first on the sheets. She couldn't go to him. Not before she told him.

"Babe—"

"You're so far away," he blurted.

She knew to go to Grant would weaken her resolve, but her body was its own beast. It folded like origami into its nook in his right shoulder.

"For Joey," he'd once said, "I'll drill a little plaque so no one takes your space."

"Just the right shoulder," she'd replied, savoring how cozy her head felt there. She liked the musky scent of his deodorant. "You can chop off your left shoulder and I'll live, but the right let's be careful about."

"How did it go?" asked Grant.

"How did what go?" asked Joey, startled.

"You said you were gonna sketch after G's?"

He ran his foot against hers, and she suddenly realized that she was capable of separating them, the two lives she'd begun to live today. The angel inside her head knocked against her skull to query what kind of person she wanted to be. But she was too tired, or too weak, to set the angel free.

"Oh. It was fine. I went to the beach, but I didn't get much sketching done."

"So you're saying I'm about to sleep in a sandbox."

Joey managed a laugh. "I did shower."

"Somehow I predict my back's still about to feel like sandpaper."

He was right. Someday someone had to teach her how to get the sand out. Maybe a YouTube video. "I'm sorry, babe."

"It's worth it for your art, Jo."

The dark made her dark. She might have been stronger in the light.

Joey ran a hand across Grant's stomach, searching for the part in the corner near his ribs with the tattoo of ocean waves, which she'd first set eyes upon only a year and a half prior. The memory hit her like medicine: Grant in that knotty man bun, soaring down a big wave off Batu Bolong, so fixed in concentration at the tricks he was turning that he didn't see her board careening at him.

She was finding herself post-legal-career. He was there for stress release after medical boards, purely for the surf and the smoothie bowls. After a short vacation romance, they'd parted, not thinking they'd see other again, but then only months later, both in their native Florida, they'd unexpectedly reunited. That was when Joey had first contemplated something real between them. She'd had so many situationships in the years after Leo, but after leaving law, Joey had longed for something bigger. Something real. Maybe she'd finally believed she deserved it. She'd let herself accept so little after Leo because that was what she'd thought she was worth.

On one of their first dates in Florida, she'd straight-up asked Grant where things between them were going. To her surprise, he'd flipped it on her. Asked her what *she* wanted.

And Joey had said without pretense, *Everything. I want everything. And I understand if that's not where you're at.*

And he'd said with zero hesitation, *I can do everything. I want to be with you, Joey. I want everything with you too.*

"So you know how I got drinks after work with your dad? He's stressed about his wedding speech." Grant rubbed the crease her waist made when she curled around him. He was the first man in so long—since Leo probably—who didn't make her tense up when he stroked her there. "He thinks your mom will overshadow him."

"She probably will." Joey laughed.

"Anyway, I think he likes me."

"He loves you." It was true. And Grant was Jewish too. Yep, she'd hit the jackpot.

Bea and Scott didn't really care about the Jewish factor. Jewish was her grandmother's non-negotiable. "I don't want to have to say this, Joey, but if you don't marry a Jew, I won't consider you my granddaughter anymore."

G had first said this phrase when Joey was seven. She remembered it because she'd come out of the pool, teeth chattering, and G had been holding a towel and looking at her funny.

Joey had said, "Okay, Grandmama. I'll marry a Jew." This had made her grandmother beam. She'd bought Joey a chocolate Popsicle.

Joey turned her head to the shadow of Grant's face. "I love you." She ran her fingers through his hair, but instead of its usual fluffy, it felt greasy, tacky. "Did you do something to your hair?"

"Oh."

"What is it?" She went for the light.

He swatted her hand before she could flick the switch. "I bought this shampoo. It's supposed to make it…thicker."

"Babe, there's nothing wrong with your hair." She'd seen him the other day, checking out his slightly receding hairline with a pocket mirror. She hadn't realized he'd gotten so sensitive about it.

"What hair? I'm losing it all. I don't want to look bald at our wedding." His hand froze mid-stroke, now warming her waist.

Joey snuggled into him. "I think…babe, are you having a groomzilla moment?"

Grant's laugh vibrated through her. "I should shower, huh?" he said.

"It's a bit of an oil spill up there."

"Okay. I will. But first, why don't you come here?"

"I'm right here."

It always thrilled her the way two heads connected in the dark. No fumbling. No straining. A pair of lips found their mate.

She would tell him tomorrow.

chapter four
Sarah

florida

2019

Sarah eased herself to a seat atop her powder-blue duvet and gripped her pantyhose at the waist. It had been a nice dinner with her friends, she thought. And Joey's visit had, as always, bolstered her spirits. In all, capping off a nice birthday week. But gosh, ninety-three. Ninety-three was incredibly old.

Sarah rolled her pantyhose down over hips that creaked as she walked, over knees diagnosed in new unpronounceable ailments each time she went to the doctor. On the TV on her dresser, two blond girls were bickering. Her pantyhose was nearly off now, dangling from one foot with its toenails painted navy blue. It was her manicurist's suggestion. Dark polish was in fashion these days, and at ninety-three it couldn't hurt to channel the young. But did it actually look young, or rather like someone had dropped a refrigerator on her toes?

The girls on TV appeared to reconcile. A man now approached them near a fence in a field. Sarah wished her volume went higher so she could hear the dialogue to figure out which of the blond girls was playing the best-friend role and which was the leading lady this leading man was eyeing. Then the thing Sarah had to do—tonight, if she could muster the courage—pressed upon her again.

She went to the bathroom and made her eyes squint so she couldn't see her nude reflection. She reached for her soft pink robe and wrapped it tightly around her waist. Then she widened her eyes just long enough to grapple for her wig, to remove both its clips. Sarah thought she could make out the man on TV saying, "I'd like that very much." Or maybe it was, "My lawyer will be in touch." Presumably the latter. Sarah knew how these Hallmark movies went. The man would be a developer, set to demolish the farm left to one of the blond girls as an inheritance from her estranged father. Before long, the farm would be saved and a fairy-tale love would unfold on the heels of a passionate kiss.

Actors didn't use tongues on Hallmark movies, Sarah had read somewhere. And one could tell.

Oh, it was all far simpler on TV.

Sarah started toward to the kitchen to give the counters a final wash. She did this every evening, prepare the house for morning. There had to be order in life, Sarah felt strongly. Routine. Otherwise one's mind wandered.

On the way to the kitchen, Sarah passed her display case, and her chest tightened. Sometimes she wished she could torch that thing—a past strapped to her like ballast. The worst were the mini statues perched so defiantly for over seventy years. There was one of Hades in white stone. Another of a surly-faced Grecian lady, a bust. Sarah called her Dagny. She couldn't remember when that nickname had arisen, whether she or Sam had coined it. The statutes had once belonged to Sam's mother. They'd survived the ransacking of Sam's childhood home after he and his family were taken to Auschwitz. Her own family's home hadn't experienced the same fortune. It had been fully appropriated, her past eradicated.

If only erasing the memories were that easy.

Sarah retrieved a sponge from the side of her sink. As she rubbed it across the marble, her eyes latched onto her rose-bushes. They were so pretty—bushes seemingly divided, some pink, some purple, but over time, Sarah thought they'd blended, the pink parts acquiring a purplish tint, the purple flowers now rimmed in pink.

Sarah had arrived in Delray seventy-three years before, because Sam had a far-removed cousin who lived in South Florida and secured the permissions they needed to immigrate. But despite living in America the vast majority of her life, Sarah still couldn't rid herself of Corfu's long shadow. This she knew even more assuredly given the letter that had arrived in the mail the week before.

Sarah set down the sponge and opened the drawer where she kept miscellaneous things. Carefully, she removed the letter from its envelope covered in foreign stamps and that familiar handwriting—a ghost in Greek cursive.

She took the letter to her computer and navigated to the Facebook using the clicker. She clicked on his picture again. She brought her eyes closer to the screen, closer still, until her forehead brushed the monitor. She stared into those eyes. Those startling green eyes.

Eventually, Sarah leaned back in her chair. She began to type.

Well, hello there, Milos. Hello. Here we are then. A lifetime later, and yet I would recognize you anywhere.

I was very surprised to get your letter last week. It arrived on a night I was going to see a movie with a girlfriend. She was calling me that night, Doris is her name, saying hurry up, and can you bring those caramel candies? This time I'd packed a box all for her so she wouldn't have to keep interrupting me during the best parts for a candy. But then I saw your letter hidden below my water bill. And I saw it was a Greek address. No one writes me from Greece. I held the letter in my hand for a very long time, and I thought about not opening it. You understand that, don't you, Milos? It's not about you, but that's a lie. It is about you. It's about so many other things too.

Oh, Milos. It's all so strange considering these things at the end of a life. At the end of a life you don't have anything to do besides put on another black outfit for another funeral and get annoyed at your friend who asks for caramel candies twenty times in a movie. You can lay down fully at the movies now. Has that come to Lefkada yet? A person could move into a movie theater here and sleep in such warmth and security.

But yes, your letter. You may be surprised to hear this, but I haven't spoken a word of Greek since I arrived in America. I was twenty when I came here. Now they say forty is the new twenty, eighty is the new forty. They want me to live forever, but it's all very tiring. At twenty, I felt so old. But I felt, this is my fresh start. Fresh starts can be deceiving though. I suspect you know something about that.

It gave me a deep pain to force the Greek back to read your letter. I said, just this once, I will do it. I saw your name on the outside: Milos Christakos, plain as day. But even before that, I knew it was you. I thought, what have you waited for? As much as it shames me, I did want to hear from you. Even after everything, yes I did.

Well, you know what you wrote. You wrote to locate you on the Facebook. That messaging is easier that way. Faster. You asked what has happened in my life. To tell you *ta panta*. Everything. You underlined that with a double line. *Ta panta*.

You wrote that you think of me. That you have always thought of me.

Is it true, Milos? It made me feel a lot of things I thought I was too tired to feel. And then I couldn't go to the movie. I just lay in my bed staring up at my ceiling, thinking about one thing you wrote. You asked for my forgiveness. You wrote that you know how much you hurt me, how much your actions destroyed me.

Well, they did.

You didn't mean to destroy me though. And you had help. They were the real destroyers. But can I forgive you? All I can do is give you my warm feelings. I don't know if I can forgive you, Milos. I want to forgive you. I've wanted my whole life to forgive many people and forget many people but ultimately I've come to understand that it's not up to me. This may sound strange, but it's actually up to a sad old lady who lives inside me. She can't forgive or forget. I can't forget either, Milos, but maybe I can soften her to forgive. I will see what influence I can have. She can be a stubborn mule, that old lady.

Oh Milos, I'm being silly. I am that old lady, of course.

The truth is, I've had a nice, full life. I was married to a good man, but he is long gone now. And I have a daughter. Just the one child. Bea. We have a complicated relationship. Complicated because I love her to the ends of the earth with no feelings of complication, whereas she loves me, it seems, with endless amounts of complication. I have two granddaughters too, and my three girls make up the whole of my world. I will tell you more, but first I am compelled to go back. There are so many things you don't know. And some things you do know, but you don't know to the core.

So I have to start way back at the beginning, Milos, don't you think?

chapter five

Sarah

corfu

1942

Every Sabbath morning, Sarah Batis watched the great big beard of Rabbi Iakov Nechama. As he stood on the *bimah*, his beard vibrated with the fervor of his prayers, igniting something in her heart. Sarah was at the grand Scuola Greca synagogue on Velissariou, in the women's partition, on the same bench on which she always sat with her best friend, Rachel.

Only Rachel was unusually late this morning.

As Sarah's gaze panned the crowd, searching for her friend, she noted the back of her own mother a row ahead, in her one nice black dress with rose corsage embroidery, eyes surely boring into her Mahzor Romania, allowing no distractions from her prayers. And then in the men's section, Sarah could make out her father's head, with its bushy red mop now torched by gray, and the raspberry curls of her little brother, Benjamin, beside him. Sarah listened to the recitation of the Shema, tapping on the wooden pew as September's potent sun streamed through the windows, casting hazy beams across the herringbone oak floor.

Soon the holidays would arrive. The Jewish quarter, the Evraiki, would be suffused with the solemn magic of a new year, and Rabbi Nechama would blow the special shofar made in the mountains of Epirus from a wild black ram.

As Rabbi Nechama's prayer reached a tremendous crescendo, Rachel slid beside Sarah, with another girl in tow who looked to be around their age, sixteen.

"My mother will kill me." Rachel retrieved a faded black prayer book and flipped it open. "Is she looking?"

"Not now," Sarah reassured her, spotting Rachel's mother, Roza, a few pews away. Anyway, she didn't know what Rachel was afraid of. Unlike Sarah's own mother, whose forehead summoned grooves at the most minor of infractions, Roza was lauded for her smile, trotted out at all occasions, even sometimes inappropriately at funerals, which she called celebrations.

Roza worked for the Jewish community, keeping up the synagogue and caring for the community's elder members at the old age home. The girls would often help her change bedpans and sweep the sanctuary or wash its windows. When they were younger, they used to play hide-and-seek across the temple grounds. Once, Sarah had hidden in the *aron* for the Torahs, and when she'd popped out, expecting Rachel, Roza had stood there instead. Sarah had feared Roza would scold her like her own mother surely would, but Roza had just tut-tutted and said in the future the *aron* for the Torahs wasn't a play spot.

"Who is she?" Sarah motioned to the girl beside Rachel who, like her friend, had straight black hair in plaits, but brown eyes to Rachel's green. She wore a dress nearly identical to Rachel's own, with a starched white collar and red plaid pattern.

"That's my cousin Stemma," Rachel whispered. "From Saloniki."

Stemma. It was a name for a daughter with many sisters before her. The name had its root in the Greek word *stamata*, meaning "to stop." Stop sending us daughters. Sarah already felt sorry for this Stemma, and she didn't even yet know her.

"*Yia sou*, Stemma," said Sarah. "Welcome to Kerkyra."

"*Yia sou*," Stemma said, but her eyes didn't match her lips when she spoke. She stared off at the *aron* on the synagogue's east wall.

"She's visiting?"

"No. She's here for...for a while, I guess."

"A while?" Sarah knew everything about Rachel, she'd thought, but not about this phantom cousin Stemma from Saloniki. Saloniki was on mainland Greece and home largely to Sephardic Jews, who had escaped Spain during Inquisition times. Whereas Sarah was a Romaniote Jew, whose ancestors had resided in Greece for millennia. The communities didn't often intermarry, although Rachel's parents had, her Romaniote father and Sephardic mother. It's why Roza's bourthetto was so delectable; the meal of little fishes in spicy red sauce was a Sephardic specialty.

"Stemma escaped." Rachel bit her lip. "She escaped from the Germans, who invaded Saloniki."

The Germans.

The congregants rose for the final prayer, and Sarah rose with them, or her feet did on their own, divorced from her head, because she felt utterly incapacitated by this information.

"And what about her parents?"

For what seemed like forever, Rachel didn't speak. There was just the deep, beautiful voice of Rabbi Nechama, but for the first time maybe in Sarah's life, his prayer didn't bolster her.

"Her mom died a few years ago, and her father was taken," Rachel finally whispered.

Sarah glanced over at Stemma, shorter than them, miniature really, when Sarah caught the whole of her. Stemma stood ramrod-straight like a statue, as if she belonged on a pedestal somewhere.

"Taken? How?"

"They made him convene at the square and beat him, and he had to do these humiliating exercises at gunpoint—"

"They beat him?" Sarah's heart thwacked her chest. "At gunpoint?"

Rachel nodded slowly. "Stemma has barely spoken since she arrived, but she finally told me the whole story this morning. That's why we were late. She said the Germans invaded a year and a half ago, and it's been terrible. First, the Jewish press was banned, and Jews weren't allowed into cafés."

"They were banned from cafés?" It wasn't like Sarah frequented cafés. Her family didn't have the money for a frivolous coffee or pastry, but she was friendly with Spyro, the owner of a café on Scholemvourgou Street, who sometimes slipped her a cheese bourekas when she visited her grandmother at the sanitorium next door.

"Yes. But then it got worse. They moved the Jews into a ghetto, by the rail tracks. Took their apartments, jewelry, everything. They had to wear yellow Jewish stars sewn to their clothing always. And the Germans destroyed a big

Jewish cemetery and took the gravestones for construction materials. And then Stemma's father was taken, to work. Her sisters' husbands were taken too. Then one night, the German officer boarding in their house got drunk and told Stemma and her sisters to leave before it was too late. Before they were deported. Stemma's sisters are all married and didn't want to leave their husbands. But they sent Stemma here. And she doesn't know what will become of them."

"That's horrible. Absolutely horrible." Sarah chewed on her nails. "I wish we could do something."

"Me too."

"At least we have the Italians, right?" They'd known the Italians for centuries on Corfu, from the Venetian era, and the Italians had re-conquered Corfu a few years prior. Bombs had rained down on the Jewish quarter, and Sarah and her family had fled to bomb shelters. But eventually life had carried on as normal.

"We have the Italians. Yes."

"So the Germans can't come here." Sarah balled her fists and willed Rachel to agree, vehemently so.

But instead her friend looked off vacantly toward the candelabra perched atop the bimah. "Sarah, now I'm afraid the Germans can come anywhere."

～

When services concluded, the men congregated around the bimah to drink coffee and ouzo. Sarah waded through the dispersing congregants toward her mother, kissing cousins and aunts and uncles along the way.

"Mama, I'm going to have lunch at Rachel's. She invited me earlier in the week."

Sarah saw her mother hesitate. It wasn't that she didn't like Roza, but her mother disapproved of Roza's marriage outside of the Romaniote community.

"You are not permitted to be with that Matathias." Matathias was Rachel's older brother, as handsome as his sister was beautiful, and he had never given Sarah a second glance. With her riotous red hair, Sarah certainly didn't meet the conventional Corfiot beauty standards.

Sarah groaned and gazed around, to be sure Matathias wasn't privy to this conversation. He'd probably laugh hysterically at the prospect. Anyway, she had her eye loosely on Solomon, her sweet, serious Romaniote school friend, who'd once pulled her from the barreling path of a donkey cart. His family happened to be the wealthiest Jews in Corfu. They owned half the real estate in town—an unimpeachable prospect for her mother. "There's absolutely nothing between me and Matathias."

"Be sure there isn't. You have plenty of cousins who are suitable marriage partners. You will marry a Romaniote Jew. That is your destiny."

"I know."

Her mother reached out to stroke Sarah's hair. "You are beautiful, Sarah. I want you to have everything good in life." Sarah allowed herself to savor it. Her mother didn't often say things like that, or touch her hair tenderly besides.

"I'm not as beautiful as you," Sarah said.

"Hush," said her mother, but Sarah noticed her mother didn't dispute it. Her mother was incontrovertibly beautiful. It was a fact of life. She wasn't that old, only thirty-six, with cheekbones chiseled like a Michelangelo statute, thick, shiny black hair, and blue eyes the turquoise of Garitsa Bay. Sarah's father always said that, whenever a customer complained about a garment he tailored, he imagined floating in a sea as blue as her mother's eyes and immediately calmed. Sarah too had eyes that blue, but she suspected her red hair negated their wiles.

"I'll see you at home, Mama." Sarah kissed her cheek and went to find Rachel. Her taste buds were activated for Roza's bourthetto.

On her way out, Sarah spotted her brother sitting on the floor in the corner, nose deep in Homer's *Odyssey*. Benjamin was only ten, six years her junior, but absolutely brilliant and with a book perpetually in hand. He was teased sometimes in the schoolyard of their Jewish school because of how ruddy his face got, implying a state of perpetual embarrassment, and for his hair, even more vibrant a red than Sarah's. Just this week, a boy had shoved him into a puddle when Benjamin was just sitting innocently on a rock with his book. Sarah hadn't witnessed it because girls finished school in the eighth grade. But when Benjamin had told Sarah about it, she'd marched over to the school, chased down that younger bully boy, and lifted him off his feet—yes she had—decreeing that Benjamin Batis shall be left alone. It had felt quite good to put that weaselly little monster in his place.

"*Latria mou.*" Benjamin looked up, and his whole face transmuted to a smile. That was how it was between them, their love simple and essential. They slept side by side on a cot, and sometimes their limbs entangled, and Sarah would wake disoriented for a moment, impossible to distinguish where she ended and her brother began.

"Are we going home now?" he asked.

"I'm going to Rachel's for lunch. I'll see you later."

"And then we'll walk to the sea?" It was a thing they did together, every Sabbath afternoon.

"We'll walk to the sea." Sarah touched the place where his hair met his forehead, sweaty now with the energy he expended reading, that thrill of imagining foreign worlds. He blew her a kiss—a thing he did only to her. He hadn't yet come to think of it as babyish, even if others observed. Sarah blew him a kiss in return.

Then she drifted through the crowd, searching for Rachel. She stepped outside to Solomou Square. It abutted their apartment buildings, which all huddled together slightly off kilter, like mini Towers of Pisa. The buildings' stucco was scorched in places from the bombings a few years prior, when Mussolini's Italians had invaded Corfu, but now the residue of war was blessedly faint. Outside the Sabbath, the cobblestone alleys making up the Jewish quarter abounded in stalls of fruit, vegetables, cloth, and silver, with streets so narrow that marketgoers hugged the walls when donkeys waddled by. Above the alleys, green shutters flung open from windows edged by flower boxes, with nosy aunts typically poking out and calling down below, where heated haggling and the clucking of hens resounded against the bustle.

But today the Evraiki was its charming Sabbath-quiet, with the exception of the wild dogs barking and cats mewing from all resting surfaces. As a child, Sarah had taken a liking to a cat and fed it bits of bread until one day it bit her, necessitating a painful shot. After that she didn't much like anything with teeth, other than humans.

Gazing northward, past the Evraiki, Sarah could make out a slice of mellow sea and Pontikonisi island beyond it, half a mile from shore. It was referred to as Mouse Island because of the white stone staircase shaped like a mouse's tail that wove through a tangle of cypress and olive trees, leading to a Byzantine chapel. Sarah had never visited the island, but her father always promised that one day they would take a boat and go.

Finally, Sarah spotted Rachel and Stemma leaning against a pillar across the square. She skipped over. "Shall we go to lunch?"

"Oh, Sarah, shoot. Solomon asked me to lunch today. I'm going to take Stemma too. I forgot to tell you." Rachel pulled a regretful face. She looked even prettier when upset, a fact Sarah suddenly resented. Jealousy was such a wretched emotion, because you wished you didn't feel it, at the same time you wished for a face that got even prettier when scrunched up—a face you certainly didn't have.

"Solomon asked you to lunch? But...you know I like him!"

Her friend's perfect half-moon eyebrows shot up as the sun danced in her windswept hair. "I thought that was ages ago. You know *I* like him."

If Sarah were to search herself, then of course she would admit she knew Rachel liked Solomon too. It was why the friends had avoided the topic, waiting for him to do the choosing. Well, he'd chosen, all right. And Sarah was surprised to find that the anger riling in her wasn't at her apparent rejection by her friend Solomon, but instead at the fact that Rachel was more beautiful and lucky.

"I didn't!" Sarah said. "And you should have told me. I planned to come to your lunch."

"Sarah, wait." Her friend reached for Sarah's arm, but Sarah shoved it away. She knew she was acting childishly but felt incapable of rewiring herself so quickly, to switch personae to Perfect Sarah, the one who didn't feel the ugly things she now felt.

Sarah stalked off, ignoring Rachel's pleas. She quickened

down Velissariou, aware only of the world inside her head. When she reached the sea, she turned left, a way she didn't often walk, muttering aloud about how much she hated Rachel and then how angry she was at herself. Rachel was a wonderful friend, and Sarah had treated her terribly. Why didn't she want her to be happy with Solomon, when really, if Sarah dug deep, she didn't even love Solomon? But she recognized that he was an eligible, nice, cute boy, and Sarah was enduring this crazy mental loop when she caught a glimpse of a fisherman, a boy she'd never seen before.

He was by the water, hauling teeming nets off his *kaiki*, wearing a navy cap, a white shirt, and tan trousers pushed up on bronzed calves—and Sarah could not breathe. She ducked behind the trunk of a cypress tree and watched as he joked with a couple older men. A donkey brayed, pulling a cart along the walk, and a few boys whooped at the shore before diving into the swell, but the noises barely blipped on Sarah's radar.

He wasn't Jewish, of course. For one, he was working on the Sabbath, and he had blond hair besides. Red hair was a rarity among Greek Jews, but blond a near impossibility. Sarah watched the boy toss the nets into his long *kaiki* boat painted sky blue. He stepped on in and put a hand gently on its side. Sarah could tell it was a thing in which he took great pride.

All of a sudden, the boy's attention was drawn to the sea. Sarah's eyes zoomed out so the boy no longer consumed the whole of her vision. A little girl was shrieking and pointing toward Mouse Island. Sarah crept closer to shore, startled to watch the boy whip off his shirt and dive into the sea, making fast, furious strokes. A crowd gathered amid murmurs and points. Sarah's heartbeat quickened as she searched the horizon. What was going on?

Finally, she saw the splashes of a struggle and something massive and hairy erupt from the surface. She strained to make it all out, as the blob of the boy wrestled with the creature. At last, joyful shouts resounded. Eventually, the boy emerged with a huge, black, shabby dog in his arms, whom he deposited at the little girl's feet. She threw herself atop the mass of wet fur, burying her face into his. Her parents must be rich, Sarah knew, to keep a dog as a pet.

Sarah watched the boy shrug off accolades, pat himself dry with a rag, button his shirt, and return to his fellow fishermen. And that was when she fell in love with him.

No, she didn't love him because he made her laugh or because he had striking eyes and soft hands. Those things were true, but she learned them later. She didn't have a choice. God didn't ask her if she wanted to love a non-Jewish boy from Lefkada who came to Corfu to try his luck for the season. To see if their fish were any better.

If Sarah had known then what she and this fisherman had in store, would she have run far? Would she have run home?

Seventy-some years later, Milos, and still, the answers to those questions elude me.

That was our beginning, but there is so much more to tell. Can you write me back in English? Maybe you can have someone translate. Please, I can't read more Greek. It makes me feel, well, unbearable. If you can't find a way to write in English, send me one of those little yellow faces the kids use these days. My granddaughter Joey, she's a girl, not a boy, it's short for Josephine—she helped me set up my computer so I could talk with you. She told me there is one face that means laughing and crying at the same time. Have you ever heard of anything so stupid, Milos? Back then we laughed and we cried, but only separate, didn't we? We laughed so hard and then I only cried.

I am tired now, Milos. I think I will go watch my rose-bushes.

I hope you are well. I hope you have been loved.

chapter six
Joey

florida

2019

Joey looped her sandals on her thumb and crossed the sand already scorching in the morning sun. She'd asked Leo to meet her at the pier at Lighthouse Point because it was private and far from Delray, minimizing the risk of encountering anyone she knew. The beach was vacant aside from an old man sculpting a sandcastle by the shore. Ahead, a lighthouse presided over a row of white-shuttered beach rentals. A silhouette hovered in the shadow of the lighthouse, near the end of the pier. Joey's body lurched like there was something it remembered.

"Leo," she whispered, covering her mouth with her hand. "Holy shit."

Joey walked slowly toward the pier, adjusting the half-tuck of her flowy white blouse into her burnt-orange high-waisted shorts. The man at the end of the pier turned. He tossed up a tennis ball, and Joey watched its trajectory, higher and higher until clapping back into his open palm.

"Hey, Jonesey." A smile unfurled on lips she once could map in her sleep.

Jonesey. The nickname traveled through her exquisitely slowly, dragging with it the bittersweet memory of its origin.

Joey stepped closer, farther down the pier, until she dead-ended into a chest, into arms, and something more than gravity swept her inside them.

⌒

"You look good, Jones." It sounded deeper, this Leo voice, and Joey tipped her face up in curiosity. His lazy, teasing smile was so utterly the same that it took her breath away.

Leo slipped from her arms and started back down the pier toward the beach. Joey followed, dazed, beside him, the hairs of her arm sweeping the hairs of his. As they walked, Joey was struck by flashes of before—floating in the sea on their backs, staring up at an azure sky, the wind dancing in the awning at their one-year anniversary dinner. Their last Corfu night.

But then here was Leo in the flesh, now more Daniel Craig to his early-aughts Joshua Jackson. He wore a green T-shirt and gray jeans slung low, skinny and rumpled. A couple of black rope bracelets clung to his left wrist. His face bore pale scruff, sprinkled by a few silver strands, and one cavernous wrinkle bisected his forehead. Somehow, though, the wrinkle lent him wisdom, worldliness, an invitation to unearth the adventures that had shaped it.

"You got edgy, huh, Jones?"

"What?" Their arm hairs were still hugging each other.

"This." Leo touched her left earlobe, where she had three

delicate gold earrings in a row, plus two in her cartilage that had hurt like hell in the piercing.

She had fewer piercings in her right ear, only two in the lobe, for an asymmetrical vibe, not too precious or perfect. Her dad liked to call her piercings jazzy. Joey still couldn't work out if that meant he liked them or not.

"When did you get them?"

Joey's heartbeat thrashed in her ears. She could tell Leo about quitting her big law job, about craving a drastic change after all those years shellacked and suit-straitjacketed. About how the ear piercer had tried to talk her out of getting all five additional piercings at once, but she'd insisted. About going to Bali and meeting Grant and one of the piercings getting infected so Grant had taken her on the back of his motorbike through twisty rice paddies to get antibiotics from a clinic.

But no, Joey couldn't tell Leo all that. That story required a thousand others to preface it. And Leo had chosen to bow out before those thousand other stories.

"I've always been edgy," she said. "I'm an artist. It's basically in the definition." Her left hand twitched. She extended it. "One thing that did change, though, is I'm engaged. Well, you already know that, I guess. His name is Grant."

Leo took Joey's hand to check out her ring. Their fingertips brushed, and Joey saw things at work in his head, as if his brain were on the outside and the gears were all interchanging, as if he were about to come out with something meaningful. But then she sensed his resolve weaken, and a weary certitude overwhelmed her, that she shouldn't have come to see him. Leo released her hand. It flopped to her side.

"My parents send their love and regrets they can't make

it to the wedding. They're so happy for you. I'm happy for you too, Jonesey."

"Thanks."

"A dermatologist, huh?" Leo raised an eyebrow. "Nice."

"How did you know?" They'd invited Maisy and Rand to the wedding for old times' sake, although not Leo, for obvious reasons. But Joey didn't think their two sets of parents had kept in touch much in the decade and a half since their Corfu days, at least not sufficiently for Leo's parents to know the particulars of Grant's job.

"You didn't think I was going to come all the way to Florida without Googling you, did you, Jones?"

"Oh." She tried to picture him scouring her digital footprint like she'd done to his but couldn't conjure it. It was a thing she'd always resented him for: Leo was better at letting go.

"You've Googled me too."

"No…" she said, but smiled and knew it was unconvincing.

"Sure, Jonesey. Sure." Leo laughed with all his teeth displayed, his front two teeth the same length as the two that hugged them. He'd been self-conscious about that. Some mishap by a dentist who'd gotten overzealous shaving off a chip. Leo tugged off his high-tops and socks before wading into a soft wave, past the line demarcating wet sand from dry. "Come sit with me, Jonesey."

"In the water?"

"It's a special occasion. My first time in the Atlantic in a long time. Just put your feet in."

"What the hell." She eased herself down beside him. They sat in silence until a wave came that looked simple and nice and instead thrust a sheet of sea into her face.

"Oh God." Joey scooted back and blinked salt from her eyes. "How am I going to explain my wet-rat look to Grant?"

"You didn't tell him I was coming?" Leo tossed up his tennis ball. It landed with a thump in his palms, and he sent it up again.

"I'm going to." A lump lodged in her throat. "You didn't give me much notice."

Leo shook his legs in the water. "I know, Jonesey. I'm sorry."

Joey's eyes fixed on his jeans, clinging like spandex to the twists of his muscles. She waited for Leo to say more, but he didn't so she thumbed through her fifteen years' worth of questions. Had he fulfilled his dream of becoming a captain of his own ship? Was he happy? But what came out of her was, "Did you ever wonder about me, Leo?" She immediately wished she could take it back. Just that little bit had induced a whiplash of vulnerability. "I mean, how I was doing and stuff."

His face looked pained but almost dumbfounded too. "I wondered about you, Jonesey. Of course I did. That you'd think I didn't…" He shook his head. "That's the whole reason I'm here. I…I didn't break up with you because I didn't love you. I loved you so much. I guess, well…the truth is that I still do."

Joey had imagined Leo saying just that for so many years, but somehow hearing it now only twisted the knife. "You still love me? That's what you came to tell me? Just when I'm happy, you swoop in to ruin it?"

"Jones, wait. I've thought about seeing you for so long. A million times I wanted to tell you the truth—"

"No!" The ferocity with which it emerged almost scared her, that something could live so dormant inside with such rage. "No. No. You can't do this now. You don't have the right. You know what? I need to leave." Joey stood and brushed sand from her butt.

Leo stumbled up to a stand after her. "Wait! I know it wasn't fair of me. Maybe I shouldn't have come. I just found out you were getting married, and I don't know, something in me snapped."

"Right," she said, unable to couch her bitterness. "Fifteen years later and something in you snapped."

He stared down at the tennis ball now stationary in his palm. "I realized it was now or never, I guess."

"It's never, Leo." She was surprised, still, at the sharp edges of her anger. "Let's get one thing straight. You and I will never happen again."

"Okay. I get it. Loud and clear, I do. But Jones, I've come to Florida for more than just seeing you."

A wave slapped her calves. "I don't know what that means, Leo."

"I know. It's just...I need to do the right thing, Jonesey. I need to finally do the right thing."

"You're speaking in riddles, and frankly it's annoying."

"Will you stay and listen? I promise, if you stay and listen, you'll understand why I had to come."

Joey looked into his green eyes, still boyish and hazy, inviting her to fall back inside them. But falling by its nature entailed that inevitable crash back to earth. Falling was once the only way Joey knew how to love. With Grant she'd finally learned how to love on solid ground.

She had to trust in that solid ground now because she couldn't rewind herself away from the beach. It was inevitable. She was always going to stay for the next part.

Joey sat back down on the sand. "Okay, sit, Leo. Talk."

chapter seven
Joey

corfu
2003

How Joey came to be Jonesey was a story that told almost everything. The beginning and, if you looked close enough, the ending too.

It was late morning on Corfu the summer they were eighteen. Joey wandered bleary-eyed onto the terrace abutting the Abrams and Winn families' neighboring apartments, with their postcard vista of town, harbor, and mountains.

She surveyed the array of mostly empty plates and glasses and only Leo at the table, his shin propped against the glass table pane. His legs were tan, bulkier in appearance when he contorted them so, the little hairs adorning them bleached by the sun. He put a hand to his brow and gave her his trademark languid smile. "Half the day has passed, Joey. Fancy seeing you awake so early."

"Ha. Some of us need our beauty sleep." She scraped back a chair and sat. "Been out on the boat?" She could smell his intoxicating Abercrombie cologne. During the school year, on trips to the mall with her friends, she often lingered by the entrance to the store with its strong scent she associated with Leo, eagerly anticipating the summer.

"Yep. Let's do something fun this afternoon, J. Got plans?"

"Not yet," she said, her insides their usual tangle of hopes and fears.

"Great. Wanna go to Sidari? I rented a motorbike."

Sidari. Wasn't that the place with the stunning beaches and the Tunnel of Love? Had Leo finally figured out she'd had a crush on him since they were ten? If he didn't kiss her at last, she'd combust. Die. Dead.

Okay, stop the crazy, Joey ordered herself.

As casually as she could muster, Joey said, "Cool." She stared out at the view as familiar as her face in the mirror. They lived right in the heart of Old Town. The tallest building with the grandest terrace. They were the luckiest people in the world.

Before Joey was her favorite marigold building with intricate, wrought-iron white balconies that resembled Chantilly lace. And then beyond it, in the sweep of town that led down to the sea, endless sherbet and copper stucco blazed into view, bookended by the two Venetian fortresses that for centuries had guarded the island against foreign invaders. Olive trees sprouted in roadside squares and bougainvillea wove around trellises. Steeples and clock towers thrust through the skyline; only the Church of Agios Spyridon was visible in its grand entirety. It had been narrowly spared destruction by Allied bombs in the forties, and according to Joey's art teacher, legend had it that Saint Spyridon walked the cobblestone *kantounia* at night, protecting the island and her people.

In the distance, sailboats bobbed in Garitsa Bay. And not far beyond hovered the misty outlines of mainland Greece and Albania across the strait, with villages baked into lush green hilltops. At a certain line, the villages petered out and the mountains stood proud watch over the Ionian Sea.

Joey peeled off flaky pieces of a leftover croissant now hot from the sun, her eyes in their typical bounce between the vista and Leo. After breakfast, while Joey went to her bedroom to slip into her favorite coral bikini, the danger occurred to her of allowing optimism to overtake things. She and Leo were just friends, and had been for years. But oh God, the hope of something more swept her away.

Joey went to the kitchen to assemble snacks into a basket. Her mother padded in.

Joey's father was in the States still, presenting at a conference on the latest techniques for minimizing estate taxes, or something equally boring. He usually spent all of June with them in Greece and came out for a week one other time.

Bea's long dark waves were piled on top of her hair in a messy bun, and she wore just a peach lace bra and matching high-waisted panties with a silky robe atop, splayed open. Even compared with high school girls, her mother was objectively hot.

"Your abs look amazing," Joey said.

"Thanks, JoJo! You think?" Bea clasped her ribs with her forefingers and thumbs and appraised herself in the stainless-steel gleam of the countertop mixer that had been used over its lifetime far more frequently as a mirror than as a baking tool. "When your dad is away, I have time to do sit-ups."

Even though Joey thought that was a bit of an exaggeration about the tightness of Bea's schedule—she had a nanny come most days to care for two-year-old Lily—Bea did generally allocate a lot of time toward her art. Sometimes she was in a research phase, or the actual creation, and sometimes she was just sitting around staring at a canvas or a wall, seemingly not doing anything. But actually, that was Bea's prime time for inspiration, she said, when ideas had space to attach. As an aspiring artist herself, Joey admired her mother's passion and devotion. Bea wasn't a wallflower stay-at-home mom like many of Joey's friends' mothers, and no one would ever say Bea Abrams didn't have a point of view.

Bea held up two dresses—a long red one with a plunging back and a black mini that Joey had once borrowed to go clubbing with Leo at the resort town Benitses in the south. "Which one?"

"The red is nice."

"It's for the presentation I'm giving at the gallery on Sexuality in the Era of Impressionism. Thirteen people signed up."

"Oh. Cool, Mom." Joey waited for Bea to launch into some diatribe about how that paltry sign-up meant Corfu needed to get with the times. That even in the nineteenth century, Manet created some scandalous stuff. Then Bea would backtrack and say, but we should be careful about using the word *scandalous* because it carries negative connotations, and nudity is natural.

Instead, Bea said, "Where are you going?"

"With Leo, to Sidari."

"Oh, it's gorgeous there. You know, Joey, if you're sleeping with Leo—"

"I'm *not* sleeping with Leo!"

But I want to be sleeping with Leo. I desperately want to be sleeping with Leo.

She'd had sex before, a grand total of once, throwaway sex in a friend's basement with a guy who was sweet and sort of chubby. The next morning, she'd nearly gagged as the heat of his stale beer breath had tunneled against her neck. In the dark, lulled by angry hip-hop and floating in the pool at one A.M. in some random girl's spare bikini, staring up at a starless sky, it had seemed the natural segue when arms wrapped around her waist, when she swiveled her head to see that guy on the football team who always seemed oafy. Or maybe she'd just slept with him to get it over with, to not look a fool when she returned for the summer and presented herself to Leo. Joey knew Leo was not a virgin.

Bea said, "Well, if you do sleep with Leo, it's your prerogative."

"*Mom.* For the last time, Leo and I aren't together." It worried Joey, how transparent her desire was and also how fragile—she was china teetering on a table's edge.

Bea dolloped yogurt into a ceramic bowl she'd made; she'd etched into the clay HEAR ME FUCKING ROAR. "Well, don't feel pressure to have sex. There are other ways to enable each other to orgasm."

"Mom, seriously, stop! I'm leaving!"

Joey clamped her hands over her ears and lifted her basket by her teeth, laughing a jittery laugh because the truth was that she didn't really know how to get Leo to orgasm, or herself for that matter. Joey crossed the peach-tiled hall to grab Leo at his flat.

He was in his kitchen, and he gave her one of those smiles she slipped in her pocket to use later, in the privacy of her bedroom with her eyes closed when her longing for him threatened to unmoor her. Leo didn't know this of course. Unaware of the power his smile wielded, he returned to slathering peanut butter and Merenda onto bread. Merenda was the Nutella of Greece, a chocolate spread made of hazelnuts, but tastier.

Joey sank onto a honey-colored wicker stool. Her friends at home all knew about her summertime crush. They each maintained rationales about why Joey and Leo hadn't yet consummated their flirtation. Leo wanted to play the field. He wouldn't make a move until he was sure he was ready for commitment because he wasn't the type to jerk Joey around like that. That was one school of thought. On the other, it was *Joey, if he wanted you, you'd know.* Joey felt a hit of anger at the memory of her friend Dalia sitting on a purple beanbag chair in her basement and saying that so matter-of-factly before taking a long drag on a joint.

While Leo rinsed his hands, Joey poked her head into the living room to say hi and bye to his mother, Maisy. His father, Rand, was out on the terrace. Joey could see his thick swoop of dark hair, white linen button-up, and tan slacks, and the backs of his Italian moccasins. Rand relished his alone time—always off on some solo sailing excursion, shouting at his brokers, or poring over investment tomes.

Maisy was lying on the cozy yellow-and-white-striped couch with her hefty black laptop on her stomach. She'd grown her golden-brown hair long this summer, and it fanned out pin-straight on a white grass-cloth pillow. The computer screen was the homepage for Maisy's Mary Kay sales thing. The two apartments sprouted an endless parade of Mary Kay lipsticks courtesy of Maisy, who was a rep. "There aren't enough lips in these families for the lipsticks" was Rand's favored commentary. He'd once confided to Joey that Maisy's Mary Kay venture yielded only enough profit to fund her annual expenditure on greeting cards. (In her defense, Maisy always did send thoughtful greeting cards.)

The TV blared a Charlotte freak-out from a *Sex and the City* DVD. "Have fun, kids." Maisy waved.

After they'd gone, Joey said, "Your mom wears a silk dress to watch TV."

Leo grinned. "My mom wears a silk dress to take out the trash."

They bounded down the stairwell and then out into the alleyway across which lines were strung with drying laundry that functioned doubly as address panes. The shopkeeper who owned Papagiorgis with the rainbow pillowcases. The old man who smoked cigars on his stoop with the light-blue undershirts.

"Shit." Leo froze mid-stride toward his bike. "I forgot the sandwiches."

"I'll go." Joey reached back for the doorknob. "Anyway, I wanna go to the bathroom."

"Okay, grab us some beers too? Let's have fun today."

"Fun sounds…fun," said Joey, but she hovered there awkwardly, not moving. She felt weird taking beers out of Leo's parents' fridge. Not like Rand and Maisy would care, but still.

"Okay, I'll come too," said Leo, following the way her mind had devolved.

Such an innocuous plan. If only she'd just agreed to go up herself and grab those damn beers.

When they walked into the apartment, the shadows of Maisy and Rand bounced on the wall of the living room visible from the kitchen island.

"It sickens me," Joey heard Maisy say, "all those Polish women who would have had the ability to choose what took place in their own bodies. And now they're saddled with motherhood, even if they don't want it. You weren't the one who had to make the choice, Rand. Leo wasn't even a year old."

Itchy from the tension, Joey opened her mouth to make their presence known, but Leo put his finger to his lips. Joey stilled against the fridge.

"I'm just saying, Mais," said Rand, in that monotone way he had, never riled up, never affected by anything anyone said, positive or negative alike. "That doctor was an idiot. She wasn't even set up for operations—"

"Abortions, Rand. You can call them abortions."

They were talking about abortion? An awful premonition swept over Joey. She vaguely remembered something her mother had mentioned the other day. A female doctor had boated to Poland, where abortion was illegal, to set up a floating operation room for women to get abortions. Apparently something had gone awry, and the doctor hadn't been allowed to proceed. Was that what they were talking about?

"Fine, abortions. The fact is, it was all sensational. This woman—a gynecologist is she? Well, I'd call her a drama queen. What, are the Poles going to decide to legalize abortion because of her stunt?"

Joey motioned her head to the sandwiches on the counter where Leo had left them. Through the Saran Wrap, she could see that Leo had sliced them on the diagonal. Leo shook his head and pressed a hand against the wall done in pale-yellow sponge paint.

"You just don't get it, Rand. What that doctor tried to do was courageous! I feel for those poor women she could have helped. Instead they'll be saddled with motherhood against their will. Having that abortion seventeen years ago was the best thing that ever happened to me. I would have died—*died* with another child. We could barely make it with Leo. He was, what, nine months when we found out I was pregnant again? I never regretted that abortion,

Rand. Let's be honest, the two of us weren't meant to have children. Women should have the right. Women should have the right!"

Joey was going to be sick. She glimpsed Leo's face; it was stone. For a few terrible moments, there was the sound of the clock tower down below. Three quick tocks. Joey wished for tocks forever.

Finally, Rand spoke. "I don't even know what we're fighting about."

The sound of ice cubes clinking against glass. Glass meeting coaster.

"I don't either, to be honest." Maisy laughed a normal laugh. Joey hated her for that laugh.

"Okay, honey," said Rand. "I'm going out on the boat."

Leo grabbed the sandwiches and slid out the front door. Joey followed him down. She had never known less in her life what to say. So Maisy had had an abortion after Leo. That was bad, but it wasn't the worst. The worst was the cavalier way she and Rand had framed Leo's entire life. Like having kids was a burden. Like Leo himself was a burden.

"Are you sure you still want to go to Sidari?" Joey asked as Leo slung his leg over the motorbike.

"Yeah." He handed her a helmet and buckled his. She got on the back and clutched him around the waist.

As Leo drove north past sea-battered cliffs, Joey finally said his name with a question mark at the end of it. It was chicken to force him to lead the way, but every other thing that occurred to her to say, to defend Maisy or Rand or explain their conversation away, was stupid, and she couldn't advocate for any of it. But either Leo didn't hear her speak or he pretended her appeal had been lost in the column of wind.

They drove steeper into the mountains, the morning's mist suspended over the bucolic countryside, the quiet punctured only by the tinkle of a goat's bell and the cicadas orchestrating their chorus from orchards of fig trees. If he'd been his normal happy self, Leo would have recited trees. Olive. Myrtle. Strawberry. Kumquat. Judas. Holm oak. When Leo was stumped over a clump of green, Joey always found it endearing when he retrieved his botany book and surfaced sheepishly with, "Just cypresses."

The entire way to Sidari, Joey composed a single sentence. She would say, "They can't have meant it." She arrived at a follow-up too. "Your mom having an abortion had nothing to do with you."

But it did, didn't it? Rand and Maisy weren't kid people. And Leo was a kid. Theirs. So by implication, Rand and Maisy weren't Leo people.

How anyone couldn't be a Leo person, Joey would never understand.

He was so special. An image flashed—the day Joey first set eyes on Leo, when their families met in the stairwell of their common apartment building that first summer in Corfu.

The Abrams threesome had been on the way in from the sea, the Winns off to some fancy dinner reservation. Leo wore a Red Wings T-shirt four sizes too big, while Rand and Maisy oozed rich, important vibes in formal clothes. Joey imagined the scene that had preceded this strange fashion array. Perhaps a bow tie thrust upon Leo that he'd obstinately refused, opting in protest for the most inappropriately casual and ill-fitting item in his closet.

The four adults chatted—sussing out their American origins and status as neighbors in the rooftop apartments, marveling that both kids were age ten.

"How did you all wind up in Corfu?" asked Maisy. "As Leo has reminded us often, it's not the normal vacation spot for Americans."

"We were supposed to go to Mackinac Island," said Leo, his sea-glass eyes blazing premature teen angst. "Their fudge is really good."

"I love fudge," said Joey, to which Leo peeped out a smile.

"My parents are from here," said Bea. "I visited only once, but I fell totally in love. Corfu in the summer is…magic, and untouched by Americans."

"We think so too," said Rand.

Bea nodded. "I want Joey to feel the same. Corfu is part of her, and my husband's never seen it either. And I'm an artist—inspiration strikes me most in new settings. The light is fantastic on the terrace, isn't it?"

"Oh, it's out of this world," said Maisy.

Over the adults' chitchat, Leo said, "Hey there, Joey. What do you like to do for fun?"

She started. Her mind went fully blank. What in the world did she do for fun? "Art!" she said, remembering. "I really like art. Painting especially."

"So you're like…an artist? That's so cool. I suck at painting."

Joey smiled. "Yeah. I'm an artist." Previously she'd only said it in a different way: I want to be an artist when I grow up. It felt good to take the future condition out of it, like Leo had. She was an artist *now*. "What do you want to be?"

Leo shrugged. "Something with the stock market. Business. Boats. I like boats."

Rand said, "Time to go, son. We're going to be late for dinner."

"Boats?" *Think of something to say about boats, Joey.* "Boats are really…wet and cool."

Wet and cool? She'd wanted to be cool for this boy, somehow, but she suspected she hadn't achieved it.

Leo started down the stairs after his parents, but then paused and turned back. He stared at Joey straight-on so that eventually his green eyes consumed everything else. "I made up a secret language this year. If you want, I can teach it to you."

"Really?" Joey's heart soared. "Sure!"

"Okay." Leo nodded. "Gagoose then. That means see you later."

"Gagoose." She smiled a little at him, and he smiled back, and she felt in their gaze that there had been some kind of test, followed by a mutual understanding that she'd passed.

Sidari, on Corfu's rocky western coast, revealed itself in a sweep of endless beauty that felt wrong, twisted. Joey and Leo dismounted the bike in quiet and followed the blacktop trail to a secluded pocket of flat, sandy rock. The water glittered calm and green below.

Leo said, "I'm gonna walk a little." He struck off. Joey shed her cover-up, squinting at Leo through the glare of the sun. His back was to her, shoulders slumped. At some point, he moved farther, a speck against the Monet-idyllic watercolor of a day. If they were intimate already, if even they'd kissed, it might have been different. Joey might have known how to touch him. But she didn't, so she sunned alone for a bit, her towel a too-thin barrier against the scorching rock.

Finally, Joey climbed down to the sand, pausing to investigate a colony of clams. Then she waded into the sea, out to a shallow reef hosting clusters of spiky, purple sea urchins— but nothing could distract her from the sick feeling that Leo's parents didn't really want him. Sure, her own mother could be a trip, to put it lightly. But Bea wanted Joey, and she wanted Lily—and so did their father.

Periodically, Joey started in the water, her eyes seeking reassurance that Leo was still out there somewhere. She'd thrash a bit and then latch onto him and calm. After she'd exhausted her capacity for swimming, she waded back to shore and sat for what seemed like an eternity on a rock, waiting. It was only when the sun went down though that Leo finally returned.

"Ready?" His tone betrayed nothing.

On their way home, they stopped for gelato by St. George's Bay.

"I'm sorry," said Leo as they waited in line. He rubbed his eyes, the green of them not their usual lively but deadened, like a lawn that hadn't been watered all summer.

"For what?" said Joey. "Leo, they can't have meant—"

"J, I appreciate you trying, but it's not such a shock. My parents aren't terrible people, but they suck as parents. What really got me though is that I could have had a sibling. You can't imagine how cold it is all alone with Rand and Maisy."

"You have me though. Leo, you—"

"Not in Michigan, I don't. I only have you guys in the summer."

The ice cream scooper girl handed them their cones. Joey tried to think of some way to flip it. To make it okay for him. "But you can't—"

"Stompoo," said Leo in a flat, calm voice. Joey looked into his eyes, and he didn't move them away from her. They hadn't talked like this since they were kids, having come to some unspoken agreement to abandon their secret language as they ascended into their teenage years.

Joey felt the fight deflate from her. "Ikodiko," she replied.

They walked outside, licking their cones on the sidewalk as night dropped its curtain. Leo got gas for the bike, and impulsively, Joey bought a fedora at a tourist shop next door. It was gorgeous, tan with a pale-blue ribbon.

"Move over, Indiana Jones, here comes Joey Jones," said Leo, legs straddling the bike, working on his cone. It was so nice to see his smile, like a spark plug to his eyes.

"It's cute, yeah?" She swiveled her head, modeling.

"It is. Only because you're wearing it, Jonesey."

Leo leaned in to touch her hat, but in the process, some of his strawberry gelato plopped onto the lid of her fedora. Joey's mouth opened to yell, but before the words tripped out of her, Leo licked the ice cream right up.

"My brand-new hat! You *licked* my brand-new hat!"

A fit of giggles overtook her, and then Leo joined in. At first his laughs were tentative, but soon they stacked atop each other like building blocks.

Joey examined the hat. The webbing was pristine—not a trace of ice cream residue.

"Good as new."

"Leo!"

"Just saying." He looked at her, and even in the dark she could sense something headier, but she swallowed it down. She couldn't handle the roller coaster of hope anymore.

"Magical saliva," she finally relented. "We should bottle it. The slogan will be…for even the toughest gelato!"

"Jonesey."

Joey still hadn't gotten it. "See, this is why you should eat your cone faster. I literally don't understand how you take so long to finish—"

But all of a sudden, Leo was kissing the words quiet, was kissing her, his lips on hers, full-body tingle, this was crazy, this was falling. This was falling down a chute inside herself.

Was it his parents' conversation, was it the fedora? Or was it simply meant to be? Later she would think it was sadly poetic. That their beginning foretold their end.

chapter eight

Joey

corfu
one year later, 2004

At last another summer had arrived. The families had reunited on Corfu, with preparations under way for their annual First Night Dinner.

Until landing in Corfu late the night before, Joey hadn't seen Leo for over two months, not since she'd visited him at U of M over her spring break from Penn, their breaks luckily coinciding. After the prior summer, it had been torturous to separate for college, to see each other only for occasional spurts. But anticipation of the summer had kept Joey going. She'd spent many hours in her dorm room's tiny, dark closet so as not to bother her roommates, winding the telephone cord around her finger, talking and listening to Leo but not getting to feel him.

Now that was done. Last night, she'd leaped into Leo's arms, soaked up his sunshine smell, and felt herself relax into the eternity of summer, where moments no longer had looming expiration dates. The fall semester felt eons way, with three months stretching out ahead in her favorite place on earth. Joey felt the happy and kind and generous that seemed to come naturally when your entire being was one giant exclamation mark.

Her gaze skittered across the terrace, at all her favorite people. In the corner, by the door that opened into her family's apartment, Rand and her father, Scott, were playing Lily's favorite game, Tossing Lily and Sinead.

Sinead was Lily's imaginary best friend, and Lily didn't find it fair that she would be tossed and not Sinead. So what happened is that Scott gathered Lily, limbs like an octopus, and essentially passed her to Rand, who stood a foot away on the terrace.

Rand's eyes lingered on the stock ticker floating across the screen he'd rigged so he was never far from his markets. Then he set Lily down and said in a cartoon voice, "Now it's Sinead's turn, Lily Pad." He gathered an imaginary Sinead, hands quaking. "I think Sinead's going through a growth spurt."

"No, silly," said Lily, licking a Kinder Egg. "Sinead's littler than me."

Joey smoothed her fluorescent-green tee, excited for Leo to see her wearing it again. Leo hated the color. Despised it. He believed fashion-oriented neon to be a bastard of those shades of green that arose in the natural order. He'd said it like gospel one summer, when that botany book was his fifth appendage and he'd scrutinized leaves and trees so that a walk to the sea could swallow the morning.

So naturally, Joey's old, worn, neon shirt got a lot of wardrobe mileage in teasing him.

Joey was sitting at the long glass table that was the center point of their lives, atop the chair with the bad leg. When she shifted, the chair rocked. Her feet met the stone ground, wet with afternoon rain. She opened her hefty paperback copy of *Anna Karenina*. She'd been reading it for two years, always in Corfu between the hours of six and seven in the evening. That was when Maisy and sometimes Bea prepared dinner.

Maisy was once a literature major at Barnard. She thought it was *crucial* that young women read. That was how they absorbed a slice of wider society. That was how they grabbed feminism by the horns.

Whenever Maisy spotted Joey reading, she said, "Good for you, Josephine. We've got dinner."

Of course, Joey never confided that half the time she read was spent returning to page one. The terrace was too distracting for immersing herself into literature, especially by the Russians. Someone was always pulling up a chair and slipping a glass into your hand, so Joey would lose her place and return to the first page, starting from the famous happy and unhappy families line that she knew by heart. Today she stuck on that line, reading it a few times in unusual contemplation. She decided that her family was happy, despite their quirks, her mother's in particular. As to Leo's family, Joey's gut said they weren't happy, not as an organism unto the three of them. This was a sad, sobering thought, but in the summers, the Abrams and Winn families became one. So the happy family would lift up the unhappy one, right? Or maybe that was just something a person from a happy family could think.

Maisy slid a glass of white wine into Joey's hand, snapping Joey out of her analysis.

"Oh, thanks, Mais! Can I do anything?"

Maisy sipped from her tumbler, depositing an imprint of red lips on the glass. "Nope. I got it! You know I'm back in my element now."

Maisy loved to helm dinner, with Bea as her occasional sous-chef. Each of Maisy's summer days passed in a *Groundhog Day*–flavored loop. What happened was that Maisy would rouse around eleven, waiting out the siesta with some light Mary Kay work and *Sex and the City* DVDs. As the gal pals clinked their Cosmos on the screen, Maisy would nurse in unity her own drink or, as Joey suspected, by the culmination of the day's reruns, her own four or five. Then, once the shops reopened, Maisy would spend hours perusing and considering. Giorgios had the best seafood. Polermos for cheese. Ionna for baklava. After unloading all her spoils, Maisy would pour herself a tumbler and set to work on the night's feast. Coq au vin. Beef bourguignon. Sometimes she'd tackle a Greek specialty like spanakopita or pastitsada or cheese souvlaki with a drizzle of thyme honey. The latter was Leo's favorite. Joey pictured him saying, *Are you sure you want another piece, Jonesey? The honey tastes off tonight.*

Down by the water, the clock tower began to chime. Sometimes it chimed once, sometimes eleven times, sometimes an incessant series where you had to stop counting because the chimes were going too fast and berserk. *Clock tower guy forgot his meds today*, was their common refrain.

Joey and Maisy counted together up to five. They laughed.

Maisy leaned over to check on one of her new plants. The Winns had arrived in town a few days before the Abrams family because Joey's father had an important meeting that couldn't be pushed, and in the interim, Maisy had adorned the terrace in terra-cotta planters. She'd announced that gardening was her new hobby, with her aim to grow ingredients for the families' meals.

The breeze played in the pleats of Maisy's black dress. "This one's gonna be basil."

"Ooh. Yum. I like what you've done, Mais." Joey gestured to the pots. "It makes it even prettier out here."

Maisy smiled. "I thought it would be nice. I love plants."

"That must be where Leo gets his obsession from."

"Oh! That's funny. Didn't ever put it together. Genetics, huh?"

Joey laughed. Her mind flickered with the conversation she and Leo had eavesdropped upon the summer prior, but she pushed that memory back down.

"My garden in Michigan is where I do my praying, so I thought I'd make one here too."

"Praying? Like to God?" Joey was surprised. It seemed a little off-brand for Maisy, with her pert nipples shimmering through her slip dress, that Joey was trying to avoid looking at, and her penchant for a couple of drinks too many.

Maisy nodded vaguely. "Where's Leo, by the way?"

Joey still loved that she was the person anyone asked when they wanted to find Leo. They'd been together nearly a year, but so much of it had been apart that they felt shiny new. Or maybe they would always feel shiny new. Joey knew with a gut conviction that, given their natural chemistry and ease, they were starting ahead of other relationships some-how. And moreover, they'd been friends from childhood, a special bond that other couples could rarely achieve.

She'd heard parents of her single girlfriends foist advice about giving a guy another chance. Always accepting a sec-ond date. Like, love can grow. Attraction can mount. Joey had felt a little guilty telling her roommate to, sure, go on that second date with a guy she didn't really have the desire to kiss. Because inside Joey had cringed, grateful and maybe even smug that it wasn't her situation. The world paused anytime she saw Leo, and that fact hadn't changed in the ten years she'd known him.

"Leo's down at the boat," Joey said. "He'll be back any moment, I'm sure."

Sure enough, Joey caught the silhouette of Leo slipping onto the terrace. Her whole body gave off a little sigh.

"Ah, there's my boy." Rand slapped Leo's shoulders as he crossed the terrace. Then Rand bent down to scoop up Jefferson the Cat. That was another thing he and Maisy had done this summer before the Abramses' arrival: adopt Jefferson the Cat and bestow upon him his mouthful of a moniker. Jefferson the Cat had gray-striped fur and green eyes and an objectively ugly face, but Maisy and Rand were obsessed. They spoke to Jefferson the Cat in this bizarre French-accented baby voice.

Leo draped an arm over Joey's shoulder. "That shirt is blinding me, J."

Joey laughed. She peered back. Leo was wearing his board shorts and a white Michigan tee, a *tsitsimpira* ginger beer in hand. He looked the happy way he always did after he'd been tinkering on Rand's sailboat. His freckles were extra prominent against his tanned skin. That was the telltale sign.

Tomorrow Joey would go to see her art teacher, Demetris. Painting with Demetris made her happy too, a different kind of happy than Leo did. Demetris was Joey's freckles-inducing equivalent.

Maisy set lamb kebabs on the table. They rested in a ceramic evil eye platter with concentric rings of alternating blues and greens, in the center of which was a black circle. The edges of the platter cradled grilled pita, tzatziki, grilled onions and tomatoes, and fried potatoes with rosemary.

"Nice, lovie." Rand plucked a fried potato.

Maisy set out a few ramekins with sea salt and herbs. "I was just waiting for a new batch of lamb. Perfect timing for the Abramses' arrival."

"Stavros killed the little lamb this morning," joked Leo, reaching for a kebab.

"Mary's little lamb?" asked Lily. She'd been tapping her spoon against the glass table like it was a drum. Now she looked up with really wide, curious, innocent eyes.

"Not Mary's little lamb, little L." Leo laughed.

"What lamb?" Lily appeared less interested than the two seconds prior.

"Steve the lamb." Leo mussed Lily's wild red curls. "Never met Mary the Lamb. From very different farms."

That seemed to satisfy Lily. She went back to spoon drumming.

"Cut it out, Lily," said Bea.

Lily drummed harder. Her toddler superpower was that she could continue doing anything in the face of admonishment. Bea wrestled Lily for the spoon. By the time she wrenched it away, she was sweating. Lily leaned back with an amused look.

"Steve the lamb?" Joey giggled. "I'll send you my sister's therapy bills."

"To family." Scott lifted his glass. "My favorite day of the year is when we're all back on this terrace together. *Yia mas.* To a summer we'll never forget."

"*Yia mas,*" they all echoed.

Joey put her hand into Leo's. Her body felt like it was quaking with joy. "To a summer we'll never forget, Winn."

Something flickered across Leo's face; Joey wasn't sure what. But then he reverted to his typical smile with a bit of mischief inside it, like his ten-year-old self was never far. He clinked his wineglass against hers.

"Or to a summer we'll forget, Jonesey. Maybe those are even better."

After dinner, Joey and Leo went to the pebble-spackled beach near the New Fortress, by the trees that looked like pineapples. (Date palms, Leo said.) In the day, you had to jostle for a spot to lay your towel. In the evening, there were no towels—only cameras. But once the sun eased under after its last plum tones, all the people who came, not to look at the sunset, but to capture the sunset, filed out.

Leo tore off his shirt. Joey's eyes lingered on his back, her favorite male body part, besides eyes, of course. Leo's back was strong, hairless, nicely medium-size, and sporting the first hints of a tan. He was like a radiator, she'd told him the summer prior. Good for winter. She'd finally confirmed it was true when he'd visited her at Penn for Halloween weekend, their first taste of winter together. They'd dressed up as tennis players, both fine to go the route of a cop-out costume because neither got the appeal of spending time and money on anything elaborate. Then they'd left the party early and made hot chocolate back at her dorm, and after some TV show she hadn't paid attention to, Joey had drifted into a warm sleep, her face pressed against Leo's back.

"Check out who's here," said Leo, and Joey followed his finger point to Nikos, the gorgeous, infamous-on-the-island son of the owner of the taverna neighboring their apartments, who was mid-flirtation with a pretty brunette.

"Oh God." Joey laughed. Tourists tended to flock to

Nikos's black hair and dark skin and dimples that didn't discriminate by age. Joey had watched his dimples flash for fifteen-year-old acne-riddled girls and just as deeply for all the grandmas clad in black. Nikos had a whole shpiel for presenting the taverna's olive oil, proclaiming it the best olive oil in Greece, the best in the whole world. But the olive oil was actually from the Aegean.

Joey knew this because she'd had a little thing with Nikos before she and Leo had gotten together, and Nikos had confided the secret.

"Think he's doing his olive oil demonstration?" Leo winked.

"Who knows." Joey laughed. "Who cares."

Joey knew Leo wasn't actually jealous, and she both loved and sort of resented that. She loved his confidence, how he moved so assuredly in his body, inhabiting it like something he would have chosen even had he been consulted before his birth. Joey didn't feel that way about her body, so connected to it, and surely not so in love with it. It was fine, but she found herself noticing her trouble spots more, especially when the magazines told her how to conceal them. But maybe that was just a girl thing. Either way, Leo's confidence extended to their relationship. He knew that Joey was his. And while he gave her no reason at all to doubt that he was hers, she didn't feel the same nonchalance toward the French girl with big boobs whom Leo had dated a couple of times before he and Joey had gotten together. Leo had explained it to Joey: He'd wanted to kiss Joey long before the prior summer, but he'd waited so long to do it because he was terrified of ruining the special bond they had. Nonetheless, whenever Joey saw the French girl, at the Pirate Bar or wherever—Corfu was small—she felt a twinge of jealousy.

Leo dove out to sea from the most treacherous point. He always chose the spot slippery from moss and rising above punishing rock. As he disappeared below the water-line, Joey's eyes met Nikos's. He waved cheerily, and she waved back.

Joey pulled out her sketchbook. She swept charcoal across paper as Leo's arms knifed the water. She didn't know what she was drawing.

She started with a pair of evil eyes.

Joey's fascination with evil eyes began when she was ten. Her first summer on Corfu. Her father took her to the narrow alleys of the old Jewish quarter where her grandparents grew up. He led her past a bunch of scorched buildings—partially demolished with black smoke burrowed into weathered white and yellow stucco. Then a square with refurbished buildings in rose and peach. A taverna on every corner. He wanted to show her the synagogue on Velissariou.

"This is your history, Joey," he said. "These are your people."

"I'll wait outside," she said.

Her grandparents didn't really talk about Corfu. But when Joey was nine, she was allowed to sleep over at her grandparents' Delray Beach condo. The sleepover was a special occasion. Before it, her mother had forbade her to sleep away from home. This was because Joey's grand-father, who grew up on Corfu, once knew a girl who slept over at a friend's house. There was a fire in the house, and when the family escaped the house, they forgot the guest.

Joey always said to her mother, "That doesn't make sense," and her mother said, "Maybe the friend slept in the guest room," and Joey said, "Didn't Grandfather live in a one-room apartment before the war?" because so was his storied youth, and her mother just said, in uncharacteristic strictness, "I am in charge," and Joey said, "I'll sleep in my friend's room so they can't forget me." But Joey's attempts to convince her mother never succeeded until her father finally said, "Bea, this no-sleepover thing is ridiculous. At least let her go to your parents."

Her mother obviously trusted Grandmama and Grandfather enough that, if there was a fire, they would not forget to grab Joey—especially Grandfather, Joey supposed, whose story had so spooked her mother. So this was how Joey landed at a sleepover replacement.

The next morning, she was in their bathroom, looking for tissues. She found an empty tissue box under the bathroom sink. Inside was a picture of suitcases.

Joey went to the kitchen where her grandmother was stirring a pot on the stove. "What is this, Grandmama?"

Her grandmother turned and went very still in her yellow house robe. She said, "I don't like talking about some things, Joey."

"Okay." Joey put the picture back in the box and sat at the table with its window onto the front yard, where a neighbor boy was mowing the lawn.

Her grandmother came over to the table and removed the picture from the box. She clasped it by the edges. "Joey, do you know Grandfather's numbers on his arm?"

"Yes." Joey wiggled in her chair. She didn't want to talk about her grandfather's numbers, the ones that looked like black-and-blue marks. And she especially didn't want to talk about her grandfather's numbers when he was watching TV in the other room and could enter at any moment to chime in on the topic of his numbers. She dug her fingers into the box of Lucky Charms to find the mini Pez dispenser the front of the box promised.

"Well, he got the numbers at a place called Auschwitz." Her grandmother's eyes looked like the eyes of the homeless woman who sat with her cat on the side of the clubhouse in her grandparents' development and got delivered cups of ice water by the golf caddies.

"I took this picture at that place. Auschwitz. I went in the sixties because my family was taken there. I had nothing of theirs. Of ours. I didn't want to go to this place. Terrible things happened there. I went with a mission. I went to find things they once had touched. Can you understand that?"

Joey nodded yes, but no, she didn't. She loved her grandparents an amount that was so big she could feel it inside her, in a place in her stomach that now pulsed, straining for its exit route. She didn't want their lives to consist of some place called Auschwitz, and her grandfather's numbers, and terrible things.

"I went when your mother was young, alone. Your grandfather didn't want to come. We're different. He wanted to go back to Corfu, to show your mother the streets we once walked, the great synagogue we once prayed at. I wanted nothing to do with that version of the past. But I wanted a piece of my own past. My past was not in Corfu anymore. My past was in Auschwitz. I saw a room of hair. Can you imagine? Their hair was probably inside. My father's. My mother's. My mother had the most beautiful, shiny, dark hair. I didn't see shiny, dark hair. It had been a long time. Maybe the hair got rotten."

Joey wondered why there existed in the world a room of rotten hair. Her forearm immersed in cereal, she finally felt the Pez dispenser. She pulled it out and licked the Lucky Charm coating off her fingers.

Stop talking, she screamed inside.

"Don't lick your fingers, darling. It's not a nice habit." Her grandmother frowned. "So I went to another room. There were a million suitcases. A million. I spent hours in there. I walked inch by inch, looking for a name. My last name used to be Batis. And do you see it here?" Joey squinted. She saw it: BATIS. The suitcase was gray and square, like a large briefcase.

"This is all I have of my family. A picture of their suitcase. They took it with them when the Nazis ordered them to gather in the scorching heat at the *platia*. That was a grassy area with walking paths between the Old Fortress and—"

"Grandmama, my stomach hurts." Joey pushed the photograph away, and as it flew off the table, she realized the magnitude of her action. She dove to catch it, but she was too slow, and the photo flopped onto the linoleum.

By then, her grandmother had already bent over. She grunted. She brushed off the floor lint from the picture of the suitcases. Joey's breath caught in her throat as she saw a patch on the upper right quadrant where she'd deposited Lucky Charm residue. She'd ruined her grandmother's favorite picture.

"I'm so sorry, Grandmama," Joey said, her eyes blurring with unexpected tears.

"It's all right, my darling." Her grandmother ran a fingertip over the Lucky Charm smudge. It wasn't on the Batis part, at least. "We won't speak of this photograph again. What shall we talk about? Not these awful things."

"My birthday party." Joey started talking fast, eager to change the subject and to brighten her grandmother's mood. "It's going to be ceramics. And Mom's not going to lead it. We got a professional. We're going to glaze and everything. You'll come, won't you? And Grandfather?"

"That's nice," said her grandmother. She put the picture back in the empty tissue box. She put the box under her arm. "Of course, we'll come. I'll be right back."

Joey never saw that picture again.

But a year later, when she was ten and in Corfu that first summer, she stood outside the Romaniote synagogue, waiting for her father. An old lady wove through throngs of people. A tour group in knee-length shorts and white orthopedic shoes. A man shouting, "Spyro, ya Spyro." Another man dragging his daughter's pink wheely suitcase.

But the old lady went straight to Joey.

"Open your hand, child."

Joey yanked back her palm, but the lady crept her strong, bent fingers around Joey's and pried them open anyhow. Inside she placed an evil eye charm.

"You know what it is, child."

Joey backed away as spittle flew into her face. She suddenly longed to get back to Leo and their beautiful terrace where the sun dappled through the cypress trees.

The lady said, "It's to ward off the evil eye. Today is Tuesday, yes? The worst day of the week. The most unlucky. You must keep this with you. Then you will have good luck. You understand? You be safe. Poo, poo, poo." She spit three times. Joey was too stunned to duck.

Her father emerged, oblivious to the old lady not a foot away. "You missed a nice visit. It's something special, the synagogue. They restored it after the war, when it was bombed." He shoved his hands in his chino pockets. "They're thinking to do a memorial for all the Jews murdered in—"

"That's nice." Joey brushed spit that was not hers from her lip. She watched the old lady shuffle away, her ankles pooling skin folds over her scuffed black shoes. The old lady didn't give anyone else the evil eye charm.

Just her. Just Joey.

chapter nine
Joey

corfu
2004

Joey lugged her canvas to Demetris. Her art teacher owned and operated a fruit stall for extra income, but his true love and talent was painting, which happened to be Joey's favorite medium too. He'd been teaching her to paint since she was ten, since she'd told Bea she wanted a painting teacher who wasn't her mother and Bea had gotten a recommendation from a colleague. Demetris had gone to Paris in his twenties and begun to make a significant name for himself, but he'd soon returned to Corfu because, as he put it, Corfu was where his sunshine was. Bea always said that Demetris could have made it big, in sort of a disapproving way, but Joey respected how he'd followed his happiness.

Demetris listened when Joey said she didn't feel like oils, when she asked, could she paint only in yellow today? He taught her to feel fruit with her eyes closed, to feel its energy, and he taught her the same with the pencil.

"Use the brain that is in your hand," he always said in those early years, loosening her death grip. "Your head is the servant. Your hand is the master."

Demetris lived in a historic burnt-orange building on the main thrust of Liston, the area boasting posh cafés, with a series of arches replicating the Rue de Rivoli in Paris. Demetris's third-floor apartment had one small window that overlooked the *platia*, the grassy expanse between Liston and the Old Fortress, in the part of town most emblematic of the island's French and Venetian influences. His apartment was adorned in the black-and-white paintings of townspeople for which he was renowned across the island and mainland Greece.

Joey moved aside two empty espresso cups in the corner that got little sun. She plunked down the canvas.

"Hi, Demetris!"

"*Yia sou* to you too, Joey *mou.*" Demetris wore baggy Dad-style blue jeans, although he was not one, and black work boots.

"I'm so glad to see you. *Yia sou!*" Joey kissed both his cheeks.

He looked amused. "Demetris is glad to see you too." For some reason, he sometimes spoke in third person. That was part of Demetris's charm.

"How are you?" she asked. "How is Bella?"

"No complaints." He smiled and turned his attention to the canvas. "What have you brought to me?" This was quintessential Demetris—down to business fast.

"Well, I think I'm onto something with these eyes. But obviously I want your opinion." Joey watched him as he studied the canvas. "I want them to be bigger. Sort of evil eyes, but sort of real eyes. Out of scale on a human head.

There's something in them, don't you agree?" She scrutinized an iris. "But I don't know. Something's off."

Demetris's face didn't flicker. "Joey *mou*, you come to
Demetris for a reason, no?"

"Yes."

"You trust Demetris, no?"

"Yes."

"Please, put the canvas on the floor." She obeyed. "*Ella,*
take a pencil."

She groaned. "I know where you're going with this. It's
like when I was ten."

He cocked his head at her. "You did some of your best
work when you were ten."

～

"Close your eyes," said Demetris.

"This is strange," said Joey.

"Accept the strangeness."

Yes, they were not strangers to strange. When she was
younger, Demetris liked to play games to train her perspec-
tive. He'd hand her string and a scissors. He'd draw a line on
the wall. On his own living room wall! (*Bella will kill you,*
she'd say. *I'll paint it a new color,* he'd shrug.) He would
make her stand ten feet away. *Cut the string to the size of
that line.* She would cut too short. *Go back, do it again.*
She would cut it far too long. *Back. If this game was good
enough for Da Vinci, it is good enough for Joey Abrams.*

Now Demetris pried the pencil from her hand and re-
instated it beneath her fingers. "Loosen up, *paidi mou.* You
don't have to create now. The pressure is off. You just have
to see what will be on the page. Eyes closed, Joey."

She closed them. She imagined sliding into the sea, down beneath the surface, and resting way below. This was one of Demetris's tricks to get out of her head.

"I want you to draw a mountain. Do you see it?" Joey didn't see it. Down, down, down, deeper in the ocean.

"Relax your eyes, Joey. Focus on the sound of the pencil. That's the only thing in your world. It's a lovely sound. How lucky we are to live in a world with pencils." Demetris hummed some tune that was presumably the Ode to the Pencil.

"Do you see the mountain?" asked Demetris again.

"Yes." Slowly one appeared. The mountains of Corfu.

"Good. Start adding things you see in your picture. Don't skip, Joey. It's a continuous line." Now his voice became more distant. She smelled espresso brewing. Her pencil moved. "Start creating a horizon. Something in order to put the sea under the mountains. So forget what is on your page. It doesn't matter. Just make a horizon. Bravo, Joey. Bravo." The voice was nearer now. Hoarse. "Accept whatever comes, eh, Joey? Now, slowly, you realize on your right side there is something. Yes. Yes. Draw that."

Joey saw a pig on the side. Her hand drew squiggly ears.

After some time, Demetris said, "Now open your eyes. Leave the pencil. So what happened?"

Joey blinked open her eyes to a tangle of indecipherable lines. "I drew a mess."

"That's a mess." Demetris motioned to her canvas. In punctuation, he stepped on it with his boot. She gasped. "There. That's better."

"Why did you do that?" Joey felt the prickly onset of tears. There was an unmistakable boot smudge by the left iris. "I worked so hard on that eye!"

"Yes. You did. Sometimes you try to control too much. You know what I think? I think this mark my boot made is very interesting." Joey took a deep breath. She knew that arguing with Demetris would be futile. They'd go back and forth, each with sentences that would better fit into other conversations. Anyway, as irritating as the fact was, Demetris was usually right. And he stretched her as an artist like no teacher ever had.

Demetris put the canvas on the table. He slid the pencil in her left hand. She always drew with her right.

She gave him a look. She didn't want to draw with her left hand. "It will turn out terribly."

"And maybe it won't, Joey *mou*. Have you considered that? Maybe it will turn out to be the greatest thing you've ever made."

⌒

The terrace glittered with lights strung on the railing and votives on the table. Joey stacked dessert plates scraped clean of their *pantespani* sponge cake. *Zorba the Greek* played from the stereo in one of the apartments; Joey couldn't tell which. They never locked the terrace doors, just floated in and out of rooms, the maze of the top floor.

Rand lifted Jefferson the Cat onto his lap and said into his fur, "Bonjour, my boy."

"I'm going in to paint. I still can't get this nipple right. It's pointing oddly to the right." Bea wandered to the door. Then she glanced back, as if they might chime in with thoughts on nipple placement.

"I'll be in in a bit, sweetheart," said Scott.

"I'm just getting started," said Maisy. She stood and

swayed, her martini sloshing over its glass. "Who's going to dance with me?"

"Not I." Rand stubbed out his cigar. "I gotta call my broker."

"Scott, you've got your dancing shoes on." Maisy set her martini down and clapped her hands in glee. "I know it. Come on. I'll put on music for the *syrtaki*."

Joey's father stumbled up and waved his arms in the air. He had long, slim arms that never tanned, like glow sticks in the night. Joey didn't think she'd ever seen her father dance. He must have had a second glass of wine. He was doing a half Roger Rabbit, half Irish jig. He was an atrocious dancer, especially in comparison with Maisy, who in her younger years had danced for the New York City Ballet.

Joey sipped her wine and watched the silhouettes of Maisy and her father. She stared at the bouquet of sunflowers in a chipped green jug on the table.

Then it hit her. Then she remembered.

It was vivid like it had happened the night before. But it hadn't.

Joey had been eleven—too old to call out for her parents when she was having a nightmare. But she'd had the nightmare again about the camps that were not camps. In the nightmare, she'd been sleeping on straw with other human scarecrows, and you couldn't escape because outside in the dark was an electrical fence that would shock you. There'd been evil men shouting and then the shouting had closed in. Boots pounding dirt. Closer and closer.

Joey sprang up in bed, panting. She watched the shadows

play on the old soldier's brick barrack walls and registered that she was in Corfu. But then she gasped because still she could hear the footsteps, and her heart jangled in her chest to their beat.

Sleeping was terrifying. You had no control where it took you.

In Joey's fifth-grade class, just a few months prior, an older boy had given a presentation about his family's trip to Auschwitz. Before that, Joey had known about Auschwitz in only a tangential way. Her grandfather's numbers were from Auschwitz. There was a horrible room full of human hair there. Her grandmother had a picture of suitcases there.

But this boy had shown pictures of barracks and impossibly emaciated people and things called gas chambers. Where people were *gassed*. He'd told about an evil man who sent people right to live, left to die. He'd talked about families wrenched apart, experiments on twin girls, death. Murder. Basically everyone was murdered for a thing they couldn't change. For being Jewish. Even if you converted, it didn't matter. Jewish blood condemned you.

Joey was Jewish.

Joey had always despised scary movies. In kindergarten, her teacher had called her mom in for a conference because Joey refused to watch the movies at rest hour. Her mom had protested that the teacher was showing scary movies. The infamous line the teacher had said in response was, *"Petey the Dog?"*

But this wasn't about scary movies. Her whole way home from school after the slide show, Joey had thought of just one thing. "They gassed them like nothing," her grandfather had once said at the dinner table. "My family." Joey had already finished dinner so she'd been playing with a yo-yo in the corner and hadn't seen his face. She'd had only a vague thought: *I wonder who farted on Grandfather's family.* But then her yo-yo had yo'd, and the question had vanished.

The day of the slide show, Joey had returned early from school to her father in the kitchen, reading a brief at the kitchen counter.

He'd said, "How was your day, baby?"

She'd whispered, "Why didn't you tell me people murder us for being Jewish?"

And her father had held her and said it was a very long time ago, but that hadn't made her feel better.

The images from the slide show had refused to leave Joey's head. She'd asked her grandfather one night on his porch, "Will it happen again?"

"Absolutely not," he'd said.

"But you can't promise," she'd said.

Her big, strong grandfather had just looked at his black leather shoes.

She'd gotten him.

Now Joey palmed her forehead of sweat. She was eleven, ostensibly grown up, somewhat assuaged by her solid Corfu surroundings but easily swayed back to that camp in a dark, distant Poland, some cruel commandant's footsteps closing in. When her breathing slowed from its rapid heaves, Joey crept to the main room. She smelled the fumes of paint from a drying canvas. She heard voices on the terrace.

"Mom," she called. "Dad." She reached for the curtains. Shadows. Cicadas. Laughter. She slid open the screen door, on the verge of calling for her parents again, and then she felt hands atop her shoulders.

All she remembered was lying back in bed with her

ratty stuffed bear Nacho Chip, whose nose she'd long since chewed off. Her father's face hung over her. He said, "It's okay, baby."

She wasn't speaking. It was excruciating—having a scream inside you couldn't get out.

He said, "Let's get these nightmares out of you, okay?"

Yes. She wanted the nightmares out. All of them.

He said, "Let's count some sheep." Joey closed her eyes and counted the sheep her father described. The fluffy one. The scrawny one. The fat one. The one with lots of fleas. They counted millions of sheep, it seemed. She felt her eyelids flutter.

Her father said, "Now I want you to imagine a field of sunflowers, okay? Remember, like we saw last summer on the way to Kassiopi?"

Joey remembered. She'd run alongside a row of them, and her father had taken her picture and framed it for his desk.

"There are sunflowers in every direction," said her father. "The sky is really blue, and you're running in the sunflowers, and you're so happy. That's all you remember about tonight. Your mom and dad love you. We love you so much. Nothing else is real. Do you see the sunflowers, baby?"

Joey didn't speak. She did see them. But the sky wasn't blue, and she didn't feel the happiness he was describing. She felt Nacho Chip's cold nose poke her arm.

Her father said, "Good job, baby."

Then he said, "Good night, Joey. I love you more than you can imagine."

He said, and she remembered it now, "You didn't see anything."

◡◡

Joey didn't know if she'd ever witnessed sunrise in the summer. Sunrise, period. She stepped onto the terrace where her father was drinking a blue smoothie. Before them rose Corfu Town in the peek-a-boo of morning, the sky shredded in orange.

"Hey, sweetheart." Her father laced up his sneakers. "Want to come running with me?" Joey shook her head. "Everything okay?" He was wearing the T-shirt she'd made for her parents' tenth anniversary, with a picture of them in their twenties, looking happy and slightly red in the face, squinting at the sun.

Was everything okay? Well, yes, life was wonderful, but still, sometimes Joey's mind dove into the crevices. Demetris called her a Sensitive Person. *Life is harder for a Sensitive Person*, paidi mou. *But life is more beautiful for a Sensitive Person.*

Joey wished she were not a Sensitive Person. That she was more like Bea, who only heard the good things people said. *Your painting is beautiful, but why is there a green blob on the right half and do you think the lines of the butt should create more of a Victorian shape, and maybe you want to reconsider the facial structure, the jaw is a bit square.* All Bea heard was, *Your painting is beautiful.*

Joey, on the other hand, heard the criticisms. Demetris said, *Your life will be difficult if you can't believe a compliment*, paidi mou. But she couldn't change who she was.

"Yes, of course, Dad. Everything's good." She didn't ask, *Who was on the terrace that night when I was eleven? What exactly did I not see?* "Did you and Maisy dance late?"

"Dance?"

"Yeah, you were still dancing when I went to bed."

"Were we now?" Her father grabbed his wrists to the right and stretched his hips left. "Well, that's funny. I'm a terrible dancer."

"No arguments here," said Joey, immediately flinching at how unnecessarily mean she'd sounded.

The look on her father's face was almost tragic in its hurt. The thing was, he was a great dad. He came to her plays, even the one where she played cowgirl number four, with exactly one line. He came to her swim meets with a video camera, even though she gave him a look every time he panned in as she mounted the starting block.

But then she quit acting. She quit the swim team. She needed to get serious, to fill her schedule with advanced art courses. He still came to all her shows, proclaiming everything she made "Beautiful! Beautiful!" Although he'd once added jokingly, "All those squiggly lines look the same to me."

Lately he'd been urging Joey to take the LSATs, saying things like, "You know, Joey, in our family, Mom is not the breadwinner. She makes beautiful things, but that's not what allows us to eat."

Now her father said a quiet, "Okay." He started off the terrace.

It was the sunflowers. The stupid sunflowers made her say it.

"Dad," she whispered. "I'm sorry for saying that thing before, about your dancing."

Her dad turned. He put a hand to his brow to deflect the sun's first sting. "It's fine, Joey. It's fine."

chapter ten

Sarah

corfu

1942

In the month after Sarah saw the dreamy fisherman, she took often to the port under thin rationales. She was eager to retrieve lamb for her mother from the butcher by the sea, eager to collect pails of water from the well in the synagogue courtyard. And suddenly she was weaving an indirect route past the port toward the place of her employ—the apartment of a widowed gentleman on Solomou Street, for whom Sarah laundered clothes and then ironed them, even his handkerchiefs and socks.

Sarah hadn't shared her fisherman sighting with anyone, not even Rachel, although she'd wholeheartedly apologized to her best friend, reassuring her that of course it was wonderful she and Solomon had a burgeoning romance.

The High Holidays passed, and a new year begun, as all the while Sarah ruminated upon her own burgeoning something. But so far, her eyes hadn't latched upon him again.

She told herself it was a good thing, as she walked along

the sea with Benjamin in early October, on their typical Sabbath stroll. That boy wasn't Jewish, and she didn't know him besides. Maybe he had a voice like a girl and a stench of fishy fish, besides. But Sarah wasn't much convincing herself because, after family lunch, she'd donned her finest blue shirtdress and brushed her hair with the hundred strokes that was Rachel's professed beauty secret.

Now the sunshine baked Sarah's arms, freckled from the frolic of a carefree summer concluded. As Sarah's stomach groaned with the weight of her mother's veal sofrito and fasolia green beans, Benjamin paused beside a light post. He set his book upon the rail and wiped his hands against his black trousers. Then he peered down at the tiny ripples of cerulean sea and eventually squinted out at the distant lumps of forested mountains and land.

"Sarah, on the Sabbath we rest, but the sea never does. It's always moving to new places."

"That's true." Sarah watched the sea and its gentle waves, and wondered where they were off to. She'd never been outside of Corfu, whereas the sea had such exotic stories to tell. "It's a very wise thing to say."

Sarah went to pat Benjamin's hand, but before she could do so, a cluster of boys around Benjamin's age ran past. One of them, a tall boy with a face sharp like a fox, sang, "There goes Benjamin Batis with his flaming-red hair and his lovely, little dress." The other boys pealed with laughter, trouncing along the shoreline.

In a flash, Sarah's feet took off. When she caught up with the fox boy, she grabbed him by his sleeve.

"Hey!" he protested. "You'll rip it."

"Rip it! I have a mind to rip it right off! Don't you *ever* speak to my brother like that again. Don't you ever! Do you hear?" Sarah tightened her grip on his sleeve and was assuaged when the boy's face paled, sufficiently spooked.

"*Signomi, signomi.* I didn't mean—"

"You *did* mean. Next time you pass my brother, you don't even look in his direction, you understand?"

"I understand."

The fox boy swiveled his head, like Sarah was going to punch him or something. Not so brave after all, fox boy, eh? "Good." Sarah released her grip. "Go."

But the fox boy and his friends didn't move, frozen as a column of Italian soldiers marched by with their long rifles and circular hard hats. Sarah recognized one, a kind general for whom she'd helped bargain for strawberries in the market because she knew Italian and he didn't know Greek.

Once the soldiers had passed, Sarah shouted again, "Go!" and this time the bullies darted away without laughter in their wake.

Sarah returned to a pensive Benjamin, staring off at the sea. She fingered one of the curls that wrapped around his ear.

"Do I look like a girl, Sarah?" Benjamin asked.

"You don't," she said firmly. She could just murder those boys. She really could.

"My pants are baggy. Like a dress, must be."

"They don't look like a dress. But perhaps we'll have Baba make them tighter. You need to eat more!"

She smiled, but Benjamin didn't smile back. "Why do they say things like that to me?"

"Oh." A heron craned its long neck from its perch on the branch of an olive tree, like it too was curious at how Sarah was going to explain this. She thought about how she'd reacted to Rachel weeks ago, how her anger at her friend had stemmed from jealousy. "You know, maybe those boys are a little scared inside, or sad, and then being mean to people is a way to distract from how they feel. But it's not the brave way."

Benjamin nodded, and Sarah was relieved when his face settled back into innocence. As she smoothed down her hair rumpled by a whip of wind, her eyes caught a glimpse of *the* fisherman.

Her heart went immediately berserk, and she stumbled back, drinking him in. This time he wore black slacks with a white-collared shirt and was transferring fish from his nets into baskets. He was tall, Sarah decided, taller and thinner than her father at least, who served as her barometer thus far for all things male. Sarah fanned her face and decided this was how people died, from too much excitement heaped upon their organs. She'd thought herself gutsy the past weeks, stalking about for him, but now she understood, she didn't have it in her to approach him. She would hasten home for the close of the Sabbath and sink to the floor as her father strummed his bouzouki and forget she'd ever set eyes on the fisherman.

As Sarah steered Benjamin back toward town, a shout emanated from the seaside. "Are you going to leave again without saying hello? It's not a very polite thing to do."

Sarah gazed around. There was no one else. He pointed at her.

Sarah took Benjamin's hand and walked over. "I am the most polite girl you will ever meet."

The fisherman smiled. She was his in that smile. It was blankets and ice cream and meadows, all in that smile.

"You weren't so polite when you didn't say hello last time. A month ago now, was it?" He set down his net of fish and raked a hand through sea-sprayed hair.

"You saw me?" Her heels faltered on the unsteady pebble beach, and the boy grabbed her arm to keep her from falling. His touch sent electricity down her bones.

"How could I miss you?" he asked.

Sarah sifted in herself for something clever to say in return. She'd never had a conversation like this before, never known what it would be like to stand in the spotlight of a boy's affection.

"My name is Milos." The fisherman stuck out his hand to Benjamin. His eyes were a stillness of sea green, like the spots in the sea beyond the darker blue, and Sarah could understand now what her father meant, how easy it could be to fall inside someone's eyes.

"Benjamin." Her brother shook Milos's hand solemnly.

"And you are?"

Sarah thrust her shoulders back, projecting a confidence she didn't feel. "Sarah Batis."

"Sarah." Her name sounded delightful on his tongue. She was in so much trouble.

"We have to get home now." She stepped away but then burrowed her heel back into the pebbles because her feet were shouting that they didn't want to move.

"What was that before, though? Those boys?"

"Sarah told them to stop," Benjamin said. "They were making fun of my red hair."

"Your red hair?" Milos's eyes didn't stray from Sarah's as he said, "But why ever would they make fun of that? Why, I happen to think red is the nicest shade of hair that exists."

They bid goodbye to Milos and walked up from the port, with Benjamin blessedly oblivious to the import of the meeting. He chattered on about Robinson Crusoe, speculating on whether pirates lurked in their own Ionian Sea. Sarah made some *mmmm* noises and finally gazed back to see Milos standing where they'd left him, staring after her.

"I think I left my shawl. Let me just go back to see."

"Okay." Benjamin plopped on a bench, and his book sprang open.

Sarah walked the white gravelly path back to Milos. The sun was doing its spectacular sleepy dance, with two fiery stripes emanating from it on the diagonal, like wings.

"Hello," said Milos.

She stopped in front of him. "Hello. I thought I might have forgotten my shawl."

He looked around, indulging her excuse. "Don't see it."

"Yes. Well then, I'll—"

"Meet me tomorrow. Won't you, I mean?" He smiled, and his dimple flashed, the shadow of it covering briefly the mole on his left cheek. She was beginning to take inventory of his features and qualities, and that was not a good thing.

"Meet you? I don't know a thing about you."

"What do you want to know? I'm from Lefkada." Sarah filed it away—the island seventy-some miles to their south. "I came here to try my luck for the season. See if your fish are any better."

She laughed. "And?"

He shrugged. "Fish are fish are fish. But maybe I've just been waiting for my good-luck charm." She blushed and looked off at Mouse Island. "I'll tell you anything you would like to know if you meet me tomorrow."

Sarah twined her fingers into her dress. "I have to work."

"After work then."

You're not Jewish, she wanted to say. But her mouth wouldn't expel it. Instead she said, "Where?"

"The Frourio, how about?" The Old Fortress was a Venetian landmark from Byzantine times but not far enough in Sarah's opinion from the Evraiki and prying neighborly eyes. "Let's meet at four o'clock on the bridge, and we can picnic on the channel."

"How about the meadow uphill from the bridge?" She went there sometimes with Rachel, where it was less traveled.

"That suits me, if it suits you."

"It suits me, I think."

"You think?"

Sarah blushed. "I'm bad at this. I've never...I've never really done it before."

"Talked to a boy?" He smiled, and then his smile faded, as smiles inevitably did. Sarah immediately wondered what she could say to make him do it again.

"Talked to a boy like you."

She hoped he wouldn't tease her more and was gratified when he said, "Come to the Frourio with me so we can talk more."

And Sarah couldn't quite believe it when she heard herself say, "Okay."

⌒

Sarah walked slowly back to Benjamin. Without looking back, she could feel Milos's eyes bore into her back.

Benjamin closed his book. "Did you find your shawl?"

"Oh. No, I must have left it at home."

Her father's oft-repeated words rang in her ears. *All you have in the world is your good name. So be a person who always tells the truth. Just like your grandmother. You are wonderful and honest just like her.* Sarah was named for his mother, who died in childbirth delivering his baby sister and whom Sarah apparently resembled from her vivid red hair and long fingers, down to her stellar negotiation skills.

Sarah would always remember it—the day she became a bad person. The first of her lies. It wouldn't be her last.

⌒

After their picnic at the Frourio, Sarah and Milos were inseparable. *But as friends*, Sarah told herself firmly on a daily and hourly basis, when her mind piped up to remind her what trouble she was starting.

They had to sneak around, of course. As Sarah told Milos from the start, her parents would disown her for even carrying on a friendship with a boy who was not Jewish. But they would walk along the sea, on a remote stretch far from the Evraiki, and then Sarah would cry no and run off, and Milos would go fishing, and then she'd be there waiting for him, after all.

The winter was coming. Milos would be returning to Lefkada. They couldn't be, and yet.

The day before Milos was to leave, Sarah offered to pick up metsovone cheese for her father's birthday celebration. Metsovone was a hard, smoked cheese from the mountains of mainland Greece, delicious on the grill and a delicacy of rare appearance in the Batis home. But her father adored it so Sarah's mother gave her ten drachmas to spend for the special occasion. Sarah retrieved the metsovone and then met Milos at the port as he roped up his *kaiki*. They wandered westward even more, farther from the Evraiki, which was their unspoken practice.

Finally, they plopped beneath an olive tree. Sarah watched a lizard scamper across the parched grass as a few peasant girls in their colorful wares hitched their donkeys to a nearby rail.

"They look sad, don't you think?" Sarah asked.

"The girls?"

"No, the donkeys."

"What makes you think so?"

"Look at him." She pointed to a particularly droopy one, his ears doing some sad slap against his neck. He was smaller than the others, a baby it appeared, with chunky, unsteady legs. Sarah was struck by a wish he was doing baby things, like resting and playing, rather than working to transport these peasant girls on the Sabbath. "He probably doesn't even have a name, that's how little he matters in this world."

"So give him one."

"A name? But what does it matter if I give him a name? He'll never know."

"Oh, I think he'll know." Milos put his hand gently on hers. It was the first time he'd ever touched her, the first time she'd let herself be touched, and it sent a wave of pleasure crashing over her.

"Okay, then I name him Spyro Moustakas."

Milos laughed. "Spyro because he is a Corfiot donkey?"

Sarah was still acutely aware of their hands touching, unable to find the will to tell him to move his away. "Yes, he is blond. So clearly not Jewish. Therefore, he must be named after the island's patron saint."

"Logically sound," agreed Milos. "And Moustakas because…?"

"Because he looks a little bit like my father, and my father has a mustache." Sarah was satisfied. "Yes. It suits him, Spyro Moustakas, doesn't it?"

"I wish I could meet your father," said Milos. "To be certain."

"I wish you could too." And for a while they held hands, watching Spyro Moustakas buckle his legs and settle to the ground, by all appearances content with his newly christened name.

"I love you, Sarah, for how much you care. Not just about people. Now I discover you care about donkeys too."

As the words assimilated, the first time he'd said them, Sarah's heart thundered in her chest. Milos wore his pale-green shirt marred post-fishing by blue-black squid ink stains, that Sarah nonetheless loved because it acted as a big arrow sign to his eyes. In Milos's eyes, she could forget there were things like Germans deporting Jews on the mainland and rules about who you could love. She recognized the crossroads they were at, and that she couldn't dismiss the love feelings growing in her too. They weren't just friends. The friend label had been a bandage her mind had invented.

Sarah retracted her hand from their clasp and stared down at the grass. "I don't mean to hurt you, but it's just impossible, you and me."

"Nothing is impossible if you want it enough. That's what my father says."

Sarah knew about Milos's father, who worked in the granite quarry, and his mother, who prepared food at the winery and whose oven-baked swordfish and stuffed aubergines Milos salivated over after such a time away. Sarah knew about their house with chickens roaming outside that Milos killed on a stump, and his married older brother and new-born baby sister, and his island's chalky white mountains and unspoiled string of beaches with cliff-backed coves where they could swim together without seeing another soul for miles.

Sarah debated between having an honest conversation about their future or instead chattering on about something stupid, like the cheese she could see poking out of her knapsack. The sight of the cheese made her realize she was very hungry, in fact.

"Shall we have a tiny bit of metsovone?" She unwrapped it from the brown paper and broke off a crumbly piece, handing half of the piece to Milos. "Just a little, because it's for my father."

Guilt immediately assaulted her, over subtracting even a little bit of her father's birthday joy. Sarah quickly put her little piece back with the big wedge and wrapped it all in its paper. She placed the cheese in her knapsack and reclined against the olive tree. "Hey, tell me about your novel again. It's a story at sea, right?"

"Yes!" Milos reliably loved this topic. "A boat's going to get lost. It will be a gritty survival tale."

"How does the protagonist survive again?"

"Ah," said Milos. "A lady's blouse is used to collect rainwater."

"Brilliant," said Sarah.

"Well, I don't know if I would put me at the brilliant stage. It's only funny ideas."

"You will make it happen. Of that I have no doubt."

"I should like to. You know, one day, when the Germans leave Paris, we should go there!"

"Really?" It sounded completely fantastic, like the end of the world. Until Sarah met Milos, her dream had been singular and small—marry a Romaniote man with a trade and bear him children. But Milos fanned out cards offering dangerous, cosmopolitan, alternative hands.

"Yes! I'll write my novel. I'll be like Hemingway. And your brother will join us too." Milos had met Benjamin, of course, once—insufficient to capture his kind, curious cleverness. But Sarah had regaled Milos with many Benjamin stories since. "Benjamin will write his own masterpiece. We'll be the new literati."

"And what would I do?" Sarah teased.

"We'll have children," Milos said, matter-of-factly. "A girl and a boy."

Children together. Sarah's heart constricted at all the steps that would have to come before children. Her parents approving of them, to start.

Tears sprang unexpectedly in her eyes. "I need to get home for my father's birthday."

"So . . . this is—"

"I wish you wouldn't leave," she blurted. "I wish so much you wouldn't go." Her stomach was unhappy with her, and it wasn't just the metsovone. Milos had done something to it, mixed up all her chemistry.

"This is only *see you later*," he said firmly. "I'll be back in the spring."

"The spring is forever away."

"I'll miss you terribly. I want to be with you forever, Sarah *mou*."

Milos drew her to his chest, and for the first time she allowed herself to rest against it. His chest was sturdy and strong, just like she'd imagined, and she savored the sound of his heartbeat before some force outside of her lifted her head, and Milos bent down to kiss her. The kiss turned her inside out with its right-ness, like carving out a place that was now confusingly home. But she had another home, and the two could never merge.

They kissed, hungrily then, until Sarah broke from him and ran along the sea now slashed with moonlight. She forced herself not to look back, making her legs cycle faster, and faster yet, to beat down the terrible knowing that had surfaced, as to which of her two homes she might now choose.

When Sarah returned home, she paused just outside her door, noticing that her knapsack was open. Her chest seized in fear as she rifled inside to discover that, sure enough, the metsovone was gone. It must have fallen out somewhere in her dash home, to make it on time for her father's birthday. She considered turning back, retracing her steps, but chances were someone had found it, already delighting in their good fortune.

Sarah stood outside the door, tears collecting in the corners of her eyes. Surely this was punishment for breaking off that piece of metsovone for her and Milos to eat. And a punishment for more, she realized with dread, for even carrying on with Milos. Sarah thought of her father's unrelenting admonishments: how important it was to maintain their insular Jewish community; that she was not even to be friends with boys from the outside.

But this punishment of the metsovone wasn't fair! Because it affected her father, who in the rare instances Sarah had watched him eat it, closed his eyes in rapture as he did so.

⌒

That evening, after delicious stuffed tomatoes, grilled fish, and potato bourekas, Sarah sat on the floor beside the fireplace wedged between their two family beds, listening to her father strum his bouzouki. Her mind was an inferno of the metsovone incident, and then Milos and perhaps never seeing him again, but her father's voice lent familiar cadence to her despondence.

At first, he was murmuring, notes without words, and then he added some.

And so it is.

I am old.

Life has been beautiful.

"You're not that old, Baba." Her father was thirty-six, the same age as her mother.

"If he is old, then what am I?" asked her mother, her blue eyes unusually teasing. She had finished the dishes and was now in an uncommon perch, sitting doing nothing on her bed, below her favorite framed painting of pink roses. Sarah, Benjamin, and their father would often pick her fresh bunches, sometimes competing to deliver the grandest assortment, because pink roses, both real and inanimate, proved the surest way to make her smile.

"You are young, *agapi mou*," said Sarah's father. "You are young and beautiful forever. Come, Benjamin. Dance with me."

Sarah's brother had lit the kerosene lamp and was now reading in the window nook with his beloved bunny rabbit,

Penelope, in her cage at his feet. Her mother called the spot God's window; in the daylight, you could see the buildings all nearly kissing with golden light spilling over the ceramic rooftops, but now just the crescent moon hung in view beyond the slats.

"Dance?" asked Benjamin, clearly not eager to leave his book.

"It is my birthday, and I wish to dance!"

Sarah smiled in spite of her sorrow over the metsovone and Milos as her father began to hum the "Kokoraki," an upbeat song about animals at a fair. *Ki ki ri ki ki*, he sang, bopping around their room with his eyes shut, so handsome in his nice black suit that he usually reserved for the Sabbath.

Sarah loved seeing him happy because her father was the type of person whose pain sometimes got turned inside out for some time. His mother had died in childbirth when he was seven, and then his younger sister from tuberculosis when he was thirteen. He always said, *I am happy. I have my wonderful family.* But Sarah was too sensitive a person to accept it. Sometimes she gazed at her father and his ears that stuck out a bit, and she could see him as a child. And then she would feel unsure for a moment, about who between them was protecting whom.

"I gave you ten drachmas for metsovone!" her mother said quietly, leaning down from the couch to Sarah's perch on the floor. "We don't have money, Sarah. You know this. And it's even more dire with the war. On the mainland people are dying, Sarah. And here I saved money for your father's metsovone."

"I'm so sorry, Mama. I…like I told you, it just fell out." She hung her head.

"You were careless, Sarah. Things don't just fall out. When they are important, you pay close attention to them."

And Sarah didn't say anything because she wholeheartedly agreed. She wished so badly she could turn back time and guard the metsovone with everything she had. Sarah watched her father dance and eventually coax Benjamin up too, and the pair of them went round and round their small little room, pausing with an *Opa* beside their handwritten family tree chart composed of concentric circles, like rings on an old tree. The chart was a tradition among Corfiot Jews, and Sarah had grown up on the stories behind the names written in careful script in each little box.

Sarah closed her eyes and listened to their footwork resume and the loop of *ki ki ri ki ki*, and her thoughts shifted to Milos. Only to Milos.

chapter eleven

Joey

corfu

2004

They stood before the turquoise beach at Paleokastritsa, on Corfu's western coast. The sky glowed in gradients of white. Taxi drivers hunched over a folding table, playing vigorous backgammon. Joey still had no clue why they were there.

"I want to show you something, Jonesey!" Leo said, bouncing her arm.

Leo led her through a maze of docks across the harbor. They stopped at a yacht that gleamed white and blue. "This is my yacht for the summer."

"Your yacht? What do you mean?" Her chest twitched with mild alarm. Some people loved surprise parties, which Joey couldn't fathom. She liked time to prepare herself, and besides she was generally too hyper-perceptive for a surprise to work before she'd sniffed it out. But in this case, she hadn't seen it coming. Leo's *yacht*.

"Come on, Jonesey. Let me give you a tour." Without explaining, he hopped on and helped her over. She glimpsed the nameplate. APOLLO.

Leo led her to an impressive salon adorned in Missoni throws and then down a flight of stairs. He pointed out the staterooms (tiny cabins best suited for midgets) and the galley (a kitchen the appropriate size for Lily to bake up some mean pretend brownies). Okay, Joey acknowledged her crankiness, but a sense of foreboding had gripped her. Leo mixed them screwdrivers, sprinkling words like *gunwale* and *hawser* with mounting enthusiasm.

"Leo," she said, after they'd returned to what he'd called the stern, and he'd clarified that this meant the back of the boat. "What did you mean it's *your* yacht?"

"Oh." Leo jumped off the boat and extended his hand. "The thing is, Jonesey, well…I've sort of been nervous to tell you this. I'm dropping out of Michigan."

"You're what?" She stuck in place, and it took a few moments for the disorientation to lift. "Leo, wait up. Wait up, Leo!" She ran down the dock and turned him by his shoulder.

"It's not my thing, Jonesey. I gave it a try, and it wasn't for me."

"What do you mean? College is for everybody."

"Not me." Leo grimaced. "All that, *Hey dude, hey bro, swallow this goldfish so we can be like brothers. Do pushups and don't shower for a week. Now some sorority pledges are gonna whore it up for us! Pass me a cig, man.* They're all just so terrified someone's going to figure them out."

"Figure what out?"

"That they're little babies inside. That they have no idea who the fuck they are, what the fuck they want, so they swallow goldfish to get people to be their friends. To validate them."

"Okay…" said Joey slowly. "So de-pledge your frat."

"I did de-pledge my frat. That's not it, Jonesey. It's all of college. These kids are just stupid. Privileged and stupid. They couldn't give a shit about careers or having conversations about things that matter. All they care about is football, beer, and sex."

"So you're saying you don't care about sex?" Joey laughed a tentative laugh.

"That, I do still care about." Leo pulled her into a half embrace. "I misspoke, Jonesey. Please don't think I've turned puritan on you."

"What are you going to do if you drop out? I don't get it."

"This!" Leo gestured back to the boat, to the sea. The look on his face scared Joey. It was like the one he had sometimes when she came onto the terrace after a shower, all scrubbed with wet hair. "The captain, Dave is his name. He's American too, actually. I met him last summer at the port in town. He's based out of Monaco now—that's the most sought-after port for charter boats. Dave's in his fifties, but he also quit school when he was our age. He knew a life at sea was his passion. That boating was his passion. And lectures on calculus and Western Civ weren't going to get him there."

Right now, Joey was internally cursing this Dave and all his passions. "So a life at sea is your passion?"

"Well, yeah," said Leo. "It is. It's always been, if I think of it. I'm gonna help Dave with his boat now. He's refitting it because some idiot guest took the wheel and rammed the boat onto a sandbar. So it's kind of a lucky break."

"Lucky," she said, unable to conceal her sarcasm.

"Don't be like that, Jonesey." They'd reached the beach now, and Leo pulled her down to the sand. "Look at all this."

The waves discarded black detritus at the shore. A piece stuck to Joey's foot. She touched it without removing it.

"This is going to be my life now, J."

And Joey didn't know what to say because she thought she was going to be his life now.

As if reading her mind, he said, "Jonesey, this doesn't change things for us."

She nodded, but she didn't know what that meant. "So after this summer, you're going to—"

"The Caribbean, yeah. Monaco's the dream, but Dave's doing winter down in the Caribbean. It won't be easy. I'm going to start at the bottom. A deckhand. I have a lot to learn, but I want to get my captain's license and..." He couldn't squelch a goofy grin. "I'm really excited, J."

"Did you tell your parents?"

"Yeah." His smile evaporated. "I told them in Michigan, before we left for Corfu."

Joey nodded, stung that he'd told them first but not wanting to make a deal out of it. "And what did they say?"

"My father thinks it's his fault. That he never should have given me the idea that boating is blissful. Because boating is a hobby." Leo mimicked Rand's lulling drawl. "A hobby you get to partake in once you become a success. And you only become a success if you go to college and get your MBA and prove yourself on Wall Street and then, of course, take over the family business.

"*You won't be able to make a living and have a stable life, Leo.*" Leo cast his eyes out to sea. "He's hoping he can change my mind still. Get me back to Michigan. He'll probably never do the Leo Winn thing again. Thank the Lord."

Joey laughed even though this was clearly not funny. "Leo *what*?"

"You sound like a chain-smoking football coach."

"I said Leo what?" She had to keep going with the shtick or she was going to lose it. "I can't hear you!"

"Winn," he said drily. "Leo Winn. Only now I'm a big fucking Loser to my father. It's okay. I don't care. I'm not him. I don't want to be him."

"And Maisy? What did your mom say?"

"Maisy." Leo sighed. "Maisy said she'd forgotten something in her garden."

"Oh." The sun was fiery on Joey's shoulders, and yet she shivered. "But, like, Leo, I don't get it." She shaped sand into a mound and then punched it spontaneously with her fist. "If you do this, you're gonna be living in the middle of oceans. And if we're going to stay together..." The *if* part paralyzed her. She didn't know how to continue.

"We'll figure it out, Jonesey. I don't know how, but we will. I want to be with you. You're the best part of my life. This doesn't change that."

Joey nodded. She didn't trust herself to speak.

Leo touched her hat. "I like that you're wearing the Jonesey hat."

"It hasn't been the same since the strawberry gelato incident." She tried to crack a smile but couldn't force one out.

She was in a mood, clearly. She remembered a day last summer. Lily had stepped on one of her paintings with the paint still wet. That had been beyond infuriating. And then Joey had gone to lunch with her mother and a strong wind had sent Bea's skirt up to her chest, and it had been clear to Joey, and the whole of Liston, that Bea wore no underwear underneath. It had been really embarrassing, and the worst part was that Bea hadn't even apologized! She'd maintained it was her right to exist sans lingerie at any time or place of her choosing. That actually she should be praised for unbinding the shackles of modern women. She'd had the audacity to suggest that Joey might find herself a little less uptight if she were to abandon her underwear too.

Leo had been on the terrace when Joey got back. It had all been a swirl, a raging swirl, and Leo had said, "Sit down, Jones." She'd sat. "Tell me," he'd said.

"I'm just...*ugh* at my mom and Lily!"

"Okay, tell me more."

"If you really want to know, I feel all...like...annoyed... and down. Really angry. Distraught." She'd felt herself getting even more riled up. There had been an overall feeling surging, a very particular one, that she hadn't been able to wrap inside words. "I feel all *zigzaggy*."

"Yeah," Leo had said, and she'd been able to tell by his voice he was taking her seriously, "zigzaggy. Sounds bad. So, which way is it zigging?"

"Here." She'd pointed to her chest and felt his hand settle on the part of her that was zigzagging like crazy in a downward motion, toward her left foot.

Leo had said, "Is it still zigging?"

She'd said, "It's zagging now, really fucking sharp."

And he'd said, "I can feel it," and so they'd sat like that for a little, as the zigzags came, and she'd felt like they were attached to a string and there was someone outside her pulling at the string, unfolding the zigs and the zags until they settled in a straight calm line and ejected right out of her, landing in a heap at her left foot.

She'd been so grateful then to have her person—the one she could tell about all the strange things that lived inside her.

But that had been last summer. And right now on the beach at Paleokastritsa, Leo didn't feel like someone she could tell about her zigzags. He felt like a person vanishing right before her eyes. They'd had plans—finishing college and then moving to the same city. New York probably, because its urban possibility was so far from their sleepy hometowns in Florida and Michigan. But maybe on reflection now, those had been her plans, and Leo had never seemed sure about a settled-down life.

"Hey, Jonesey, why don't we go swimming?"

"I don't feel like swimming." Joey looked at her sketchbook. She looked at Leo. "How about I sketch you?"

"Sure, Jonesey." Leo retrieved their towel from the beach bag and laid it on the sand. Joey dug in the basket for a pencil. She selected a 0.3-millimeter one. Demetris said it was a good starting pencil. It left only a thread of a line.

That was all Joey felt herself capable of now. A thread of a line.

Leo stared off at the mountain sloping over the turquoise bay.

"Look straight at me," she said.

"Really? When you sketched that woman at Lacones, you had her turn her cheek to the side."

Joey flicked her pencil back and forth, a warm-up for her fingers. "What I've learned, Leo, is that I'm really good at figure drawings. That woman at Lacones staring at the castle, her face was in shadows. The mother and son in Liston walking toward the Spianada. No faces. Only backs. The only face that interests me in the slightest is yours."

"Understandable." Leo sucked in his cheekbones and swiveled his head comically. "It's a pretty stunning face."

"I'm serious, Leo." She debated saying the thing that had

plagued her of late with her art. "I'm afraid something's wrong with me."

"Yeah, Jonesey? What's that?"

She finally said, "I think I can only sketch the face of the person I love." She was glad she had her sunglasses on.

There was just the lull of the waves as Leo reached over and removed her sunglasses. He put a hand on her thigh. He lifted her chin in a way that was so slow and tender she thought she might faint. "Jonesey, I love you too. You have to know how important you are to me."

She bit her lip. Finally, she nodded.

"This yacht thing, it's really scary. I need you to understand it. It's like…" He touched his neck, the part right below his Adam's apple, the part she avoided even brushing against because he always flinched. "It's like this whole year I've felt like someone was strangling me. And now, well, I think I'll be able to breathe again."

A tear plopped onto her sketchbook; the source of it was Leo.

Joey reached over to touch him. And as she stroked his back the way she knew he liked, she had a sinking feeling that the future she'd been counting on had surprised her by shifting askew, and she had no clue how to get it back upright.

chapter twelve

Joey

corfu

2004

"But you know," Bea was saying, knees clasped to chest, "you only have to look so far as the Greek language itself to see how the Greeks place enormous value on femininity."

Maisy poured them all more wine. Greek music wafted from inside. To Joey, it was the language of love as she knew it, suffused with emotion, as if the singers were soap opera stars belting out their lines instead of saying them.

"How is that, Bea?" asked Rand. He'd just returned from a sailing trip to Albania, and he'd turned a color suited to a man discovered on a deserted island with just a palm frond strung around his waist.

"Well, in Greek, words themselves are either masculine or feminine."

"Is that right?" said Scott. "I'm impressed, sweetheart."

"So what words are masculine?" asked Rand.

"Ah-ha! I'll tell you." Bea gave a dramatic pause. "Anger. Fear. Pain. All masculine. How's that for you men?"

"I don't know what that proves," said Rand. "So they arbitrarily assigned genders to these things."

"Arbitrary? I don't think so," said Joey. She realized she must have read the same article as her mother. "How about the feminine words though? Love. Beauty. Art. Truth." Bea smiled at her, but a tight smile. Joey felt uneasy for a moment, like she'd inadvertently stolen her mom's spotlight.

"Impressive, Jonesey." Leo whistled and gave her one of those mock bows that made Joey feel like she'd earned a gold star. "Truth. Feminine, you say? That's very interesting."

"What you see is what you get." Joey laughed. "Right, Mom and Mais?"

"Well, beauty is a woman's purview, I'll give you all that," said Rand. "I wouldn't ever try to convince you I'm beautiful."

"No, you most definitely are not at the moment, my friend." Scott pressed a finger into Rand's skin. "It's like Lily's Etch A Sketch."

"Thanks, bud," said Rand, his smile jarring, the white of his teeth against the red of his skin. "Here's what I don't get. Why all the negative masculine words? Anger, pain. What did we ever do to piss off the Greeks?"

"Yeah!" said Scott. "We're teddy bears, us men."

Joey snorted.

"Because you men don't deal with your pain and anger, and it doesn't go away, it just simmers below the surface," said Maisy. She didn't pipe up often in these sorts of debates, so when she did interject, it was noted.

Jefferson the Cat made a growling noise underfoot.

"No, I'm not giving you my chicken," said Leo in the cat's general direction.

"Sibling rivalry." Rand laughed. Joey couldn't look directly at him.

"How about hate?" asked Leo, in a tone befitting the word he'd tossed into the arena. "Is that feminine or masculine?"

There was some shifting in chairs and drinks being drunk. Leo stood. "Never mind. How about a walk, Jonesey?" She eyed the clouds moving in. "She who wilts in the rain," he said, reading her mind. "If it rains, we'll duck into a bar."

"Okay." Joey stood.

"Don't forget, JoJo," said Bea. "Tomorrow is the reunion of Corfiot Holocaust survivors at the synagogue."

The reminder filled Joey with an immediate, uncomfortable dread. "I'm not sure I can make it."

"JoJo, you have to come," said her mother.

"You're going," said her father. "They're unveiling a plaque in dedication to everyone who died. You have two grandparents—your only living grandparents—whose families will be on that plaque."

"I'll come too," said Leo.

"Sure, Leo," said Bea. "We'd love it."

"Yeah?" Joey asked him, feeling something settle inside her. "That's really nice."

"Of course," he said. "Wouldn't miss it."

The next day, on the way to the synagogue, Leo asked Bea about the progress of her show. Then he listened patiently as Bea spent the whole way down Nikiforou Theotoki Street talking about her new pieces devoted to a woman's menstrual cycle. He kept an inexplicably straight face as they passed the tourist shops selling soaps and dream catchers and sesame peanuts as Bea used the words *womb* and *flow* and *indigenous cultures* and *menstrual cup*. He made *mmm* sounds as they traveled north, beneath a canopy of brilliant fuchsia bougainvillea, past the homemade hat store and the barber and the tavern with lime-green tablecloths that served the best aubergines with feta, as all the while Bea described a particularly tricky time she was having mixing the right shade of crimson early-menstrual blood.

It felt like something of a deliverance when Joey glimpsed the Jewish star insignia on the hunter-green door, the pristine yellow stucco building with its gabled roof that gleamed astride its neighbors in disrepair. Even though the walk from home took five minutes, Joey hadn't crossed the east part of Velissariou since their first summer when she was ten and had waited for her father outside the synagogue.

She followed her parents up the staircase that spilled into the main sanctuary. There milled about thirty or so people whom Joey estimated to generate an average age of eighty-five. Here and there were scattered a few younger ones, presumably progeny of the senior generation.

"It's pretty in here." Leo ran a hand over a wooden bench with intricate armrests.

Joey lingered by the stairs. She fingered the evil eye charm in her pocket that the old lady had given her just outside when she was a kid. She plucked a few orange sugary peanuts off a plate on the bimah.

"Joey, come look at this," said her father. Reluctantly, she crossed the room to a white marble plaque. Beside it, stained-glass windows adorned in a Jewish star and hamsa streamed in films of yellows and reds. Joey crunched on the peanuts.

"This is why we're here, JoJo. After all these years, they've built the memorial statue by the waterfront, and here's the plaque commemorating the ones who died."

"The ones who were murdered, Dad," said Joey quietly.

"Right, you see"—her father pointed—"your grand-mother's maiden name, Batis. And then of course, their last name. Bezas."

Bea was studying the plaque when a man hovering around the average age of the attendees to this somber reunion tapped Bea's shoulder.

Bea turned. "Yes, hello there."

"*Kalimera*," said the gentleman. Good morning.

He was tall with kind, crinkly green eyes, wearing a yellow tweed blazer, matching pants, and a brown cap. He motioned to the woman next to him, who looked to be around Bea's age and wore a floor-length brown dress smattered in pink flowers.

"My father thought you looked familiar," said the woman in English. "He thought you looked like someone he used to know."

"Oh really?" asked Bea. "Who?"

"Her name was Sarah Batis."

Bea smiled. "Well, how about that, that's my mother! Everyone says we have the same eyes." She shook the man's hand.

"So you're here for the reunion?" asked the woman.

"Yes," said Bea. "My parents couldn't be here, but I wanted to come in their place. To be honest, neither of them spoke of the Holocaust much when I was growing up. But you get the gist when you're the kid." She twisted her hands.

"Lucky me, who got a pair of survivors as parents. Probably just means I'm doubly fucked-up."

The woman's mouth parted but then closed. The older man let out a stream of Greek.

Joey and her father strayed back as the trio continued talking.

"Dad, is G a survivor?" asked Joey.

"You know the answer to that, JoJo, don't you?"

Joey's eyes settled upon the white wooden ark that held the Torahs. "The Holocaust gives me nightmares, you know that."

"Well, your grandmother's not a survivor in the sense that she went through it. But her whole family died in the war. They all got sent to Auschwitz."

"And G escaped?"

"Right."

"How?"

"You know, Joey, I don't know the answer to that question. I don't think even your mother knows the answer to that question. G has never liked talking about it."

"Does Grandfather talk about what happened to him? About…" She didn't want to say the word. Auschwitz.

"He has to me. You could ask them, you know."

"You *should* ask them," said Leo. "It's your history." Joey had almost forgotten he was there.

"Maybe," said Joey, although she knew she would not.

"I think it's important to know our ancestors," said Leo.

"Why?" asked Joey.

Leo scrunched his nose. "I think who they are is a little of who we are. And if we want to be like them, then we know a little bit of how to get there. And if we want to be different, well, we get the clues for how to change course."

"But we're not living with the Nazis in charge now!" Joey was surprised to find this anger, or whatever it was, boiling to her surface. "Knowing about all the evil my grandparents experienced doesn't help me. It just makes me so..."

Joey turned away, unable to pinpoint the feeling, and took in the airy space with light-blue walls and yet a pervading eeriness. Everyone was so old. Everything was so sad. There were fewer than a hundred Jews left in Corfu to pray here. Before the war, there had been two thousand. But over sixty thousand Greek Jews, including seventeen hundred Corfiot Jews, were murdered in the Holocaust. Those were the statistics her father had mentioned on the walk over, when she was eager to give her ears something other than menstruation to latch onto.

Suddenly Joey was inside that old nightmare that barraged her in the night, snatched from the synagogue where her grandparents had once prayed. It was night where she'd flown to, back in the barracks, to the soundtrack of boot steps closing in. "I'm gonna wait outside."

Her father said, "But Joey, we're going to say kaddish for the victims soon, and then—"

"I'll be back. I just need air." Joey felt a thing rise up in her chest, a beast virulent and familiar. She barreled past a few old people on the steps and heaved herself through the exit. The heavy heat of late July folded her in.

Leo joined her outside a few moments later. Joey sank down to the sidewalk.

"I'm proud of you, Jonesey," said Leo.

Joey kept her eyes trained down at her feet. "Oh yeah? For what? Coming here? You have a low bar for pride, if that's the case. I was essentially forced." She dug her sandal into a moss-covered stone.

"For being a good daughter." The shadow of Leo hovered over her. "For being a good person. I think you're a really good person, Jonesey."

"Why? I don't even want to know my own grandparents' Holocaust stories. I can barely stand to visit the synagogue they used to go to."

"You know, Jonesey, for being as crazy smart as you are, you're missing something that's pretty obvious to me."

"Oh yeah?" she asked softly. "What?"

"You're only avoiding that stuff because you love your grandparents so much. Your brain doesn't want to accommodate all their pain. I hereby diagnose you with an excess of love, Jonesey."

"Oh." Joey was quiet. She didn't have a word for the feeling she felt. It was like she was an X-ray, and Leo could see into her.

He leaned down and squeezed her hand. "I think you're the best person I know, Jonesey."

chapter thirteen
Sarah

corfu

1943

Nothing ever happened in winter, and Sarah endured that nothing in a tangle of longing. Milos had said he'd return after Easter, and Easter had come to Corfu with trumpets blared by marching parades and clay pots thrown from balconies amid raucous applause.

After Easter, Sarah took to the sea every day. Milos had promised that, when he returned, he would wrap a scarf in the branches of the olive tree under which they used to sit. But slowly the snowcapped mountains of neighboring Albania melted to green, and sunlight stretched the days, and still no scarf.

Then the island rolled out its carpet of flowers in bloom, and Sarah's favorite holiday, Pesach, came and went. Thirty members of her extended family gathered for the Seder, to read in Hebrew from the Haggadah. Sarah's mother made her famous panada beef broth soup with matzah pieces — and yet no scarf in sight.

One late afternoon in mid-April, Sarah buttoned her

pale-blue overcoat and paused at her father's sewing machine. It was siesta time but he'd already conducted his
afternoon snooze, the apartment rumbling with his snores.
Now he bent over, adding darts to a shirt with the familiar
spools of thread jumbled at his side, stray strands littering
the scuffed wooden floor.

He did most of his work at his shop down below but
occasionally brought a project home. He had been teaching Sarah to sew since she was child, and she loved to
watch him immersed in a garment, his tongue stuck out in
concentration as he formed each stitch, the perfect distance
from the ones before and after. Customers raved about the
precision of his stitches and came from far and wide for his
craftsmanship.

"Where are you off to, Sarah *mou*?" he asked.

"To do Yanni's ironing." It was truly her plan, but she'd
omitted the indirect route to the sea she'd take to get there.

"Yanni likes even his underwear ironed, eh?"

"I don't mind."

"I am proud of you, *chriso mou*."

"I'll see you later." Sarah kissed his scratchy cheek.

"Your ears will get cold. Put a hat on."

"It's not that cold, Baba. And it will ruin my hair." She'd
wrangled it in place, and it was almost even obeying. A hat
would just smush it.

"Put a hat on, Sarah," her father said again, without looking up. "We may not have money for much, but for a hat to
keep your ears warm, yes we do."

Sarah pulled on her brown wool cap, resisting the urge to
tell him she'd take it off the moment she cleared the door.
When her father was a boy, he'd lost his hat, and to teach
him a lesson, his father had refused to purchase him another.

It pained Sarah now, the thought of her father's icy ears, and she found it quite endearing, his perpetual concern over the temperature status of her and Benjamin's ears.

She walked to the sea and saw the scarf first in the tree. Her heart soared as she spotted Milos in his cap, chatting with other fishermen by the white bobbing masts of their trawlers. She burst forward to him like a marathon runner, and he tossed aside his nets and ran toward her just as fast. Their chests met like magnets. His arms welcomed her back in.

"I can't believe you're back," she whispered, over and over, as she gripped his nice shoulders and sucked in his particular scent of fish and sea and man. She caught a glimpse of sky overhead—blue at last. She hadn't seen blue sky in months. Well, it was spring. Maybe it was the first blue sky. But it was more than that.

Milos set her arm's length in front of him, and Sarah grew shy as he took her in because she knew how fantasies could embellish things, and she was no model, after all. Perhaps now, back with the reality of her, Milos would feel differently. But his translucent green eyes glimmered—those eyes, those eyes—and inside them was something she could read plainly before he spoke it. "Every thought I had this winter was of you, Sarah *mou*. Whatever it is now, we will be together."

They were sentiments that wrapped blankets around her heart, and words she felt too, but she had other words, darker ones, adjacent in her brain. It was the perfect match, she would realize much later: one person who surfs a perpetual wave of sunshine and the other who peeks her head out into this sunshine but then has no choice but to dive back into life's murky corners.

"Stemma got a letter from Saloniki yesterday," Sarah told him, a thing that had been plaguing her ever since Rachel relayed the news. "Her whole family is being deported from the ghetto. The Germans say they are sending them to work in Krakow."

"Poland?" Milos's face was the same infuriating calm of her mother's when they'd discussed it the night prior. "Well…maybe Poland won't be so bad."

"Maybe," Sarah whispered. "What if they deport my family to Krakow too?"

"They won't," he said, sure as day. "I will protect you. Anyway, we have the Italians. The Italians are wonderful." As if on cue, a few Italian soldiers marched by, and Milos saluted them.

The moment felt almost laughably cinematic. Who could imagine bombs and deportations when now there was only love and sea and beautiful young men meant to protect them, solemnly marching in their backdrop? When you were the protagonist of the story, it had to include a happy ending, didn't it?

Milos took Sarah's hands. "You are the most sensitive, loving person, Sarah, with a million things in your head."

"A million," she agreed, with a tentative laugh.

He paused, his face suddenly solemn. "Will you marry me, Sarah? Say you'll marry me!"

"Will I marry you?" She shook her head, both floored and also unsurprised, because wasn't this where things led? Love didn't exist for love's sake, after all. The object of love was to create something more than just two people standing together with hearts in their eyes. "You can't be—"

"I am certain. I want to marry you, Sarah. I'd marry you tomorrow."

"I need to think," she finally said, dizzy at the speed with which they were now moving after months when she'd almost convinced herself she wouldn't have to pick one of her two worlds. "My family…"

"When they see how much I love you, they will accept it." He said it with a man's unequivocal certainty.

"They…it's not so easy."

"Try. Please try. I've told my family about you. They can't wait to meet you." His enthusiasm was so contagious she could almost catch it.

"My mother will kill me," she whispered.

"It's never as bad as we think it will be. That's what my father says."

Sarah thought about Stemma. It could be so much worse than they thought it would be. But she resisted the urge to say it.

"Please, Sarah. I don't need much in life. A little house one day. Some children running around. Whatever it will be, my love, we will be safe and together."

And Sarah rested her cheek against his chest and tried to believe it.

The next evening, as Sarah climbed the steps to their third-floor apartment just before their weekly Sabbath meal, she decided she would have a calm conversation with her parents. She had prayed the whole winter that she would see Milos and feel differently, that their love would have gone. Sarah stood in the cool, dank hall, staring at the doorknob, unable to turn it. Their love hadn't gone. She had to explain it to her parents in a way they would come to understand and accept.

But when she walked inside the apartment, instead of her mother at the stove, her cheeks flushed with soup steam, and her father in his chair, stretching his wrists—both her parents stood in the entry, a united wall of fury that matched the teakettle blaring on the stove.

"Are you carrying on with a not-Jewish boy, Sarah?" Her mother grabbed Sarah's hands, her turquoise eyes frenzied with rage. "Tell me your thea Elpis imagined it when she went to fetch Leon at the sea yesterday and saw you embracing a blond fisherman."

"Thea Elpis didn't imagine it," Sarah finally whispered, frozen still.

"Sarah!" was her father's thunderous eruption. He took her by the shoulders. "No, no, no. *No!* You will end it."

"I tried, Baba. I tried. Please, just listen. His name is Milos. He is a fisherman from Lefkada, a wonderful person. When he left for the winter, I tried to forget him, but I couldn't." Tears spilled from her eyes. "Please—"

"No, please. Forget please! There is only, *I will never see him again, Baba.* There is only, *I made a terrible mistake and will never upset you again, Mama.*"

Sarah knew it with a sick certainty—the familiar stubborn position her father's features had assumed was the same position now arranging on her own. She shook her head slowly and dreadfully, a conviction rising in her, that her heart was presenting her no other option but to follow its compass. "I can't, Baba. Please. Please try to understand. I cannot not be with him."

"Then you will leave." It released from her father like a gust of wind, the kind that knocks off your hat and seems to rattle the wind too at the revelation of its sudden might.

"Leave?" The words ran a jagged knife across her throat.

"Yes, leave. You will leave now, Sarah." Her mother crossed her arms over her chest so she almost appeared like a stranger standing there, incompatible with the mother who had placed warm compresses on Sarah's forehead when she was ill and buzzed around every hour, every day, her whole being attended to their family. "And you won't be our daughter anymore."

Sarah shook as she crossed the room to where Benjamin sat weeping on the floor, stroking his bunny rabbit, Penelope, through the wooden slats of her cage. Askew on Benjamin's head was the round red hat of his Purim costume. Their father had made it to accompany the tan shorts suit of a Greek freedom fighter he'd painstakingly sewn. Benjamin had loved assuming the dress of a freedom fighter, loved imagining he was someone brave and strong. He'd donned the hat often at home ever since.

"No, Sarah." He dove to Sarah's leg, clinging to it like a toddler. "Sarah, you can't leave. Please don't leave, Sarah."

"I have to leave now," she got out with gasps between words. "Just for a little while." Where was she even going? she wondered. Milos lived in a room with several other fishermen across town, and they weren't even married yet, besides. Would they go to Lefkada? That seemed the natural conclusion. They could go to Lefkada and stay with Milos's parents, and Milos could fish there instead and work in the granite quarry too, and eventually, when her parents reconciled themselves to the new facts presented, life would peacefully rearrange. She would go, just for a little while. Sarah beat back the dread that arose, that her decision would splinter them all forever, with each spinning like a Hanukkah dreidel toward their own separate graves.

So dramatic, Sarah—to go right to death from all of this.

Sarah opened the dresser. She tried to see her clothes, her items, to pack some of them, but she was crying too hard to make them out.

Benjamin was shrieking now, pulling on her leg, trying to drag her to their bed adorned in the patchwork quilt their mother had stitched while she was pregnant with him. Sarah could recall her mother in the act of it—her belly slowly burgeoning as the quilt came to life.

Her chest suddenly seized, a crushing sensation, like the ceiling had collapsed and pinned her beneath it. She couldn't go. She couldn't leave her family.

But then she thought of Milos, and his arms around her, and how somehow the one plus one of them equaled something more than two.

She stuffed a few things into her bag and forced herself to hug Benjamin goodbye. "My special little brother, I'm going to Lefkada, just for a little while." She crouched down, feeling his small back in her hands, all the tiny bones whose cricks she had memorized from a lifetime sleeping beside him. He stopped sobbing and stared up at her in eerie quiet.

"Baba once told me ancient Ithaca is Lefkada now."

Sarah tuned out usually, when her father and Benjamin discussed Greek mythology. "I didn't know that."

"Say hello for me then, to the home of Odysseus. Maybe one day I will go too."

"I'll be back, and we'll go together," she choked out, and squeezed him tighter. Then somehow she mustered the strength to extricate herself.

Benjamin wiped his eyes, his chest still heaving. "Please don't leave, Sarah," he whispered. "Please don't go."

Through her cascading tears, Sarah blew her little brother

a kiss, but Benjamin was shaking too hard to blow her one back.

Her parents stood by the door, immobile in their prior positions. Sarah crossed the room to them but then didn't know what to do when they stood there so still, already out of reach. "Please, Mama. Please, Baba. I love you so. I'm so sorry for disappointing you. But I can't help how I feel. Please don't make me go." Nothing in response but the persistent shriek of the teakettle.

Finally, Sarah gathered her bag and gazed around her home, at her parents' wedding ketubah framed above their table, taunting her with the thousands of years of Jewish lineage from which she was now threatening to break. "I'll see you soon. Please..."

Her parents looked off, anywhere but at her.

Benjamin ran to the door, stopping right before Sarah, his face smothered in tears. "I love you," he sobbed, and this time he blew her a kiss.

"I love you dearly," she managed, and blew him another one back.

She knew if she didn't leave now, she never would. She took one aching look back at her family. "I'll see you all soon," she said again, and wasn't sure if the promise was for her or for them. Then with a force of strength that seemed to come from outside her, Sarah opened the door and stepped out. The door clicked behind her.

She knew it even then—she would always remember the click behind her.

Sarah was a babbling mess when she surprised Milos at his guesthouse by the church. After he'd delivered some optimistic platitudes, Sarah endured a sleepless night on a cot in the room of the proprietress's daughter. The next morning, at the rooster's first cry, she went to Milos, who greeted her happy as a clam. He didn't have to give up his family for her. His family were nice, lovely Greek Orthodox. Apparently they didn't care if Sarah had three heads or prayed to idols. All Milos had to do was give up fishing season in Corfu. Well, Lefkada had plenty of fish.

His face shone as he packed his few things and bid good-bye to his fellow fishermen. Sarah loved him to the ends of the earth, but perhaps she already resented him. They took the ferry to Igoumenitsa. As a drizzle pelted them on the bow, Sarah thought of what Benjamin had once told her. On the Sabbath, the Jews rest, but the sea never does. It's always a new sea.

She watched the waves crisscross each other, heading out to new places. Her leaving Corfu—it was irrevocable. Even her Jewishness had seeped out of her somehow, she realized with dull horror. Today was the Sabbath, and Sarah was violating it with the ferry ride, not one bit at rest. She knew these things, and yet she tried to brush the knowing away.

From Igoumenitsa, Milos's cousin picked them up and drove them to the main town on Lefkada. In the back of his cousin's truck, Milos clasped her hand. "I swear, it will be wonderful, my love."

chapter fourteen
Joey

corfu
2004

"What do you think?" asked Joey.

"What do *you* think, Joey *mou*?" asked Demetris.

Joey exhaled, fluffing up the bangs she'd tragically allowed a local hairdresser to snip. "Like, you see the right eye. The light is hitting there, so I've shaded the other half, but the left eye looks more real. More potent. But still off, a bit. What I really want is to merge evil eye geometric intensity into human form." This summer, she'd been playing with a more geometric style and studying the greats of geometric abstraction, like Kandinsky.

She thought about telling Demetris that Leo was her inspiration, that his eyes had woken this in her, but she held back, not ready to reveal it to Demetris before she'd even revealed it to Leo. That piece felt fragile somehow. Maybe *she* felt fragile, ever since Leo's bombshell about dropping out of school for a yachting career.

Demetris brushed his fingers across the bottom part of the canvas, where Joey had begun to outline Leo's right forearm. Joey could tell he was waiting for her to say more.

"I think it's an interesting start," she said.

"But…"

"But I want to capture more." She closed her eyes and thought about everything that had been simmering in Leo, of which she hadn't been aware. "Fire, and also peace. But can I possibly show both?"

Joey wavered, a stage of the creation process with which she wasn't very intimate. She often felt that she'd emerged from the womb with an artistic compass. People always marveled at her clear talent, passion, and dedication. Maybe it wasn't humble for Joey to say, but she was just really good at art.

"Why am I in doubt now, Demetris? I'm not usually in doubt."

Demetris just smiled. "Joey, people resent doubt. Have you noticed that? *Doubt! You go right in the corner and get out immediately.* Am I right?"

Joey smiled a little. "Maybe."

"When doubt comes, what you do is you switch to ink."

"Ink? I'm only still sketching."

"You see? You think ink is an unforgiving medium. You see how you regard ink!"

Joey gripped her canvas. She didn't want to expose it yet to ink.

"You have a doubt, *paidi mou*? It's all good. Some artists have analyzed so much what comes naturally. Some artists think all it takes is a little more pain and suffering."

"I don't want to suffer," said Joey. "Art is fun. Art is light." She felt her body release something in response to those words.

"You realize sometimes things are put so easily down on paper? The Masters. We refer to them again. They let themselves play a lot. People think, *Enough play*. But it's the mind that tells you that, because life is a game. Life is the biggest game of all, Joey. Tell me, have we played a lot here?"

"We always play here."

"So you don't need the tricks. There is nothing to measure. Because once we have played, things come automatically. And you can achieve your intention immediately with one stroke. This pen." He held it up. "Do you know how it performs?"

Joey nodded.

"Okay, so we use ink." He slapped the pen into her hands. "And we will Be the Explorer." That was another Demetrisism. "As if nothing is known about art or drawing and, for some reason you have this ability to put things on paper. Tell me, *paidi mou*. What makes an artist most attractive to people?"

"Hmm. Passion. That's a big one. Patience. Letting our art show us where to go, instead of forcing it to take a certain form…"

"Yes, exactly. Artists who are more attractive are the ones who find a consortium with the medium they are using. They let the medium do its thing. They don't push it. *No, go there! No, do this!*"

"I've never heard a pen speak before." Joey smiled.

"Oh, the pen speaks, *paidi mou*. The pen speaks, the pen sings, the pen loves. You just have to move into the brain in your hand to feel it."

Joey hovered the pen over Leo's right eye. "Demetris…"

"Yes?"

"Do you think I'm going to make it as an artist?"

Joey held her breath, wanting so badly for him to say

that he believed she could achieve anything. She didn't need fame or fortune; that wasn't what she was asking. But when she imagined her life, her art was at its core. She just wished there was some sort of guarantee that she'd make enough money to live simply upon, to enable an eternal string of these kinds of moments, where her passion jiggled and jangled.

"You know what I think, *paidi mou*? I think you're doing basically okay, and you don't even know it."

"I'm doing okay?" Did he not get that, in American lexicon, *okay* was about a C-plus?

Demetris plucked a sesame peanut from a doily-covered dish. "Tell me, who do you love most in this world?"

"Is that a trick question?"

"It's a question, Joey *mou*. Don't analyze."

"Leo," she said softly. "I love Leo the most."

"Wrong answer," said Demetris.

Joey didn't understand.

"You love Joey the most. The answer must be that you love Joey the most. Then it doesn't matter if you make it as an artist. Because when you love Joey the most, and you play, life is just wonderful.

"Life is simply grand, Joey *mou*."

⌒

Joey was in a Demetris hangover.

She dropped her canvas at home that Tuesday afternoon. She said hello to the statue of Bea, studying her own canvas but not painting it. In the throes of pre-show chaos, the living room was dotted in various incarnations of the menstrual flow. Leo now referred to their apartment as the

Womb. He said the paintings were scarring to any man who might at any point in time wish to bed a woman.

Joey changed into a floaty white tank top, white capri pants, and her new espadrilles. Then she appraised herself in the mirror and decided to add a funky necklace. She selected one with chunky, wooden, emerald-green beads and fastened it around her neck. She went into the living room.

"Bye, Mom! Leo and I are going out for a picnic at the Old Fortress. I'll sleep at the Winns' tonight. You know it's our one-year anniversary?"

"Oh yeah? Wow, one year. That's a beautiful milestone. Have fun, sweetheart. You know what, JoJo? Have *too* much fun!"

Lily was an angel sprawled on the couch with zero trace of her earlier tantrum when Joey had taken her to the supermarket.

In a spurt of love, Joey picked up her sister and whooshed her around in a circle, kissing her on her soft cheek before setting her back down. "Tomorrow let's build another sand-castle, Lil, how about it?"

Lily removed the pacifier from her mouth. "Castle!" She clapped her hands.

"Yes, castle! Maybe we can even drag Mom along with us again." Joey laughed.

"I'm in. It will do me some good to get a break from the Womb." Bea winked. "You thought I didn't know? Say hello to Leo for me."

Joey giggled. "Will do. Love you, Mom. Love you, Lily Pad."

"Love you, Oey."

The city was bathed in pink when they stepped out onto the cobblestones after aperitifs at Leo's place. "Guess what?

We're going to Salto after all, Jones," Leo said with a giant smile, like he'd been bursting with that surprise.

Salto was Taverna Salto, with the famous chef Joey had read about in a magazine and mentioned offhand to Leo weeks before. They'd booked in a reservation but then decided last week to cancel. It wasn't prudent for such a splurge with neither of them earning money in the summers and Leo saving all of his for his yachting business plan.

"We're not doing the picnic?" She'd been content with their low-key plan. "I like gyros."

"Then we'll do them another night. I want tonight to be special. It's my treat. Are you happy?"

Joey could tell Leo really wanted her to be happy, and she was, with either plan. "Ooh, really happy!" She kissed his cheek. She considered broaching if the money aspect was really fine but then decided to avoid the topic. "This is such a nice surprise!"

"Do you want to change into comfy shoes? It's a pretty far walk."

"No, I'm fine. Oh, I'm so excited!"

They arrived at Taverna Salto. Joey soaked it all in—the string quartet, the crisp linen table settings, the enchanting garden vibe, the hideaway location.

Most of all, Leo, who was wonderful and hers.

A few moments of bliss, and then Leo's eyes went strange. And all of Joey's happy went poof.

They fled the taverna, with Leo pulling Joey along in some baffling race of his life. When they finally stopped, the taverna out of sight, Joey's heart was racing, her nerves all screwy. She tried to meet his gaze, but Leo's eyes skittered around, anywhere but at her.

Leo, come on. Please tell me the truth.

I have a headache. That's all.

They walked in silence back home, with Joey berating herself for not turning around, for not having seen what Leo saw. But maybe she was inflating things? Leo was tight on money, after all. Maybe he just hadn't quite anticipated the prices. Maybe it wasn't such a big deal.

When they returned to the hallway with both their apartment doors side by side, there was a terrible moment when Joey didn't know if Leo was going to invite her in. But then he turned his key in the lock and, without meeting her eyes, said, "Coming, Jonesey?"

She followed him down the dim hall to his bedroom. There, he didn't switch on the lights, just stripped to his boxers and slipped beneath his navy coverlet. Joey wriggled out of her pants and debated going to the bathroom to rinse her feet. Having walked barefoot across town again to avoid her killer espadrilles, it would now be revolting to skip a good rinse, but Joey knew that Leo would be sleeping, pretend or otherwise, by the time she'd returned. So she opted for dirty.

"Leo," she started, joining him in bed but not sliding across the invisible barrier between them that had been so quickly erected, "can we—"

"I'm tired, Jonesey. Let's just go to sleep."

"But is everything...are we okay?" She squeezed her eyes shut, steeling herself for his answer.

"Yep. We're fine, Jones."

Leo rolled on his side to face the window. And Joey just stared at his back, praying he'd wake up in the morning back to normal.

chapter fifteen
Joey

corfu

2004

The morning after Taverna Salto, Joey woke to Leo staring at her from within a hazy beam of sunlight. Her mouth felt cotton-ball-parched. As if reading her mind, Leo said, "I put a glass of water on the nightstand."

She grappled for it, relief soaring inside her at the normalcy of his sentence and gesture. As she chugged the water, she listened to a gecko croak and watched it scurry into a ceiling crack. She set the glass down and slid against Leo's warm skin.

He pushed her slightly back. "Jonesey, we need to talk."

No good thing ever followed that sentence. Joey felt her throat constrict with fear. "Leo, please don't—"

"I can't do this anymore." His eyes cast down to his pillow. "We—"

"No, Leo! Please, no." Her chest seared with pain, like someone had taken a chain saw to it. "We're so good. Please don't do this." Maybe it was pathetic to beg him to be with her, but she didn't care. "You *know* how good we are."

"We are good, Jonesey." Leo still wasn't looking at her, and his words were dry, almost unfeeling. "But I talked to Dave yesterday. The boat's finally done, and I'm gonna join his crew. I need to start my life. Dive headfirst into this new career. That has to be my priority now, over summers on Corfu."

"No, Leo! No." Joey grabbed his face and made him look her in the eyes. There was wet between their chests, and she realized it had streamed there from her face. "This is because of last night. Don't pretend it's because of Dave. Tell me what happened last night. Did you see another girl or something? That French girl you dated? Tell me the truth, Leo! Is it someone else?

"What gi—Jonesey! You're so wrong." Leo kept his eyes fixed on hers, but they were different somehow, already gone. "That's not it, Jonesey. Please don't come up with stories that aren't even close to true. Part of me wishes we had met later in life. We're just too young. We're about to be split across the world. Think how hard this past year was apart, but at least we were both in school in America. I'm going to be in the middle of oceans now. You know it's impossible."

Something about the way he said *impossible* absolutely zapped her of hope.

She didn't know how long she cried. She felt him dab at her face with a tissue. "My grandmother will be happy about you breaking up with me, you know. Before I left this summer, she grilled me. *Promise me you're not going to look at this Leo boy.*"

Even with Joey's eyes closed, she felt Leo smile. "What did you tell her?"

"I said, *I'll try, G.*" A wave of desolation overcame her. "She would like you, is the thing."

There was a rap at the door. Joey struggled up in the bed to see her mother poke her head in. "Mom?"

Bea had never interrupted them like this, especially not in Leo's apartment. Unlike her friends' parents who freaked over the topic of sex, Bea felt it was of feminist imperative that Joey own her sexual choices. Yes, there were some key benefits to her mother's extreme feminism, despite Bea occasionally being embarrassing as hell.

Joey took in her mother's unusual, tearstained face, a mirror to her own.

"Grandfather died." Her mother bit down on her lip. "He had a heart attack and died last night." Bea dove into the bed and clutched Joey with the same intensity that Joey had just clutched Leo.

"No," Joey whispered as the words slowly sank in.

"Oh God, Bea, that's terrible! I'm so sorry," Leo said, amid his tossing aside of sheets to scoot closer. "Jonesey, I'm so sorry. I'm so…"

Joey felt stroking on her back in addition to her mother's grip that she knew was from Leo.

Her lovely grandfather whom she adored. Her lovely grandfather in his black polished shoes.

"It was fast, baby. He didn't suffer. But we need to go home now. They're waiting for us to have the funeral. You know, the Jewish custom is that burial has to happen as soon as possible after the…death. We need to pack up and go home."

And her mother went off on a fresh spate of tears as Joey sat perfectly still in her mother's crushing embrace, her tears all dried up.

⌒

Later Joey lay on her bed, clutching her teddy bear Nacho Chip, who usually didn't get much love. Her bedroom door opened, streaming light like shards of glass into her eyes.

"Jonesey?"

Joey wanted to tell him to go away. But more than that she wanted him still, for as long as he would stay.

Leo didn't seem to know how to approach her. He sat on her bed against the wall but then made a wincing sound. Joey twisted slightly to see what had happened and watched Leo remove a tack that protruded from the wall. With it came the picture it had attached—a Polaroid of Leo from the summer before.

They'd climbed up the famous castle on the northwest coast, the Angelokastro, and then dipped into the sea. She'd skipped down the caramel sand to their knapsacks and said, *Let me take a picture of you, Winn.* Joey thought about it now, that maybe she'd wanted to capture him completely, in a way she wasn't allowed to do to a person, or supposed to. Leo had stopped in the break of a wave, facing her straight-on. There was something so vulnerable about that, Joey felt, hair slicked back, eyes blinking salt, everything you try to be or think you are scraped away. Leo didn't smile, but it was always his eyes that held all of him. His eyes were content.

Now Leo's eyes were unreadable. "Can I hold you, Jones? I know I shouldn't be allowed to, but—"

"Yes." She blinked back tears, feeling the bed shift as Leo got behind her to be the big spoon. He plucked the fluorescent-green tee she'd migrated into after discovering it crumpled in her covers.

"This is a horrible shirt, Jones, but somehow you still look cute in it." When she didn't respond, his arms tightened around her. "I'm so sorry. I'm sorrier than you will ever know, J."

"My grandfather survived Auschwitz. He was one of my favorite people in the world."

Leo stroked her hair. "I'm so sorry, Jonesey. God, I...well...I have terrible timing."

Leo held her as she shook, and Joey imagined that Leo's arms were stitched together with her inside and he could never move them, not ever.

That evening, Leo helped carry all their suitcases to the curb. Even though the sun had gone, Joey put her sunglasses on. The taxi pulled up.

Leo's eyes were focused on her, like willing her to be normal and okay because he needed her to be. "I love you, Jonesey. I know you don't believe me, but I really do love you."

Joey just nodded, not trusting herself to speak.

"Bye, little L." Leo knelt down to hug her little sister. "I love you too." Then he whispered quietly to Lily, "Don't forget me, okay?"

There were more goodbyes. Rand and Maisy and words and more words. Then Leo, again, hands on Joey's waist. Even though she didn't want to, Joey tilted forward like a plant to the sun.

"You're amazing, Jonesey. You're the most amazing girl I know. Be happy, okay? Be really happy. You'll find some other guy who adores you. I know you will. And you'll forget me." His voice broke, like he was genuinely heartbroken at the thought. But then why was he doing this?

Joey wedged her cheek into Leo's neck. "I wish I could forget you. I really wish I could."

chapter sixteen

Joey

florida

2019

The sun was its late-morning fierce, and Joey questioned why she'd picked the beach for their reunion. The beach had been their spot, she supposed, the axis on which their childhood had spun. But staring out at the waves now next to Leo made Joey think of a hundred different moments. They should have just gone to a Starbucks.

"Remember Taverna Salto, Jonesey?" Leo pulled at the collar of his shirt. It was only a crew-neck tee, but Joey knew how he hated when anything pressed on his neck. She thought how bizarre it was to know intimate details about a person who was now essentially a stranger.

"How could I forget it?" The trauma of the twenty-four hours after that dinner would never be easy to revisit— losing Leo and her beloved grandfather in one fell swoop. "You saw someone, didn't you?" Joey's heart hammered her chest.

"Not someone, Jones." Leo squeezed his tennis ball so tightly his face contorted like a bodybuilder. "Someones."

"Okay. Who? Did you cheat on me with…" She steeled herself. "That French girl you dated?"

A boy and girl, all scrawny legs and arms, ran past them toward the sea. They reminded Joey of her and Leo, when she still thought that summers meant magic.

"No, Jonesey." Leo laughed a laugh that sounded desperately sad. "I can't believe that's what you would have thought all this time. What I saw was two people—two lovers—having dinner together."

Joey was growing impatient for the punch line. "Who?"

A long pause. The little girl shrieked with glee as the boy pulled her under.

"Our parents. Well, one of yours and one of mine."

"Huh?" Joey's brain scrambled. "My dad was in Florida then. What do you mean one of—"

"Bea and Rand. They were having an affair. I'm sorry to tell you this. That night at Taverna Salto, I saw Bea and Rand."

"I can't believe it. It can't be true," Joey heard herself saying, over and over, as she kept clumping and then destroying the same mound of sand. Her mind buzzed with flip-book scenes from all their Corfu summers as she picked apart moments and laughs and smiles for clues. Only nothing suspicious surfaced. Finally, she dared to look up at Leo, praying for him to admit this was all a sick joke. But his face was solemn.

"I just can't believe it." A chill traversed her bones. "No. It's just…it's not…I mean, when did you even find out?"

"The summer before our last. Right before the end. That's why—"

"That's why you were kind of distant at the beginning of school. I knew something was off, but I chalked it up to college starting." Joey remembered sitting in those giant lecture halls, her stomach in knots at his sudden lag in communication. Pieces were slotting into place, and her disbelief was giving way to rage. All of Joey's pain, all those years of sadness—her mother was responsible for it.

The word *mother* caused an association. *Father.* Joey let out a strangled sound that was for her father. Her sweet, trusting, endearingly nerdy father who'd been back in Florida making money so Bea could play artist in Corfu and sleep with his friend behind his back.

"That's why. I'm so sorry, Jonesey."

"Yeah. You said that."

Joey pictured Rand now, not a strand of his dark coif out of place. She pictured him clapping her father's shoulder as they drank margaritas. *My friend!*

She pictured him kissing her mother.

She remembered them all out on the terrace, eating and laughing. It still didn't make sense. There were too many holes. "How did you even find out?"

"I saw them, Jonesey, the summer before our last. They were out on my dad's sailboat. I followed them to this place they'd rented on the other side of town."

"What? Where?"

"South. Closer to the airport."

Joey digested it. They'd rented a place, and their affair had lasted two summers at least. "When did the affair start?"

Leo drew an audible breath. Joey found herself holding hers. "Since the beginning. It's why they orchestrated both our families to vacation on Corfu. They deliberately got neighboring apartments."

"No." Joey gasped. That couldn't be true. She sifted through her memories. "You're saying when we met in the stairwell—"

"It was intentional. This was how they could arrange to be together. Get us all to Corfu. Then the two of them would sneak off."

"Oh God. I don't…" She was going to be sick. "How do you know all this? Did you confront Rand?"

Leo nodded, his eyes tilted vacantly toward the sun. "It felt so isolating, being the only one to know. Wondering what I was supposed to do with the information." His voice cracked. "I confronted my dad after I found out. Told him that I wouldn't spill the secrets, but that he and Bea had to be done. No more contact. No more affair." Leo paused. "Maybe I should never have gone back to Corfu the next summer. But I came back, hoping I could put it behind me. Hoping they could do the right thing. I came back to see *you*, Jonesey. I tried to block the affair out of my mind. But they wouldn't let it go. Seeing them at Taverna Salto proved that. I was so shocked that they'd gone back on their promise."

Leo shook his head and gave a dry laugh. "I don't know why I trusted my dad the first time when he said he would end it, but I did. I really thought they would just do the right thing. But of course they couldn't stay away from each other. Later, my dad told me they figured it would be safe to go out for dinner that night because you had told Bea we'd planned to picnic at the Old Fortress. Bea got a last-minute babysitter for Lily, and they decided on Taverna Salto because they knew the owner or something. They took a cab over and beat us there. They were just as shocked to see us. Anyway, I was just so relieved you didn't see them. But that's why I broke up with you the next morning, Jonesey.

I realized, if we kept dating, there would be no getting around you finding out, and I just...I needed to protect you from that."

Joey's head was spinning. "I'm still so confused. When did our parents even meet?"

"My father backpacked the Greek islands one summer with his friends. The summer of nineteen eighty-three. He was twenty-two. I asked your mother if she'd spent time in Corfu before. She came with your grandfather one summer, did you know that?"

"Yes," whispered Joey.

"Do you know what summer it was, J?"

"Nineteen eighty-three," she said, but it didn't feel like it was coming from her. It felt like the person with the ability to speak was a separate entity than the person who was processing this affair and reframing her entire childhood on Corfu. Nineteen eighty-three. That was two years before her parents got married. Her mom would have been twenty-one.

"Oh God. This is so insane. So you came here to tell me this, Leo? I don't get it. Why now, after all this time?" Leo opened his mouth to speak, but Joey jabbed him in his shoulder with force that surprised her. "And don't you *dare* tell me that you're in love with me again."

Leo sighed. He reached forward to retrieve his tennis ball from where it had rolled across the sand. Joey watched his biceps flex, her eyes inadvertently tracing his muscles, bigger than before. Heat that wasn't from the sun torched her neck, spreading up to her cheeks.

"There's another reason I came now, Jonesey. I suppose I could have waited until after your wedding for this part. Maybe it was selfish of me to come before."

She gave him a pointed look.

"Okay. It was. I'm sorry." He did sound sorry. "But I didn't just come for you."

"What else did you possibly come for?"

Leo's face twisted. He looked so sad.

"What else could you possibly have come for, Leo?"

"This fucking sucks, Jonesey. I won't tell you what else I came for though. I'll show you."

He was speaking Swedish. She needed the subtitles.

He showed her his phone with a screenshot of a picture. The picture looked like it was from an old Kodak roll, with AUGUST 14, 2003, in the corner. It was of a wooden plaque bleached white with blue hand-painted letters. Joey read it.

"Okay. So?"

Leo said, "This was the plaque outside their place. They rented it every summer from this British lady who lived on top. Then they stole away there when they could. During the days, sometimes at night, if my mom was passed out, if your dad was out of town, if my dad was on one of his sailing trips." Leo put *sailing trips* in air quotes.

"How do you know these things?"

He shrugged. "I had time, Jonesey. Eons of time to put it together. You haven't had time."

She read the plaque again. Her stomach turned.

"Oh my God."

⌣

She staggered up. Leo stood too and took her hand.

Joey knew he took her hand because she saw it, but she didn't feel it. Suddenly she threw her head to the side and vomited up her morning omelet. She felt Leo scrape back her hair.

"Lily's Place," Leo said. "They were having their affair at Lily's Place."

"Lily Pad," whispered Joey, and pressed her face into her palms.

Now Joey was irate.

"Not only do they have an affair," she ticked off, pacing the sea in front of Leo. "Not only did they freaking arrange all of it in advance. Premeditated. It was all so disgustingly premeditated. Not only did they trash their marriage vows. My poor dad. My poor, sweet dad who probably had some sort of Rand STD but didn't think to get checked."

Leo didn't say, *Hey, now.* He just seemed relieved she wasn't going off the deep end. Joey didn't know what going off the deep end would look like. She wasn't opposed to it.

"Maisy!" she said. "Sweet, innocent Maisy. She didn't deserve this."

Leo grimaced. "No, she didn't."

Joey stomped the sand. It felt good to stomp her bare feet. Stomp, stomp. Joey stopped. The anger went as fast as it came. A desolate sadness swooped in. Anger was far better. She stomped a few more furious stomps to summon it back.

"Not only all that. No. They conceived a child. They conceived Lily and passed her off as my father's."

"Scott is a better father than mine," said Leo softly.

Joey didn't know what to say. Rand was fine. She'd always thought Rand was fine. A bit aloof. Okay, a lot aloof. Obsessed with sailing and stock markets. Not super obsessed with his wife or son. But fine. Not, like, an abuser or something.

"Maybe she's not really Rand's. Maybe she's my dad's and the Lily's Place thing is a coincidence."

"No, Jonesey. She's Rand's. When I confronted him, he confirmed it."

"Oh."

"Anyway, think of Lily. She has those blue eyes."

"My mom has blue eyes. So does my grandmother."

"But I swear if you look at my father's and Lily's side by side, you'll see the similarity. And Lily's birthday, J."

"May twenty-second."

"May twenty-second. That's a late August conception date. Your mother—"

"My mother was the only one of us who stayed longer in August. To do gallery stuff." She was going to throw up again.

"There's something else. She has this smirk face, you know? Or she did. I remember it about her." Leo drew circles in the sand with his tennis ball, and Joey had an astounding revelation. Lily was Leo's sister. "Her smirk face is my father's face when he's negotiating and he's waiting for the other party to cave."

"Oh." How hadn't Joey seen it? It was so strange and twisted. Lily was to Leo as Lily was to Joey.

"I'm sorry, J. I wanted to tell you, all those years I wanted to tell you, but why should I ruin your life too?"

"You should have told me." A sob shuddered through her. "I had a right to know."

"But then what? We'd stay together with this huge secret? It would have eaten us alive. I know that because it was eating me alive. So at least I could spare you. And it would have gotten out somehow to Scott and Maisy, and I just didn't want that, to ruin their lives too. And especially…I didn't want the whole thing to affect Lily. I know what Rand was like as a father, Jones. I wanted better for her."

Joey absorbed it. His explanation made sense on its face, but something in her—maybe something illogical—couldn't forgive him. "You don't think?" She had a sudden, vile thought. "You…" She couldn't finish the sentence. "Me?"

"No," said Leo quickly. "Of course not. They're not that disgusting of parents. We were sleeping together. And besides, there's a whole backstory about why they got separated after they first met and then ran into each other before we started coming to Corfu. My father wrote Bea letters that she never got. You'll have to ask your mom for all the details."

"Oh, I will. Trust me, I will." Joey stared at her legs adorned with late-summer souvenirs: mosquito bites and sun freckles. "What about us, Leo?" she whispered. "Why didn't you take us into account in your whole calculus? Did you ever think about destroying us? About destroying me?"

"It tore me apart to do that," Leo said quietly. "I just didn't see another way. I was trying to protect Lily. And trying to protect you."

"What if I didn't need to be protected?" Joey heard herself shout. "What if what I needed was someone to tell me the house of cards my life was built on?" She wanted him to know what it had been like for her in the aftermath, really, really know, but how could he possibly understand? Those years couldn't be distilled into sentences. And anyway, she knew now on some level that she'd needed those years to teach her how to be happy by herself. She wouldn't have broken if she hadn't already had so many of her own cracks.

Joey stood. A wave slapped her calves.

"Joey, I…we need to do the right thing. Lily just turned eighteen. I've had that date in my head since I found out, as a deadline or something. She got her childhood with Scott, but I've always felt like she deserved the truth. And I've always wanted to know my sister. So when I found out it was your wedding, and Lily was finally eighteen, I don't know, I just leaped. Booked a trip here. Maybe it…I don't know, when I hear it out of my mouth, it sounds impetuous and selfish. But it felt like what I needed to do. We need to tell Lily, you do agree, don't you?" Leo reached for Joey's hand. The one with her engagement ring. Their fingertips brushed.

Joey jerked back her hand. She was light-headed from his betrayal. And especially from her mother's. "I have to go."

"Joey, please. I'm sorry. I truly am. I wish I could take this pain away from you. That's why I kept it from you all this time. Please stay, and we'll figure all this out. Igloo seedok." He tried a weak smile to disarm her.

"No. No secret language." Joey backed away and started running. Her calves burned. The footsteps behind her quickened. This was always going to be the fucking scene in the movie where he caught up to her.

Leo made it astride. Joey bent over, hands to shins, panting. He wasn't even breathing hard. "I'm staying at the Boca Beach Club."

"I lifeguarded there in high school," she managed as she stared into her knees.

"I know."

Joey felt something close around her throat. It was a

sensation that had surfaced for years after their last summer, that had arisen on every date she'd pep-talked herself into going on. She'd be drinking a frozen yogurt shake with a guy at that place on campus decorated with the goofy customer Polaroids, and all of a sudden, the panic—like the arc of a dive into a pool with no water. After a decade enduring it, she'd finally gotten a therapist who'd prescribed anti-anxiety meds.

As Joey returned herself upright, an unexpected sentence dangled on the cliff of her tongue, trying to scramble back to safety. But then unwittingly, it tumbled down.

"I saw you everywhere, Leo."

"What's that, Jones?"

Joey could pretend she hadn't said it but suddenly she needed it out, needed him to know how much she'd been affected. "I saw you everywhere after our last summer," she whispered, and felt herself slowly deflate.

Was she really going to be vulnerable like this to him, after all the secrets and lies? She attempted to pull the sentences back down her throat, but already they were sliding out. "I walked into a convenience store in Philly, and there you were, picking out deodorant. You were at all the big milestones. My graduation from college. From law school. I'd chase you around the corner, and I was always heartbroken when a stranger peered back at me. You know, I once...once I went to Nice."

"You...came to Nice? You knew I lived there?"

"Yeah. I convinced a few girlfriends. I promised them glitz and glam. We'd go to the casino. We'd find hot French lovers." Joey burrowed her foot into the sand. "It was the worst trip of my life. The last night I pretended I was sick so I could stay behind at the hotel. It had been ten years since

I'd seen you. Ten. And I hated myself for still thinking about you, after you broke up with me so abruptly like that. I hated myself for the real reason I'd orchestrated the trip."

"Jones..."

"But the worst part was that I didn't see you! Facebook said you lived there, but you were nowhere. I made my friends walk the harbor. I had all the excuses—exercise, scoping celebs. But of course I was just hoping to...I don't know...accidentally-on-purpose bump into you."

Joey paused, reliving every beat. She felt utterly transported, and dizzyingly sad.

"But eventually I had to fly back to New York. Without you, Leo, but also without me too, in some ways. Am I even making sense? Anyway. Yeah. Sorry if I'm ruining some fantasy you had, that I sailed off from that last summer into some un-fucked-up life."

Leo's smile was achingly sad. His mouth opened without words emerging, like trying on different things to say. Finally, he said, "You're not the only one who saw ghosts, Jones, but I—"

Before he could say another sorry, she put a hand out. "I can't do this. Talk about telling Lily, before I've even processed this myself."

"Okay. Of course. I get it. I—"

"Do you, Leo? *Do* you get it? Dropping this on me before my wedding? I'll talk to you when I talk to you. You're on my timetable now. For once."

Joey gathered her sandals and walked to her car. She looked back only once to see Leo standing in the same place she'd left him, just like the last time, watching her go.

chapter seventeen

Joey

florida

2019

Joey maneuvered her Jeep past a park where mothers pushed children on swing sets—mothers who probably did not have lengthy secret affairs and children with falsified paternities. With a quick left after the park, there it was: Joey's childhood home, one of the last remaining traditional Southern-style houses in Delray, with her mother inside it.

Joey parked beside the row of hedges and switched off her ignition. She could see Bea in the living room window by her easel, absorbed in her latest canvas, oblivious to Joey's arrival. Writers needed a room of their own, wasn't that the saying? Well, Bea had appropriated the whole main floor as her art studio.

For Joey's entire life, she'd thought her mom a bit loud, a bit out there, but talented and gregarious and confident. Joey had been proud that Bea was her mother, and proud of her mother's art, no matter how offbeat. Joey knew intimately the vulnerability it required to create something from the truest part of you and then splash it out into the world. For a long time, Joey had been too distraught and disconnected from herself to create anything real. But since leaving law, she'd bonded with Bea again about the passion they both shared. Only now the varnish had gone. Her mother had taken everything Joey held dear—Leo, her art, and her family intact.

Joey bit her lip, white-knuckling her steering wheel. She so desperately didn't want to cry. But her chest refused to obey and gave a heaving convulsion.

The tears came fat and hot. When they'd finally petered out, Joey lifted her head from the steering wheel. She slowly rearranged her Cousin It hair. She wiped her face with a makeup towelette and surveyed herself in the visor mirror.

Well, the glowy effects of her pre-wedding facial had gone, that was for sure.

Joey forced herself out of her car and across her parents' driveway. As a child, she'd found her home magical, starting with its romantic origins—purchased in the loved-up throes of early marriage because Bea had a thing for *Gone with the Wind* and Scott had a thing for Bea. There was the yellow stucco box-style house, its Palladian windows framed by hunter-green shutters. The expansive front yard with the two stately sycamore trees. The cracked tar driveway and the basketball hoop with the off-kilter net on which Joey and her father used to play endless games of Horse. The garage where she'd once scraped her Jetta going in and then told her parents that someone had keyed her car.

Joey stepped atop the gray-brick porch and inserted the key she'd retained, even after so many years in New York.

"Hi, JoJo!" Her mother swept open the door before Joey could push it open. Bea dove in for a hug, but Joey sidestepped it. The scent of pumpkin spice stormed Joey's nostrils. Her mother had never met an autumnal room diffuser she didn't snap up for year-round use. Bea wore black leather leggings and a black lace camisole, purple paint smeared up her right forearm. Her skin was, as ever, an I-spent-a-week-in-the-Riviera caramel, owing to a mix of genetics and spray tans.

"I'm so glad you wanted to come over. We have a few wedding things to discuss! And I made banana bread. How about a slice?"

Joey took an unsteady step forward. "Dad's at work, right?"

Her mother's eyebrows raised. "Yes, Dad's at work. And Lily's filming content in Miami. What's going on, JoJo? Why are your shorts wet?"

"Leo came to town to see me," Joey said without preamble. "He told me about you and Rand. And Lily." She could barely get it out, it was so vile. "He *told* me about Lily. How *could* you?"

Bea's face crumpled in like quicksand. "Joey...oh my God...Jo—" She stretched out a hand, catching Joey's forearm.

Joey flinched at the touch. "Don't *ever* touch me again! Don't fucking ever." She wasn't a huge curser but now all she wanted to do was pull variations of *fuck* out of a hat. *Fuck you! Fuck both you and Rand! Go fuck yourselves. Literally, I'm sure.*

They stood in silence, like the panting aftermath of a race. "I owe you an explanation," Bea eventually said. "A big explanation."

Joey caught a flash of the scrunched lines between her mother's eyebrows that had survived the latest round of Botox. "You owe me a lot of explanations."

Bea nodded as an Academy Award–worthy tear rolled down her cheek, cutting a swath through her blush. "I know. I do."

~~

Bea sat slumped on the living room couch. It was rare to find Bea just sitting like a normal person. Usually she arranged herself in a very conscious way. Cleavage aimed. Stomach sucked. Lips pursed. Face on. Face always on.

"I can't believe you know," Bea said softly, more to herself than to Joey.

"You can't be so stupid to have thought you'd keep your secrets forever," said Joey, and she almost gasped at her vicious tone.

"I deserve your anger, Joey. I deserve it. I can take it."

Joey sat beside her mother on the couch. She slid left so she hugged the armrest, putting more space between them. She balled her fists and her nails dug into her palms. "I need to understand. I need the whole story."

"Yes." Her mother fixed her eyes on a family picture framed on a side table. Her father holding a smirking Lily. Her father looking like he might explode with love for his girls.

Joey felt her heart constrict.

"I met Rand even before I started dating your father."

"On Corfu."

"How did you know?"

"Leo told me, Mom." The word that was Joey's first, her most familiar, felt sour on her tongue.

"Right. I can't…so Leo's actually here? In Florida?" Joey didn't reply. "Okay. Well, when I was going into my last year of college, I went to Corfu with your grandfather. You know, my parents grew up there, and despite the tragedy of their lives, I always held rather romantic notions of Corfu."

"I see. *Romantic.*"

"Yes. Your grandfather didn't despise it like G. Even though his whole family was murdered, somehow he could separate it from the happy times of his childhood. G can't. She had, and still has, no desire to ever go back to Corfu.

"So after years of begging, Grandfather said he would take me. We planned to go for three weeks, and I was so excited. It was my first time out of the US other than Jamaica. And you know G. She hovers. My dad was different..."

Bea lit up in that way she used to around Grandfather. He would kiss her forehead, and she would look soft and lovely. That's what Joey had always thought—her mother had looked her loveliest around Grandfather.

Fuck her mother looking lovely! Her mother was a horrible person.

"Grandfather got a place for us on the water, right by Markas. He showed me around, and I was besotted. It was the first time I fell in love, and it was with a town. We wandered the alleys, and he got me this wide-brimmed hat with a pink grosgrain ribbon and, I don't know, I felt like some sort of princess wandering around." Bea gave a wistful smile. "He showed me the synagogue where he met G, and the street he grew up on, and the place where his dad was a butcher. He even showed me the spot at the Old Fortress where the Nazis took them, at gunpoint, to wait all day under the scorching sun. Then those monsters squeezed them onto death boats and sent them to Auschwitz."

"The Old Fortress?" Joey flinched. That was where she and Leo had gone to the meadow sometimes. She suddenly remembered being there one summer on a day Leo had decreed that every fifth word out of their mouths should be *mulberry*. She wasn't sure she'd laughed as hard since. That such a day shared a history with the extermination of her grandparents' families made her body jerk with a shiver. Maybe their whole island had been cursed.

"On our second week of vacation, I went to the beach without Grandfather. I wore this pink polka-dot bikini with my new hat, and I felt very fresh."

"This is where you meet Rand," said Joey, recognizing the beats of a story.

"Yes, Rand was with two friends. They'd graduated from Michigan and were traveling the Greek islands. They were only supposed to stay two days but wound up extending to ten." Bea studied her lemon-yellow fingernails. "I suppose it would be cliché to say it was love at first sight."

Joey felt herself getting riled. "It would be. Let me save you the trouble. Rand couldn't take his eyes off your bikini. He said something suave and Rand-ish. He wined and dined you, and when Grandfather was sleeping, you sneaked off."

"I guess."

"Okay." Joey twined her fingers together. "So then what?"

"Well, Grandfather wasn't an idiot. Eventually, I had to introduce him to Rand, and he gathered immediately that Rand wasn't Jewish. Now, Grandfather wasn't particularly bothered by this, but his allegiance was clearly to G. He told her on the phone."

"And?"

"And what do you think? G said things like *extremely disappointed* and *this is what they died at Auschwitz for*. She ordered us directly home. Grandfather did one thing for me

though. He said, *I'm going to sleep*, and he kissed my forehead. It was six P.M. He gave me one last night. Our flight
was the next day. I've never been so upset."

"Upset," Joey whispered. "*You've* never been so upset?
Do you remember when Leo broke up with me? It was all
because of you. To save you and Rand from your lies. You
ruined our lives, but who cares about us kids, right?"

"Oh, honey." Bea stared at her hands. "I can't believe…I
didn't know that was why Leo broke up with you."

"Yeah, right."

"Really, I didn't. Not at the time, at least. I didn't realize
Leo had seen us at Salto. Rand only told me later. And it
was the year Grandfather died. I was a mess. I didn't know
what I could possibly do to fix things for you."

"That's why you guys never went back to Corfu, then?"
Joey said, rolling the thought around in her head. "I thought
it was in solidarity with me, that because I didn't want to go
back, you and Dad didn't either. But—"

"It was Leo's condition to Rand, for keeping our secret.
Yes. I told your father it was time for a change of pace. That
he was missing far too much of our time in Corfu. We—"

"You started going to Vermont for a couple of weeks in
the summer." They'd tried to convince her to join, suddenly
all presidents of the Vermont Tourism Department. But Joey
had been on a mission then, her quest to get into law school
becoming her singular life purpose. Her dad had been so
proud when she'd announced she wanted to try following
in his footsteps.

"Oh, Joey, I'm so sorry for all of this. I can't believe…oh
God."

Joey bit her lip. "Go back to the Rand story. I still don't
understand how it happened."

Bea's eyes went away somewhere. "Well, when we had to split that summer we met, Rand and I were a mess. We had to figure out a way to be together. We knew Rand couldn't call. I was living at home then, going to Nova, so we decided he'd write and use a code name. Harry Berry."

"Harry Berry," Joey said, processing it.

"Yes, well, I never received a letter from Harry Berry. Every day, I came from summer session and looked through the mail on the table, and my mother said, *Nothing for you, dear.* I believed her. Well, what reason did I have not to? I didn't hear from Rand. I didn't hear from Harry Berry. I stopped eating."

"You stopped eating." The venom in Joey's voice scared her.

"I tried writing him too. After all, who said men got God's gift of initiating things? But no response. I thought of going to Michigan. We'd made promises. We said it had never been this way before. But what would happen, huh? I'd catch him with another girl? I'd be made a fool? He didn't want me—clear as day.

"Every day I used to roller-skate around the neighborhood. It was sort of the way I'd get out my sadness. And, well, your dad lived next door. I used to see him, and we'd catch up, casual, really. He'd just finished law school and was studying for the bar. G and Grandfather adored him. He'd asked me out over the years. It wasn't that I didn't like him, but just, he seemed like the boy you'd be serious about, not the boy you'd have fun with."

"Well, it seems like you got to have a lot of fun," Joey said, but even as it came out she was wincing at her cruelty.

Her mother gazed at her nails again. "Not long after I got home, a few weeks maybe, a month, with no word from

Rand, I was roller-skating and bumped into your father. He said he'd gotten two tickets to an art show at the Miami Art Museum. You know your father. He only goes to art shows to appease me."

"Dad was pulling out the stops." Joey had heard this version of the story before. "I know where we're headed now—unexpected pregnancy. Me."

"Yes, well, so you know then."

"No, I don't know! I don't know, Mom." A sob caught in her throat. "I don't know how our adulterous family vacations originated."

"Well…that part was unexpected."

"Unexpected." Joey grimaced. An ice cream truck outside began to chime.

"When you were nine," her mother said, "I gave a few guest lectures at a college in Carmel. They paid to fly me out, even hosted me at a gallery opening. It was really flattering at a point in my career when I felt I was floundering. It felt like I was just this, well, mother…. I was at this tiny airport in Monterey. I was eating cheese fries of all things when I saw Rand. I felt, well, my heart stopped. I considered not saying anything—"

"*That* would have been the right answer."

"I can't reinvent history now, darling, can I?" Bea said it almost wistfully. "I said his name, and he broke into the biggest smile. I felt so happy. He'd been in San Francisco for a real estate conference and had driven down the coast to check out a property. The first thing he said was how sad he'd been that I never answered his letters.

"*I never answered your letters? I said. I waited for those letters every day. And I sent you my own too.* You see." Her mother got a vacant look in her eyes. "That was the day I began to hate my mother. I understood it then. She'd known me too well. She'd known about Rand, and she'd had to thwart him. *Nothing for you today, dear.* He wrote at least five times before he gave up. And G must have deliberately taken my letters out of the mailbox, as well."

Bea tucked her feet under her hip. "There were storms that evening. Our flights were delayed. We sat there wondering if they'd be canceled. Hoping maybe. Ultimately, our flights weren't canceled, but we decided to tell Scott and Maisy they were. We got a hotel room. It was…well…magic."

"Magic." Joey was going to be sick.

"But you have to know, Joey, how conflicted I was. I was so ashamed I had done it. The next day, you and Dad were all I thought about on my way home. I did love my life. I *do* love my life."

"You have an interesting way of showing it. Making us both the backdrop of your affair. Making us…I don't know…footnotes."

Her mother sighed. "Corfu. It was never supposed to be like that."

"Like what? The incestuous Brady Bunch?"

"It snowballed. It snowballed, and we snowballed. JoJo, have you ever had two things you loved so desperately?"

"No." A thought floated toward her, though, that she quickly flicked away. "I haven't."

"No, I suppose you haven't."

Joey fiddled with her thin gold bangle that she never took off, that she'd bought in Bali and had stamped with the words SHE BELIEVED SHE COULD SO SHE DID. "So finish the story."

"It was Rand's idea. He wanted us to get away together after Monterey, but I didn't see how that could be possible.

We both had families. I loved your father. I did. I mean, I do. I really, really love your father. You know I do. Just differently from the all-consuming way I loved Rand..."

That she threw around her love for Rand so casually was a sucker punch. Joey endured another swell of nausea. Her foot nudged a piece of cracker in the couch. She dug it out from under the cushion.

"Rand said, *We have kids the same age. They could play. Just this one time. We'll spend the summer together, and when Scott's back in Florida or Maisy is under the weather...*" Her mother made air quotes. "I know how terrible that sounds."

Joey set the cracker on a side table. "Not how terrible it *sounds*, Mom," she said quietly. "How terrible it is."

"I agree, Joey. I don't know, maybe part of us wanted to get caught that first summer. Wanted to make it so we could be together. But it seemed so impossible. We both had lives we liked. Rand and Maisy got on less so, but he'd also met her right after me. They'd also gotten pregnant soon and built his business. She was loyal, as far as I knew. This was supposed to be our summer in the place where we fell in love."

"And then?"

"And then we couldn't fall out of love. And then our families grew to love each other. Your father and Rand had a genuine friendship. Me and Maisy too."

"Come on, Mom? Genuine? You were sleeping with her husband."

"I know. It was awful." Her mother put a hand to her chest. Her hand had prominent veins and little brown age spots Joey had never noticed before.

Suddenly Joey thought of something. "And did you meet

during the year too? Did you rendezvous while I was in school and Dad was at work?"

Bea went back to staring at her nails again. "We did a couple of times after that first summer, but to be honest, there was something wrong about it. We decided we could only be a summer thing."

Joey's jaw clenched. "Let me get this straight. There was something wrong about cheating on Dad when he was far away, but not when he was sitting across the table?"

"Oh, Joey." Her mother wrapped her fingers in the fringe dangling off a throw pillow. "All I can tell you is that Rand and I met a few weekends outside the summer, and it just felt so deceptive."

"But you liked the adventure. It almost sounds like...like you wanted to get caught."

"I don't know, Joey," her mother whispered. "Maybe sometimes you have to risk hurting people you love in order to be happy."

"Hurting me, you mean. Hurting Dad. But I don't get one thing." Joey forced herself to say the word. "Lily."

Her mother buried her head in her knees. "You were never supposed to find out about Lily."

"I think it's a miracle no one found out sooner. Well, Leo." Joey took a deep breath. "Did you always know Lily wasn't Dad's?"

After some time, Bea lifted her head back up, her eyes smeared in mascara. "I was pretty sure. I stayed later on Corfu that summer. We had sex once, your dad and I, before he took you back to Florida to start school, but I wasn't ovulating then.

"I hoped, I prayed, it was your dad's. I had nightmares all that year that the baby would come out Rand's twin.

I thought about aborting it, but I wanted her. I just…I wanted her. Lucky for me, she came out Lily. Just herself. But I knew immediately. She's mostly me, of course. But Rand's eyes. His smile."

"Rand knew too." It wasn't a question.

"Rand knew too."

"And he just gave her to Dad? Like that?"

"It wasn't as easy as that, JoJo. Look, Rand's a good person. He knew I loved your dad and what a good dad your father is. And Rand has a lot of strengths, but maybe fatherhood isn't his top. He didn't want to start again. And what were we going to do? Break up our families and raise Lily in some dysfunctional mash-up? You weren't even out of high school yet. I didn't want to do that to you."

"Oh, thank you so much for that consideration."

Her mother's hand went to her throat, her face stricken. "Please don't tell your father. Please, JoJo. It would break him. It would tear up Lily's life. Please, JoJo. I know it's not a fair request. I know what I've done is unforgivable. But after Grandfather died and we left Corfu, I never saw Rand again. We put a stop to it fifteen years ago."

"Because that was Leo's condition! Because Leo forced your hand."

"Well, either way, we listened. We tried to do the right thing."

"For Lily," said Joey very softly. "Listen, Mom, I'll let you know what Leo and I decide to do about all this. But I'll tell you one thing. Whatever we decide, I just…I don't know if I can ever forgive you. And at my wedding…" A fresh pain sucker-punched Joey. Her wedding. It felt inconceivable to fast-forward a week or so, to imagine being happy and carefree.

"At my wedding, I'm sure I'll hug you and enjoy with you and you'll think this is over. But this isn't over. This can never be over. You made it that way. We can't come back from this, Mom."

Joey stood, thinking how that was the most unfair part of all—that life didn't give rewinds, even when you really deserved one.

chapter eighteen

Joey

florida

2019

Another call. Was there no end?

Eighteen-year-old Lily had been stalking Joey, intensifying her calls in the last hour. She was in the don't-let-up camp of communication, her persistence likely why she now stood on first-name footing with Anna Wintour.

A heavy dread shuddered through Joey. She silenced her little sister and propped herself up on her pillow, now covered in dried tear splotches.

After having it out with her mother, Joey had flung herself into her bed and prayed for sleep. But sleep had been like, *Ha ha ha.* It was hard to conceive that only ten hours prior she'd sat with Leo on the beach, entirely oblivious to the Swiss cheese foundation of her life. Joey had to protect Lily, and she would. But first she had to process things herself. However in the world she was supposed to do that?

Joey scrolled to Siya's contact. She hovered over the number, imagining her best friend's shock (disapproval?) that Joey had agreed to meet Leo, and then of course Siya's disgust at Leo's revelations. She'd start to dash off opinions—Siya had endless, strong, well-meaning opinions—and no doubt she'd want to pick things apart with forensic scrutiny. She came by it honestly; her father was a detective and had raised Siya to believe she was a legitimate Nancy Drew. But Joey didn't want to pick things apart even more. She needed to forget for a while. To the extent possible, distract.

Joey threw off her covers and went to the second bedroom that she used as her art den. She sat on a stool before the canvas propped upon her easel. She'd spontaneously grabbed the canvas from her parents' house before leaving that afternoon. The canvas was a sketch of green eyes.

Lily kept calling. With each call, Joey's charge between pencil and canvas fizzled. The phone rang again, and Joey considered flinging it at the wall. Now the screen read KATRINA—Lily's assistant, older than Lily by a decade and perennially kind.

"Hey, Kat."

"Finally," came the soft, authoritative voice of Joey's little sister.

Joey's pencil slipped from her fingertips. Her throat felt like a clogged drain. Lily was Rand's daughter, arguably the biggest victim of their mother's lies—it was still so inconceivable to absorb. Joey imagined Lily, in her prime in the spotlight of their father's affection. How could Bea have done it? Joey imagined her devastation if it were her in Lily's place, how it would cast questions across her entire life. But Joey also couldn't shake the tiny, mean voice inside her, saying that if not for Lily, Leo wouldn't have broken up with Joey and sent her on a downward spiral all those years prior.

"Oh. Hi, Lil." Joey closed her eyes. "Sorry, I was sketching."

"It's okay. But I hope you don't wait this long to respond to your clients."

"My clients don't leave thirty seconds between calls." *And I have no clients at the moment.*

"Sorry, that wasn't fair." Lily prided herself on being fair. *Fair* was her favorite buzzword. Next to *feminist.* And *ethical fashion.* "How are you?"

"I'm good," Joey said and almost laughed. *Good.* "How are you?"

"Oh, good too. Busy. Listen, I have a business proposition. You know Edith?"

"The older lady?" Joey brushed pencil shavings from her thigh. She conjured a vague image of Lily with her hair teased into a purple beehive beside a woman seventy years her senior sporting the same 'do. Something about friends straddling generations. The Saviors of Feminism. It had been in one of those big magazines.

"Yeah. So listen, Edith moved into a huge place on the Intracoastal. I was there the other day for kombucha. We're hosting a party together, for the launch of this jewelry made by rural Sri Lankan women. The design of the collection is amazing—all types of lariats made from cord. Anyway, Guy Lazant's heading up the art. He's got her some major pieces, but Edith has this huge foyer. It's a grotto vibe, and there's this blank wall, and none of Guy's suggestions are *important* enough."

"Wait, back up. Who's Guy?"

"The art cultivator. So I showed Edith your evil eye stuff from Bali. Edith was intrigued. She's interested in having you do an evil eye wall. Something striking. The party's next Thursday so you'd have to get on it fast."

"Next Thursday! Have you forgotten I'm getting married next Saturday?"

"The timing sucks." Lily sounded genuinely remorseful. "But Joey, she'll pay you twenty thousand dollars. And *Vogue* is sending a photographer."

"Seriously, Lil?"

"I'm always serious," her sister reminded her, and it was true. Lily Abrams was serious, indeed. Tackling fashion and feminism on her Instagram and YouTube with an authenticity that had earned her millions in social media followers. By age fourteen, inclusion in 30 under 30 in the Media category in *Forbes*. At fifteen, anointed by *Time* as one of the world's most influential teens. At sixteen, photographed beside her new friend Anna Wintour at New York Fashion Week. And at seventeen, designed a well-received fashion line at Kohl's "for the teen who aspires to a Parisian wardrobe with a croissant budget."

"Edith wants you to meet with her in a couple days. She had to go out of town briefly, but in the meantime, you can start to prep like the commission is yours. I really think she'll give it to you. Kat will shoot you details of the meeting. Are you in?"

"I'll be there. Wow. Really appreciate it, Lil."

"Of course. See you tomorrow to shower you, big sis!"

Oh God, her bridal shower. Organized by her mother. And Joey still hadn't even told Grant about Leo. Suddenly she longed for a Rip Van Winkle amount of sleep.

"And Joey, if you need help picking out something stylish to wear, I'm here!"

"Thanks, Lily, I'm stylish on my own," Joey said, bristling, that tiny barb burrowing into her skin. She and Lily were close. Close-ish. As close as you could be, really, to a sibling sixteen years your junior. But sometimes Joey felt like they were competing for their parents' attention and love and like Lily came out ahead, especially since Joey had left law, her high-flying career of which her father had been uber-proud. Maybe all siblings experienced it, a standard jostle for their fair-share slice of the pie. Or maybe Joey was a bit jealous of her little sister's wild success, like everyone presumed.

Joey set down her phone. Evil eyes? It was like Lily had a spy camera on her. Twenty thousand dollars? *Vogue*? Holy shit. But how was she supposed to paint some epic wall with her wedding in eleven days and Leo the Minefield now traipsing around town?

She needed to tell Grant. That was the critical thing. She tried to rouse the will, to box herself into the task by calling him. He'd be out of surgery by now, eating a Tupperware of egg salad with that Paleo mayonnaise he bought in bulk. He'd be spent, but his voice would be light at the sound of hers.

She should have told Grant about meeting Leo before she went to the beach. That was the part she was dreading. She was going to have to explain why she'd kept it secret when she'd had plenty of opportunities to share, to give him time to weigh in. And then of course there was another thing, Leo's confession of love that Joey was certain he didn't mean. He didn't even know her now, besides. He knew a version of Joey that was long gone. Still, she was going to have to tell Grant about the love confession too.

She couldn't do it. She just couldn't call him now. Not after the day she'd had.

She considered the canvas again. The eyes flashing at her were intricate. Big. Larger than his real ones. Leo eyes with evil eye flair. Just the eyes had taken her weeks. The lids. The shadows. The crinkles. There was the outline of a face.

Some lines of hair. The beginnings of an arm. The curve of a back. A smudge by an eye.

Joey smiled at that smudge. She remembered it well.

This was the one portrait Joey had ever begun that she'd liked. She loved the idea of a portrait, the turning of a person inside out. And she was good at certain frames: the backs of a mother and child walking away. A woman on a paddleboard with just her right cheek in the frame. But Joey wasn't so good at portraits so exposed. Head-on. Her faces came out flat, her eyes uniformly vacant. *No movement*, Demetris had once agreed. *No life.* For some reason, this facial portrait was the sole interesting one that she'd ever produced.

Correction. That she'd begun.

Because in the midst of birthing it, she'd traded art for law. And when she'd returned to her old friend a year and a half back, it wasn't with verve but with care. Like her art was something that could be shattered again.

She would do evil eyes, she'd contracted with herself, but without faces attached. Evil eye walls. Those safe, distant portraits, yes. But now she'd violated the contract. The past couple of hours, she'd sat in front of this strange, unfinished, distorted Leo face. She'd sketched and remembered and considered. Her cheeks blazed.

The same thought returned to plague her: *I should change this to Grant.* She flipped open her sketchbook and hashed out some ideas. She slashed a line at the jaw for him. Grant's jaw was what people called chiseled.

Joey's pencil hovered over the page. Quickly, she flipped it so the point aimed up. She busied the eraser over the jawline, hating her relief as it reverted to Leo.

Joey slammed her sketchbook shut. She eyed a pile of

candy boxes. She could work on wedding stuff—the few items her mother had delegated. What she needed to do was dole Hot Tamales (Groom's Favorite!) and Sour Patch Kids (Bride's Favorite!) into welcome bags and affix the tags with calligraphy that had consumed hours in emails with an Etsy proprietress. Joey turned a Sour Patch box around in her hands, already tasting the salty sweet of a little bear on her tongue. Knowing how one bear would turn to one box, would turn to two, would turn to ten.

No. No no no no.

Joey knew she should feel her feelings—that was what she'd learned to do to defuse a binge. She bit her lip, reminded of that first binge, in the dark all alone after she was back at Penn and Leo and her grandfather were gone. But Joey didn't want to feel her feelings now. What was she supposed to do, she wondered, when her feelings felt like they were killing her?

Her heart beating fast, Joey stuffed the candy in a drawer and darted to her walk-in art closet. It was edged in cedar oak shelves, with special slots for canvases to rest, with thoughtful compartments for paints and pens. Joey had created the many canvases that now occupied the shelves for a show a couple of months before, but the gallery had backed out. She'd been devastated, her faith dampened that against all odds she'd make it as an artist.

Joey plopped on the floor carpeted in a cream squiggle print. She ran her hand across an empty shelf, contented at the granulated wood dust that adhered to her fingertips. It smelled like her grandfather's wooden shoe trees that she used to help him slip into his beautiful wing-tip shoes.

His fine shoes now sat on her shelf. She liked to hold them from time to time, talk to them. Italian leather, he once told her proudly, when they snuck away from dinner. Joey didn't think of her grandfather as an adult then. He was her buddy who led her to the back laundry room where his shoes lived. He showed her how to polish and buff them and insert the shoe trees. He only had one pair of special-occasion shoes. He didn't need more than that, he explained. All his shirts went with black. If a shirt didn't go with black, well, he wouldn't buy it, simple as that.

He was such a simple brick, her grandfather, such an unassuming Jenga piece. Joey shifted to a recline across the carpet, slipping a stray sweatshirt under her head. Her eyes felt like they had anchors attached to them, dragging them down. She reached for her grandfather's shoe off the shelf and cradled it to her so the soft leather rested against her cheek. Then her eyes fluttered shut and sleep finally came.

chapter nineteen

Sarah

corfu
1943

They arrived in Lefkada as the sun dwindled, still bright enough to experience the assault of colors, places, and people. As Sarah was hugged by people of varying shapes and smells, she endured the panic telling her that something was very wrong. Her whole life she'd known the Jewish quarter of Corfu Town, and now here she was, smothered to the bosom of Milos's mother, whose brass breastplate on her velvet outfit threatened to take out Sarah's eye.

"Oh, it's so wonderful, just wonderful! Our new daughter."

"*Efharisto*," Sarah said, thank you, thank you, thank you, to the myriad wishes of *na zeesete*. May the both of you live long.

On their way from Corfu, she and Milos had decided to tell his parents they'd already married. His family would expect that cemented union to accept her into the fold, and Sarah had no intention of a real wedding until her parents came around. She was still convinced that eventually they'd soften to a marriage.

Milos found her hand, and his squeeze administered a little balm to her wounds. He led Sarah to his house, a stone affair with citrus trees outside, a garden in the front, and the day's thunderous sea in a wide sweep beyond. On the main floor, dust stormed them like a welcome party, and when it cleared, Sarah saw a brick fireplace, a scuffed black piano, ramshackle furniture upholstered in a range of sun-beaten, primary-colored velvets, and books stacked floor-to-ceiling in the corner.

"My father loves to read," said Milos with evident pride. "He thinks I can be as good as Tennyson and Joyce, if I apply myself. I wonder if…I mean, do you think I can, Sarah?"

Sarah heard the import of the question mark. It wasn't soft and light, like requiring confirmation of something he already knew. No, Milos needed Sarah to inform him what he was capable of. He'd recited passages to her before, which she'd thought wonderful, albeit commentary drenched in bias. When you loved someone so newly and completely, it was quite impossible to conceive of a critique.

"I know you can," she said, and when Milos smiled, she was struck by her power, to make him and to break him. And if she wielded that power over him, then couldn't it work vice versa?

Sarah paused at a teetering pile of books, wishing Benjamin was there to delight in the bounty. She could just picture him, assuming the preparatory stance of an Olympian to conquer every last tome.

"The attic is over here." Milos led her away, and somewhat reluctantly, Sarah followed him up rickety stairs to the tiny alcove on the very top, large enough only for a bed made up in yellow linens, framed by an oval window onto a garden. Sarah sat on the bed, atop a creaky spring. They hadn't been together yet, like a married couple should. Well, they weren't married. And what did it even mean, to be together? She was supposed to have a mother and friends to help her decipher how these things were meant to proceed.

Rachel. Sarah's heart panged, thinking how she hadn't even said goodbye to her best friend.

"You can put your things in the dresser." Milos opened a drawer, and a moth scattered out.

"My things?" Sarah remembered her bag and peered inside it, suddenly eager for a memory of home. Slowly, she removed a pair of pajamas and then the fancy dress her father had made her for a cousin's wedding. He hadn't even protested when she'd selected the cobalt brocade fabric that cost more than her mother had said she could spend.

"That's all you brought?" Milos extended his hand for the dress. "Here, I'll hang it."

But she couldn't bear to part with it yet. "It all happened so fast. I…I didn't—"

"It's okay, *kardia mou*." Milos sat beside her and slipped an arm around her shoulder assuredly, as if her wardrobe was all that was plaguing her. "My mother will have something for you to wear, I'm sure. She said…"

When he didn't finish, Sarah said, "What?" She was alarmed, all of a sudden, that she'd made a negative impression on this woman who was about to exert significant influence upon her life.

"Don't worry! She said you are wonderful. Beautiful. Of course, she would like you to convert to the Orthodox religion."

"I won't. We talked about this, and I—"

"Don't worry," Milos soothed. "I told her that. But she did say you should wear the kerchief in your hair."

"Oh." Sarah had noticed it, the women all bedecked in white headscarves.

"If you are married and don't wear it, it gives the wrong impression."

"Okay." Sarah fixed her eyes on her nails to distract them from spilling tears. "Should we go down for dinner?"

"Not yet. My mother knows we would like some time alone."

"Yes." Well, it was to be understood. Milos was a man, and she was committed to him now. Sarah tried to psych herself up to the task. "How should we—"

"No!" He laughed. "You think I've brought you up here to make mad, passionate love with you?"

At his joking tone, Sarah's chest heaved relief. "Are you telling me you didn't?"

"Sarah, we have our whole lives for that. This is a huge sacrifice you've made, to come live with me—"

"Until my parents change their minds," she reminded him.

"Yes. Until then. I just want you to feel safe. All I want in the world is for you to feel happy and safe."

And when Milos put it that way, and wrapped his arms around her, and the sun wrestled from the clouds and warmed them through the window, Sarah found she could feel happy. In the interludes she didn't fixate on what she'd left behind, she could feel quite happy, indeed.

⌒

And so Sarah's life went from her parents and Benjamin and Rachel, and laundering and ironing for Yanni the widower, and the Evraiki and synagogue and Jews, to Milos and his parents and his colicky baby sister, and Sarah's new job baking pastries in the shop of an old lady with a large mole on her chin who smelled like the cheese she produced—and no Jews. Sarah was the only one on the island.

For those first months, she and Milos just slept side by side, sometimes hugging or touching hands or feet, but not fully conjoining. Sarah thought how interesting it was, how different she felt when her foot touched Milos's foot versus Benjamin's. Missing Benjamin always made her sad and sober then, and she would write her little brother long letters to which she hadn't yet received a response. Milos would watch her rush to the post office and return empty-handed and dejected so he began leaving her notes. He left Sarah notes in her apron, notes in her shoe. He left her notes in the pocket of the dress his mother gifted her, a folksy affair that made Sarah feel perpetually in a Purim costume.

I am so happy.

The red of your hair is my favorite color that exists.

I'm sorry you can't have all of the people you love at the same time.

It was the last note that did something to her, made Sarah attune outside of herself, to sweet Milos and how her despondence was hurting him. It was fall by then, the air cool and pine-scented, and Milos was out fishing. That evening when he returned, he undressed in the dark and slipped into bed. And this time Sarah turned to him.

From then on, every evening they came together in a symphony. They clung to each other under the gnarled brown blanket with the moon unpeeling little slivers of their limbs for the glimpsing. They were drunk off their love. It was the happiest time of Sarah's life.

The happiest time of her life came to a swift end in September 1943. Sarah stood in the kitchen of the bake shop where she worked. She was pulling ladokouloura, olive oil cookies, from the oven when her favorite patron, Costas, swept inside, bringing with him a crisp fall gust. He requested his usual baklava, which was the bane of Sarah's existence to produce. The phyllo dough required inordinate patience. It was prone to tearing and drying and mandated a quick assembly with the local thyme honey.

But Sarah loved serving Costas so she excused him his vice. He was old, in his fifties, and he seemed to be a man who liked to talk and had few people with whom to do it. He reminded Sarah of her father a bit, with his expressive eyebrows, grand mustache, and white hair combed neatly to the side—except Costas was gentler and thus far had found no aspect of Sarah to critique. Well, easy to be gentle when you are not the father, perhaps, Sarah thought. She'd noticed herself becoming wiser since leaving Corfu and longed to present herself to her parents and say, *Look Mama, Look Baba, I am a person you would be proud of.*

As Sarah served Costas baklava on a blue-flowered plate, he said, "Have you heard? The Italians are out. The Nazis got them. And the destruction is terrible, especially on Corfu. It's such a shame. Such a crying shame."

Sarah's body went rigid. Of course, they'd heard the bomber planes. They'd crouched under the table with their hands over their heads. But she didn't know the Nazis had won. She'd thought the Italians strong, powerful, capable. But apparently they too had toppled like dominoes.

"They've killed all the Italian soldiers. From the generals on down."

"All…all of them?" Sarah thought of the general she'd

helped bargain in the market—how he'd given her straw-berries to take home to her family.

"Yes. The Nazis are here too, you know."

"Here?" Sarah whispered.

"Yes, they've got all our Ionian islands now." Costas shook his head. Over the yammer of her heart, Sarah noticed how his hair should have moved but didn't because it was so shellacked into place. "But their main objective is the Jews, and as you know, no Jews reside on Lefkada. I fear for the Jews of Corfu. I fear for them deeply."

"For the Jews of Corfu?" Sarah didn't feel her tongue form the words, but she heard them emit from her mouth.

"Yes. They've made all the Jews in Corfu register. Nothing good comes from that, I tell you. Why do the Nazis need a registry? To invite the Jews to a party? No, it's a sinister thing, a list. Mark my words. I wish there was something we could do. I just need to do something." He lowered his voice. "Stop these German animals. It reminds me how powerless we are, this thing called war. Don't you think, Sarah? I mean, tell me, have you ever felt so powerless?"

And somehow Sarah's head managed a small shake in reply, because it was quite true that she hadn't.

chapter twenty

Joey

florida
2019

In her thirty-four years, Joey had attended many bridal showers, but none had involved barefoot guests sitting on poufs on the floor. And to Joey's knowledge at least, none had been hosted by the bride's mother who'd been recently exposed as a lying adulteress.

"Joey loves Indian food," her mother was explaining into a microphone to the thirty or so guests who had gathered to shower her.

"I also love sushi," Joey whispered to her best friend of over twenty years, Siya, who occupied a yellow pouf to her right. "I mean, I do like Indian food. I like your mom's, obviously."

"My mom's rasmalai is better," said Siya as she ate the dessert on which she and Joey had grown up, made of ricotta cheese soaked in condensed milk and flavored with pistachio nuts and saffron. "Or it used to be."

"Agreed." Joey placed her hand over her best friend's. They weren't touchy-feely friends, but it felt important to convey her solidarity. Joey knew what they were both thinking, how unfair it was that Siya's mom had recently lost dexterity in both her hands due to her MS diagnosis. Joey found it almost inconceivable to imagine Siya's warm, giving mother doing something other than puttering around her kitchen.

Joey could feel Siya's we-can-stop-holding-hands telepathy so Joey lifted her hand and checked her phone. She saw a text from an unknown number that was now wholly known to her, but that she hadn't yet added to her contacts. Her stomach somersaulted. *Can I see you again tomorrow, Jonesey? It was unfair of me to come to Florida before your wedding, I realize that now. I'm sorry. I'm also sorry for how many times I'm telling you I'm sorry. But now that you know everything, we really need to talk again, don't you think?*

"What?" asked Siya. Joey's fingers hovered over the phone. It could all slip so easily out to Siya, but Joey wasn't ready for Siya's judgment, however well meaning.

"Nothing," she said, maybe too brightly.

Joey shot off a quick text in reply. *Tomorrow at 9am?*

She couldn't see Leo again before she told Grant. Which meant she had to tell Grant. Tonight.

Joey slid down her silver pouf and smoothed her olive-green silk midi skirt so she didn't flash all her guests. She'd found it for a steal at a local boutique going out of business and paired it with a simple chunky cream sweater, which perhaps wasn't weather-appropriate for August in Florida, but the air conditioner was on full blast. Joey adjusted her three gold coin necklaces so the coins all lined up uniformly in the center of her chest. She and Grant had discovered them at an antiques fair in Sarasota, from a dealer who'd told them an elaborate, questionably true, but nonetheless romantic story about each. Grant had surprised Joey for Valentine's Day, both with his thoughtfulness and for knowing her taste, by having the coins strung on thin gold chains of varying lengths.

"Jo, why are you being so secretive? Who were you texting?" asked Siya, and Joey was quiet, at a loss for a response.

A welcomed distraction—somewhat—was Lily now striding across the mahogany wood, calling, "Siiiiiiiiya!" Joey's sister wore her Power Lily jaw clench, a rose crushed-velvet jumpsuit, and mules with big, black, furry straps that resembled Chia Pets. She looked like some stern but sultry headmistress roused out of bed at an all-girls boarding school. Her hair ran in copper crimps to her waist. She had twenty necklaces draped in her cleavage, but they were all so delicate it was like gold and diamond webbing.

"Siya, I need your help." Lily thrust a pile of bows from presents Joey had unwrapped earlier into Siya's lap. "Can you make this into a hat?"

"Why, are you gonna stick it on your Insta, Lil?" asked Joey.

Lily's microbladed eyebrows raised in a look of disdain that was so Rand, it nearly took Joey's breath away. How was it even possible she'd never noticed? "No offense, Joey, but I have two million savvy followers. They aren't captivated by some basic shower ribbon hat."

Siya snorted. Joey pressed a hand over her chest, her heart pounding. "Then you can take Siya off ribbon hat duty, Lil. It's not really my thing."

Siya took the ribbons. "It's fine. I like an art project."

"Thanks!" Lily burst off, flagging a server.

"She's something else, isn't she?" Joey watched her little sister gesticulate to the poor server who'd apparently committed some sort of infraction. As ever, Joey was both amazed and appalled at the way Lily walked through the world, claiming everything and everyone she wanted. Maybe it was the Rand in her asserting itself, Joey thought with disloyal dread. An image flashed of her own father in his trademark sandals with socks, proudly walking into the kitchen to display an impressive tomato from his garden.

"Lily's just trying—" Siya was interrupted by a shrill of the microphone.

"Sanjeep, where is Sanjeep?" Bea shouted amid violent taps to the microphone. Joey could barely look at her without seething. For a moment, Joey wondered why such a happy event felt a little like being tortured. Her mother wore her multicolored, embroidered artist's cape, which she'd apparently retrieved from the bowels of her closet. Joey's memories were rife with memories of her mother painting in that cape, especially on Corfu. Her mother now swept an edge of her cape in much exaggerated fashion so it came to rest over the same shoulder on which it had previously resided.

It was a practiced Bea move. Draw Attention to Thyself.

Sanjeep appeared from the kitchen, his round face steamy and bashful. He wore a long tunic made of thick yellow silk with navy embroidery adorning the neck. "Here I am, Madame Bee."

At that, Bea executed a curtsy. She said into the microphone, in booming good humor, "Sanjeep, you've known me my whole life. How many times must I tell you? It's *Bay-uh*."

Joey said, "He's younger than her. How is it possible he's known her all her life?"

Siya shrugged, a purple ribbon clamped between her lips. Up front, by the windows onto Atlantic Avenue, Sanjeep dragged something cloaked in a sheet out of a closet.

"G." Joey tapped her grandmother's hand at her right. "Did you intend for Mom's name to be pronounced *Bay-uh*?"

G smiled, and her aggressive swipes of blush smiled with her. "Your mother is a force, isn't she? That's what I always say, a force. A dynamo!"

"But seriously, G. Her name is pronounced *Bee*, right? *Beeeeatrice*. We're Greek, not Spanish."

But G was rifling in her cream leather purse. She drew out her phone, and a party of crumpled tissues flew out after it. "Joey, I need you to explain something to me."

"G, you're so beautiful," said Joey in a spontaneous flood of love. Her grandmother might have been overzealous with the blusher, but her creamy skin was in far better shape than her advanced years would suggest, setting off her kind, aqua eyes.

"Oh please, Joey." G scrolled through her phone. "Look closer. Even my wrinkles have wrinkles." She frowned. "This! This is what you have to explain. What the heck is this?"

Joey saw a Facebook conversation with lengthy text. At the end was embedded a poop emoji. "You're really doing the Facebook thing? Who are you messaging?"

G jerked back her phone. "What is that *thing*?"

"You mean the poop emoji?"

"The poop emoji," repeated G with a doubtful curl of her lips. "But what…what does it do?"

Joey stifled a giggle. "It's just meant to be funny."

"Ah." A smile took hold of G's face. "I see. And what about all those different hearts?"

"What do you mean? Like, heart emojis?"

In her periphery, Joey could see Bea greeting a line of her friends, no doubt reveling in their praise over the lovely shower. Joey sighed. It *was* in fact a lovely shower. Just, it felt like a lifetime of love for and from her mom had gone in an instant, leaving a cold, gaping hole.

"Emojis?" asked G. "The faces? But there are a bunch of them with hearts."

"Oh," said Joey distractedly. "Well, if it's just a big heart, it could mean love, especially if it's coming from a romantic partner. And if there's a face with a little heart that's kind of winking, it's a kissy—"

"Okay, darling. You can stop. Who knew a face could do so many things?"

"G, who are you talking to on Face—"

There was a tap on her shoulder. Joey swiveled to see the round, probing face of Doris, her grandmother's best friend and personal trainer and the benefactor of Joey's Jeep. Doris's vision had become too impaired to drive, but not to personal train, so she now walked to houses in G's little cul-de-sac to conduct sessions with seniors that consisted mostly of deep breathing and gossiping with an occasional grunting side stretch.

Joey hugged Doris and helped her into a chair. "Tell me, dear." Doris leaned in, and now Joey remembered this— Doris's tendency toward close talking. "Tell me how you met your fellow."

"Oh, yes, tell Dor the story." G abandoned her phone and now looked rapturously upon Joey.

Joey smiled. She did love her love story. For a moment, a cloud drifted over, and she was somewhere else—telling Grant about Leo, and he was mad she hadn't told him sooner, and worse, he was sad. And then, the cloud didn't lift so much as assimilate, so Joey could recount things, but with an element of wistfulness.

She began with Grant's gorgeous tan, omitting his man bun (the over-fifty set thought it was a variety of hamburger encasement), and she skated heavily over the surfing into him part ("But how dangerous!"). She was practiced at the climax—when Grant approached her on the beach.

"So there I was, every bone in my body hurt. Lolak, my instructor, had gone. He'd told me he could get anyone to surf, but after I rammed into Grant, I think he gave up on me. There's something about the sea though. I was spent and content. I found this stick, and I drew my name into the sand. I was admiring it, when this guy came over."

"Grant," said G triumphantly.

"Grant." Joey smiled. "His calf was wrapped in a T-shirt, and I recognized him immediately. I said, *Did I do that?*, and he nodded, and I felt so terrible. It was really embarrassing. And so I said, *It's my first time.* And he said, *No? I wouldn't have guessed.* But he was laughing, and he held out a beer for me and had one for himself, and then I understood. He'd sought me out.

"I said, *Are you going to be okay?*, and he said, *I think I'll live.* And then he looked at what I'd written, and he said, *So Joey?*, and I said, *And you are?*, and he gave me this gorgeous grin, you know Grant—"

"Very handsome," said Doris, with a knowing look.

"Very," agreed Joey. "So Grant didn't answer when I asked him his name. He just wrote with his finger in the sand next to my name one of those ampersands and then followed it with his name. So it read—"

"Joey and Grant," said G and Doris in one united swoon.

Joey felt the cloud lift entirely now so she could pretend

to herself a little longer that this sweet Bali love was all in the world there was. "So we had a romance, but only for a couple of days, until his flight out. And I knew he lived in Florida, of course, but I didn't know I'd be coming back here."

"But then not too long after I had my surgery," cut in G, as her starring part arose. "You remember, Dor, on my aorta?"

"Of course."

G nodded importantly. "Well, Joey came back from Bali for my surgery and was visiting me in the hospital. And she walked right into Grant!"

"Literally right into him." Joey laughed.

"He's a doctor," confided G to Doris. "A dermatologist."

"Oh, my." A knowing glance passed between them.

Joey stifled a laugh as her mother rapped on the microphone again. "Attention, attention, please."

"What now?" said Joey, since she'd already opened presents, and Bea had already delivered a lengthy and meandering speech that Joey had endured with her fists clenched at her sides. Siya shrugged, not looking up from her bloated ribbon thing.

When the room had quieted, Bea said, "I just have one final gift to present." Joey saw a stand had appeared, along with that thing Sanjeep had lugged out of a closet. It looked like a canvas. With a flourish, Bea unveiled it.

Oh shit. Joey froze.

"Is it…a flower?" Doris squinted.

"Is it a mountain?" asked G. "That's quite a beautiful mountain." G leaned forward so far that her chair tipped, and Joey somehow grasped her faculties fast enough to right the chair.

Oh no. Oh *no*.

"It's a vagina," explained Bea, but Joey had already put together the pink and red and *oh*, she couldn't look. She wished for sunglasses. She wished to disappear.

All Joey could do was whisper, "You painted me a vagina?"

"*Your* vagina," said Bea, as the restaurant filled with nervous laughter. "Well, of course it's not your wedding gift. That's the wedding, from your father and me. This is just sentimental, sweetheart. I know your vagina, of course. I gave birth to you."

"Ah!" said Sanjeep, and Joey gave an involuntary glug as she saw him try to absorb it all. "Brilliant! Bea, how about that, you are very talented, I did not know—"

"I thought you could present it to Grant." Bea paced the room now. "You aren't giving your vagina to him, of course. That belongs only to you. Remember that, Joey. You *own* your vagina. But if you have a fight, or you're out of town. Or if you have babies. It will never look this fresh. See the depth I was able to create." Bea appraised her work with a look of satisfaction. "It took a long time to shade the labia…"

"It's…lovely, darling," said G with a loving but dubious look to her.

Bea said in that tight tone she reserved only for G, "Lovely is a little…condescending for this piece, Mother."

Bea smiled at Joey, as if she actually believed Joey would accept the vagina thing as a peace offering. Joey felt the silence in the room get louder, awaiting her reaction.

"Thanks, Mom. It's…fab."

"Mic drop," said Siya, and plopped something atop Joey's head. A ribbon flopped into her mouth.

Joey spit out the ribbon and pressed her fingers into her temples. "Total mic drop."

chapter twenty-one
Joey

florida

2019

They found themselves in a sea of blenders and mixers and one extremely odd vagina painting.

"What are we going to do with all this stuff?" asked Grant.

"You're going to use it to cook me ten-course dinners, of course." Joey slipped her hands under his T-shirt at the base of his spine.

"And what are you going to do?"

"Eat," she said into his chest. "I'm going to eat all of your masterpieces."

"How generous." He cracked his neck back and forth.

Her mouth opened. The words to tell him about Leo in town hung in the back. They hid behind her tonsils.

She and Grant had such a simple relationship. Her first simple relationship.

Grant knelt beside the boxes, sifting. He held up a white ceramic mezuzah. "I'll hang this up, yeah?"

"Sure." Joey went to the kitchen for a glass of water. The refrigerator was leaking murky purple again. She put down a towel to sop it up—a stiff white towel covered in yellow smudges, a towel of suspicious origins. From Grant's bachelor life, probably.

"Mezuzah is up," he called. "I even Googled the prayer to say."

When she returned to the foyer, Grant was holding up the painting. "Now where should I hang my gift?" He smirked. "It deserves a place of prominence, don't you think? In our marital home."

"Only if you want me to paint a picture of your dick to go beside it. Then we'll be *those* people. The strange genitalia people."

"Well, what kind of studying is going to have to occur to render that painting?" He pulled her into him with one hand and set down the painting with the other.

"Don't you wish." The moon outside hooked over Grant's head.

Grant kissed her forehead.

"I have to tell you something," she said.

Joey hadn't known that her last day as a lawyer would be her last day. In fact, she'd just reached the pinnacle. Partnership. Her father had shown up from Florida with champagne. They'd alerted him first—the King of Estate Planning. Scott toasted her. "My big-deal daughter. You've worked so hard for this." It was eleven A.M. The champagne fizzed down Joey's tubes the wrong way.

She got flowers from her biggest client. Not flowers so much as a garden. It took up her whole desk. Two mailroom guys had to carry it in.

"They'll fit into your new office," said Mark Delisio, the managing partner who'd come down to slap her shoulders. He slapped them twice before halting, presumably coming to the realization that she was a woman with shoulders as delicate as tissue paper.

He smiled with his mouthful of veneers. No woman had made partner in her group in twenty-eight years.

Joey's new, partner-size office with an actual city view was being prepped down the hall. (The view was of another office building in Battery Park. But sunlight peeked between the office buildings at certain times, she'd heard.) Office fairies had installed her new nameplate as her partnership was being announced.

"Now I wish I could say *take the day off*." *Wish* wasn't a word you wanted to hear out of Mark Delisio's lips. What followed was a string of semi-platitudes like *last minute* and *it's out of my hands*.

At four the next morning, as Joey sat on the floor of her office, double-, triple-, quadruple-checking the myriad org charts and agreements that had to be reviewed and signed at eight A.M. by a client launching his new hedge fund, her chest arrested.

I'm having a heart attack, she thought. Her second thought was, *I hate my life*.

That she hated her life came as a surprise to Joey. When I make partner, I will love my life, she'd told herself all along. I'll be able to save for a West Village walk-up. I'll take more vacations. I'll go to Bali. I'll have more sex. Better sex. More discriminate sex.

That she'd made partner and still didn't feel happy was surprising.

Joey glanced at the blue sheets of paper they used to

fasten the agreements. She stapled four sheets together. Then she thrust an agreement across the room. The pages fell in a disappointing heap on the carpet, only one paper poking out, not even out of order. Joey grabbed a permanent marker from her table, sending pens flying across the cherrywood. She wrangled the floral arrangement to the floor. It smelled like summer. Like the outdoors.

What were those things?

Joey sprawled on the floor and began to sketch. After some time, she filled all four stapled sheets so she added new ones. Eventually, there wasn't enough floor space. She moved chairs to the hallway. She wedged her bookcase between her desk and a file cabinet. Her hand flew across the sheets. When Mark walked into her office the next morning, she knew he was there because his $1,500 John Lobbs approached her blue canvas. She didn't look up.

"What's going on, Abrams?"

She didn't try to conceal her painting. It was jammed with evil eyes. Scrawny ones and bloated ones. The evil eyes she'd started to draw back in Corfu. "I think I'll be taking some days off, Mark."

"How many days?"

"All of the days." She stood, suddenly extraordinarily happy. "All of the days in the future, I'll be taking off."

She collected her blue sheets of paper and followed security out of the building. She put her things in storage and went to Bali the next week.

Having to tell Grant the truth now was even scarier than that day Joey gave up everything she'd tried for so many years to want.

chapter twenty-two

Joey

florida

2019

"You remember I told you about Leo?" she said quickly because she was going to lose all her nerve if she didn't.

"Leo. No? Should that name ring a bell?" Grant walked back over to the door to check out the mezuzah. He seemed pleased with his handiwork.

"He's my old boyfriend. From Corfu." She wiped her sweaty palms on her sweater. "He came to Florida to see me yesterday."

Grant's eyes caught hers. They flickered with shock. "You saw your ex from Corfu yesterday? And you didn't tell me?"

"Kind of." She walked over to the couch and sat down, hoping he'd follow.

He didn't. "You either saw him or you didn't, Joey."

"I did," she admitted. "But he had a crazy thing to tell me, about—"

"Crazy, like, he's still in love with you?" Grant laughed,

but it was a laugh with an edge of *maybe I'm right, tell me I'm not right.*

"More crazy, like severely fucked-up stuff about my family."

"So he's not still in love with you?"

She opened her mouth, willing the right thing to come out. But nothing did.

"He is. God, Joey! I can't believe you went and met with him without telling me. How would you feel if I was telling you the same story about Lauren?"

Lauren was Grant's tiny blond yoga-instructor ex who also owned a gluten-free bakery in Hollywood that Joey sometimes stalked on Instagram and once had even gone to and confirmed Lauren's tiny blondness. She'd pretended to herself she was just getting a cake to surprise Siya for a lunch date on her birthday, even though Siya was all about gluten. To add insult to injury, sweet, bubbly Lauren had insisted on adding one of their new peanut butter chip cookies free for the road. It had, of course, been delicious.

"I'd feel shitty," Joey admitted. "Really shitty."

"That about sums it up for me right now," Grant said. "Do you…I mean…do—"

"No! Of course not. I love *you*. Only *you*. Look, I need to tell you the full story. What I learned about my family. The real reason Leo came back was to tell me why—" She had been about to say *why he broke up with me.* "Why our families stopped going to Corfu. Basically, my mom was having an affair with his dad, Rand, for like, the entire decade we summered on Corfu."

Grant froze, hovering over her, still not sitting. "Your mom was cheating on Scott?"

"Yeah," Joey said quietly. "For ten years. And that's not

the worst part. Lily is their daughter. She's not my dad's. Can you believe it?"

Finally Grant sat beside her. He didn't say anything.

"I guess Leo has been waiting on telling me until Lily turned eighteen. Which, you know, happened recently."

Even as she said it, she was digging her nails into her palm. It still didn't feel real. Just two days ago, Corfu had seemed a million miles away, like everything that happened there was locked away under key. Or maybe she'd just locked it away. Or thought she had, or could.

Grant didn't say anything, and his silence was freaking Joey out. He walked to the bar cart by the balcony and selected the decanter she'd picked out on a flea-market trip with G. She remembered how fun it had been, to buy a few things to adorn her and Grant's new conjoined life. White milk-glass goblets. The crystal decanter she'd imagined Grant using to do this very thing—pour himself scotch—but not in this weird, distant version.

"Say something, babe," she whispered. "Please."

Grant finally joined her on the couch. He swirled his whiskey on his knee. "Leo." He seemed to be turning the word around on his tongue, unsure of which direction to fling it. "God, that's just insane about your mom. And Lily. It's horrible."

"I know." Joey laughed, a laugh that had tears spilling out along with it. She was so glad he could go there, that he could start there, instead of with Leo.

"Oh, Jo. Come here." Grant set down his glass and tugged Joey into him, and she sank gratefully into his embrace. But the hug was achingly short. Grant pulled back, his face clouded over. "And so...Leo knew this secret in Corfu. It's why he broke up with you, isn't it?"

Joey so didn't want to say it. "Yes. Grant, I'm—"

He put out a hand this time. To stop her, but also to keep her away. "It's like, I know I'm supposed to comfort you right now. And I want to, Joey. I really do. But I'm pissed at you, and I'm pissed at this Leo character. I'm mad this is all happening right before our wedding. And honestly, I'm mad at myself for not just…like, part of me just wants to hug you forever."

Joey inched closer to him at that. She wanted so badly for him to hug her again too. She'd nearly closed their gap when he drained his glass and got up to pour another.

Her chest felt paralyzed with desperation. "I just want you to know…I just want one thing not to be in doubt. I've always wanted to marry *you*. None of this changes that."

"Doesn't it though?" He spoke in such a strange tone. Not an angry one. Just curious. Like he was probing her to see whether she preferred peanut butter over almond butter, New York City over LA.

"No. It has to do with a lot of people—it affects a lot of people—but not us."

"Huh. That seems wrong." Grant returned to the couch. "He…Leo. You loved him."

"It was fifteen years ago." She tried to smile. "You've loved other people too."

"But none of them have returned telling me they still love me." Grant winced. "That's not your fault, no. But you decided to see him right before our wedding. And you took away my opportunity to decide how I'd feel about it. Admit it, Joey. You didn't tell me because you knew I'd say how uncomfortable I'd be with it. And so instead you just did it. That's not how a partnership works. That's not how I want *my* partnership to work."

Joey opened her mouth but couldn't think of a thing to say to defend her behavior. She slid across the leather toward him, forcing herself into him, she knew, but Grant's love language was touch. Maybe if he felt her skin again, she could fill in their cracks. She slipped herself under his arm, hoping for that imperceptible shift, for him to allow her back inside. But he didn't, not after a few uncomfortable minutes. So she slowly untangled herself.

"That's not how I want our partnership to work either," she finally said. "I swear it isn't, Grant. But I think..." She tried to choose her words carefully. "This doesn't have to change anything. I've told Leo in no uncertain terms that his...declaration is not reciprocated. I didn't ask for it, Grant."

"I don't know, Joey. I think you wanted to see him. Leo." Grant put his thumbs to his chin and his forefingers to his temples. His other fingers dangled, and then he pressed them all into his face. "Admit it. You couldn't see him for fifteen years, and you wanted to see if you still felt something. Hedge your bets."

"No! That's not true!"

But wasn't it? Joey trembled on the couch. Wasn't it a little true?

Grant cradled his head in his hands. Joey realized she'd never seen him cry. On their first date in Florida, he'd told her about his older brother, Sean. How Sean was a marine in the Gulf who'd returned believing he was still at war. How Grant was fifteen when Sean came back. How twenty years later, Sean still had bouts of thinking he was at war. They'd been at dinner, a romantic place in Mizner Park, and Grant's eyes had bored into their slice of key lime pie. He'd said the only time in his life he'd cried was the day his brother had come home. It wasn't his brother anymore. Just some prisoner of a faraway war. Grant had said it was an irrevocable day. She'd wanted to throw her arms around him then, but she couldn't in that fumbling beginning stage. Later when she could, she'd hugged him extra hard for his brother.

Joey feared Grant thought this too was an irrevocable day.

"Look," she said. "Look. I'm not going to lie to you. I loved Leo once. I did. When we left each other that last summer, it was hard. For a long time, I thought about no one but him. But fifteen years is a long time. I moved on. Especially with you, I did."

Grant lifted his face. His soft, brown eyes she called Baby Bear Eyes were shot with streaks of red. She'd discovered the Baby Bear Eyes soon into dating, when Grant told Joey that he didn't think he'd really loved another person since Sean came back from war. That he'd believed scary things happened to the people he loved. That it had taken Joey to show him it might be worth it to risk it.

"I don't know if you moved on," said Grant. "I wish I did, but I don't. It feels like I don't know a lot of things about you."

"You know everything about me. Everything! You know watermelon," she said, referring to their time in Bali when Grant had asked her simple questions to get to know her, and she hadn't been able to spit out the answers. Watermelon versus papaya, he'd posed, and she'd found herself at a loss. He'd helped her find herself. What they had was so good, and real. How could she make him see that the two of them were the realest thing she'd ever had?

"We don't have to let Leo affect us," Joey whispered.

"Is he still here?" When she didn't answer, Grant said, "He's still here. Of course. Because the two of you are sitting on a bomb of a secret that you have to figure out. And because he still loves you."

She didn't want to pursue that one again. "Nothing has to change with you and me," she whispered.

"You think Leo in town isn't going to change things? We're getting married in ten days, Joey."

The *we're getting married* soothed her a bit. "We'll table the whole secret, obviously. Deal with everything after we get married."

"If we get married," Grant said, just as there was a clatter by the foyer.

"If?" She felt the same stunned terror as the night Leo pulled her from Taverna Salto.

Grant went to the door and returned holding up two pieces of their mezuzah. "Looks like I did a shitty job nailing it." He didn't smile.

Another time Joey would have teased him about his subpar handyman skills. Anything he tried to fix eventually collapsed. Bookshelves fell. Toilet rolls clanged to tile.

"Doesn't bode so well for us." He sat back down on their couch and slapped the mezuzah fragments on the coffee table. One broke into more pieces.

"Lucky we got gifted a few others," she said with a weak smile.

He didn't respond.

"Grant…please don't say the *if we get married thing* again."

"I don't know." Grant stood. He pulled her up with him, his hands drifting languidly to her hips. Gratefully, Joey sank into his chest. "I'm so sorry about your mom," he whispered. "About Lily. I really am, Jo." His voice broke, and she pulled him tighter even as she felt him go. Sure enough, he set her back at arm's length. "I need to get my head straight. I'm gonna sleep at Evan's tonight."

"Don't leave! Please, Grant, don't. I won't ever see Leo again! He asked me to meet tomorrow, you know, to discuss when to tell Dad and Lily, but I'll tell him I can't!"

Grant just stepped his way through the maze of shower gifts without glancing back. "Well, this Lily thing has made that all moot, don't you think? You're gonna have to see Leo eventually. So go ahead. Meet him tomorrow. If we're so strong like you say we are, it shouldn't change anything, huh?"

When Joey was left alone in the dark, she knew he was right. She had wanted to see Leo before her wedding. Before she committed. Joey might be furious at Bea, but right now that paled in comparison with her fury at herself. She'd finally put Corfu behind her, only to let it come right back through her door.

In the morning, no call or text from Grant. Just a reminder from her mother of their *long-standing appointment* for lunch and *urgent* wedding decisions. Joey responded *I'll be there, but please don't think what I know now is in any sense of the word dropped.* With a hazy detachment, she surveyed her puffy eyes. They begged for concealer. She indulged them.

When she made it outside, there was Leo straddling a motorcycle, his face to the sun. The moment was almost intimate in its rapture. Leo returned his head upright and blinked a few times.

"Hey there, Jonesey."

"I should have known you'd be on a bike." She took the helmet he extended but hesitated. It felt too intimate, the two of them squished together on a bike. She should have just told Leo she'd meet him wherever they were going. But it seemed too late to back out now.

"Why go for aircon blasting in a box when you can get the real thing for free?" Leo started the motor. "Climb on."

Joey clicked the helmet straps shut and slipped on a pair of round see-through orange sunglasses that Grant joked made her look like she was eighty and a beetle.

"I need to be back by noon. Lunch at the parents'."

"That's fine."

"And I don't want to touch you." Joey didn't know that was going to come out. Her cheeks flamed.

Leo grimaced. "I suppose I deserve it, Jonesey. But that's a little impossible given what we're working with here."

"Yeah, fine." She climbed on behind him. "Groovy." She didn't think she'd used that word before, ever.

"Groovy," he repeated. "You can hold on to the bar in back."

"Is it as safe?"

"As what?" She didn't want to say *your waist*. "Hold on wherever you want, Jones. The world is your oyster."

"Is it?" she asked lightly.

But Leo had already started the motor. Joey gripped the bar behind her. Then, as they sped off, her cheek rested against the fuzz of Leo's shirt. So quickly, so lightly, that maybe it didn't happen at all.

chapter twenty-three
Joey

florida

2019

Leo parked the bike beside a row of yachts bobbing in the Fort Lauderdale harbor. The world rang in Joey's ears.

"Nice, yeah?" Leo collected her helmet and stored it alongside his own beneath the seat.

"Yeah." She wove her fingers through her hair, working out the tangles. "What are we doing here?"

Leo pointed and started walking. "We're here for that."

She trotted to catch up, following his finger point to an astoundingly large boat. "For a yacht?"

Leo stopped at the yacht, called *Arthur*. "Yep. It's mine now."

"You came to Florida and randomly bought a ginormous yacht?"

"Not randomly, exactly. I've been thinking about it for a while, and Fort Lauderdale's a good place to buy. You know how I am, Jones. I get an idea and—"

"Ten seconds later it's done." Joey smiled but was still in shock over the massive boat being his.

"I'm gonna gather up a crew to take it to the Bahamas for the winter." Leo leaped onto the platform and stretched out his arm.

"So coming to Florida is killing two birds with one stone?" Joey left his arm dangling and hopped up on her own.

Leo squinted as the sun took its aim. "I guess. Leave your shoes and come on up." She followed him around the Jet Skis docked in the back and then up a couple of stairs. Leo went to the captain's wheel.

Joey sank down to a couch, stretched out her legs, and pointed her toes. The couch was covered in the softest cream leather and flanked by a table. "Wow, Leo. You've made it, huh? What you always dreamed of."

"Oh, I don't know if I've made it, Jonesey. I have investors. It's not just me in this game."

"Funding aside, you're buying a huge, luxurious yacht. I think if you look up *making it* in the dictionary, this would be it."

"Actually, I already have one yacht. That one's in Europe with my crew. So this will be my second."

"Wow." She digested it. "I'm really proud of you, Leo." She meant it so thoroughly that she felt sad Leo couldn't experience the soar in her chest, like it was happening to her, the fruition of his long-held dreams. "I *really* am."

"Thanks." In a minute's span, Leo had pulled levers, twisted knobs, and checked the satnav. Now he crouched on the floor, unsnapping covers adhered to the boat's sides.

"Can I help?" she asked.

"Sure." He handed her a cover. "Fold this and stick it in the salon."

Joey took care folding it and carried it into the serene, well-appointed space he'd motioned to. The salon. She could imagine celebrities in it, tech moguls, nibbling on olives and drinking from fizzy flutes, talking and complaining about nothing.

The carpet was tan, fresh, and luxurious. In her lawyer life, she'd glided atop carpet like this. Thick carpet cleaned each night by a troop of underpaid fairies. Perhaps the part she'd detested most about her old life was the way her peers had ignored the help. The men and women tasked with grunt jobs would enter offices to empty trash, to deliver mail, and would exit as ghosts, as if garbage cans refreshed themselves, as if mail flew in on the backs of storks.

It had been the brightest part of Joey's day when she'd gotten to chitchat with the mail guy Salvador—about his mother, Jasmine, who was going through chemo, about the controversial new sculpture installed in the elevator bank. Then Salvador would reach for the door. *Okay, Josephine,* he always said to signal his exit, sheepish in his keeping her from her Very Important Work. He pronounced the first part of her name *Joss* and enunciated each syllable so fully it was like even her name itself was a thing he cared for. She was always sad as he slipped out the door, the click behind him practiced in its softness. She hadn't thought about Salvador all this time, and somehow his memory made her feel sad.

All this had filtered through the sieve of Joey's mind by the time the Florida sun again kissed her shoulders. Sometimes she wondered about it—how big were the things that jangled around in her head. Not just big as in numerous, but big as in important. Salvador was important, and she didn't think she'd ever told a soul about him.

"You know, I once had a friend named Salvador," she said to Leo, without realizing he was talking to someone on land. "Oh, sorry."

Leo turned to her with a look of distracted curiosity. He unscrewed a handle of vodka and poured some into the two red Solo cups that had materialized. "That's Lucas. He's responsible for the upkeep of this beaut until I officially take over."

From down below, Lucas lifted a hand from the hose he was spraying on the pavement and waved.

"So how about it, Jonesey?"

"How about what?" She eased herself into the chair across from the captain's seat.

"A little spin? I'll have you back for your lunch."

"Oh. Well, okay. Might as well have some fun on the side of our not-fun."

Leo handed her a Solo cup, then he pulled a lever, and the boat rumbled to life. "Exactly."

As Leo maneuvered them out of the harbor, baby waves lapped at the side of the boat and then crashed in pools of white froth.

"So Jonesey?" said Leo as they sped toward open water.

"Yeah?"

"How about you tell me about your friend Salvador?"

They anchored far out, the waves knocking periodic love taps against the yacht, having opted for a level of intensity to complement Bob Marley crooning aboard.

"I love that you already have a plant on the boat," said Joey, touching the glossy leaves sprouting from the gray concrete pottery on the floor. "It's so you."

Leo was applying sunscreen to his chest in lazy swipes, employing no obvious method at achieving full coverage.

"It's the first thing I did to christen it. Buy a ficus. Plant and sea. All you need in the world. Blue and green are the best colors."

"Is that a fact?"

"Of course." Leo turned up the volume on Bob.

For a while, they just cruised to the soothing reggae. "So can I ask you something?" Joey finally said.

"You can ask me a lot of things, Jones. It's time for talking."

"We're talking," she said, irritated he was framing it otherwise. "We covered Salvador. We covered my family. You told me about yours. Shall we recap? Your parents: divorced. Maisy quit drinking ten years ago and remarried. New husband is our age and a personal-trainer-slash-green-juice entrepreneur. Rand is still trading. Basically living off the grid. But with WiFi. Also now a sheep farmer."

Leo laughed a small laugh, his lips barely parted. "That about sums it up. Did my dad win Biggest Departure from the Old Days on Corfu?"

"No doubt. Rand turning into a reclusive shepherd, not what I would have voted him up for in any yearbook awards."

"You know my dad though. Prickly around people."

"Prickly indeed."

"Better with sheep," said Leo, and they both laughed. "Hey, how's your grandmother?"

"You remember G?" Joey laughed, but she didn't feel the laugh spread to her whole face like the prior one had. "She hated you, sorry to say it. *The not-Jewish boy.*"

"Some things are immutable, I guess." Leo smiled. "But I remember when we went to that reunion of the Corfiot survivors at the synagogue."

"Wow. I haven't thought of that in ages."

"I thought about it a lot, actually, after. I always wondered if you found out how your grandmother escaped the Holocaust."

Was it possible Joey still didn't know? "I'm ashamed to say this, but honestly, I still haven't broached it with her. It's always felt painful to me, my grandparents' stories. But that's not an excuse, is it? I have to ask her."

"You should. Before it's too..."

"I know. I will." Joey winced, before making a mental note to do exactly that. Then she steeled herself and said, "Hey, Leo, who's Arthur?"

"He's my son," said Leo, just as a fish soared from the water. "Hey, a marlin!"

Joey twisted to watch, but she caught only the piddly splash as the fish plunged back into the depths. The water churned with its piercing and then stilled. "Your son?" she said softly.

"I guess that didn't show up in any Google searches."

"I guess it didn't."

Joey absorbed it, this son of Leo, named Arthur. She pictured a sweet, bucktoothed kid with thick black glasses posing on the edge of a chair for some school picture. What could have been swooshed through her, like a gust through the slats of an abandoned house. "Wow, Leo."

"He's such a cool kid, Jones." Leo smiled a smile she knew well—his lips pressed together, the light oozing out his eyes. "He's seven. I met his mom when we worked a Med season together. I was the first officer then, and she was a stew. Janna's her name."

Janna. Joey cycled that name through her stuffed file of inconsequential factoids accumulated from Facebook-stalking

Leo's profile came up dry. She felt stupid, and a little sad, at how far off Leo's reality was from the fiction she'd spun, of his cavorting with the supermodel, graduates-of-Ivies girls on his friends list.

"Anyway, it didn't work out, but we got Arthur, and he's amazing, the most inquisitive kid. He won't stop asking questions."

"Sounds like someone I know."

"Yeah. Takes after his Old Man. Sometimes you want to be like, *Arthur, buddy, give me a breather*, but he has to know things. Everything. Why sometimes people cry and say they're okay when they're not really okay. How a weed is different from a plant." Leo shook his head. "God, I love that kid."

"So when you're in season, he's with—"

"His mom. Yeah. We both rent apartments on the same street in Monaco. When I'm gone, I FaceTime with Arthur of course, but the distance is hard on us both. It's funny, Arthur's into ballet these days—"

"Ballet? That's awesome."

"He's obsessed. He's teaching me how to plié." Leo stood and did a bouncy thing with his toes turned out.

Joey giggled. "Do that again, please."

"Sorry, Jones, that ends the entertainment portion of this boat ride."

"Given the evidence, I think Arthur needs to up his teaching game."

"Yeah." Leo looked out distantly to sea. "Well, he's not here to teach me. He had a recital recently, and he was so bummed I wasn't there. Janna had me on FaceTime, but the connection kept cutting out, and I missed his big solo. Later he was like, *Did you see me, Dad?*, and I pretended I had, but I wasn't describing his big leap or whatever, or how elongated he had his arm, and he knew. He *knew*. And you know what, Jones? I felt just like my father."

"Come on, Leo, you're nothing like Rand. I may not have seen you in fifteen years, or with Arthur, but if you ask me what I know for sure, it's that you're a good dad."

"I don't know, Jones. I really don't. What if that's just what I tell myself to be able to live with myself? Because the truth is, I'm not around a lot. I'm out here."

"You're working to provide for Arthur. And you're there when it counts."

"Maybe. I like to think being out at sea makes me a better dad. You know how I am…"

"You need it." She gestured around. "You talk to them."

"The waves?" He sounded surprised that she knew.

"I know you. Or I used to."

"Yeah. You did. So…what about you, Jones?"

"Me? No playmates for Arthur over here."

"But you're getting married." Leo's back was to her as he said it, cranking up the anchor. "And about that. Jonesey, I don't want you to worry. I'm not here to ruin your wedding."

Over the roar of the anchor ratcheting up, she said, "Well, that's good to hear."

"I just mean, we can deal with the fallout after. I want you to have your day. I so want you to be happy, Jones."

Joey exhaled a breath she hadn't realized she'd been holding since she saw Leo on the pier. "You can stick around until after?"

"Yeah. They're still fixing up the boat, and anyway I'm getting *real* good at shuffleboard."

"Now, that's a skill that will come in handy. You're welcome."

Leo grinned. "But Jonesey, after the wedding, we need to tell Scott and Lily. You agree, don't you?"

Joey nodded slowly. "It's the last thing I want, to break their hearts like that, but I can't un-know what you told me. My dad deserves the truth. And so does Lily."

Leo visibly exhaled. "I'm so glad you feel that way too. I can't live like this anymore. Hiding it."

Joey kneaded her knuckles into her thighs. "So we'll do it after the wedding. There are a few days before we go to Bali for our honeymoon."

"How do you think Lily's going to react?"

"No idea." Joey grimaced. "Probably awfully. Hey, Leo." Something had occurred to her, but she felt guilty saying it. "What if you go to the market or something? Like—"

"What if Scott sees me? I'll just tell him I'm in town to buy a boat. That should do it, don't you think?" The motor sounded, and the boat spurted to life. Leo's hands finessed the wheel, one over another, like art in their fluency in the language of the sea. "Tell me things, Jonesey."

"I've told you lots of things." She snuck a glance at her phone. Still nothing from Grant. Just a confirmation from Edith's assistant regarding their meeting later that afternoon. Oh God, Joey wanted the commission. She deeply did. But since Lily's call, Joey had hardly achieved a single preparatory sketch. She couldn't conceive of how she was going to pull off some massive piece in the lead-up to her wedding.

"Tell me some real things, Jonesey." Leo mixed her another vodka lemonade.

"You're trying to get me drunk so I'll spill dirt." Joey wiped her sunglasses on her shirt. She wished the lenses weren't see-through so her eyes weren't so on display. "What do you want to know?"

"How did you and Grant meet?"

"Oh. Okay." It was bizarre to tell this story to Leo, like two worlds meant to orbit apart now colliding. "We met in—"

"Bali. That part I know."

"How?"

"The Delray Jewish News."

"Stalker." They both laughed. A speedboat flew by on Joey's side. An older couple waved; the wife raised her beer. Joey knew how she and Leo must appear—lovebirds. Rich lovebirds.

In another world maybe. Another life.

"So we met in Bali after I left law because—"

"Tell me how you met, Jonesey. The real story. You know?"

She knew what he meant. "Well, I was..." She had to stop because telling this part of the story brought her back. It felt dangerous, this slice of her life, like it had been tended to and bandaged so beautifully after leaving law but then since Leo's return the bandages had begun to fray. "Leo, I was totally fucking lost. I surfed into Grant—you know that part from our engagement notice, I guess. I told him I'd buy him a smoothie bowl to make up for it. So we were at this café in the rice paddies. I was telling him about my law days and how I was going to start painting again, but I didn't know where I wanted to live, or what I wanted to do, or really who I was."

Joey smiled at the memory of it, the two of them on stools by the window with its shutters perpetually swung open. The sun had sopped up all their wet, leaving two sandy, very tan Americans, stray dogs at their feet, with reams of shirtless Australian men roaring up on motorbikes.

"Grant said, *Well, if you don't know who you are, let's figure it out.*" This was the part that demanded a reaction — a chorus of *so cute* echoed from friends of her mother to women in supermarket lines alike. Leo just looked ahead, riveted to the sea as if he hadn't seen tidaling blue in this iteration a billion times before.

"So Grant said, *Papaya or watermelon?*"

"Papaya or watermelon?" repeated Leo.

"Yeah, like which is your favorite? And I couldn't figure it out, Leo. That's how long it had been since I thought about what I liked. And so Grant shouted through the place, *Waitress, can we have two of your finest pieces of papaya and watermelon?* It was over the top, but that's him. Or it was. Bali Grant was really...free. So anyhow, she brought over two plates. One had watermelon. One papaya. And I ate fruit upon fruit, and you know what? I liked the watermelon more." Leo's eyes didn't stray from the sea. "Now's your cue to smile, Winn."

"So you figured out you're a person who likes watermelon more?"

"Yeah." Joey's cheeks warmed, and it wasn't the sun. "Why are you knocking my love story?"

"Not knocking anything."

"Grant brings me watermelon-flavored stuff a lot, actually. It's sweet. Watermelon Jolly Ranchers. Watermelon gelato. And he asked me bigger stuff too, by the way."

"Like?"

"Like beach or mountains?" She heard the bitterness suffusing her tone.

"Beach," said Leo. "A thousand times, beach."

"It was actually a tough decision," she shot back. "In

my law days, I used to go on hiking vacations too. I did Kilimanjaro, did you know that? And part of the Camino de Santiago."

"I didn't."

"Yeah." The fight deflated from her. "But I did choose beach." She hated giving Leo that satisfaction. Like she was so simple to deduce. Joey tried to remember Grant's other questions. At the time it had seemed magical, the way he'd revealed her to herself. This was the first time it felt a little bit stupid.

"City or country?" she eventually said.

"Country. I can't believe you lived in Manhattan, Jones. Someone's gotta fire your college career counselor."

The anger reared in Joey. "Guy on top or girl on top?"

Leo crunched his face. It didn't feel nice, having said it. "That one I'll leave to Grant," he finally said, and she didn't reply.

For a while, the sea was the only one doing the talking. Joey downed her drink. At last the fuzzy outline of land filled the horizon.

Leo finally said, "And how's it going with the wedding?"

"Great!" she said, forgetting for a moment where she was, and with whom. The stock answer accustomed to being trotted out echoed against the hull, swept back out to sea. Echoed. Echoed.

"I haven't been able to sleep the past few nights," she finally admitted. *Don't ask me why. Don't ask me if I want to get married because the answer is I do. If ever in my life I am meant to become a wife, it's now, to this man, and I don't want to betray Grant by discussing it with you.*

Leo said, "Oh." Casually. Like she'd explained how she operated her dishwasher. "What does it feel like?"

"What does it feel like? It's a dream I've been having, and it feels like I'm the only person in the world." Leo nodded, and then she realized he was motioning his head to the wave hurtling at them. A curl of ocean slapped Joey's face.

The boat hopped a few times like a bunny rabbit and then sailed forward on level sea. Leo said, "You have this dream."

Joey scraped sea-drenched hair from her face. "Just a few times. It's a weird dream."

"I can do weird."

"It's just, I've been dreaming about two deserts. They're both massive, like the Sahara. That red-orange color and just, sand in every direction. And in between the deserts is a canyon. Sorta like the Grand Canyon, in size."

"Two deserts, split by the Grand Canyon. Doesn't sound so weird."

Joey had been there just the other morning, before the sun had fuzzed through their blinds, the desert filling the empty spaces between her glances at the clock and at Grant. One moment, she'd been marveling at Grant's capacity to sleep for seven hours under the microscope of the world without so much as a leg budging from its heavy diagonal drape—and then she'd flown back to the deserts again.

But last night there'd been nothing. No deserts. No Grant.

"So the thing is, there are also two of me in the dream. One of me is in one of the deserts, and the other me is in the other."

"Is there anyone else in this world?"

Joey shook her head. "No one. And the first me has fallen, and she's dangling on the edge of her desert, over this huge abyss. The other me is on the edge of her desert watching the first me about to basically die. And the other me has superhuman hands or something. She's reaching out her long hand to help the first me. And the first me is trying so hard to reach the second me's arm without plunging to her death. But she can't, and she's slipping. She's slipping off her desert."

Leo slowed the boat; the abrupt deceleration startled Joey. Leo maneuvered toward the boat's slip. To safe land, but also to what existed upon it. "And then what?"

"What do you mean?"

"What happens, when the other you tries to save the first you?"

"Nothing happens." She managed a weak smile. "It's just me trying to save me. So far there's never anything more."

Leo killed the motor. They both waved to Lucas on the land.

"Sorry, I feel a little crazy here," said Joey, shaking her head, wishing she could shake the deserts right out of her. "I haven't told anyone about the two deserts, or the two me's."

"You're not crazy, Jonesey. The two deserts, the two yous…"

"Yeah?" She needed Leo to explain it to her. This was, after all, why she'd told him. Because Leo was good at making okay the things that lived in her head.

"I know how it ends."

"Oh?" She followed Leo off the yacht. He extended his arm to help her down. "There's symbolism here some-where," she laughed, and gripped his hand.

"Both yous are safe. That's how it ends. Next time you're awake in the dark, just tell the first you to reach longer. Harder. The second you's gonna save her. And then wake up Grant. He'll distract you. Or else he'll just bring you watermel—" Leo sprouted a boyish grin that tempered Joey's irritation at his words, transporting her back to the little boy who was once her best friend, who adventured with her each summer.

As Leo went over to talk to Lucas, Joey wedged her feet back into her sandals, thinking his watermelon dig was unfair. Grant was so much more than a guy who could be reduced to some sort of watermelon bellboy.

She checked her phone, and there it was. A staid text by Grant standards, but he would be home later. That he'd called it home was a good sign.

Joey went to the bike. Her mind swished with the day. She thought about the boy named Arthur and imagined deserts. She thought about Grant coming home, and what he would say.

But mostly she thought about what her answer would be if Grant were to ask her: Who would you choose, Joey? The first you or the other you?

chapter twenty-four
Joey

florida

2019

Bea greeted Joey in the foyer. "Guess what? The cake toppers just arrived."

Joey let her fringed purse slide to her parents' bleached
Persian rug. "Is that really how you're gonna greet me,
Mom?" she asked in a low voice. "By pretending like noth-
ing has happened?"

Her mother sighed. "I'm not pretending, Joey. I just don't
know what to say. I've called you so many times, and you
haven't called me back. I'm sorry for everything. I cried all
day after you left."

"You cried all day. Okay. And now I'm just supposed to
get over it?"

"I'll do anything to make it better. Just tell me what I
can do."

"I guess there's really nothing you can do." Joey sighed.
"Is Dad home? I saw his car."

Her mother motioned her head nervously toward the
kitchen. "Yeah. He's in there."

Joey nodded. She took a deep breath. "So I didn't know you ordered cake toppers."

"I did." Her mother smiled, visibly relieved they could talk normally again. She rummaged through a box on the floor. Styrofoam packing peanuts erupted like confetti.

As if the packing peanuts were capable of generating noise, Joey's father yelled from the kitchen, "Bea, neatly, please!"

"He has a video camera on me, I swear." Bea's feet crunched on the peanuts. "Ah! Here we go." She unveiled two items. She ripped off their bubble wrap covers and tossed them down to join the party of green peanuts. "Oh, they came out so good!"

Joey peered over her mother's shoulder. The Grant topper had a man bun with his tux, and the Joey topper had brunette waves, a party of multiple tiny earrings, and her bell-sleeved, boho dress.

"You're always talking about Grant's man bun." Bea handed them to her.

"They're great." Joey set the toppers on the white marble console. "Thanks for them," she managed to add.

At the sound of Lily traipsing downstairs, Joey untied her cork wedges. Her sister now descended on the right side of the Tara-replicated double staircase that Joey considered to have been a ridiculous renovation. Lily pointed her foot dramatically like the ballerina she was not as she leaped from the bottom step. She wore a white button-down shirt that looked like she'd borrowed it from their father, but she'd buttoned it crookedly and one side draped off a shoulder. The shirt was front-tucked into tattered jean cutoffs and comple-mented by Lily's hair slicked back in one of those pop-star ponytails, with harsh slashes of bronze on her eyelids.

"Hey, Lil."

"Hey, Jo." The sisters embraced quickly.

"You're not wearing that to meet Edith, are you?" Lily asked.

"Umm…yes. I am." Joey glanced down at her moody purple floral boho dress that she'd bought in her law days, even though it hadn't meshed one iota with her then-polished, fancy life. She'd known she'd wear it someday; every time she'd seen it in her closet it had been some soothing glimpse of a future self she could still become. Now it was a mainstay in her wardrobe. Her power dress.

"Yes, JoJo, let Lily help style you," said Bea.

"I think Rei Kawakubo sent me something too big," said Lily.

Joey had no clue who that was and wasn't about to ask. "No thanks. I'm quite capable of picking my own outfits. This dress is MISA, by the way. You're not the only Abrams who appreciates fashion. I'm an artist, remember?" Joey felt herself growing more affronted than Lily's comment really warranted.

"Are you joining us for lunch, Lil?" asked Bea.

"I can't." Lily heaved a sigh worthy of a president on the brink of initiating nuclear war. "We need to put the inaugural issue to bed, and I haven't finalized the piece about genital mutilation in China. It's a nightmare, with all their internet blockades."

"Wow, so the magazine's happening?" Joey recalled vague conversations about a feminist fashion magazine for teens that Lily was launching.

"It's definitely happening," said Bea. "It's the next *Vogue*. Not even. It's the *Vogue* that *Vogue* wishes it could be."

"That makes no sense." Joey winced at the spite in her words. "But that's awesome, Lil."

"It is," said Bea. "Victoria's the guest editor too."

"Victoria?" Joey shook her head. Bea made a motion like she was swinging a tennis racket.

"What are you doing, Mom?" asked Lily.

"Her husband!" exclaimed their mother, frowning.

"David Beckham?" asked Joey, piecing together Victoria Beckham. "He's a soccer player."

"Oh." Bea kicked an imaginary soccer ball. "Whatever."

"You were identifying Victoria by reference to her famous husband, Mom?" said Lily. "Not cool. I'd argue that what she's achieved with her fashion line is far more monumental than—"

"Out-feministed, Mom," said Joey, surprised as a real laugh squeezed out of her. "I never thought the day would happen."

Bea smiled and tried to wrap Lily into her arms, but Lily squirmed away. She'd once been asked in an interview, *What is your worst nightmare?*, and she'd replied, *Group hugs.*

"The student is now the teacher," said Bea.

Lily nodded. "Anyway, yeah, Joey. Victoria Beckham."

"Right. Wow, Lil. The whole thing sounds really ambitious. I'm proud of you." Joey grabbed a piece of bubble wrap that was asking for it and crumpled it up in her hand. The pops felt like a little outlet for so many things that Joey couldn't name.

"Yeah." Her sister shrugged. "I'm sort of aging out of the teen demographic now, but I've still got my pulse on things."

"And this is your outfit for writing?"

"I need to feel myself to generate inspired content. What do you wear to paint?"

"Old jeans usually and…I guess something similar to your top, actually. One of Grant's white button-downs. I like to feel like a blank palette."

"For Godsakes, Joey," said Bea. "At least put a bra on. What will Grant think?"

"On that note, I disagree, Ma." Lily smirked. "The no-bra look is all the rage these days. Nipples are decidedly in."

"Really?" said Bea, running her fingers along her chest. "That's very interesting."

"Great, look what you've done, Lil," Joey said, and the sisters both laughed.

"So what are your thoughts on seating Evie Nicholas by Mr. Sanders?" asked Bea, sitting cross-legged in the breakfast nook. "Because they might actually hit it off, and it's a mitzvah to matchmake if we have the chance, don't you—"

"Who is Mr. Sanders?" interrupted Joey.

Bea pushed aside a plate with cold salmon to make room for her chart. "You don't remember Mr. Sanders? At Kilwins? Who always gave you an extra piece of turtle fudge? And then pulled quarters from behind your ears?"

Ah, Joey did remember, vaguely. The man who pulled quarters from behind her ears but then didn't let her keep them. She'd never understood why that was supposed to be a fun trick. "Okay, but why was he invited to my wedding?"

"We couldn't not invite Mr. Sanders! He's eighty-three and still on his feet every day at Kilwins, scooping the most perfect scoop of rocky road you've ever seen."

"If on his feet with the ability to scoop rocky road was the criterion to get a wedding invite, then we have an issue here. Anyway, we went over the list multiple times, and Mr. Sanders wasn't on it."

Her mother had the grace to blush. "He was a last-minute addition."

"Seriously? Mom, I've told you so many times, I don't want a big wedding."

Joey's dad glanced up from a pile of mail. He'd come home from work especially for "lunch with his girls" and was wearing his yellow-checked button-down that Joey privately thought lent his skin a touch of jaundice. Her father now used his brass letter opener to carefully swipe open a hot-pink envelope that looked very clearly to Joey to be junk.

"Dad, why are you opening that? Just toss it."

"You never know what's important. And sweetheart, your mom just has a soft spot for Abe. I do too, really. He has a heart of gold." Her father unleashed a paper and with excruciating care unfolded it, studied it, and turned it to Joey. "Twenty percent off slippers. Do you need slippers?"

"I don't need slippers!" Joey started at her father's pained expression, but she couldn't help but be on edge. This lunch seemed absolutely farcical—planning a wedding with her mother and her up-in-the-air groom to boot.

"Joey, we already invited Mr. Sanders," Bea said. "We can't rescind his invitation. Anyway, you gave me full creative control—"

"I don't remember that."

"I do. You said something like, *I don't care who you invite, just please stop calling me about anything wedding-related.* Does that ring a bell?"

Unfortunately, it did. That was likely on her mother's thirtieth phone call about the guest list. For not the first time, Joey wondered why she and Grant hadn't eloped, why she'd consented to this supposedly small wedding that now included the old ice cream scooper/magician of her childhood?

She knew why. Grant wanted a real wedding. He'd said, *When you find something good, you max out the celebrations.*

"Okay." Joey exhaled deeply.

"This is a lot of work for me, Joey. You could show a little appreciation."

Joey gave her mother an incredulous stare.

Her mother smiled weakly. "I'm happy to do it! Overjoyed to plan your wedding, JoJo. But it's a lot. Like, just the other night, I was giving a one-off talk on the commercial exchange of sexuality in modern art as viewed through the lens of *Olympia* and *A Bar at the Folies-Bergère* by Manet, fascinating stuff. And instead of really getting into the moment with the barmaid's expression, instead of taking this…this…*journey* with my students…do you know what I was thinking? Whether we should have gone with the lighter tablecloths."

"Huh?"

"Don't you remember? We went with black to keep with your antique, tropics-at-night vision, but I was thinking we should have gone charcoal. Yes, I'm going to swap to charcoal if they won't penalize us. It will better contrast with the deep-green vases."

"We went with deep-green vases?"

"Joey," boomed Scott, rising. "Can I talk to you a moment?"

"Sure, Dad." Joey stood in a restrained fashion so as not to underscore her gratitude at escaping. She trailed her father down the hall that led to his study. It was the hall with the light always on the fritz, that displayed old pictures of the girls. Joey was on the right side, Lily the left.

From a cross-hallway comparison, you could discern two things. First, that photography had really advanced in the new millennium. Joey's pictures were uniformly characterized by a white fade-out at the edges, like a smoke machine on its last fumes. Lily's were crisp and ethereal, like she was living in a fairyland.

The second thing you could tell was that Lily had confidence. Gravitas. Moxie. Lily age five—you would listen when she commanded you to bring her apple juice. Lily age eight—you might follow her to the moon. Joey just looked kind and sincere, like a girl with the simplest internal life. Like a girl you could read through her eyes and bouncy pigtails. She liked glitter and dancing and sunflowers.

In actuality, Joey had liked rummaging in the dirt for earthworms far more than glitter and dancing. And now she hated sunflowers. She looked into little Joey's eyes, age eight—clad in a frilly white dress Bea had cajoled her to don, clasping a bunch of daisies and smiling. Joey was relieved when the hallway dead-ended at her father's study.

She sat on the beige leather chair across from her father. How many times had she flopped down here in various states of excitement and unrest? In high school, to show off her latest artwork. Later, to exchange stories from the trenches of their mutual estate planning career. The man with the trust providing a life of luxury for his dog. The lady with the trust to dispose of her hundred-thousand-dollar handbag collection.

A Post-it hung on the windowpane. Joey squinted to see that, written in her dad's neat script, it read, *The only thing today requires of you is a smile.*

"Who's that quote by?" she asked.

"Oh." He pressed a thumb along the Post-it's top sticky part.

"One of yours?" She knew he alternated sources for his motivational Post-its. His idol Thomas Jefferson. Thomas Edison. Sometimes Scott Abrams.

Her father blushed. He opened a drawer, pulled out the pocket brush from which he was never far, and brushed his sandy-blond hair into its signature side sweep.

"Scott Abrams has some genius sayings." Joey caught a whiff of the Thomas Jefferson cologne they'd gotten him for his birthday. Past gifts had established that her father went gaga over anything bearing his idol's name, but the lesson had since been learned—Joey should have smelled the cologne before gifting it. The scent was what she imagined was the smell of old English people returning to their musty castles after skeet shooting in the moors.

Her father fiddled with his wedding ring. Joey bit her lip, trying to push what she knew from her mind. He was going to be devastated—*wrecked*—and there was nothing Joey could do to prevent it.

"Yes, well, Joey."

"Moving on?"

"Moving on. I want to say something to you. You know, your mother didn't get to have her dream wedding, not really."

"What do you mean? I've seen the pictures. You had a beautiful wedding."

"Well, I don't want to spoil any romantic notions you

have, but I think you're old enough to know. You see…"
Her father's face turned the color of the red Montblanc pen
he was twirling in his fingers.

"Mom was pregnant at the wedding."

Her father's mouth gaped open. "How did you know?"

"Dad, if you count the months till I was born, you don't
have to be a rocket scientist to figure it out."

It took a few moments for her father to regain compo-
sure. "Okay. We were a modern couple. It's not why we got
married, for the record. I loved your mother very much. I
still do, of course. I would have married her anytime, anywhere, regardless of you on the way or not. But her parents
were old-fashioned. We had to get married quickly, before
they suspected. So it was a wedding on the rush. Your
mother always wanted us to do this dance to a flamenco
band at our wedding. They played at a dive bar we used
to go to. But they were going to Mexico that weekend to
play at a quinceañera so we had a troupe of Motown singers
instead. Do you understand?"

Joey nodded slowly.

"Good. You're a wonderful daughter."

Joey managed a faint smile.

"So you see how important it is to your mother to plan
your wedding? It's making her so happy."

Joey wanted to say many things to her father now, to
make this a conversation that was genuine on both ends, and
yet she couldn't.

"One more thing," said her father. "You know, I had
drinks with Grant the other night, and I want you to know
how lucky you are." Her father's eyes blinked, portending
tears. "Grant loves you so much. Do you know how I know
it, Joey? Not just how he talks about you."

"How?" Joey whispered.

"The way he watches you." Now her father wept freely. "It's how I'm okay giving away my little girl."

"Dad, I'm thirty-four."

"It's how I'm okay giving away my little girl," he said again, louder. "Thirty-four is young like you can't imagine, Joey. And even when the two of you are in the middle of people and phones and chaos, Grant watches you. He always knows where you are in relation to him."

Joey knew this to be true. She wanted Grant to watch her again, and she didn't know if she'd ruined it.

"Do you always know where Mom is in relation to you?" she asked.

Her father's tears petered out. "Yes," he said. "Yes, I always do."

chapter twenty-five

Joey

florida

2019

In the foyer, a massive blank wall ascended fifteen feet. The floor was glossy navy wood. Windows opened onto an infinity pool perched at the edge of the Intracoastal. Scattering the lawn were sufficient white sunbathing chairs to accommodate the Palm Beach elite and dangling rope swing chairs to accommodate their leggy teenage offspring. Inside, above a midcentury cabinet that cradled a giant topiary, hung an installation of textured white.

The butler in tails who'd greeted her at the door followed discreetly behind Joey as she went to inspect the art. Her armpits pooled Florida's steam onto her dress.

A voice said, "It's made from coffee cup lids."

Joey turned to greet a very small, really miniature, woman with a teased gray beehive. The beloved Edith Lallouche. She wore her trademark giant, round navy glasses with black skinny jeans, a printed blue-and-white tunic, suede smoking slippers, and a bag made of bright-blue feathers. The purse triggered a color association Joey couldn't place.

Four necklaces weighed down Edith's neck, each strung with beads the size of golf balls. It seemed to Joey a feat of aerodynamics that Edith remained upright. Last, Joey spied the cane in Edith's hand, but her corresponding arm was so consumed by blue-patterned bangles that the cane assumed the energy of an average person's socks. That is, you hardly noticed it.

"Coffee lids, really?" Sure enough, Joey discerned the lids. "That's amazing."

"I like unusual art." Edith patted her purse. Joey had never seen a person wear a purse around her home. This devotion to style impressed her. No wonder Edith and Lily got along.

Ah! It occurred to Joey now. The color of the purse was that of Cookie Monster's fur.

As she crossed the foyer, Joey gave herself a pep talk. *You are a talented and worthy artist, you do really interesting evil eyes, and you've even gotten some great press—a year and a half ago, you were written up in that magazine in Bali!*

Against her will, her pep talk veered. *That magazine in Bali was basically a leaflet distributed in untouched stacks in juice shops.*

Joey shook Edith's bony hand. "Joey Abrams. It's a pleasure, Mrs. Lallouche."

"Call me Edith." She fingered the flutter sleeve on Joey's dress. "MISA, yes? It suits you."

Joey nodded. "Thank you. Your home is beautiful."

"I don't believe in false modesty, Joey. That is the first thing you will learn of me. My new home *is* beautiful. So thank you."

Joey moved closer to the blank wall. "Is this the wall Lily told me about? Or is it another one?"

"This is the one."

"Wow. It's very prominent."

"Joey, I don't beat around the bush. I have just one question for you."

"Just one?" Joey crossed her arms, which felt immediately off, but she didn't want to uncross them for fear of seeming unsure of herself. "Sure."

"Do you believe in your art, Joey?"

"Do I believe in…? You're asking if—"

"I'm asking, do you believe in your art? It's another way of saying, do you believe in yourself? Because I've seen your work. Your sister showed me a snapshot of that canvas with all the abstract evil eyes, different irises, some scary, others sweet. I felt you captured something there. Yes, I go by my instincts in life, Joey, and I have an instinct about you. You are not well known. You are not known whatsoever, is the fact. That doesn't matter one iota to me. Fame equates to complacency, I tend to think. But I don't do wishy-washy. I don't do, *Am I good? Am I worthy of this project?* I do confidence. I do conviction."

Joey allowed her arms to drop to her sides. "You know, Edith, if you'd asked me this question two years ago, when I was still a lawyer, I think I would have given you a glossy answer. I would have said, *Of course I believe in myself. I'm fabulous, Edith.*"

"And I would have seen through it," said Edith, not insensitively.

Joey nodded. "What I can tell you is I think every person is born with a special way of expressing herself, and this is my way. I snuffed it out for a very long time. And you know what, Edith? Now I'll bet all my money on me. I'm not yet a success in the art world, and I may never be. But

I'll never stop drawing and I'll never stop painting. And so, do I believe in myself, Edith? Well, excuse my language, but I really fucking believe in myself. I really do." Joey spoke so fast at the end that her mouth kept moving with nothing left to come out.

Edith snapped her fingers. "I like you. Done."

"Done?"

"You have the job. Ten thousand dollars now. Ten thousand when it's done." Edith reached into her purse and unveiled a stack of crisp hundreds. "I trust cash is acceptable?"

Joey nodded as coolly as she could manage. "Yes."

Edith placed the stack in Joey's hands. Joey hadn't received a paycheck in a year and a half. Her legal savings were nearly fully depleted. Lately, she'd been selling bags and shoes on The RealReal to maintain her equal contribution toward rent and expenses. Not that Grant demanded it. He said his money was hers. But she didn't want to rely on him. Joey gripped the bills, not ready to part with them for placement in her purse. Not even her astronomic legal salary had yielded this measure of gratification.

"I need it by next Thursday, dear. For the event I trust Lily filled you in on. You have complete reign. Robert there"—Edith indicated the butler—"will let you in day or night. I'll try to leave you to it, not to interfere. But as the wall lives by my front door, and I do have a thriving social calendar, we may bump into each other from time to time." Edith began to walk off, necklaces clicking like castanets with each languid step.

"Wait!" Joey called out. "But you haven't told me what you want. I mean—what you want me to paint."

Edith turned at the mouth of a hall with walls covered in round, evenly spaced 3-D spheres in pinks, oranges, and yellows. The effect was of life-size versions of old-fashioned candy dots, the kind that tasted partially of sugar and partially of the paper they adhered to.

"I thought I was clear. You believe in you, and thus I believe in you. So put on that wall whatever you like."

"Seriously? You don't want to give me any other direction? Color? Scale? Portrait? Abstract? Landscape?"

"No. It doesn't even have to be evil eyes." Edith shuffled off. "Just create, my dear. It's only a wall. It's only paint."

chapter twenty-six

Joey

florida

2019

The apartment hummed with the sound of appliances in resting states. Joey went to the kitchen, and a tangle of dirty towels nearly sent her sprawling. She righted herself and remembered that the fridge guy had come to fix the leak. She flung open the freezer and rummaged for the cookie dough she'd buried beneath a bag of frozen corn.

Hello old friend, she whispered, and she was back where she'd been so many times, right there on the edge. Lost, and then found, at the end of a cookie dough tube.

Joey placed the tube on the counter, her heart racing, transported back to when she'd returned from that Leo-less trip to Nice. When she'd flown to her client's important family office meeting in Baltimore and collapsed in their all-glass-and-chrome lobby. *Panic attack*, the medic had said, strapping an oxygen mask to Joey's face.

"It's okay not to be okay," Joey's therapist had told her a few days later, at their first session.

Joey had asked, "How?" Because G needed her to be

okay, and her parents needed her to be okay, and her firm needed her to be okay.

You just sit in the not-okay-ness and you try to be nice to yourself.

Joey had never thought of herself as a person to whom she owed it to be nice. What her therapist said had felt bold. Soft. True. Sometimes Joey wondered if things would have been different if she'd started with her therapist after Corfu instead of a decade later.

Her therapist had given her steps to take when she felt a binge coming on and also prescribed anti-anxiety meds. *You don't have to suffer, but meds aren't a cure-all.* She'd given Joey homework to do: write a list of her triggers, a list of nice things she could do for herself while allowing a stream of not-okay-ness.

It wasn't that lighting a candle or taking a bath had solved all her problems, but Joey had begun to meet a stronger, happier self in the nooks and crannies of a life gradually unstuffed. Still, her not-okay-ness returned from time to time. Joey hadn't had a true binge in years, but it would be easy to slide back down the hole.

Joey eyed the cookie dough. She felt very much not okay.

She unwrapped the yellow cover. Slowly. Then she tore at the dough. She ate and ate and ate. Her stomach throbbed, and she sank to the tile marred by dirty work boot prints and ate more. At first, she tasted all the nuances. Sweet. Salt. And then there was no taste, just more dough, and more.

She'd failed. She'd failed at kicking bingeing, and she would fail at everything else. A minuscule bite remained, calling back all those mind-fuck games of yore. If she left a little, then she hadn't failed the full extent of the tube. Joey emptied the last of the cookie dough into the garbage and sprinkled salt atop it. And then, because she knew from experience that salty cookie dough could indeed be stomached, even enjoyed, she poured the residue of her morning green smoothie from the blender over the garbage.

That familiar distended exhaustion sent her scurrying to the bedroom. Joey heaved herself onto the bed, furious with herself. After everything, how could she have done it?

A boulder trundled over Joey's eyelids.

When Joey woke, it was with the disorientation of a nap stretched too long. Her eyes blinked open to the outline of Grant. He was staring at the glow-in-the-dark constellation he'd had framed to put up on the wall when he'd proposed. It was his favorite constellation, Perseus and Andromeda with their grand love legend. He'd showed Joey that constellation in Bali and said he always wanted to stare at it with her. Stargazing together on their balcony with glasses of wine was one of their favorite evening pastimes, and Joey always felt content as Grant pointed out and explained things about all the different stars.

"I'm so sorry, Jo," said Grant as she shifted, and he turned to face her.

"What?" Joey clutched a pillow to her chest—a salve or a shield, she wasn't sure. Her stomach was now surprisingly sedate. But that was just the physicality of her binge; her shame was fresh, curdled on top.

"I'm just so sorry, babe. I'm sorry for leaving you alone last night. You told me the most awful thing in your life, and I ran."

"You had the right to run," said Joey, as a feeling flooded her. She couldn't pinpoint it exactly. Relief, but threaded with unease.

"No. I didn't have the right."

Joey breathed in his spicy Armani cologne. She buried her face in his chest. "I should have asked if you'd be okay with—"

"It doesn't matter." He tipped her head up. "I'm so sorry for what your mom did to your family."

"Yeah…" She was eager for the pillow of him. She didn't want his eyes.

"When I think about you finding out about Lily—"

"Can we not…?"

"Okay. So…you saw Leo again today?"

"Yeah. He took me out on his new yacht."

"His yacht?"

"Yeah. Leo owns yachts. He has a crew operating the first in Monaco, and apparently he's going to the Caribbean with this next one."

"Leo owns yachts," repeated Grant. "You couldn't have an ex-boyfriend who was, say, a garbage collector?"

She laughed. "Sorry."

"Do you have a picture?"

"Oh." Joey reached for her phone. She flipped through the roll. "That's Leo in front of his new boat."

Grant studied it for a few beats. "Good-looking guy. He's got big arms, huh?"

"I didn't notice." Joey squirmed against Grant's biceps. "The important thing is, he agreed to keep things quiet for now. He'll stay until after the wedding, and we'll tell them all before we go back to Bali. And…maybe you guys should meet."

"Leo? We should. Yeah." Grant was quiet, a contrast with his general tendency not to draw breath between words. "How about Tuesday? I can get out early. I'll grill."

"Okay. I'll ask him. It's probably fine. He's got nothing but time down here."

"Did you get hit by the rain on the boat today?"

"No." But Joey followed his logic. Grant always knew the exact weather in like ten different cities. It was a dorky trait Joey loved. "We were in Fort Lauderdale though."

"That explains it." His eyes fixed on the glow-in-the-dark constellation.

Finally Joey whispered, "Grant, do you still want to marry me?"

"What?" He pulled her to him and kissed her forehead. "Of course, I want to marry you. Of course I do, baby."

And then they lay in each other's arms, and Joey didn't have deserts, she didn't have two Joeys, only Grant and the safety she felt with him and the pretend night sky blinking its stars from the wall.

chapter twenty-seven
Sarah

florida
2019

"G, where did you put the mailbox?" called Joey from the kitchen.

"I moved it, darling. It's in the oven." Sarah heard rummaging and then the oven clanging. The moisturizing mask birthday present on her face bubbled. It was the height of skin-care innovation. Apparently. The mask was a frivolous thing she wouldn't have ever thought to do prior to her granddaughters introducing her to the concept of skin care. Joey and Lily had brought an undeniable light to her life, along with a little hip-ness she'd never previously embodied. Even though Sarah didn't understand most of the fashion and music her granddaughters talked about, she enjoyed listening to them and inhabiting their carefree world.

Sarah ventured a finger along her temple, and an edge of her mask curled off.

"Not yet! We still have five more minutes." Joey reappeared with her own face Martian-silver, unwrapping a caramel candy.

Sarah smiled. She removed her hand from her face. When Joey was little, Sarah had bought a kitschy tin mailbox at the flea market. She'd filled it with treats so that, when Joey slept over, and then Lily, they'd find little surprises to collect. It still gave Sarah joy to watch Joey enjoying the traditions they'd developed.

"G, why did you move the mailbox inside the oven?"

"Well, I don't use the oven anymore, darling." Sarah propped up her feet on an ottoman. Her feet were clad in blue booties after being smothered in a solution that would cause them to peel intensely in three days and then unveil baby-smooth soles. They'd planned the timing of this spa session deliberately; with the wedding a week away, their feet would have time to shed and regenerate.

"Why don't you use your oven?"

"I have that *friend* now." Sarah winked two fingers on each hand like quotation marks, as one was supposed to do to express these things. "She cleans twice a week and brings me catering. Your mother said I must stop cooking. Queen Elizabeth is my age, you know, and she doesn't cook. Never mind that she's never cooked in her life; your mother loves to send me emails about the queen to convince me. It's fine. I never much liked cooking for just myself. So the oven is empty now. It's a smart use of space."

"Oh." Joey tucked her legs beneath her. "It's just, the mailbox has been in the cabinet with the red paint smear for, like, forever."

"Things change, darling."

"Yeah. They're changing a lot."

The phone rang, and Joey's mouth pursed. Sarah would bet a million dollars it was that woman on her cul-de-sac, the drama queen Trudy. The nerve of that woman—Sarah had told Trudy just this morning about her spa date with Joey. Did she have to spell out the supreme law of grand-parenthood? When one was with one's grandchildren, one was not to be interrupted.

Sure enough, her friend's high-pitched chortle blasted from the machine. "Sarah, sweetheart, you must ring me back immediately. Ian just—you'll never guess!" There was a rustle, and then, "He proposed! I'm enga—"

Sarah yanked the machine's cord from the wall.

"G, you should have picked that up," said Joey.

"Oh, that woman has been married three times already. A fourth engagement is hardly worth disturbing our time together."

"Okay. Hey, G, can I ask you something?"

"Of course."

Joey tipped her silver face to the side. "It's kind of a weird thing to ask in my thirties. I should have asked you a long time ago. It's just, I realized I don't know how you escaped the Holocaust. Grandfather was sent to Auschwitz with his family, I know that of course, and I know your family got sent there too, but I have no clue what happened to you. I'm sorry I never asked."

Sarah's heart began to beat so violently she feared it might explode. "One day I'll tell you the story," she managed to say calmly, "but you'll indulge me, darling, if I'm not up to it today."

What strange, strange timing. Why in the world was Joey asking this now?

"Of course, G. I understand." Joey squeezed Sarah's hand. When they untangled their fingers, Sarah's skin pulsed from the touch. "Can I ask you something on a happier

topic then? How did you first know you loved Grandfather?"

Oh my. Death by a thousand questions. "Oh, Joey, I
don't remember. It was so long ago."

"But you have to remember something. Was there a
moment? Something he said? Something about Grandfather
that made you confident he was the one?"

As Sarah grappled for an answer, the alarm blasted from
Joey's phone. "Time to get beautiful," Sarah said, and pushed
herself up off the couch.

Joey followed her to the bathroom. They removed the
silver masks. Like Joey had explained, they didn't need to
be rinsed but rather peeled off like rubber.

"How do I look?" asked Sarah, picking at a few silver bits
that remained. She adopted a cheery tone. "Fresh-cheeked
and seventy again?" In actuality, she didn't think her face
looked any different, but then it was home to so many
wrinkles it was conceivable this mask had closed up shop on
one or two of them.

"Radiant," said Joey, beaming at her.

Sarah beamed back. Oh, how she loved this girl.

After they'd rinsed their feet, Sarah asked a few questions
about the computer that she'd written on a Post-it. Then
she stepped out onto the front porch to see her granddaughter off.

As Sarah waved goodbye, a thing began to nag her. At
first, she brushed it aside, waving, waving. This used to be
Sam's job—to see their girls safely off. After his death, Sarah
had assumed his role.

But as Joey disappeared around the bend, Sarah's arm
stopped its motion, and she wondered whether she'd
been selfish to evade Joey's questions before. Whether

there was something plaguing her granddaughter. Whether Joey needed to understand something, or release something, and instead of helping, Sarah had withheld honest counsel.

Sarah went to her computer, and in an act that was most familiar to her, she buried those uncomfortable questions.

chapter twenty-eight
Sarah

corfu
1943

After Sarah learned the Nazis had taken Corfu, she ran to Gira Beach, to find Milos on his return from fishing. He called it the best beach in the world, and they strolled often on the peninsula by the old windmills off the dunes, searching for funny-shaped seashells to add to their collection and watching the flamingos flock.

But that evening, Sarah didn't even notice the waves kiss the shore. The sun hovered over the lagoon, low and orange, by the time Milos stepped onto the sand, a net slung over his shoulder and a bucket in hand.

She ran to tell him but saw it first on his face. How long had he known without telling her? She couldn't bring herself to ask.

"You never told anyone you were Jewish, did you, Sarah?" She squirmed from his attempted embrace but shook her head no. Then she retched onto the sand. Milos came down on his knees beside her. "We'll get you new papers. There aren't any Jews on Lefkada. Only my parents know. No one else will suspect."

"I don't care about that!" She wiped her mouth, her knees aching from the pebbles they crouched atop. "What about my family? That's what I care about! My family!" She shifted to a seat atop her hands to keep them from throttling him.

"Your family will be okay," he said in an infuriatingly soothing tone.

"We don't know that. They haven't responded to a single one of my letters! I want to visit them right away."

Milos extended his hand. Reluctantly, she let him pull her up. They began to walk home. The sky was shredded in pink, the day erased. It was almost impossible to imagine the Nazis could mar this unblemished perfection of an evening.

"Sure, my love. Let me ask around. We'll figure out a way for you to visit them."

But a week later, after Milos's parents had vowed not to tell anyone Sarah was Jewish, after they had papers in hand declaring her Sara Christakos, she said it to him again: "I need to go to Corfu."

Milos was on the floor, mending his nets with black twine. "Theodore just went to fish there. He'll tell us how it is. Let us wait and see."

It became December with all Milos's hedging. Again, Costas came into the shop.

"We don't have baklava," she told him. "The Nazis have confiscated all sugar, flour, and oil. On pain of death, if we have it."

"I know." He nodded. "What do you have?"

"Bobota with raisins." It was a loaf made with salt, yeast,

cornmeal, and whatever other more exotic ingredient Sarah could scrounge. Today, raisins.

"Bobota would be wonderful then."

As Sarah plated it, she garnered the courage to ask him, "So what is the state of Corfu? Have you heard?"

He frowned and shut his newspaper. "Yes, I've heard a terrible thing. They closed the Jewish school." That was the school Sarah once went to with Benjamin and Rachel. "Jews have to report in for counting each week too. But unfortunately, those aren't the worst things. The rabbi of Corfu now reports to the German commandant. Each evening, the rabbi must go to the German officers' quarters. He must stand in the room as the commandant bathes. When the commandant emerges from the water, the rabbi is made to hand him a towel."

"While he's naked?" Sarah managed, unable to fathom such a horrid, shaming scene.

"Yes. It pains me to say it, but yes. And on the Sabbath, they make him work and sweep their floors."

Sarah cried then in silence for kind Rabbi Nechama, he of the booming voice at the Romaniote synagogue who kindled something in her heart when he sang. She'd subsumed her Jewish pride to be with Milos. Now she wept for Rabbi Nechama and the Corfiot Jews. She was a Corfiot Jew. She'd forgotten it, and now she'd remembered.

She went home that evening, and Milos listened to her weep. They sat on their bed, teeth chattering in the December chill. Milos was filthy from a day at the quarry, but Sarah said, "You will not bathe until we resolve this." He tried to reassure her. Maybe she wanted to be reassured.

"So they closed the school, Sarah. They will go to a different school. It's humiliating, yes, for the rabbi, but it's not the end of the world. We just need to wait it out. Soon, the Germans will lose the war, and all of it will return to normal."

"No. I cannot accept that. I am going to see my family. The ferry still runs. I cannot sit by while they are in danger."

What Milos did next was squeeze her wrist very tightly. For days after, she could still feel the place where he squeezed it. "I forbid it, Sarah. It's too dangerous now."

And so Sarah unraveled. Like one of the textiles over which her father hunched, Milos pulled the string, and she went to shreds. But did she ram her fists against his chest in protest? Did she say *You are not the boss of me! I will do what I want to do?*

No, she did not. She accepted it like Milos was her master, like she did not have two feet that could have hitchhiked a ride to Igoumenitsa and boarded the ferry to Corfu.

It is far easier to do nothing than it is to do something. So Sarah was quiet. She pretended that reality was not reality. She said stupid, worthless prayers when her own two feet could have taken action.

Days passed as Sarah attempted to shove from her mind what Costas had shared. She continued to write her family letters, with nary a reply. Maybe Milos was right. She could sometimes convince herself of that in the dead of night as she lay awake, counting the panels in their thatched roof. Everyone was saying the war was as good as over. Soon the Allies would beat back the Germans. Then Sarah would be reunited with her family.

But for now, the Germans had infiltrated their lives. People stopped looking at each other as much, just hurrying along on daily tasks, giving off fumes of fear. And the Germans existed in physicality too—waltzing into Sarah's shop with their brisk commands, commandeering free goods. She always trembled on those encounters and for hours after, terrified those severe, unsmiling men would sniff out her Jewish-ness.

Christmas and New Year's arrived, and with them strange traditions that had once lived on the periphery of Sarah's life and now moved into its forefront. The last of the celebrations was the Epiphany, the anniversary of the baptism of Jesus Christ, whom everyone kept blathering on about.

"Who is this Jesus Christ anyway?" Sarah whispered on their way to church.

She'd never been to church before, only passed by the exterior of the grand Church of Agios Spyridon in Corfu Town's center. It housed the mummified body of the island's patron saint, whom the Christians believed to perform miracles for all inhabitants. Well, Sarah wasn't a believer, but she certainly wouldn't refuse miracles performed for her family.

"Who is Jesus Christ?" Milos repeated. "You can't be serious, Sarah."

What was so crazy about the question? She supposed she'd heard the name bandied about by Milos and his parents, but she'd always tuned out the discussion. "It's okay. You can tell me later."

He laughed, a surprising, uproarious sound. "*Who is Jesus Christ?* she asks." He squeezed her side and laughed again, and Sarah laughed then too, for no reason at all. "I won't soon forget that."

After church, an entirely bizarre and disconcerting affair, the congregants spilled out toward the shore, ushered along by the island's philharmonic choir and children waving oranges by strings tied to their stalks. The sky was blue overhead, almost eerily so—a winter sky with the powers to distract and delude.

When they reached the sea, Milos and his father and other able-bodied men swept out in trawlers for the much-hyped cross throwing. The bishop read some religious-sounding words. He was soft-spoken, tall, and thin, so different from big, booming Rabbi Nechama with his particular notes of prayer and song, Sarah's foundation of home. A lump clogged her throat, recalling those old Sabbath days. As the bishop droned on, he inflamed her soul instead of soothing it.

Suddenly the crowd began to chant, and then, even though Milos had prepared her, Sarah watched in amazement as the bishop tossed out a cross, and in unison, about fifty men dove into the frigid January sea to fetch it. Sarah prayed fervently for it to be Milos who found it, Milos who won, because the one who did was considered blessed and fortunate. And just in case Sarah was wrong about her God and Milos's God was the one in charge, then she wished Milos to win because he'd promised to bestow those blessings and fortune upon her family.

But eventually a man surfaced with a shriek, brandishing the cross. He was a portly fellow whom Sarah would have bet to sink rather than rise. Milos swam furiously to the shore and darted to her, shivering. Sarah wrapped a blanket around his shoulders.

"I'm sorry it wasn't me. I'm so sorry it wasn't me, Sarah." She nodded because he did sound awfully sorry, but she couldn't access the words to console him. "Let us find the man with the cross. If you kiss it, it will bring you blessings just the same."

"It's okay." Sarah felt physical revulsion at the idea of pressing her lips to that thing.

"I'm so sorry," said Milos again, and Sarah could see how he needed her reassurance, to know he hadn't failed her.

"It's okay." Lies heaped upon lies.

In the night, the wind howled outside like pleas, and her family populated her nightmares. In her head in the dark, Sarah was convinced they should take over boats and save them. But save them from what?

In the daylight, she was sure she was overreacting. The Allies were closing in. Nonetheless, Sarah and Milos crumbled beneath the weight of what lived in her head.

He was no longer her beloved Milos, but rather the boulder obstructing her path to her family.

chapter twenty-nine
Joey

florida
2019

Joey pulled up to the pink terra-cotta clubhouse where she'd spent the bulk of her teenage years, lifeguarding and eating free frozen yogurt. She was zonked from a day at Edith's, if one could be zonked from accomplishing absolutely nothing.

All of yesterday, she'd sketched ideas, masses of evil eyes, because that had first piqued Edith's interest and they were indeed Joey's specialty. But when she'd gotten in the space today and stared at the wall, attempting to feel what it was asking her to paint, it had all seemed wrong. The foyer needed something major. Something large-scale. Not lots of evil eyes, but one thing to hold its own against the coffee lid tapestry and the giant Lucite chandelier.

She'd closed her eyes and tried to activate an image. Instead, all that had happened was that the butler had nearly tripped over her legs. As he'd said, brushing imperceptible lint off his jacket, he hadn't expected the artist to be taking a nap.

Joey knew the sign of a creative well run dry.

That morning, Grant had suggested takeout for dinner from the Boca Beach Club, and Joey had offered to pick it up after her day at Edith's. They'd decided on kale salads and turkey burgers in lettuce wraps from the club's new California-style decorated-in-all-white spot where, appropriately, the kale salad was called the Wedding Diet Salad.

Joey hadn't confided in Grant, or anyone, about her recent binge. She was putting it in her past. Never again. She just had to be vigilant going forward, especially if she wanted to fit into her wedding dress. She couldn't wait to slip on her pajamas and eat Wedding Diet Salads with Grant. They'd watch *Bachelor in Paradise*, maybe, and talk about anything other than her family, Leo, and the wall she had to paint.

Joey switched off the ignition and smoothed her oversize white linen button-down. Then she twisted slightly to examine the butt of her slashed painter jeans from her college days. Before heading inside, she wanted to be certain that the rip that had resulted when she'd contorted herself on Edith's floor to examine the wall from a non-traditional vantage point wasn't indecent. Having reassured herself that nothing was poking out that wasn't supposed to be, Joey locked the Jeep and followed behind two immaculately dressed women strutting on stilettos into the club.

Joey gazed down at her sad feet clad in navy Adidas shower slides. Other than a few hiking trips she'd taken, she wasn't one iota of sporty. Why had she let Lily talk her into this ugly trend?

Suddenly, Joey noticed a woman in a prim pink trouser suit execute an ineffective duck behind a waist-high stone garbage bin. Her teased red hair popped out atop like some exotic flower.

Was that G?

G. Definitely G. What was G doing—?

Then Joey saw her mother. And Lily. And Siya. What the…?

She saw Lily punch something into her phone, and a moment later Joey's purse bleeped. It was a text from Grant.

Enjoy your bachelorette party! I know you didn't want one, but Lily insisted she had maid-of-honor duties.

A bachelorette party. God. Surprise throttled her, and disappointment—no Wedding Diet Salads on the couch—but Joey managed to serve up a strong face. She crossed the lot, zombie-like in her enthusiasm.

A bachelorette party with her mother in attendance? She wondered where exactly that fell on the spectrum of fun to torture. But then the image of G drinking out of a penis straw made Joey spurt with laughter. She hadn't wanted one of those productions, the type that threw together twenty friends from all walks of the bride's life, each of whom paid a sizable portion of their monthly salary to attend. But maybe it would be nice to celebrate with something low-key. Chill.

And zero photos of her shower slides permitted to grace social media.

As Joey made it past the fountain in the center drive, she had a thought that made her want to run very fast in the other direction. What could she say? She was sick? She'd inadvertently dressed like a homeless swimmer?

Leo was staying at the club. Bea hadn't seen him yet, and worse—Lily didn't know he was in town.

Joey was tipsy in the way that the private room Lily had arranged in the restaurant filled with a rosy glow. But she wasn't so tipsy that she couldn't comprehend the irony. A hostess was leading Leo to a table not four feet away, in the midpoint between the bachelorette party and the restaurant's terrace. He sat, his back to them, framed by the sign strung over the private room door that read, SAME BACK FOREVER. Apparently Lily had ordered it from an Etsy shop—a play on the "same penis forever" bachelorette trope, in homage to the back being Joey's favorite male body part. It made Joey giggle each time the sign popped into her periphery.

Joey needed to text Leo ASAP to tell him to leave the restaurant. She rummaged for her bag, but it wasn't under her chair.

"Lil, do you know where my bag went?"

Her sister glanced up mid-conversation with Bea about constructing a guesthouse in the Abramses' backyard to house Lily's growing media company. "That big canvas one?"

"Yeah." Joey sipped her jalapeño margarita, her eyes not straying from Leo's back.

"I thought it was your overnight bag. I had the guy put it in your hotel room."

"How could it be my overnight bag when I didn't even know it was my bachelorette party? It had my paints and stuff in it. And my phone!"

"Your sister got you a hotel room, did you hear?" Bea said.

"Actually, I got you all hotel rooms," Lily said. "Boca Beach Club is one of my advertisers. The guy did me a favor."

"But I need my phone!"

"Why do you need your phone?" asked Siya from Joey's

side, adjusting the bodice of her fuchsia minidress. "You don't need your phone to get woke." She made a jokey *W* with her hands, thumbs together, like the sign for an angst-filled "whatever" they'd used in middle school.

Joey laughed in spite of the burgeoning Leo fiasco. "You are so uncool it's terrifying."

"*Whatever*," Siya repeated, hands back in the W-position. But she was laughing too. "Isn't woke what all the kids are saying these days?"

"I think you used it wrong. You're looking for turnt. Or lit." Joey felt only half present in the conversation. How could she tell Leo to leave without risking him swiveling around and being seen? Maybe she could write a note and tell a waiter to slip it to Leo. She just needed—aha!—a napkin to write on.

"Turnt," Siya mused. "Let's turnt this party up. Do you want a passion fruit margarita next round?"

"Sure," said Joey absently, her eyes darting from Bea to Leo, from Leo to Lily.

"You seem so…distracted, Jo. I mean, I know it's your wedding. It's not real to me yet."

Joey's eyes flickered at her best friend. She really needed to tell Siya about Leo. She would tonight, she decided. Once they were alone. "I'm distracted because of this art commission. The timing is insane. And it's not real to me either."

Joey glanced around for a pen, but nothing. She gave up. This note thing was stupid. She'd go to the bathroom and wave Leo over from a place out of sight from the private room.

"Wait, so did I tell you that Aadesh's sister, Kyra, went shopping with me for wedding shoes? I splurged on four-inch Manolos. Me! Manolos! Do you know what they are?"

Joey smiled. Her best friend was so not into fashion that

this whole conversation was funny. "Of course I know what they are, but I'm shocked that you do."

"Well, let me tell you, Mr. Manolo knows his stuff. Somehow they were soft like pillows. I'm going to have to hide this month's credit card bill from Aadesh and do an exorcism to forget the price myself, but I'm going to be a hot matron of honor!"

"You're always hot." Joey kept a distracted eye on Leo. "Wait a sec, 'kay? I have to go to the bath—"

"Look." Siya thrust her phone into Joey's face. "Those are them." They were gorgeous, simple and caramel-toned, with one strap over the toes and another around the ankles.

"Perfect. Love."

Siya thumbed to the next picture. "Oh, that's all. That's me and Kyra though. She's a millennial, very into the animal ear thing."

"You guys are so cute. And by the way, we're still millennials." Joey was all for embracing their age, but she didn't need to be aged up.

"Elder millennials." Siya winked. "I saw the Netflix special." Siya raised her margarita. "Hey there, Team We Love Joey, I want to toast our bride. To Joey being a complete klutz and surfing into Grant!"

Joey giggled. She raised her margarita and clinked her best friend's glass. God, she still really needed to get the message to Leo. She stood just as Lily rose from her chair and tapped her champagne glass. Joey flopped back down.

Her sister was resplendent in the way only possible for a brief window in time and if you hit the genetic lottery. She wore a pale-blue mini slip dress paired with a nude suede duster coat. Her strawberry hair was flat-ironed, and her makeup Kardashian-contoured.

"I want to give a toast too." Joey's eyes darted outside. The second Lily was done, Joey absolutely had to deal with Leo.

"Joey is, as you all know, my older sister. And she may not know it, but I've always looked up to her."

Joey glanced up, surprised.

"Joey worked really freaking hard as a lawyer. She'd come home for the High Holidays, and it would just seem like all her energy was snuffed out." Lily shifted her weight so her right hip bone jutted alluringly through her dress. "I knew she wasn't happy. Mom always said Joey was a really talented artist. There was this one painting she did. I found it in Jo's closet at home. It was this face with these mesmerizing eyes. It wasn't finished."

Joey's heart went from producing unexpectedly warm feelings toward both her sister and Bea, to positively arrested.

"It was just true. It was this really true painting. And I was really proud of her when she left law to pursue her art. Jo, I don't know if you remember, but we talked on the phone before you went to Bali. I asked if you were scared. You said, *I spent the last ten years being bored. I'm excited to be scared about something.* And you know what? That's when I decided to start my YouTube channel! You may remember, my Instagram was really successful at that point, but I wasn't sure about the video component. It seemed so, like, in your face…"

As Lily went on, Joey froze. She watched the Leo back turning. The Leo back rising. The Leo back becoming not a back anymore, but a front.

They locked eyes. Joey stood cemented in place on tracks as the train chugged closer. Leo broke into a smile. He began to walk over.

Now Lily was saying, "And Joey wasn't sure about YouTube, but she's, like, Gen X."

"Elder millennial," Siya corrected loudly.

"Well, I'm Gen Z, and we are all about YouTube..."

Leo was almost at the door. Joey waved her hands a couple times and then realized her lack of subtlety and attempted headshakes to convey the urgency of the situation. Leo glanced behind him. He turned back, his face confused.

"Joey, who are you waving at?" asked Bea.

Like synchronized swimmers, heads went to the door.

Joey steeled her hands against the table edge. Leo stood in the frame, smack beneath the SAME BACK FOREVER sign.

"Hey, Jonesey." Those green eyes wandered. They registered Bea. The eyes flickered with shock.

Then, for what seemed like forever, his eyes locked onto Lily.

chapter thirty
Joey

florida

2019

Bea spoke first, in a falsetto. "Leo! Leo Winn. Joey, did you know Leo was here?"

"Leo? You're *the* Leo?" said Lily.

"That's the boy from Corfu?" said G. "The one who wasn't Jewish? What's he doing here?"

"Joey's Leo?" said Siya. "That's your Leo, Jo?"

Leo walked in. Slowly, Joey said, "Everyone meet Leo. Mom, you remember him, clearly. Leo's in town for the wedding."

"I'm in town for the wedding," repeated Leo, his eyes fixed on Lily.

Bea looked almost manic, her eyes darting and wild. "Well, my goodness! Leo!"

"This was accidental, us running into him now." Joey gave her mother a meaningful look meant to convey, *We're obviously not planning some showdown here.*

"You're Leo!" Lily rose. "I've heard so much about you! Dad told me you were one of my first words. Eo!"

Leo smiled. "I was honored for that."

Leo hugged Lily, and when they stepped apart, Joey watched their faces arrange in the same smile—lips pressed together but a sheen to their eyes.

"No one ever talks about Corfu. You don't know how lucky you guys were. I've basically only ever gone to Vermont or on press trips."

"Lucky," repeated Joey, her heart yammering.

"Corfu." G shook her head. "I never understood why you vacationed on that miserable island."

"I mean, like, I've Googled it so many times," said Lily. "There's this place, I forget what it's called. It's this rock thing you swim under with the person you love. One day, I want to do a shoot for my magazine there. It's my dream."

Leo's eyes met Joey's. "Sidari."

"Yes! I have to go there."

Bea's face turned the gray of her wrap dress. "So Leo, when did you get in?"

"Last week."

"And have you met Grant?"

"Not yet. But we're doing dinner Tuesday, right, Jonesey?"

Joey nodded. Under the table, Siya pinched Joey's thigh, or tried to, but ripped jeans were made thick back in the early aughts.

"Jonesey." Bea slapped on an overwrought smile. "This is feeling like the Twilight Zone."

"Leo." Lily put a hand on his shoulder. "You have to come by this week. I have so many questions about Corfu. I want to hear all the stories."

"I can tell you the stories, darling," said Bea.

Lily ignored her. "So will you, Leo?"

"Leo's pretty busy, Lil," said Joey, and relief shone on her mother's face. "He's not just here for the wedding. He's also here to buy a yacht."

"A yacht," said Bea. "So you're a—"

"Captain." Leo shoved his hands in his jeans. "I have a little charter business. I'm small potatoes next to a lot of the outfits, but I enjoy it. It's a nice life."

"You're a captain on yachts?" said Lily. "That's so cool. Could I maybe—"

"Lil, Leo's yachts are his job," said Joey. "They're not for photo shoots."

"What I was going to say," said a frosty Lily, "was I want to hear about it. We have practically no family, you know, Leo. Most of them died in the Holocaust. Dad always says the Winns were like family."

"We'll make something happen," said Leo. "I promise you that."

Lily beamed. Joey felt an irrational hit of annoyance toward her. Like they were competing for Leo, and again Leo was going to choose Lily.

"What is Leo really doing here?" Bea had displaced Siya from her chair and now whispered half an inch from Joey's ear.

Joey sipped her margarita, trying to calm down her nerves. "You know he's in town. That's the whole reason all your lies unraveled."

"I knew it, but to see it is another thing. I don't get what you both are planning to do. Destroy all our lives? Now? Before your wedding?"

"No. Not before my wedding. We'll tell Dad and Lily after. Lily's eighteen. She has a brother, Mom. She has a biological father she doesn't know about. Leo has kept your secret for fifteen years."

Bea rolled a piece of hard gold confetti between her finger-tips. Then she dug the edge of the confetti into her forearm, carving two lines into an X-shape. She stared at the X like it held answers. "I know this is my fault. I knew long ago this day would come. I just didn't expect it on your wedding." Her mother slid her wedding ring up over her knuckle and then pushed it back down again.

"Well, that makes two of us." Joey watched Leo and Lily talking. Seeing them for the first time together as siblings was such a weighty reality to digest.

Suddenly G rose from her chair. "I have something to say. Now, this is my first bachelorette party, but I did think it was going to be more fun. Where is the dancing?"

"Yes." Lily rose. "G, you're totally right! Do you want to try to twerk?" She smiled slyly at Joey, and Joey managed a tiny smile in return.

"A twerk, you say. Yes. Lily, turn the music up!"

Bea wandered off, and Leo slid into her abandoned chair. He said, "Will the real bachelorette please stand up?"

Joey motioned to a gyrating G. "She must have missed out her time around."

"No twerking for you?"

"No twerking. I'm just kicking it over here with my margarita."

"I'll kick it over here with you then. If that's okay."

"It's okay," she said.

⌣

Much later, after a surprise performance orchestrated by Lily of an apparently on-the-cusp-of-superstardom local pop singer, everyone left.

Siya and Lily helped G out in a chain of linked arms. Joey wasn't surprised that Siya was heading off to sleep. Since they'd been kids, Siya had favored a grandparent-hour bedtime, and her four-year-old twins had only pushed it earlier. On her way out, Siya whispered in Joey's ear, "Tomorrow. Me and you. Every. Last. Detail." She had that menacing look, like when Joey accidentally drove her car over the prom dress that had slid off Siya's trunk.

Bea went last. "I'm sorry," she said to Leo, and had to stand on her tiptoes to achieve an awkward pat of his shoulder. "I always wanted to tell you that."

After they'd all gone, Joey teetered near the door. She wondered vaguely where her shower slides had gone.

"Careful, Jonesey." Leo chuckled. "Still barefoot, I see."

"Always." The sudden quiet of the place struck her. It was in that void that Joey realized she was drunk for the first time in years. Quite possibly wasted.

"Easy, J. How are you getting home? I'll wait with you while you call an Uber."

"I'm staying here. Lily got us rooms." She leaned on Leo's arm for support. They walked through the door. One side of the SAME BACK FOREVER sign detached as they left, flapping against Joey's head.

"I'll walk you to your room."

"Okay."

They made it to the elevator bank. "So was your bach-elorette party everything you ever wanted and more?" Leo grinned. "Other than me crashing it, of course."

"It was a nice night," Joey said. "I felt really loved."

"I sense a *but*."

"Well." Joey stared down at herself. "I'm wearing jeans

from high school, Leo. They surprised me. You know how I feel about surprises."

Leo's eyes flitted down to her jeans. "Those jeans look nice to me."

Men. Joey rested against the elevator door. Leo shifted her over to the wall.

"Lily seeing me already was disastrous," he said. "I'm sorry."

"It had to happen sometime, right?"

"Yeah. God. It was amazing to see her. She's really something else."

"You don't know the half of it."

"No," said Leo. "Other than my Google searches, I guess I don't."

Joey winced. "You will, Leo."

"I'm sorry I ruined your bachelorette party."

"You didn't. I didn't even want a bachelorette party. You know…I don't love being the center of attention. Not to sound ungrateful. It was beautiful. Just, I guess if it was up to me, I would have opted for something quieter."

Leo looked thoughtful. "What would you have wanted? You know, if you'd gotten to choose? Maybe we can still grant your wish."

Joey stared at him. "What are you now, my bachelorette fairy godmother?"

Leo smiled. "Maybe I just am. At least I can do something to make your life better, not worse, while I'm down here." Leo pressed the button to go up. Joey pressed the button to go down.

"Well then, you're on, Winn. I know what I want," she said as the down elevator dinged. "But you're going to need to take me there."

chapter thirty-one
Joey

florida

2019

Joey raced to the checkout counter with a cake and a squeeze tube of blue frosting teetering in her hands. Her biceps wedged a jar of Merenda against her chest. Joey had convinced the nice manager of Publix to import it from Greece, vowing to be an avid customer. (She'd kept her word.)

The frosting Joey had scrawled on the otherwise standard vanilla sheet cake now bobbed up against the plastic top. She ran past a shelf with Doritos. Gosh, Doritos were delicious. But Nacho Cheese Flavor versus Cool Ranch? Pausing to ponder, Joey set the cake down beside her bare feet. The cake had previously been adorned with HAPPY JOEY DAY! Now the entirety of the *H* clung to the plastic top, so the cake just read APPY JOEY DAY!

"Jonesey!" Leo's voice tore through the vacant market.

"Coming!" Abandoning the Doritos, Joey lifted the cake and ran. Then she changed her mind and swiveled backward into a Roger Rabbit. After a few moments, she was breathing hard, but it was very fun to Roger Rabbit. But God, it was also exhausting to Roger Rabbit.

Joey stopped, panting in the produce aisle beside a crate of interesting objects. They were waxy yellow-green, shaped like stars. Joey picked up a fruit, twirled it around. It was fascinating, in a way. Star fruits? Huh.

"Joey!"

Joey went to the checkout line in a manner she felt to be restrained and sober and un-Roger-Rabbit-like. She placed the cake, frosting, Merenda, and star fruit on the conveyor belt. The checkout girl had already rung through Cinnamon Toast Crunch, milk, Sour Patch Kids, wooden spoons, paper bowls, and two bottles of water.

Over the beep-beeps of the scanning machine, Joey said, "Leo, what are *you* going to eat?"

"There's an entire cake here, Jones."

"It's my cake!" Joey's stomach rumbled at the threat of him. The cake wasn't even that big. "If you want cake, Winn, I suggest you get your own."

Shit, was she really going to eat all this crap? But she'd hardly eaten all day. And it wasn't necessarily a binge if it was in full view of Leo.

Leo laughed. "So I'll have cereal. Or are you going to eat the entire box of that too?"

"You can have cereal," she allowed.

"Maybe I'll even eat this," said Leo, tossing the star fruit into the air and then catching it as they exited the market.

"You can't eat the star fruit. It's my inspiration."

"For what?"

"A star fruit show. Maybe I could be a...sculptureress? Sculpturrrr...you know." Joey plopped onto the pavement by a row of shopping carts.

"Jones. Let's eat at the hotel."

"I don't want to eat at the hotel. It's Joey Day! You promised me it's Joey Day. Can't we eat right here where I want to on Joey Day?"

As Leo sat down beside her, Joey's head did a washing cycle spin, and the stars came down to dance with the happy shopping carts.

"Have some water." Leo handed her a bottle, and after a tiny struggle, she popped open the top and chugged. Leo composed their cereal bowls. "I have such a memory of you, our first summer. You were up in arms that Corfu didn't have Cinnamon Toast Crunch. Remember how we protested?"

"Oh God." Joey crunched down on Cinnamon Toast Crunch deliciousness. "I totally forgot that. You were such a good sport. I made you march with that insane poster."

Leo slurped up a spoonful. "You made me a believer, Jones. You wanted it so badly that I got all riled up too. Didn't we march for days until old man Kristo finally capitulated? *I'll see what I can do.* He was so peeved."

"Super peeved. But the next summer, he had Cinnamon Toast Crunch."

"You were so determined, Jones. Passionate when you believed in something. Full of big, unique ideas that came to life when you painted them." Despite her inebriation, Joey had a lucid certainty that she was indeed those things once. In a strange way, she felt closer now to the kid who'd campaigned for Cinnamon Toast Crunch than to most of the stages she'd occupied since.

Somehow, the memory of strong, little Joey emboldened her. "Leo, you know that day on the beach, when I told you I looked for you in Nice?"

There were a few spoonfuls of cereal-worth of silence before Leo said, "Yeah."

"You said I wasn't the only one with ghosts. I couldn't let you finish then. I was going to jump out of myself or something. I don't know why, but I need to know. Did you…did you ever look for me too?"

Leo stared beyond her, beyond the lot, at Federal Highway. A green car careened by, then a white one. Then no cars at all. "The truth is, after we split, I spiraled, Jones." Leo rubbed his eyes, his cheeks, made fists with both his hands—and then slowly unfurled his fingers.

"I mean, I put on a good front. First, I got that gig as a deckhand. Then I got promoted to second mate. I was throwing it all into work, but if I'm truthful, I saw you at the bottom of every beer I downed. I was angry. Scary angry. Pissed off at the world. Especially at my father."

Joey had thought hearing that Leo had suffered too would make her feel better, but it didn't. She bit her lip and tasted frosting. The artificial sweet roiled her stomach.

"I punched a guy in the supermarket once. He took the avocado I wanted."

"Good avocados are serious business." Joey forced a smile.

Leo raked a hand through his hair. "Yeah. Well, at some point, I was on a ship called *Checkmate*. There was this older woman chartering the boat one week—pretty, thirties, the wife of some gazillionaire. Her husband was negotiating deals on a satellite phone at the most ridiculous hours, and she kept trying to lure me into her stateroom. It's not that I wasn't attracted to her, but I wasn't about to go there, you know? I was so one-minded on making it then, on getting to wear the captain's hat one day. The problem was I was still in such a dark place. Anyway, one day the charter guest tried to kiss me, and I guess I kissed her back a little. I don't know…the moment ran away with me. And then the cook—this girl named Tess—happened to see us from the galley. It looked bad, Jones. It *was* bad.

"Tess and I had had this little thing, and it didn't end well. Anyway, yachting is an incestuous industry by its nature, and Tess ran to the captain. When the captain came down to see what was going on, the woman who'd been pursuing me denied she'd started it, and I just…"

"You snapped," Joey said quietly.

"I snapped. I totally snapped. This job was the only thing I had in the world, and now my integrity was being threatened." Leo nibbled so slowly on a Cinnamon Toast Crunch square he was like some *Top Chef* judge teasing out its subtle notes. "I'm still so ashamed about what happened. I was in such a frenzy, and I shouted at the woman, *You're the one who wanted me!*" His eyes grayed. "You know that's not me, Jones. It's so not me to shout at a woman, or to get into some inappropriate work romance."

"I know." She wanted to touch him but couldn't bring herself to.

"I got fired. For a long time after, no one would hire me. Those were rough times, but finally I got back on my feet. I had to take a step back, do the deckhand thing again. A Russian hired me. One of the new tycoons who didn't know the European scene. So I started over. But more than that, I finally clawed myself out of this hole I'd allowed myself to descend into. One night, I looked at myself in the mirror and said, *Are you going to let what happened define you?*"

"You weren't talking about the woman on the yacht," Joey whispered.

"No. No, I wasn't. So I decided that no, I wasn't going to

let what happened on Corfu define me. I was going to try to stop being so angry. You know... I meditate morning and night. Almost twelve years now. Yoga too."

"My therapist always tells me to meditate. I've tried a few times, but my mind is too crazy." Her mind was a pressure cooker now, about to blow up between her ears. Joey thought about how Leo had once sat there with her zigzags. How she'd felt like she could control the things pulsing inside her because he had witnessed them.

Leo said, "I have this guru in Monaco. Jim. He's Australian. The kindest, wisest guy. He says the crazier your mind, the more you need to meditate."

"Well, my mind's been an insane asylum ever since you got into town so..."

They both laughed. And as Joey picked at the hole in her jeans and her head continued to pulse, she wondered why it had never occurred to her to give herself an ultimatum too. "I think I let it all define me," she said.

"What?" asked Leo, slurping up the last of his cinnamon-y milk.

"Nothing." But suddenly Joey couldn't pretend anymore. She kneaded her hands together. "You know, after we broke up, the pain was so... well, bad. Not to make you feel guilty. It was just a really dark time in my life, and to cope, I used to... well, binge."

"Binge as in, eat?" Leo stacked their cereal bowls and leaned back on his elbows on the pavement, seemingly unfazed at her confession.

"Yeah. I had gotten it under control finally, you know? It took years, but it felt handled. Behind me. And then with you coming back and all this stuff about my mom and Rand and Lily, not to mention the wedding, I've... well, I've—"

"You've eaten some stuff?" Leo wasn't trying to be funny, she knew, but he was smiling.

Joey gave a small smile back. "Just once. But yeah."

"You wanna know what I think, Jonesey?"

"I do," she said quietly.

"I think you're not perfect," he finally said, and for the briefest of moments, he put his hand on top of hers. "And I think you're perfect that way."

chapter thirty-two
Joey

florida
2019

The morning after her bachelorette party, on her way home from Boca Beach, Joey called her best friend. Siya answered on the first ring. "Abrams, what the hell?"

The shout rattled Joey's head. "Indoor voice, por favor."

"I can't use my indoor voice when you've been keeping bombshells from me."

"I know." Joey cringed. "I'm sorry."

"Does Grant know?"

Joey's stomach turned over itself, because of the special bachelorette cupcakes that had been waiting in her hotel room when she'd returned there alone, that she'd devoured one after another. Because of everything. "Grant knows. But it's not like that."

As she drove down Federal, she unloaded the whole she-bang. For a while, there was only silence in her earbuds—so all Joey heard was the guy outside dressed in a hot dog costume, talking in a strange voice that was presumably that

of a hot dog, distributing flyers by the Publix where she'd
gone with Leo the night before.

"So Lily doesn't know?" Siya finally asked.

"Not yet. I can't…oh God. I wish I could do something
to protect her from it."

"I can't believe your mom. I wish you'd told me
sooner, Jo."

"I just…it's been a lot the past couple, few days. Si…I've
been bingeing again." Siya would know what that meant.
How hard Joey had worked to free herself, and here she
was, right back there again.

Silence for a while on the other end. Finally Siya said,
"Joey, you know what I think?"

"That I'm falling apart?" she whispered.

"No. Not at all." Siya said it so fiercely that Joey almost
believed it. "What I think is that you're basically the strong-
est person to deal with all this right now. And it's so unfair
it's come before your wedding. But you still get to have
a happy ending. That part, the most important part, hasn't
changed."

"Yeah. I guess."

"I *know*. And you know what a binge means, if we drill
it down?"

"I'm going to look gross in my dress?"

"No, Jo. Stop. It means you ate a lot of food. That's all.
You don't need to assign it some profound meaning."

"I ate a lot a lot."

"So, you ate a lot a lot. So fucking what? If I was in your
shoes, there wouldn't be enough pizza in the world. I think
what you're forgetting is that there's a cycle to everything.
A beginning, a middle, and an end. And maybe you're in
the middle right now, of something, but there's no law that

says you have to leap to the end. Because you have to wade through the middle first."

"But I don't want to be in the middle anymore! How do you know I'm even going to get to the end?"

"Maybe the end is overrated. And also maybe we're talking in riddles now. The bottom line is you and Grant, forever. Just stay focused on that."

"Yeah." As Joey said it, a song came on. She didn't know what song exactly, because songs, their lyrics and their titles, had always eluded her. She only knew that she'd heard it a hundred million times, and its familiar happy tune confided something small.

"Jo, can you promise me you'll stop beating yourself up? That you'll cut yourself some slack."

Joey gazed down at her puffy stomach. "I'll try. Si, can I...?"

"I just got home. Get your butt over here."

So Joey did.

~

The evening after the bachelorette party, Joey was sprawled out in a tangle of sketchbooks, paints, pencils, and a canvas when Edith trailed down the hall. Joey shot up. On Edith's arms were bangles the size of bricks, giving her the appearance of a shackled marionette.

Her hand on the door, Edith turned. "You do realize the event is in three days? And you do realize...the wall is still blank."

Joey could barely get out the words. "I do."

"Mmm." Edith hobbled out without a backward glance.

At the door's click, Joey sank back to the floor. The

navy wood floor with which she'd become intimately familiar.

Joey's phone rang.

"Hi, Dad." She wedged the phone between her ear and shoulder. "I'm at Edith's."

"JoJo! Real quick. Lily told me Leo's in town." Joey froze. "Leo Winn."

"Yes." Her pencil slipped from her grip. "Leo's here for the wedding."

"I had no clue you were still in contact with him! How wonderful. I haven't seen Leo in…oh, it must be—"

"Fifteen years."

"Fifteen years! My goodness. You must invite Leo over for dinner this week."

"Oh, I don't think so. Leo has work stuff this week, and I've got Edith's and last-minute wedding—"

"Tuesday night works though, right? Lily told me Leo was planning to come to you and Grant on Tuesday night. So that night should be clear for all three of you. And now you won't have to cook, or Grant won't have to, so I'll take something off your to-do list. I'll barbecue, and we'll all catch up! Just like old times."

"Uh…" She grappled for an excuse, but none arose. "I'll see if it works for Leo."

"Of course it will work for Leo. Just find out, he hasn't gone vegetarian on me?"

"I'll find out, Dad. I gotta go."

Joey hung up, her head in a tailspin. There was the family dinner with potential bombs abounding. There was the white wall in front of her. There were oils, a bamboo stick, a long piece of charcoal, and her notebook of evil eyes. One of the eyes caught hers. Maybe it spoke to her.

Joey thought of the email that had arrived from Demetris. She'd contacted him in a panic. She was going to fail, and in turn, she would be defined by this failure. By Edith, by Lily, by critics, by *Vogue*, sure, but worse, by herself. She was going to give up on herself, and then who would be left believing in her?

When was the last time you were inspired, paidi mou? *My advice is simply to follow your curiosity. If you fail, fail epically. Fail having placed your heart on the platter. Fail having said to your brain,* Brain, you and I need a little break now so I can create.

Or maybe you won't fail, Joey mou. *Imagine that. Allow yourself to entertain the idea that maybe everything in your life has prepared you for this. And remember, an artist delights herself first. She pleases herself, first. She has fun. She has great fun. Remember that,* paidi mou, *and fly.*

Joey watched the waves ripple through the window. She knew what she had to do. She selected a pencil and walked to the ladder propped against the wall.

She began to climb.

chapter thirty-three
Sarah

florida

2019

Sarah was in the midst of a raging sea. She plunged again below the surface, the waves thrashing her as if she were an insignificant rope of kelp. She kicked her feet in a fight to the top that mustered every last ounce of her will, because Benjamin was there. Benjamin needed her, and this time she would save him.

She made it to air. Her ears emptied water and heard, "Sarah!" It was unmistakably her brother's shriek. "Sarah!"

Sarah swam in the direction of his voice, but at every stroke, the ocean slammed her back. *Oh no, you don't. Who do you think is in charge here? Our waves need to move, and you are standing in our way.*

"Sarah!"

She was choking on the salt, or maybe her own tears. Why was Benjamin swimming in the dark? She had to get to him! She could make him out now, head bobbing in white froth—his translucent skin, his lively blue eyes.

Suddenly, he stopped moving. He met Sarah's eyes. He

didn't smile—just blew her a little kiss. Then in an instant, the entire ocean stopped. Halted. Stilled. It was all a pool of nothing, and Benjamin was gone.

Sarah sprang up in bed. Her mouth grappled for air. And as the air hit her lungs, she felt that dormant swell of pain—like she was stealing a breath that belonged to her baby brother.

My dear Milos, It is the middle of the night and I cannot sleep. So much is plaguing me, I almost can't bear it. And perhaps worst of all—I am writing to thin air. I am writing my deepest feelings to be returned only by little faces and hearts. It isn't enough, Milos! I want to hear from you. I want you to find someone who can type English to me. Someone you trust to bare your own deep feelings to transcribe them. I want more than a little house with a shrub next to it, Milos. That was trite, as far as those little things you send me go.

I could use a hug, Milos. A very long hug. I haven't been hugged tightly, long, so you can hear the other person's heartbeat, in—oh, Milos, it's been a lifetime. You want to know a sad secret? Sometimes I get a massage just to feel a hand on my skin that is not my own.

Well, Milos, we've gotten this far, eh? It is black outside, and inside too. There is nothing more to do than write.

chapter thirty-four

Sarah

corfu

1944

In June 1944, Sarah had not heard a word from her family in over a year, and a film played constantly in her head. In it, Benjamin barreled toward her, his cheeks rosy and his eyes dancing with light. Her parents followed closely behind, so that soon all three sets of arms wrapped around her, fusing her back inside her family. Sarah soaked in their familiar smells: her mother's perfume she made by crushing petals from her beloved pink roses; the meaty tinge to her father's breath that lingered after a meal, when he sucked the marrow out from the lamb.

But the scent she imagined the most was the sweet sweat of her little brother, and in her movie, she hungrily dipped her face to his raspberry curls. Benjamin wasn't a climber or a traipser or a runner; his sweaty perfume derived from all the energy he expended with his nose inside books. He would read *Robinson Crusoe* and get worked up from the excitement of spearing fish by hand even when he was too afraid to poke a toe in the sea.

In Sarah's wishful daydream, her parents accepted Milos. The Germans, their long separation—all of it had lent time to building new understanding. Her being with a Christian man was no longer an insurmountable problem. She still believed in happy ever after then. She just had to look forward and trust that soon her movie would be real.

Sarah was still in her movie when Costas and his grandson walked into the cheese lady's shop. The house was stifling, with the mingling of ovens and a hotter-than-normal June. The air Costas let in from outside, even steaming, was a welcome fan to Sarah's face.

Costas fingered his thick gold chain with its ruby cross nestled in the bird's nest of his chest hair. "Hello, Sarah. Wonderful to see you."

"And you, Costas. Bobota with orange zest today?"

"Wonderful," he said, as usual acting as though the cornmeal loaf were as grand as his prior baklava.

His grandson raised on his tiptoes to peer over the counter. "Kourabiedes, please."

Sarah almost salivated at the memory of kourabiedes cookies—buttery shortbread made with local almonds and dusted with icy sugar. Sarah used to think their recipe to be overly sweetened, but the cheese lady had liked it that way. So had the grandson.

"I'm afraid we don't have kourabiedes now."

The boy frowned.

"Soon, when the war is over." Costas patted his grandson's shoulder. "In the meantime, we have tasty bobota."

"Mama makes bobota." The grandson sighed and sank into a seat.

"Don't tell your mother, but this bobota is the best there is." Costas winked at Sarah, and then his face sagged. "I have terrible news to share, I'm afraid. The Jews of Corfu are here."

Sarah's hands froze over the table as she set down the plates of bobota. There had been word of another bout of bombings over Corfu that had caused her to nibble her fingernails to bone. Later, Sarah would understand the bombs were the work of the Americans, intended to be a diversion from their Normandy landings. "Is it because of the bombings?"

"Unfortunately, it does not have to do with the bombings."

"What do you mean then, *the Jews of Corfu are here*?"

For a few terrible moments, Costas didn't speak because he had bobota in his mouth. Her friend was too polite to speak about Sarah's family with a mouthful of crumbs. Finally, he said, "They've rounded up the Jews of Corfu. Oh Sarah, it's just terrible."

Sarah felt her hands move and her feet step, and yet her extremities seemed divorced from her core. Time stretched and bloated. Finally, she managed to say, "Rounded them up to go where?"

"Nowhere good, I'm certain about that." Costas tipped his head up toward the crumbling ceiling that sometimes shed powder onto Sarah's ugly maroon dress, gifted by Milos's mother. Sarah had tailored it to her body that had subsequently fleshed out from consuming the things she was baking. But with the cruelties and hardships of the German occupation, the dress now fit once again.

"I don't understand. How could…how…" Sarah tried not to betray her emotion. As Milos reminded her incessantly, the fact of her Jewishness had to be assiduously concealed. But Costas was talking about her parents and Benjamin like they were a period at the end of a sentence that was already written.

Costas caressed his grandson's cheek. He ate his bobota so quietly and carefully in a way that made Sarah despise him. Benjamin should have been there instead, eating bobota and relishing every bite.

"What I heard is that, a few days ago, the Nazis made all the Jews of Corfu gather," Costas said. "No exceptions. On threat of death, they had to surrender their possessions. Gold, apartments, everything. The Nazis took it all. They put the Jews in the fortress, the old one. Anyone who wouldn't go willingly was shot on the spot. It was horrific, I understand. Just horrific."

"Shot on the spot?" Sarah's hand migrated to her throat.

Costas nodded, and his face shaded with disdain. "The next day, the mayor issued a proclamation. He announced to the people of Corfu that at last the Jews are gone and now the island may return to prosperity and the land to its rightful owners."

"The Jews are...gone?"

"Some of them are here on Lefkada now. But it's just temporary. The Nazis will move them again soon."

"What do you mean...*here*?"

"On the edge of town, northwest of the port, in an area barricaded by fences. My wife and I brought some food to them and are organizing more provisions. *Filotimo*, yes? We have to do what we can, don't you agree, Sarah? We can't just stand by and watch. These Jews...they are our people too. We are bound by compassion and humanity to help them."

Sarah nodded but couldn't bring herself to speak. When at last Costas and his grandson had finished their bobota and gone, Sarah threw up the crushed olives she'd eaten in the morning. The cheese lady had returned from outside with a pail of warm, fresh milk in hand from their last remaining cow, just in time to watch Sarah get sick. Sarah didn't correct her misperception that it was a baby and not olives.

The cheese lady said, "Go home."

So Sarah ran down the stone village paths still abjectly foreign, past the lemon trees wafting their horribly pleasing fumes. She arrived home to Milos, grilling fish in the dim, musty kitchen. He hadn't yet left for the quarry.

"They're here! My family's here." Sarah grabbed a sack and started gathering fruit to place inside it. "I'm going to hug them so hard. We'll get them out, won't we? We have to. We just have to."

Milos tried to halt her, but she sidestepped him and kept gathering and babbling. She was a tornado, and Milos seemed to think he could pause her whirling by resting his hands on her shoulders. He could not. Sarah had tried to wait out this war, sitting on her hands. Talking to God. Stupid, useless God. Now it was time for her feet to take action.

"You can't go see them, Sarah. It's far too dangerous. You can't help them."

Sarah felt herself erupt—a volcano of emotion she'd shoved down inside in their year of blissful, ignorant house-playing. "Don't you ever speak of my family that way. Don't you ever! They're here and they're alive and I'm going to save them. It's a miracle of miracles."

Milos removed his cap and looked out the tiny window onto the garden, where his mother was snipping grape clusters off a vine. He said nothing. That was when Sarah realized Milos already knew her family was on Lefkada.

"Where are they?" she demanded.

Milos spoke so quietly and sadly, but it did nothing to soften her toward him. "They are behind fences at the edge of town, by the sea. They are surrounded by Germans, Sarah. I gave them food."

"You gave my parents food?"

He nodded. "Others did too. There are good people on Lefkada."

"Oh, really? The mayor of Corfu said they were happy to be rid of the Jews!"

"Well, here on Lefkada they are giving food and trying to help."

"And how were my parents? How was Benjamin?"

Milos reached toward her again, but Sarah stepped back. "You can't go there, Sarah. You can't save them."

"Oh yes? Watch me!" She yanked him by his collar with strength that surprised her. Yes, she'd been a strong, stubborn girl once, defending her family and the values she held dear. Milos had fallen in love with that girl, and now she resurfaced. "Take me there now! I demand you to take me there now!"

"I will not." Milos wasn't usually stubborn. He was easy. He told Sarah often that all he wanted in the world was to please her. But now he crossed his arms over his chest.

"Then I will go out to find them myself!"

Milos grabbed for her, only reaching the pleats of her dress. But then he stopped because he knew she had won, impossible as it was to prevail against someone willing to risk everything. And she was.

"I will take you there, but only if you stay back. We will give them this food, but that's all. You will see. There's nothing else we can do."

Her love for him washed over her again, but she couldn't follow it down the dark alley this time. Nor could she muster any promises. "Take me."

Milos led the way out of his house, past the empty spot upon which their piano had once stood, which his parents had sold in exchange for two liters of contraband oil. Sarah's entire soul tingled in anticipation of her impending reunion with her family. She followed Milos out the front garden, down the trail covered in dry grass. Past normal people spewing normal chatter as if her family were not prisoners nearby. They walked very far, to the edge of town and then west along the sea a bit. What Sarah saw first was a boy in uniform, a swastika on the band around his arm, just like German soldiers who now frequented her shop. She registered his eyes—surprisingly boring, the color of mud. She had expected palpable evil, but what greeted her was a baby in the body of a soldier. This boy, just a little older than her with plain eyes, wouldn't harm her family. She began to walk to him.

Milos hissed in a low, harsh voice, "Sarah, you will not. I beg of you, no."

But she was just going to talk reasonably with this boy soldier. She was going to say she would give him everything she had. She had nothing, of course. But she did have some savings from the bakery. She would give that to him, and he would give her back her family. Her eyes were on the lookout for her family. *Where was her family?*

The boy soldier had watched her approach, but now he was diverted by something. A priest had walked up to the barbed-wire fence. Sarah recognized him, in fact: Pope Dimitris Thomatzidis, with his long black robe, giant, bushy beard, and tall black hat. He was a refugee from Samsun in coastal Turkey and a customer of the cheese lady's shop. Once, before the German occupation, Sarah had accidentally omitted sugar from a batch of bougatsas, and she remembered how kind he'd been, praising the custard pie, even asking for another slice, when the following customer had made a warranted fuss about it. Sarah had winced when she'd tasted it, but the pope had already gone.

Maybe the pope could help now. Maybe the Nazis would listen to him. Sarah nodded at him in recognition and tried to formulate a plan of attack. Her head grew wild with charts and thoughts, none of them coalescing. The pope nodded back. Then through the fence, he handed a cigarette to a man in his forties. A man whom Sarah gleaned was a Jewish prisoner.

But then she noticed a little boy sitting on the ground. Benjamin! He was playing with nothing. He was playing with dirt. He was not off dancing or reading. Beside him Sarah saw her parents. Her father in his brown tweed coat. It was so hot for a coat! Why was he wearing a coat? She started to trot that way. Milos reached for her.

"Leave me," she hissed. She walked faster, but Milos hung on to her arm. He was not letting her go, and all she wanted to do was go to her family. She hadn't seen them in over a year. A year!

She called out, "Mama." Benjamin looked up. His face broke into a giant smile. He nudged her mother's arm. Sarah was nearly there. She was nearly to them.

This was the moment that could have gone a thousand different ways. In the years since, Sarah had cataloged those ways—her fingers touched Benjamin's through the fence; Baba kissed her cheek through the fence; Mama said, *It's okay, darling. We love you. We forgive you.* So many permutations. So many chances. Maybe all of that happened, and then still Milos pulled her away. Or maybe all of that happened, and then the boy soldier took her. He understood she was Jewish, that she belonged to these prisoners, and he put her behind the fence with them. To die with them, but never to wonder what she read in their silent eyes.

Instead, none of this happened because the boy soldier saw Pope Thomatzidis approach the fence and hand the cigarette through the slats to the Jew. The boy soldier whistled, and as Sarah said, "Mama," as she ran to her family, a gunshot pierced the day's blue-green idyll. Then shouts— commands—that she didn't comprehend. She watched in mute horror as the Jew who had accepted the cigarette keeled to the ground, his head something bloody and terrible.

The boy soldier advanced toward a Jewish couple behind the fence, who had simply been standing in the vicinity of the fallen man. Sarah's screams froze inside as her eyes locked on the woman in a black-collared dress, a little girl's hand curled into her own. Her husband in a beautiful coat like the ones Sarah's father made.

Sarah pinched her thigh, aware of the specter of Milos behind her. Do something, she pleaded in mute telepathy. *Do something.* Her eyes closed at the screams. This time no gunshots, but the sound of something heavy crushing bone. When Sarah peeked her eyes open, at first she couldn't be sure if she was dead or alive. But her fingers fluttered and her toes curled, sending a message to her brain, that alive was indeed what she was. The couple now sprawled on the ground, and the boy soldier stood over them with his cane. The little girl was screaming *Mama, Mama, Mama,* in the most chilling shrill that had ever accosted Sarah's ears. An older girl clapped a hand over her mouth and moved her back.

Sarah searched wildly for her family, eventually locating them again—her mother with her turquoise eyes like Sarah's, so eerily still, with no bourekas to make or cucumbers to chop; her father with his ears that stuck out, that froze up as a child when his hat was stolen. And Benjamin—wise, kind Benjamin, who had longed to visit Odysseus's Lefkada. Oh, but not in this horrific way!

Again Sarah's attention was diverted as the boy soldier stalked back from the fence. Each stomp of his boots against dirt strummed the tenuous strings that connected Sarah to her parents and Benjamin. As the boy soldier passed Pope Thomatzidis, he yanked him by his beard and threw him to the ground. Sarah felt herself crumple down too, her ears thrumming with her heartbeat. She blinked open her eyes just in time to watch the boy soldier jump atop the pope's prone body, yielding a sickening crunch.

The boy soldier screamed something in German. The only word Sarah gleaned was *Juden*. Jews. A rumpled man approached from outside the fence. He was the translator, a prisoner, Sarah later understood. In Greek, he said, "You must go. You may not give gifts to the prisoners. Otherwise he will hurt more of them."

"She is frightened," Milos said to him, crouching down beside Sarah. "We will go."

But Sarah's eyes stayed locked on her family. She wished to die right there and then. She didn't know everything—in later months she'd learn of concentration camps and Auschwitz—but she knew the rumors from Saloniki. She knew that Jews were disappearing. And kneeling there, amid the dead and beaten Jews and the pope, she knew somehow that her family's fate was already sealed.

Milos pulled her up, and her limbs betrayed her, clicking back into her core to hold her up. Milos lifted Pope Thomatzidis to his feet and said, "*Ella*, we will help you."

Sarah's eyes stayed riveted to her family. She watched Benjamin put his hand to his mouth. He blew Sarah a little kiss. He didn't smile again. Just the kiss. Before Milos led her away, Sarah put a hand to her mouth. She couldn't feel her hand. She couldn't feel her lips. She blew her little brother a kiss in return.

◠◠

The next thing Sarah remembered was waking in their attic room. She was screaming, sobbing. Nightmares when she was awake. Nightmares when she was asleep. She didn't speak, to Milos or to anyone. Milos told the cheese lady she was expecting a baby. She was very sick. She needed some time off.

Sarah lay there in the bed where symphonies had once played as she and Milos had wound and bound their bodies with love. Only now, she prayed desperately for the courage to commit suicide. A few times she took a knife and ran the jagged edges against her neck. But she couldn't bring herself to do it.

Her family was gone, and even in joining them, she was a coward.

◠◠

A few weeks later, Milos came home from fishing. He sat on the bed, and Sarah inched away to its farthest border. He said he'd heard something he thought she should know. That he'd debated telling her, but he couldn't keep this from her. The night after they'd seen her family on Lefkada, Greek Resistance had helped a few Jews escape. The Jews were then hidden by local fishermen and had managed to flee to the mainland.

"Do you know who?" They were her first words in weeks, and they scraped her throat as she spoke. Her heart leaped a little with possibility, and she hated it anew, for the hope she thought she'd beaten out of it.

"I don't." Milos studied his hands. He'd once taken her eyes into his at every opportunity, but her eyes weren't accessible anymore.

"Do you think there was a young boy? A couple?"

His eyes didn't stray from his hands—hands that used to fill her with pleasure. "I do not think so."

And they both looked anywhere but at each other. They'd been children, really, whose only crime was that they'd loved each other when the world had gone insane. If not for Milos, Sarah would have been with her family. Then, if not for him, she would have died with her family.

And if I could wave a wand and choose a past without you, Milos, would I do it? It is a question that has plagued me for seventy-some years—and I am still no closer to an answer.

chapter thirty-five

Joey

florida
2019

Joey kept reminding herself that they weren't in Corfu anymore, but the evidence urged otherwise. There was Bea's easel on the taupe stone patio, with an unfinished rendering of the nude backside of a woman bent over a table. There was the long wooden farm table adorned with ceramic jugs of sunflowers. There was Leo, deep in conversation with her father about barefoot ultra-marathons.

And there was Bea, emerging from inside holding a water pitcher with lemon wedges. She wore teal separates comprising a midriff-baring bustier tank and a floaty, tea-length skirt.

Grant whispered, "Bea's abs can work it. I bet you inherit those abs, babe."

Leo broke out of his conversation with Scott to interject, "There is no question that Bea has ageless abs, but she's wearing a terrible shade of—"

"Green." Joey laughed, even though the topic of ageless abs had made her remember her bingeing again. She patted her stomach—puffy, the abs buried deep. She told herself that was okay and tried to believe it. "You're so predictable, Winn." She explained to Grant, "Leo used to walk around Corfu with this botany book. He has a narrow concept of valid shades of gr—"

Joey was interrupted by a startling sound, like a thousand frogs croaking in unison. Bea set down the wooden thing from which she'd created the noise. She bent her knees in the way of a small curtsy. "It's a didgeridoo."

"A what?" asked Joey.

"A didgeridoo." Her father went to the barbecue and lifted a burger with his tongs, checking its doneness and apparently, by its drop back onto the grill, deciding it needed more. "Lily must have left it behind."

"Where is Lily, anyway?" asked Leo, and his nonchalance didn't fool Joey. She shot him a look.

"Our creative Lily is at the seminal cover shoot for her magazine. She was so sad to miss this dinner, Leo, but the shoot couldn't be shifted. She had a really interesting concept." Scott crunched his nose, as if to summon Lily's fashion-speak. "I think it was juxtaposing offbeat musical instruments with flower outfits."

"Not flower outfits," said Bea. "Victorian-era high fashion."

"That's some enterprising girl you have." Leo glanced at Joey. "Two enterprising girls."

"Leo." Joey flushed. "You don't have—"

"Two enterprising girls is right," said Scott. "But truly, Leo, Joey here, she's a brilliant lawyer."

"Dad, I'm not a lawyer anymore," said Joey, prickly at the cavalier way her father sometimes treated her art—as if it was a hobby, as if she didn't have the right to her high level of devotion.

"Now I'm hoping for some grandchildren," said Scott, stamping out Joey's hurt with another sensitive topic. "No pressure, kids, but of my best friends, I'm the last man standing."

"Maybe you should have had more kids," muttered Joey.

Grant put a hand on her thigh. "We're working on it."

"You are?" said Bea, at the same time Leo said, "Are you guys now?" in a calm, toneless voice, and Scott said, "Bravo!"

"We are?" said Joey tightly.

"Well, at some point. We've talked about this."

"Yeah." Joey did want kids. That was the thing. And every attendee over fifty at her shower had given her some variation of *you're not getting any younger*. But she didn't want that pressure. She wanted to nurture her art now. She *needed* to nurture her art first, and she needed everyone to back off.

Grant said, "You can do both. Art and kids."

"Can we talk about this later?"

"I have to say, I disagree, Grant," said Bea, and Joey eyed her mother in surprise. "It's very difficult to care for your kids at the same time you're creating. A painting requires all of a person. You have to be in a very specific zone."

"That's right," said Joey slowly.

"You just don't want to be called *Grandma*." Scott chuckled.

"I won't be *Grandma*," said Bea. "And none of those cutesy variations like *Glamma*. Nothing that starts with a *G*. I'll be something nice, like Unicorn."

"My kids are going to call you *Unicorn*?" asked Joey.

"Unicorn it will be." Scott kissed Bea's cheek. "I can hardly believe the whole gang's together again." Scott's phone buzzed on the table. He checked it briefly and turned it over. "Well, minus a few players..."

"And plus one," said Grant in a breezy way.

"The plus one is the most important one." Scott walked back over to the grill.

"The plus one is definitely the most important one," whispered Joey into his ear. She watched Leo watch them. She glanced down at the burger her father now put before her.

"To Grant." Leo raised his beer. "To Grant and my old friend Joey. I'm honored to be here for your wedding."

"We're honored to have you here, Leo." Scott finished doling out the burgers. "Now tell us everything that's happened the last fifteen years, son."

"A son!" said Scott. "You have a son, Leo. I can hardly believe it."

Leo showed a picture on his phone of a kid with floppy blond hair, bright-blue eyes, and a toothy smile.

"He's so cute, Leo, wow." Scott flipped through the photos. "A lot of Rand, eh?"

"His eyes." Leo zoomed in. "The eyes are pure Rand."

"The eyes…" It was so obvious to Joey now. The eyes were pure Lily too. Everyone always said Bea, but their mother's were almond, clear, without nuance. The wider shape, the murkier quality—that was all Rand. That they could look at this picture of Arthur and still skirt around it revolted her. She was glad it was all going to come out soon. Joey felt Bea watch her with trepidation.

"The hair is Maisy," said Scott. "But much lighter even."

"The hair is actually his mother's," said Leo. "His mother has very blond hair."

It was a new fact about Grown Leo. Grown Leo liked women who had very blond hair.

Bea looked up from her planner open on her lap. "JoJo, we still have so much to do this week."

"Do we? Because I don't really have time. The painting for Edith is my top priority."

"What Joey means is, her painting is her top priority, after getting married." Grant propped a loafer on his knee.

"Of course, that's what I meant." Joey squeezed his hand. "I don't care about the details. Give me a sunny day with no rain, and beyond that, Grant and I don't care."

"What Joey means is, she cares very much, but not about the minutiae. And by the way, babe, forecast says eighty-four and partly sunny with only a seventeen percent chance of rain."

"I don't like that seventeen percent. Do you—"

"Well, Joey, I don't care that you don't care about the minutiae," said Bea. "I'd like you to care about it for five minutes."

"Fine," Joey said. "Just…fine."

Bea sighed so heavily that her outfit fluttered around her, giving her the appearance of a peacock on the precipice of flight. "So, just to clarify," said Bea, standing and stretching in such a way that her abs peeped out to say hello, which Joey was sure was the entire point, "you've made the Hot Tamale and Sour Patch Kid bags, and that is about the extent of your contribution to this wedding?"

"I wanted to elope, Mom," said Joey. "You were the one who said you'd plan the whole thing."

"Joey," said Scott, "show a bit of gratitude to your mother. She's running herself ragged."

Joey appraised her mother. She did not look one iota of

ragged. For all Joey knew, her mother was going to show up on Saturday in her own wedding gown. Her second coming. The viciousness of her thoughts swelled Joey to a height from which she swiftly plummeted. She wished she wasn't so damn angry.

"Sorry, Dad," she started to say, as her father stood up. Scott didn't anger quickly. She hated to be the one hurting him.

"Everyone, please excuse me. I have to run a very quick errand," Scott said.

"You have to go now? I said I'm sorry."

"I'll be back in a jiff, Joey." He gave a half smile. "Now don't anyone move a muscle, okay?"

The screen door closed, and Bea slumped her shoulders. "I don't know how much longer I can keep up this charade."

"Stop. Dad could come back any moment."

"Oh, I *know* where he went, Joey." Bea flicked the pages of her list and then with her fist smacked it onto the table. "He has some surprise for you. Some *big* surprise photo book thing, which I'm sure you'll appreciate to the nines and lavish attention on him because he's your perfect father and I'm just the mother who birthed you without an epidural and planned ninety-nine point nine percent of your wedding."

"We're really grateful," said Grant at the same time as Joey said, "This isn't a fair contest at this stage, Mom. Dad's not the one who had an affair."

"Let's not go there today." Leo set down his phone. Arthur and his blue eyes lit up on the screensaver.

"We haven't really gone there yet," said Joey. "That's the problem."

"Jonesey…"

"What, Leo? Lily's going to be home later, you know. Your *sister*, Lily. Your sister is going to walk through that door in some outlandish outfit with those same blue eyes. With Rand's blue eyes. With Arthur's blue eyes. And you're going to have to keep quiet yet again. You're going to have to look at your sister and give her back to us because she doesn't know she belongs to you too. Doesn't that just kill you?"

"*Your sister, Lily?*"

Joey swiveled to the voice, to Lily standing in the sliding door in a majestic floral headdress. She had a hand on her didgeridoo. Her blue eyes were soft, contemplative, like an adult helping a child finish an easy puzzle. Joey watched those blue eyes melt from curiosity to confusion.

"Your sister, Lily? But...?"

Joey died in the span of the poison reaching Lily's brain.

When no one spoke, Lily slammed the didgeridoo into the ground. But then all of her seemed to deflate, and Lily's hand released the didgeridoo. It fell to the ground with a clang. She whispered very softly, "Please will someone tell me what that means."

chapter thirty-six
Joey

florida

2019

"What do you mean I'm Leo's sister? So…Leo is my brother?" Lily's headdress slipped crookedly on her head. Still, no one spoke.

"It's over." Joey placed a hand over her wild heart. She could hardly believe it had been expelled into the world.

"Holy…" said Grant.

"So you're not my mother?" Lily asked a white-faced Bea.

Joey got up and put an arm around her sister. "Come here, Lil. Sit."

"I don't wanna sit, Joey." Lily threw her off. "I want to know what the hell is going on."

"Please, Lil," said Bea. "Calm down."

"Don't tell me what to fucking do." Lily sank into the chair Grant shifted beneath her. "I just found out I have a brother. Him!" Lily's eyes fixed on Leo's for the first time. "Wait, Leo is my brother? I don't get it." That was the thing about those Winn eyes. You could see everything in them. "So you're not my mom?"

"Mom is your mom, Lil…" Joey stood on her tiptoes and stroked the fuzzy strawberry hair on the perimeter of Lily's forehead that poked out from under her headdress.

"Get off me, Joey!" Lily shoved her off and grabbed ahold of the didgeridoo. "So then, what? Daddy's not my daddy?"

"Oh, Lil."

Lily held the didgeridoo to her chest. "I want you all to tell me the truth."

"Daddy's not your biological dad." Bea took a tentative step toward Lily. "But he's your father in every way that counts. I'm so sorry you're finding out this way. I'm so sorry, baby. Lily Pad, come here. I'll explain it, and maybe you can understand—"

"Understand what? That you've been lying to me my entire life?" Bea's head jerked like she'd been slapped. "That you had an affair with—wait a minute—Leo's father?"

"Lily," said Grant. "You have to know—"

"Shut up!" screamed Lily. She clapped her hands over her ears. "Shut up, shut up! You're not even family. Shut the hell up."

"Lily!" said Joey. "That's so rude! And he *is* family!"

"You all knew?" Lily glanced from person to person. "All of you? Leo?"

Joey watched all of their frozen faces reflected in the glass door.

"Lily, I…" Leo closed his eyes.

"Even Daddy?" asked Lily in a heartbreakingly weak lilt. Joey berated herself for anytime in the past week she'd subconsciously blamed Lily for this. This wasn't Lily's fault. Lily was the casualty.

"Dad doesn't know." Bea's lips were chapped and pursed. "Dad doesn't know, baby."

"Well, that's not exactly true," said a voice from the side of the house.

Joey saw his white legs before she saw his face. Those skinny white legs in khaki shorts such a pale shade of beige they practically melded with his skin tone. He must have come from the gravel path that began at the driveway and ended at the steps on the far side of the patio.

The words weren't comporting for Joey. Joey's eyes traveled to her father's face. It was devoid of surprise, not gelling with the magnitude of the shock waves.

"I actually do know," whispered Scott, and as he hung his head, Joey's world tipped off its axis.

"You know?" said Bea. "How could you know?"

"What do you mean, you know?" said Joey.

"Scott?" said Leo.

"Daddy," whispered Lily.

Scott closed his eyes and made a humming sound.

It was Tuesday. Tuesday was the worst day of the week. That's what the old woman had told Joey all that time ago in Corfu, when she'd stood outside the synagogue waiting for her father. Then her last day with Leo was a Tuesday. Then her grandfather died on a Tuesday. Joey dug in her purse for her evil eye charm. Out came a peach lip gloss. Out came an empty Tic Tac container and a bunch of receipts she removed with her napkin because she'd read somewhere that touching them was basically akin to licking the floor of a Monsanto plant.

Where the hell was her evil eye charm? In fury, Joey threw her empty purse. She intended it to go far. At least to the potted cactus by the steps. Instead, the purse crumpled in unceremonious fashion to the ground by Joey's feet.

"Oh, *you're* upset, Joey?" said Lily. "Oh, really, *you're* the one who gets to throw a tantrum?"

"You all get to tantrum." Grant put a hand on Joey's shoulder.

Her father continued to hum with his eyes shut, rocking back and forth like a crazy person.

"Scott." Bea's mouth opened and then closed. "Scott, I don't—"

For a very long time, Joey watched her father with no pity, no pity at all.

"Someone needs to tell me what is going on!" said Lily.

As Scott buried his face in his hands, Bea walked Lily through the highlights. Meeting Rand in the early eighties. Harry Berry. The letters G hid. The reunion in Monterey. The Corfu plan. The feigned spontaneous meeting in the building on Delvinioti Street. The families becoming family. Lily's Place. The day Bea realized she was pregnant. An education on fertility windows. Welcome to the world, Lily Pad. Those blue eyes. Those blue eyes locked on your father—on Scott—and fell in love. I—we—couldn't take him from you. Leo found out. We stopped going to Corfu. Joey found out last week. The End.

"I can't believe it." Lily crunched down on her lip. "I just…"

Joey forced the word out: "Dad?"

Her father coughed a few times. Finally, he said, "I'm so sorry."

"I don't get it, Dad. You knew?"

"I knew." Her father sat down on the lawn, even though

it had rained earlier. He began plucking up clumps of wet grass.

"You knew how, Scott?" said Bea. "You figured it out what, when we stopped going to Corfu?"

Crickets. Then "Earlier."

"When Lily was born? You knew when Lily was born, and you didn't say?"

The moon materialized, like a wedge of peach with a mushy center. The mosquitoes converged on Joey's right foot. She scratched her ankle so violently that it began to bleed.

"Before Lily was born." Her father's voice was barely audible.

Joey's eyes suddenly caught on the vase of sunflowers on the table. It smacked her: the night she was eleven.

"I heard voices," she said, and everyone looked at her.

"Babe." Grant patted her shoulder like she was a delicate mental patient. "Babe."

She shoved him off. "No, stop. Listen. I really heard voices. When I was eleven. I'd had a nightmare and went to the terrace. I don't remember what I saw. I just remember being back in bed. You tucked me back in, Dad. You said to imagine a field of sunflowers. You said I didn't see anything."

"Scott!" Bea's eyes widened.

"Don't Scott me!" he shouted, and instinctively, Joey covered her eyes.

"It wasn't you," Joey said, it all dawning. "I remembered it the last summer we were on Corfu, that time when I was eleven. I think I briefly wondered if you and Maisy were having an affair. But I guess I forgot about it."

"Me and Maisy?" Scott shook his head. "Oh, honey."

"But it wasn't you and Maisy."

"I don't understand," said Bea.

"*I* don't understand!" said Lily.

"The voices I must have heard on the terrace were Mom and Rand. Seriously, Mom? In plain view?"

"We never did anything on the terrace," said Bea. "Give me a little credit, Joey."

"You deserve no credit. Zero credit. Ahhhhhhhhh." Lily let out a banshee scream. Then she gave the didgeridoo a long blast. Eventually Lily removed her mouth from the lip and propped it against the table.

"They were just talking," said Scott. He'd now torn up a sizable patch of lawn. "But they thought we were asleep, me and Maisy. So the talking wasn't normal talking. It was lovers talking—"

"Scott, that was nine years before our last summer. I don't—"

"It was *lovers* talking, Bea, and I didn't want Joey to catch on. She was such a perceptive kid. I walked you back, JoJo, and there were sunflowers on the kitchen table, so I guess I blabbered something about them—"

"I've hated sunflowers ever since," said Joey. "I don't get it, Dad."

"I don't either, Dad," said Lily. Then her face changed. She tore off her headdress. "He's not even my dad. Fuck, he's not even my dad."

"I *am* your dad. Please, Lily. I *am* your dad."

"When did you know?" asked Bea.

Scott exhaled deeply through his mouth. It was a long exhale, like blowing out birthday candles. Like huffing and puffing to blow the whole house down.

"I knew before we were married," he whispered. "I knew about Harry Berry."

Bea looked at Scott like she'd never seen him before. "But I never talked about Rand. Not to you or anyone. And definitely not about Harry Berry."

"You did," said Scott. "You were skating around the neighborhood with that girlfriend you had. Remember her? Her name was—"

"Veronica." Still Bea looked blank. "Right. With the great legs."

"Yes, Veronica. You'd just gotten back from Corfu. You wore these tiny jean shorts to roller-skate around the neighborhood. I was studying outside on a blanket on the lawn. I don't even think you noticed me. You girls stopped in front of the mailbox. You were looking for a letter—"

"Harry Berry..."

"You told the whole story to Veronica. How you'd fallen in love. How he was going to write to you in code. You weren't surprised there was no letter yet. You'd just gotten back that week."

"No." Bea put a hand to her mouth.

"It's the least proud moment of my life," he choked. "I've loved you since I could remember, Bea. You were this gangly girl dancing in the sprinklers. I loved you when my father died and you brought me a canvas and paintbrushes and told me painting helped when you were lost. Do you remember that? You sat beside me and did your own sketching, and I painted only black on that canvas. You looked at my terrible painting and said, *I'm really sorry.*

"That was the year before, Bea. I was lost that year. My mom went to pieces, and I moved home to take care of her. Otherwise, she did things like forget to shower for two weeks. That's why I was studying for the bar at home. That's why I was there when you got back from Corfu. We talked a bit then. I thought maybe you were even flirting with me. When you said the whole Harry Berry thing—"

"No!"

"Well, it's certainly the thing I'm most ashamed of in my whole life. You were at classes that summer. Your dad was working. Your mother hardly went outside. Just at—"

"Four in the afternoon," said Bea slowly.

Scott nodded. "To get the mail. But the mailman came around two. A few times, I went to your mailbox. I peeked inside. I told myself I was just curious. You remember, your mailbox was right next to mine."

"Yes." Bea put a hand to her throat.

"Oh my God," said Joey.

"A few days later there was a letter."

"Harry Berry," said Bea.

"Fuck this Harry Berry," said Lily. "Can we get to the part where we talk about what shitty people you both are? Where we talk about how you deceived me my whole life?"

"I want to hear this part," said Joey. "Go on, Dad."

"Well, you can figure out the rest. I took the letter back to my room. It was just temporary, I told myself. I'd read it and see what was so great about this Harry Berry guy. What he had that I didn't. Then I'd put it back. But I couldn't bring myself to read the letter—"

"Well, isn't that saintly?" Bea almost laughed.

"Takes one to know one," snapped her father. "I didn't mean that. Love, I didn't mean that. It's just…" He ran a fistful of grass through his fingers.

"But my mom took those letters," said Bea. "She denied it and said there were no letters, but I knew it could only have been her."

Scott grimaced. "No. It wasn't her."

"But my mom must have taken those letters," said Bea. "She must have because all this time I've *hated* her for taking those letters."

Scott hung his head. "I'm so sorry, my love."

"It was you," said Bea. "Oh my God, it was you who— wait, so you took my letters too? The ones I wrote to Rand?"

Scott grimaced. "Yes."

"How *could* you? How could you do—"

"I just thought if you got to know me, if you just got to know *me*, you would love me. If you just gave me a chance!"

"I *did* give you a chance! I gave you a chance because I was heartbroken. I gave you a chance because I needed something to hold on to."

"And you loved me. Once you loved me—and I knew it was genuine love, just as I always suspected we would have—I put Harry Berry out of my mind. You chose me."

"But I *didn't* choose you! I only chose you because you deceived me!"

"And then you deceived me. And then you took me to Corfu."

"Oh boy," said Grant.

"So you knew the whole time, Scott?" asked Leo. "But…why would you spend every summer with the man your wife was having an affair with? That sounds like some insane mode of torture."

"Did you know when we first met?" asked Bea. "In the stairwell?"

"We met in the stairwell," said Joey, to Grant and Lily as much as to herself.

Scott said, "I didn't know exactly. There was something that felt funny to me. I'd wondered why you were so keen on renting a place in Corfu that summer when you'd never expressed an interest in going back there. All of a sudden, it was *We have to do this, I found a place*, all of it. But no, I didn't know in the stairwell."

"You masterminded a meeting with your lover in the stairwell?" asked Lily.

"So when?" asked Bea, ignoring her.

"I figured it out that night, in the shower. I thought about the letters."

"I thought you didn't read them."

"I didn't at first. But then I did."

"You read Rand's letters to me? And mine to Rand? Oh, Scott."

"I did. I'm so ashamed of it. But I did. And in the shower, I remembered something. I remembered how he signed the letters. Not Rand, but—"

"Randall," said Bea, white-faced. "He went by Randall then."

"It didn't take a genius to put two and two together."

"I've heard enough," said Lily, and stood. "And don't any of you fucking follow me." She stormed inside with the didgeridoo.

"We should go after her," said Scott.

"No, you should finish the story, Dad," said Joey. "You should explain why on earth you'd realize your wife had orchestrated this elaborate affair and then stay?"

"Oh, JoJo." Her father finally got up from the grass. He walked over to her. She flinched, and he stopped. "It's complicated."

"It's not so complicated, Dad! Leo kept it secret for fifteen years to give you a life with Lily. To give Lily a life with you. And all this time, you knew! Do you know that's why Leo broke up with me our last summer? Do you know how it tore both our lives apart?"

"I'm sorry. I'm more sorry than you'll ever know to both you and Leo. But you asked me why I would stay. In the whole affair, I'm the initial culprit, I suppose—"

"You manipulated me to marry you," said Bea. "You decided who got to be with who."

"I suppose I did, but I think I paid in spades for it, my love. I stood by as you went to him. As you said you were going to spend the day drawing in a meadow and you went to his sailboat instead. When you announced you were pregnant, and I knew it couldn't be mine. I'm not an idiot, darling. I've always been good at math."

The only sound was the maniacal tap-tap-tap of Bea's fingernails on the water pitcher. "I can't believe this. Do you know how I've made my mother suffer for breaking up me and Rand? And it wasn't even her! Oh…I just…" Her face wrenched with sudden startling emotion. "Oh God, it wasn't her."

Scott went to Bea, but Bea thrust out an arm. "No! Don't come near me."

Scott went to Joey, but she also put out a hand. "Not now, Dad."

Her father stood before them like a traveling salesman, closing up his briefcase in defeat. When he turned, Joey saw his chinos damp with grass stains.

"I'm done." Joey stood and pulled at Grant's arm. Leo rose too.

"JoJo, please don't be upset with me."

"Please don't be upset with you! Dad, I don't even know how to respond to that. Lily, Leo, and I didn't ask to be trapped in all these sick lies."

"You're getting married this week, JoJo," her father said. "Please. I've dreamed of walking my baby girl down the aisle. I've dreamed of this week since you were born."

"You know who else has dreamed about this week, Scott?" said Bea. "Me. I've dreamed of this week since she was born!"

"*You know who else has dreamed of this week?*" Everyone stared at her. Joey's throat was hoarse from the shouting.

"Oh, forget it," she said softly, and walked to the door. And as Grant took her hand, she wondered even if she'd told the truth. If she ever had dreamed of this week at all.

chapter thirty-seven

Joey

florida
2019

They watched Leo speed off on his bike. Joey shoved aside Grant's boxing gloves and the tangle of his hand wraps and collapsed in the passenger seat. Her body had nearly stopped twitching when Grant said, "Oh jeez…"

Joey watched a figure dart from the house, tugging a massive suitcase on wheels that bobbed down the front steps. Lily. Grant rolled down his window.

"I just want to say," said Lily, poking her head in, subdued, tight. "You guys aren't my favorite people right now, but as favorite people go, you've got a substantial leg up on the parents."

"Lil." Joey rubbed circles into her forehead. "Do you want to sleep over?"

"Yes." Lily pitched herself into the backseat. She tapped Grant's shoulder. "Do you mind getting my suitcase? I don't have, like, an iota of energy left."

"Sure. Got it." He unbuckled his seat belt.

"That's a big suitcase," Joey said.

"Are you seriously going there now?" Lily said.

"No." Joey's eyes turned compassionately on her little sister. "I'm sorry, Lil. I'm here for you, I really am. I really want to be."

"Joey, you guys have a bed for me, right? My back doesn't do so great on couches."

Joey smiled in spite of it all. "We have a comfy couch. Two of them, in fact."

Lily sighed, like she'd just been informed they were dumping her in the Sahara with a scorpion-infested sleeping bag.

Grant got back in the car. "Lil, that's quite the packing job for one night."

"Who said I'm staying with you just one night?" she asked, lying horizontal now. Her hands cupped her head, her elbows splayed out, her copper hair a waterfall off the seat.

"I didn't mean…you're welcome to stay as long as you want." Grant started the motor. "As long as you put your seat belt on."

"Are you sure you're okay with that?" whispered Joey over the irritated clacking of metal from the backseat.

"Yes. She needs us."

"You're amazing. Thanks."

"Of course. I'm her family too."

"It's a wonder you still want to be in our family, after tonight." And then, as Grant opened his mouth to speak, Joey said, "Do you mind if we're quiet for a bit? My head is pounding."

Grant turned onto A1A from Linton, and she saw him open his mouth and then shut it like he was unsure, like his jaw wanted to work, not to go to waste. Joey just closed her eyes, and maybe it was the exhaustion or the stress, or both, but she fell into a quick, hard sleep. And immediately the deserts welcomed her in.

She was the Joey on the edge of the desert.

And she was also the Joey trying to save her.

⌒

As they lay in bed, Grant said, "We have to talk about it."

"I just…I'm not ready to talk about it." Joey shifted her head in the crook of his shoulder. She couldn't get comfortable there tonight. She wanted to curl into a solitary ball facing the wall, but she knew that would hurt his feelings.

"Babe."

She moved onto her back so she still nestled in Grant's nook, but now she also stared at the glow-in-the-dark constellation on the wall. It made the room slightly less dark. She always hesitated to raise that issue.

"I just…since Leo told me, I saw it so black and white. Mom was the terrible one and Dad was the victim. But now it's all turned on its head. And my mom's not innocent, but God, Grant. I've been kind of awful to her this past week."

"Maybe it's not up to you to dole out the blame. Maybe you should just leave that to the Big Guy upstairs. Anyway, don't you think they've suffered enough? I think things will look different in the morning."

He didn't understand. So much could happen before morning.

Grant clasped her face to his with a ferocity that surprised her. "In good times and in bad. I want you to remember that."

He held her, and for a long time, she let herself be held. "It's gonna be okay, baby. I promise you it is." And Grant rolled over to his side of the bed, leaving Joey to stare at his lovely, strong back dappled with starlight.

Joey urged her eyes to stay open, please to hang on—she really wasn't ready to go to the other side.

Lily slumbered like an angel with her hair fanned out on the pillow and her hands clasped neatly over her stomach.

"I wish she was always like this," whispered Joey.

"What?" asked Grant. "Mute?"

"Ha. Maybe that too. No, what I meant was it reminds me of when she was little. She was so cute and sweet when she was sleeping."

Lily twisted toward the door. "Are you guys watching me sleep? Because that's creepy."

"No. I had to grab some supplies for Edith's. I'm sorry if we woke you." Joey started to walk in, but Grant pulled her arm.

"Good luck today, babe." He kissed her. "Bye, Lil."

"Bye, Grant." Lily reached her arms to the ceiling in a wide-eyed sleepy stretch. "Joey, do you know this thing is like lying on cement?"

Joey didn't respond, just rifled through her drawer of oils and piled them into a canvas bag. Then she stopped, went over to the couch, and perched on the armrest. "Lil, how are you feeling?"

"Fine." Lily turned her long frame to face the back of the couch. She wore a pair of Joey's pajama bottoms that were like pedal pushers on her coltish legs.

"Seriously, Lil. How are you doing?" Joey felt emotion

swell in her throat. It wasn't fair that this had all crashed down onto Lily. It so wasn't fair.

"I'm doing terrible, Joey. I just found out Dad's not my real dad. How do you *think* I'm doing?"

"I'm sorry, Lil. I'm so sorry you have to go through this. But I didn't do this to you."

"But you didn't tell me right when you found out."

"Lil." Joey reached over to pat her arm.

Lily flinched. "Just go. Just leave." Joey got up. Lily twisted back to her. "Don't leave!"

"But...you just told me to!"

"How can you leave me at a time like this?" she wailed.

Joey had never seen her sister so undone. "I wish I didn't have to go. But I need to finish Edith's. The party for the Sri Lankan jewelry launch is tomorrow."

"Oh yeah." Lily sat up, and Joey swore that just like this, with her hair all mussed and her crop top strap askew off a shoulder, Lily could pose for the cover of her magazine.

"Maybe that's what I'll do, throw myself into work today," said Lily, chewing on a fingernail. "I had a good idea last night actually. I wrote it to Kat. I think I'll do a video blog. Something really raw. I'll pose on your sad couch with these awful walls—the aqua is way too bright, Jo, it's like living in Candy Land—and I'll tell the whole sordid thing..."

"Lil..."

"But what do I wear? What says serious and sad, but still with a point of view?"

"Lil!"

"Yeah?" Her sister folded her legs beneath her and slapped her own face, once each cheek, hard.

Joey grabbed her sister's hands. "It's okay to cry, you know, Lil."

Lily looked away. "I don't want to cry, Joey. Weak people cry."

"No," Joey said emphatically, remembering those days and months and years on her couch, eating and watching TV and not crying. Just numb. "Strong women cry, Lil. I promise you that."

"Oh," said Lily. "Oh." Suddenly she crunched her face like a wrinkled pug. Joey felt Lily's pulse in their hands, or maybe it was her own. Eventually Lily's face unfolded. "Nope. I think my tear ducts are broken."

Joey rubbed her thumb along the webbing between Lily's index and middle fingers. "Here, I have an idea. What's a place you feel really safe? What's a place you go to and it's like…it's like a big hug?"

Lily looked thoughtful. "The beach."

"The beach? Really? That's my place too, Lil. Okay, so go to the beach today, and let yourself cry. This isn't the day to do a video blog. If you don't let yourself cry, then…"

Joey stared at the wall. How had she never noticed it was way too bright?

"Then what?"

"Then I think you get really hard inside. I think you get really hard and tough and it takes forever to go sweet and soft again."

"Joey," said Lily in a small voice, "will you meet me on the beach later to cry?"

Joey felt something rise up in her throat. "Oh, Lil. I wish I could. But I've got to paint all day."

"Please."

"Okay, Lil." Joey patted her sister's hand. "I'll take a little break later."

"Atlantic Avenue at six?"

"Yeah. That works."

"One more thing. Can you give me my brother's number?"

"Oh." Joey's vision fuzzed as she thumbed through her phone. She rattled off the number.

"Do you think he'll want to talk to me?"

"I know he'll want to talk to you. He came all this way for you."

"Just for me?"

Joey didn't answer. She got to her feet, grabbed her bag of art supplies, and walked to the door. Lily rose and followed after her.

"Where are you going?" asked Joey.

Lily rolled her eyes. "To finish sleeping in your bed, obviously. That couch is horrendous. New walls, new couch. We really need to get your house in order."

chapter thirty-eight
Sarah

corfu
1945

In November 1945, the war was finally over, and the ferry deposited Sarah at the Corfu Town port.

Ever since her family had been briefly imprisoned on Lefkada nearly a year and a half prior, each day had lasted an eternity. Once the war had ended and Milos's family had deemed it safe for her to return to Corfu, Sarah had purchased a ferry ticket and bid Milos the quickest of good-byes, silently enduring his pleas not to leave.

She'd let him kiss her one more time though. Maybe it had been a gift for herself too. Either way, she'd felt a deep, heart-wrenching well of conviction that it would be their last of a lifetime.

Now Sarah trudged through her old city abounding in demolished storefronts and buildings reduced to rubble—but inexplicably alight in bustle and chatter. She sensed a palpable shift though when she crossed westward into the ruins of the Jewish quarter. As she walked the old familiar alleys, she was assaulted by chilling quiet. Once, not long ago, she couldn't take two steps without running into a friend or an aunt. But now shops were destroyed, and others boarded up. The few people she passed weren't Jewish, but unfamiliar Greeks.

There was the market where she and Rachel once scurried underfoot, haggling for textiles as entrusted by her father and translating sometimes for Italian soldiers. There was the Italian synagogue, decimated. There was the Romaniote synagogue, still standing but blackened ash marring its once vivid yellow siding.

And there, up the slope of Velissariou, was her father's shop, one window shattered but the other intact. Sarah pressed her fingertips to the rain-smeared windowpane and noticed something unfamiliar and framed hanging there. Slowly she read it. JEWISH, in bold letters. A proclamation signed by the Germans and their Greek collaborators, ensuring no one would frequent her father's shop. Without thinking, Sarah found herself bursting inside, yanking off the frame, and throwing it to the ground. The glass broke, skating across the floor. And then it was quiet again, the machines and textiles looted—empty inside.

Empty, and then teeming with ghosts.

With shaky steps, Sarah made it back outside. As a little girl, she'd stood with her face pressed against the glass, making silly faces at her father before scampering off to school. He'd chide her later, for how he had to scrub off her lip prints before customers arrived. But still, he always played along, sticking his thumbs in his ears and contorting his face into funny, ugly shapes in return.

What had Sarah thought, after all? That her father would be sitting in his chair again, threading a needle?

Sarah keeled over and had to crouch down. Her eyesight

blurred with the cobblestones polished by all those vanished feet. She *had* thought it, that they'd be waiting here for her. Or hoped it at least—by slipping briefly into fairy tales.

But as Sarah grappled to stand and walked to the entry of her old apartment building, almost peculiarly intact amid all the destruction, she feared she was perhaps the last Jew alive on the island.

It took Sarah ten minutes to coax herself up the stairs. She turned the knob—locked. The air was sweet and a bit like sewage, not the charcoal scent of kitchen fire that used to greet Sarah at the entry, pointing to her mother over the stove, stirring something lovely in their great black pot. Sarah knocked softly, and an old, sour lady answered the door with a liver-spotted face and gray tendrils escaping her black kerchief. A lady who was not Sarah's mother. "Yes?" The girth of her successfully blocked the doorframe.

"This…this is my home," Sarah managed to say.

"This is my home now, Jew!" The lady flashed gums so red they were burgundy.

"But…but I used to live here. With my family."

"Oh yes? Prove it." The lady crossed her arms over her chest.

"We have a family chart on the wall." Sarah strained to remember other things. "And my parents' wedding document. A ketubah."

"I don't know what you're talking about. And if I did know what you were talking about, I would suspect those things were gone."

"Gone?" Sarah shuddered.

"Burned, probably." She shrugged. "Hold here."

The lady disappeared inside, giving Sarah a peek of the home that used to be hers, with their art, their cheap, stupid art, on the walls! The painting of pink roses that her mother adored—and then it was eclipsed as the lady returned.

She thrust a wooden cage into Sarah's startled hands. "He is your rabbit, eh? You are lucky we fed him. Be gone now, or I will shove you in the ovens just like the rest of them."

Sarah flinched at the spite. Ovens? She didn't yet know of ovens. She came eye-to-eye with Penelope, the apple of her brother's eye. The door slammed shut as she whispered, "It's a girl rabbit, not a boy."

Somehow Sarah stumbled down the stairs. With Benjamin's bunny rabbit in hand, she wandered through the ruins of her town to the synagogue. They called it Scuola Greca. They were Romaniotes—the first Jews outside Judea. They'd been so proud of that once. It was always important to know they were Jews, Romaniotes. They'd cherished those labels, and then they were murdered for them.

Sarah walked inside the temple, past the well from which she used to collect water, and saw the back part in rubble. She heard the murmur of voices overhead, presumably in the sanctuary. She stepped down to the wing that once housed Rabbi Nechama's office, no longer identifiable if she hadn't known where he'd once sat and learned. She remembered what Costas had said about him, how he'd been made to hand a bath towel to the German commandant, and she swallowed hard and coughed into the sleeve of her folksy Lefkada dress. She walked to the edge of the rabbi's old office space to peer across a wall reduced to nothing. She'd expected to see her old Talmud Torah school, which had abutted the synagogue—but that too was gone.

She had to get out of there. If she didn't see another person soon, a Jew, she was going to leap out of her body.

Sarah felt her feet quicken, now running up the stairs. She burst into the sanctuary, initially heartened at the sight of life. Jews. Her heart quivered as she spotted a familiar profile kneeling on the floor, polishing a pew, but it wasn't until Sarah had hastened across the room that she realized who it was.

Roza—Rachel's mother.

A sob arose in Sarah's throat. "Roza?"

The woman looked up with absent eyes. She had aged immeasurably since Sarah had last seen her, not even three years prior. She wore a prison uniform—dingy white with black stripes—and her face, once perpetually alight, bore such visible pain that Sarah flinched.

"Sarah," Roza said slowly. "Sarah Batis?"

"Yes. Oh, Roza." Sarah couldn't help it. She set Penelope in her cage on the floor and dove down and threw herself into Roza's arms. She clutched Roza's shoulders, now as tiny as kumquats. "Roza, what happened?"

Roza clenched her rag to her chest, enduring the hug. Reluctantly, Sarah released her grip. "They're gone, Sarah. They're all gone."

It couldn't be. It just couldn't. Roza's face didn't flicker as she recited them. "My Menachem. My Matathias. My Rachel. My brother's girl, Stemma. Gone."

"No." The names screeched in Sarah's ears, cycling round and round. "Rachel?" Her sweet, beautiful friend. How could it be?

Roza smelled like putrid flowers. Sarah fought back nausea. "Your family too, Sarah. Your mother and father—"

"No." Sarah covered her ears. "No, please. No, no, no—"

Hands circled Sarah's wrists, to free her ears and condemn them. A voice as dry as dust. "Your Benjamin too."

"No no no no no no no." Sarah gasped for breath—breath she didn't even want.

"All of them, Sarah *mou*. Yes. Everyone is gone."

"I want to die. Take me too!" Sarah turned her face to the ceiling, to say it to God, and she prayed he would smite down from the sky and remove her from this wretched earth.

Sarah sensed Roza lifting her arm, pulling on it, with a strength that felt peculiar, even in the sea of her grief. "You will come home with me, Sarah *mou*. I have more beds than bodies now."

Sarah found that, when she swept the synagogue floor, her mind sometimes—fleetingly—could focus only on sweeping the synagogue floor. And so she came to the synagogue, day after day, to help with the restoration efforts. But one winter day, January, February, who knew, she was sweeping and got a feeling that struck her often, like her legs were going to buckle.

Sarah sat on the pew. It was still a beautiful synagogue. Looking at beautiful things made Sarah's eyes hurt. She didn't register a man approaching until he sat beside her. He was familiar—he'd been coming to the synagogue every day for maybe a month and just sitting on a pew, but not speaking. Sarah hadn't thought it strange; nothing seemed strange or not strange anymore. The man was older—thirty, maybe.

"Can I sit?" he asked in Italian, which explained why Sarah hadn't known him before the war. He surely belonged to the island's Italian Jewish community, whose synagogue now sat in ruins.

"You are already sitting," Sarah responded in Italian, which she knew nearly as well as Greek. It had been years since she'd spoken it though. She shifted away from the man.

"I just meant, do you mind if I do?"

"You can do whatever you want. The Nazis aren't here to outlaw it."

A long silence. It was raining outside, drumming onto the windowpanes. Penelope thumped her feet in her cage on the floor, where Sarah set her each morning. Thumping meant she was unhappy with something; that was what Benjamin had once said. Since Sarah had acceded to her ownership, Penelope was incessant in her thumping.

"You lost your family?" asked the man, whom Sarah had nearly forgotten was still there.

Like she had misplaced them. "Yes, they are dead. They are dead. They are dead." She could have kept going, but her mouth ran out of steam.

"My wife and baby daughter died too." He scratched his ear, and Sarah saw his arm with those horrific numbers.

"I'm very sorry." Her eyes bored into the pew. Finally, she got up with her broom.

"And now I am getting out of here to America."

"Well, then, good luck." The man reached out to put a hand on hers. Sarah's hand stung with the touch. She ripped it away.

"Why don't you marry me and come with me to America?"

She finally looked at him. He looked like all of them. Not eyes with light. Just dark eyes. Dull. No contrast. A shell with a skeleton frame and a fine-shaped head. His dark hair was sparse, and she could see his scalp. It was red in parts. It needed ointment. A caring hand to apply it. You couldn't see those places by yourself.

"Marry you?" She managed to laugh.

"You are Jewish, I am Jewish. We can start a new life in America."

"You are crazy." She swept away from this crazy man.

"Don't you want to get out of this place?" he called. "Don't you want to get away from the memories?"

And the thing was, she did. Very much so.

"I will think about it," she finally said.

He stood. He was not tall and not short, but of medium height. Somehow Sarah liked it, his medium-ness. A tall life was no longer possible, of that she was certain. But meeting this man was like tasting the first bite of some potentially medium life.

"Please, do," he said. "My name is Sam, by the way."

And Sarah watched crazy Sam walk away.

The next day, she was sifting through the Mahzor Romania prayer books, to see what might be salvaged, when she heard a familiar voice echo from downstairs.

"Sarah Batis?" the voice asked. "I am looking for Sarah Batis."

Sarah didn't think, just burst across the room toward the *aron* and leaped inside the ark. She'd once hidden there as a child, among the Torah scrolls, playing hide-and-seek with Rachel. But there were no Torahs anymore, because the Nazis had looted them.

"Sarah?" she heard. "Sarah, are you here?"

Sarah peeked through the crevice of the doors of the *aron* and watched Milos wandering through the pews. Milos, in his sweet tweed cap, searching for a person who no longer existed.

Sarah held her breath, watching him, wanting him—and yet willing him away.

When he'd gone, she went to find Sam. She said, "I will marry you."

Six months later, she found herself on a boat with him, heading to America.

Well, that's all I have for you for now, Milos. It's a relief to have written it. It's a relief to have it outside of me. I want you to know something. It's important I tell you this. I forgive you. I forgive you, Milos. It's not your fault they died. It's not your fault I died inside. It's not your fault we couldn't be together.

I loved you then and I love you now. Love doesn't die, Milos. Love doesn't even need to be reciprocated. Love just is. It doesn't get to make a choice. That's what I know to be true.

I would like to see you. I would like to put my hand to your face and look into those eyes of yours and laugh and cry. If you are married, it's okay. I respect it. If we cannot do this in person, perhaps on some video contraption. Perhaps my granddaughters can arrange it. I will talk in Greek. I want to see you right away. Please, Milos. Please.

It is peculiar, Milos, but after writing this terrible note to you, I feel a little bit happy. I am going to go sit in my garden with my rosebushes. Speak to you soon, Milos *mou*.

chapter thirty-nine
Joey

florida

2019

Joey was still thinking about the eyes when she stepped onto the sand. The eyes were the heart of her portrait. More subtle than anything she'd done before. She couldn't quite believe she was the creator of this. Maybe the nose needed to come down. Yes, the nose was slightly smaller than she'd sketched it. But she'd gotten the backdrop right. The streakiest navy—unhinged. She hadn't felt this way about a piece before, so wild, so trusting.

She'd need the entire night, but she had confidence in her ability to pull it off. She'd asked Edith to stay out of the foyer until it was done. She had to get the eyes right. And fix the nose. The rest just needed shading and coaxing.

As Demetris always used to say, *It's not you moving the brush!*

Joey saw the eyes first—blue that mirrored the water. She kicked up sand as she walked to her sister.

Lily straddled the waterline—feet in wet sand, butt in the precariously dry part. She had on a red flannel crop top, distressed black bike shorts, and massive opaque black sunglasses.

"Hey," said Lily as Joey sat beside her.

"Hey." Joey stretched out her feet to meet the wave rolling in. "Is this your beachy outfit?"

"It's all washable. How about you? Where are the five people you're hiding under that muumuu?"

Joey glanced down at her white eyelet midi dress. It was a little tentlike, maybe, but tentlike was in. "It's my painting outfit today. I wore an apron over it. And I wear it in real life too." Water droplets smattered on Joey's shoulders. She hoped it wouldn't rain.

"So looking ugly helps you paint better?"

"Thanks, Lil. Remind me why I came out here to meet you?"

"Oh, Joey." Lily gasped. "I'm *really* angry at you."

Joey piled sand into a little mound. She studied the imprint her fingers made on top. "I only found out a week before you. I thought it was best to wait to tell you after the wedding."

"Right. Everyone knows what's best for me. I didn't get to choose if I wanted to grow up with my real dad or my real brother. Maybe that would have been best for me. You know, Leo's really cool, Jo."

"He is." Joey considered reminding her sister that Leo had known about the secret for far longer, but she wanted to protect their very new bond. And Joey understood that she was an easier target right now.

"I have a nephew too! He's such a cutie. Arthur. Can you believe that? I'm an aunt."

"You talked to Leo?"

"We went for lunch."

"Oh, wow. Okay, that's—"

"It's weird. It's crazy and weird. I'm a little mad at Leo too, that he didn't tell me the truth a long time ago. You know?"

"Yeah." Joey nodded.

Lily frowned. "By the way, you didn't invite me with a plus-one to your wedding. That's pretty messed up."

"Huh?" Joey searched in her purse for her sunglasses. "You don't have a boyfriend."

"But maids of honor get plus-ones. It's, like, etiquette."

"You can have a plus-one, Lil. What, you want to take Leo? I'm gonna invite him. There's no reason now to keep him away."

"No, I don't want to take Leo. I invited my father."

Joey's hands froze around her aviators. "You invited… Rand?"

"Leo gave me his number. I called him. Leo already told him what happened so I asked if he'd come down to meet me. And technically he's not even a plus-one because apparently you guys originally invited him. His reason for declining doesn't really apply anymore."

A wave that looked like it was going to break farther off ended up barreling to their waists. Joey leaped up. Lily just reclined fully in the sand as the water swept up to her head.

A little red-haired girl ran over to them. She tapped Lily's arm. "I know you!"

"Oh." Lily sat up, drenched hair matted with sand. "Do

you want my autograph? Or a photo together?" She turned
to Joey. "It's really sweet. Moms and daughters read my
blog together as their first dabbles in feminism. Lots of
teachable moments."

"I know you fwom the movies!"

"She thinks you're the Little Mermaid," said a woman
juggling a baby and a litany of plastic beach toys.

"Oh." Lily smiled brightly at the girl. "But I am the
Little Mermaid!" She lay back down again and arranged her
hair to stream behind her. The little girl clapped her hands.
"Look at this stuff," Lily belted.

The girl darted off mid-song.

Joey smiled. "Fickle audience."

Lily slowly sat up. "She was cute."

"That's how old you were when Leo found out about
everything, Lil."

"Oh." They watched the girl hop up and down in a dance
whose rhythm was evident only to her. "Was I that cute?"

"You were even cuter. You were so cute and innocent,
and Leo just didn't want to ruin your life."

Lily shut her eyes. "I didn't mean what I said, Joey. It's
Mom's fault and Dad's fault and Rand's fault. None of this
is your or Leo's fault."

"Thanks for saying that. And Lil? Rand can be your
plus-one."

Thunder rumbled in the distance. "Thanks," said Lily. "I
told Dad I invited him."

"You called Dad?"

"No, he called me five million times."

"He called me too. I haven't answered yet."

"Well, I did. I told him I wasn't coming home. I told him
I moved in with you."

Joey smiled and inwardly cringed.

"He said Mom left."

"She did?"

"Yeah. He said they need space to figure things out. That he understood why I'd want to meet Rand."

"Wow. Okay." Joey watched a column of rain far out over the sea.

"Joey." Lily rested her wet, sandy head on Joey's shoulder. "Do you think Dad loves me less than you? You know, because you're really his?"

Joey swallowed hard. "No. I really, really don't, Lil."

"But...I don't have his blood. I'm the daughter of the man...the man his wife was having an affair with."

"Dad loves you so much. He always has. And he's known from the start that you weren't his." Joey felt her sister shake. "It's okay to cry, Lil."

For a few minutes, her sister wept quietly on her shoulder.

"Joey," said Lily after a while.

"Yeah?"

"Do we hate Dad?"

"Oh, Lil. I think we want to hate Dad. But no. We don't hate him."

"Do we hate Mom then? We *must* hate Mom! I hate her! I really do!"

Joey pressed her hand against her sister's cheek. It was wet and soft. Joey wanted skin that soft again. "Take it from your big sister. I've only had a week of it, but it's a lot of work to hate."

"I hate them," shouted Lily. "I haaaaaaate them!"

Her little admirer ran up to them from the shore. "My mom says you're not s'posed to hate." Her eyes bobbed between them. "Got it?" She darted back to her shovel.

Joey giggled. "PSA, Lil. You're not s'posed to hate. A message from your three-year-old self."

Lily shoved her sunglasses up over her hair, unveiling splotchy red cheeks. "Did you resent me a little, Jo? After you found out the secret?"

Joey felt her sister's heartbeat against her arm. It was such an un-Lily-like question. "I guess I did a little," she finally said. "I'm really sorry, Lil. It just came as such a shock. None of it was your fault, but I realized it had changed my whole life. Leo broke up with me, and we stopped going to Corfu, and—"

"So *it* ruined your life," Lily said softly. "*My existence* ruined your life."

"That's the thing, Lil. I've learned something. I think I only learned it now. No one can ruin your life without your permission. I've been so angry with Mom since Leo told me, and now there's this whole thing with Dad. Maybe it's just—he did what he did. She did what she did. They made mistakes, you know?"

"So what do *we* do?" asked Lily. A crackle of lightning shook the beach. Blankets started being gathered, beach bags packed.

"I don't know," said Joey. "But right now we go. It's going to rain."

"I don't care. I'm already wet. I'm going to stay."

"Are you sure? I have to get back to Edith's." Joey hugged her sister.

"See you at home then."

"Okay." Joey started to walk.

"Hey, Joey."

She turned. "Yeah?"

"You really loved Leo back then, huh?"

"Yeah, Lil. I did." Water streamed down Joey's face. It was just rain, she thought.

She made it to the edge of the sand and knelt to put on her sandals. It was drizzling now, her arms riddled in goose bumps. As she fastened her sandals, her hand went to the damp sand. It started to write.

It wrote JOEY.

She added an ampersand.

She went to write Grant, but she hesitated. Very quickly, she erased the ampersand with a rub of her hand. Then she erased the Joey too. Now she wrote her name even bigger, so she had to walk from letter to letter to craft them. JOEY.

She finished decisively, with a period on the end. As the rain picked up, she surveyed her handiwork. Some place deep inside her smiled.

⌒

Joey smelled coffee as she climbed down the ladder. She set her charcoal stick on the floor.

"It's magnificent." Edith was leaning on her cane by the coffee lid installation.

"Thank you."

"I did question if you'd pull it off." Edith started toward Joey. She wore pale-blue silk pajamas. Strands of sapphire necklaces hung atop. Joey had never known a person who wore sapphires while lounging around her house.

Joey's legs buckled. She sank to the floor. She removed her apron.

"You should rest, dear. Did you sleep at all last night?"

"I didn't." Joey couldn't stop looking at the wall. Couldn't stop marveling that she had created this remarkable thing.

"Well, you should go home." Edith handed her a stack of bills. "Thank you, my dear."

Joey put the money in her bag. She packed up her oils. "Thank you so much for the opportunity." She hovered at the door. She didn't want to leave her wall. She dug for her phone and snapped a couple of photos.

"*Vogue* is going to have a field day. Did Lily tell you they're sending a photographer over tonight? I'll make sure this lands in the article. Prepare for an onslaught. A well-deserved one."

"Wow." Joey's stomach rumbled. She couldn't remember when she last ate. "So...when do you think the article will come out?"

"Not for some time, I assume."

"Right." Joey reached for the door handle. "I'm really appreciative that you took a chance on me."

"A chance well taken. My instincts never lie, my dear. And congratulations are in order. I nearly forgot to wish you luck!"

"Luck?"

"You're getting married in a couple of days, no? One does need luck for such things."

Joey remembered reading somewhere that Edith had been married four times. "I am," she said. A couple of days. Gosh.

"He's a fortunate guy," said Edith.

"Oh?"

Edith pointed to the wall. "That's love. That is love if I've ever seen it."

Joey felt her cheeks go hot. "Thank you," she said, and opened the door.

chapter forty
Joey

florida

2019

Joey drove fast. Thick morning air bisected the car from all four windows ratcheted down, still not ridding the Jeep of its indelible scent courtesy of Doris, its prior owner. Joey found the smell peculiarly nostalgic, like eucalyptus air fresheners and barbells that had seen their heyday in the era of Jane Fonda workout videos.

Her phone rang. There was pretty much no one to whom she wanted to speak. She glanced at the screen: G. Well, sweet G wasn't on any shit lists. In fact, G was probably calling to check on things after Joey had filled her in on the dysfunction with a capital *D* that was their family. G had been subdued on the phone before. Perhaps now the whole vacation affair had sunk in, and G was ready to rage about everything Bea and Scott had done.

"Hi, G."

"I need you to come over," came a whisper. It was flat and lifeless—not the voice of her lively grandmother.

"G? Are you okay?"

"No," said the strange voice. "I am not."

Joey jerked onto the shoulder. "G, tell me what's wrong."
The call evaporated. She dialed G back—nothing.

Joey made a U-turn toward her grandmother's.

chapter forty-one

Dear Mrs. Bezas,

My name is Elena Kallas, and I am the daughter of Milos Christakos. I do not know how to tell you this so I am just going to come out with it. Two weeks ago, a day before you sent your first message to my father, my father was in an accident. He was walking to the fishing wharf on our island. At ninety-four, he still walked that route every day. He liked to have a coffee and watch the boats coming back from sea. But as he was crossing a street, he was struck by a car. He was admitted to the General Hospital of Lefkada, and by the time I rushed over, he was in a coma.

    Oh, Mrs. Bezas. I am so sorry to say it. My father is very loved. We were all there. I have three grown children, and my brother, Adelphos, has four. The doctor said my father wouldn't make it, that it would be a matter of hours.

    Two days later, my father still hung on. I signed into

his email. I was trying to reconstruct his life. He'd lived alone for so many years. My mother died when I was young, and he'd never had a partner since. I figured there would be bills to pay. Friends to contact. I saw an email fresh in his box notifying him of a Facebook message from you.

I instantly knew who you were. You see, fifteen years ago, my father asked me to accompany him to a reunion of Holocaust survivors on the island of Corfu. He told me that, when he was a teenager, he fell in love with a Jewish girl. That he didn't want to be disloyal to the memory of my mother, but that he'd loved this girl with all his soul. He wanted to know she was okay. He wanted one more chance to see her. This girl was you, of course. We went to the reunion and met your daughter. I'm sure she's told you. I translated as my father told your daughter that not a day goes by that he doesn't think of you. Your daughter said you were happily married. She said she would give you my father's contact information.

If there is one thing in life you should not doubt, please know how my father loved you. I watched the tears run down his face as we took the ferry back to Igoumenitsa. He told me you had once taken the ferry together.

When I saw your message, I did not know what to do. I hadn't realized my father had reached out to you. Of course, why would I know such a thing? He was a person with his own thoughts and desires. I was heartbroken when I read your letter because I knew how my father would have longed to receive it. I printed out the message, and I went to the hospital. I want you to know, Mrs. Bezas, that there had been no response from my father since he was brought to the hospital. But I held his hand as I read the letter, and you know what he did? What he did was a miracle. He squeezed my hand.

I hope you will forgive me. I couldn't bear to tell you the truth then. It seemed to me that you needed to say some things, and that my father needed to hear them. So I sent you one of those emoticons. I went along with your assumption that my father couldn't respond in English, even though my English is quite fine. And I continued to read your letters to him. And he continued to live. The doctors were surprised. They expected him to pass on quickly.

Yesterday, I sobbed as I read him your last letter. What happened to your family was truly horrific. And how that tore you and my father apart—well, I felt both your pain. None of it was your fault, but both of you took on that blame.

On this note, I must tell you, there is a story I know, that it appears you do not. On our ferry back from Corfu after the reunion, my father kept mumbling that he'd tried to save them. I asked him what he meant. He didn't want to say it, but eventually he told me, not all the contours of the story, but just this one part. That he'd joined with a man named Costas, who led the Greek Resistance on Lefkada. At night, he snuck to the place where the Jews were being held and searched frantically for your family— but was unable to find them. It was dark, he said, with the Germans on guard. They had to move quickly. There was nothing he could do. He helped others escape instead, and you cannot fathom his guilt, Mrs. Bezas. Trust me, for I saw it ooze from his pores. He didn't tell you this story because he was ashamed. It was your family he wanted to save, and he felt that he failed. Even though he risked his life to try.

Well, Mrs. Bezas, I thought you would want to know.

In any event, when I finished your letter to my father, I thought I saw him smile. I could have invented it, but I like to think I did not. I left the room to see about his medication, and when I came back, he was gone.

I think—no, I know, Mrs. Bezas—I know he hung on for you. I know he hung on for your last words. I know he left this world in peace, and for that and to you I am very grateful.

My father cannot be here to say it, so I will. He loved you until the day he died. On that I would stake my life. That kind of love is rare indeed. He was kind and good to my mother, but as I look back now, I'm not sure those things add up to love. We were his light. Once my mother was gone and his children grown, we urged my father to date. He was young and handsome. He had those gorgeous green eyes. But he said he'd had his love, and that was the end of it. Until the day of the Corfu reunion, I thought he meant my mother. But then I understood it. He meant you. He had his love with you, and that was enough for a lifetime.

I am sorry to send such a terrible message. I wish all the best to you and your family. I hope you feel my father's love from up above, and that it can provide you with some small comfort now.

Sincerely, Elena Kallas

chapter forty-two
Joey

florida

2019

The door was open.

"G?" Joey walked past the photo of her grandfather as a boy, past the cabinet stuffed with miniature Greek statues. She knocked on her grandmother's bedroom door.

No answer.

Joey slowly opened the door. Sun had invaded the rest of the condo, but here it was the dead of night, with daylight only filtering in from one narrow window that had escaped the installation of a blackout shade. When Joey's eyes oriented, she saw her grandmother sitting up in her bed.

"G, are you okay? Are you sick?"

"I'm not sick."

Joey sat on the edge of the bed and flicked on the nightstand lamp. Her grandmother was wig-less, her tiny head matted in white cotton-candy hair. G's eyes didn't shift from the reproduction of Monet's water lilies that hung across the room.

"You're scaring me, G. Please tell me what's wrong."

"I can't tell you, Joey. If you want, you'll have to read my messages on the Facebook."

Surely her grandmother was joking. But when G kept staring ahead, Joey realized she was serious. "Okay, G. Sure. Facebook messages with who?"

"You'll see. There's only one person. Start at the beginning."

"Okay." Joey's heart settled back into its cavity. She was relieved this was about Facebook messages. That this wasn't a heart attack or cancer or something equally unfixable. "What's your password?"

"My password? Benjamin. My password is always Benjamin."

Benjamin. Her grandmother's little brother. Joey had almost never heard G speak of him.

"Okay, I'll be back after I read them." Joey walked to the door.

"Joey?" said her grandmother. "Can you please turn off the light?"

~~

For a long time after she finished reading G's Facebook messages, Joey sat very still in her grandmother's swivel desk chair. Every time the chair shifted, it jerked Joey to another terrible thought.

Finally, she called her mother. Bea said hello. She didn't launch into a game of Fifty Questions: Wedding Edition. Just hello.

Joey told her she had to read some Facebook messages of G's. Her mother said okay. Joey said, *Once you finish, can you meet me at G's?* Another okay.

Joey ended the call. She read the last message again.

Then the last one her grandmother wrote. By the time she finished, her cheeks were smothered in tears.

It was some time before Joey got up the nerve to venture back into her grandmother's bedroom.

"So, you read?" The room still hung in darkness. Joey went for the light switch. G said sharply, "No."

Joey climbed onto the bed so she was flush against the headboard beside her grandmother. "I don't know what to say." She listened to the hum of the humidifier. "I didn't know any of that. I'm so, so sorry, G."

"He's dead. I can't believe it. He's dead. He tried to save my family, and I didn't even know it. And now he's dead, just like the rest of them."

"I know," Joey said, more tears spilling out her eyes. Why was she crying and her grandmother perfectly still? It was beginning to frighten her, her grandmother with her back so erect.

They sat side by side for what seemed like hours. Joey stared at the blue light on the TV monitor. She began to shiver. She was still wearing her dress from the ocean with Lily. It was maybe even still damp.

"G, can I ask you something? Or do you not want to talk about it?"

"You can ask me," said this new, eerie G voice.

"Well...how did you survive it? How did you survive the deaths of your whole family? And then losing Milos?"

There was a choking sound. A rustling on the bed. The shadow of her grandmother lifted a throw pillow from behind her back and clutched it to her chest.

"By the skin of my teeth," whispered G. "That's how. At first, I was preoccupied, Joey. I met your grandfather, and we got to America. We had to get jobs. We worked very hard, you know. He wanted to have children. He was desperate to have children. But I couldn't fathom bringing children into a world where such evil existed. Your grandfather took me to psychologists. He went to great efforts to convince me. I wanted to make him happy—oh I did, Joey—but something inside me was too hardened.

"Your grandfather accepted it at last, or pretended that he had. Then one day, he said something so innocuous, that it would have been nice to have someone to carry on our family names. And that is what turned the light on inside me. Suddenly I desperately wanted a baby to carry on my family's legacy. By then, we were older though. It was harder. It wasn't working. We went to fertility specialists. No baby. I began to resign myself, I suppose."

How had Joey never known any of this? How had she never asked?

"Then I became pregnant. It was a miracle, Joey. And when your mother came into this world and cried, I got parts of myself back that I hadn't even known were missing. I had something to live for. I had some piece of my parents. I named her—"

"Beatrice," said Joey. "For Benjamin."

"Yes. For Benjamin."

"So much makes sense. Like why you wanted me to marry a Jewish man."

There was a long empty hallway's worth of silence. "Yes."

"Can I ask you one more thing though, G? About Milos?"

"Yes."

"I just wonder…do you think, if you'd gotten to see him

in person after all these years, you would have loved him just the same as when you were younger?"

For a while, there was only the *brrrr* of a lawn mower outside. At last, her grandmother said, "I do. I do think I would have loved him as much. But maybe it's just been a fantasy all these years. A fantasy that kept me going. Perhaps a fantasy that kept me back too, if I admit it to myself. You know, Joey, maybe my longing for what once was held me back from the life that was in front of me. Who can say now? But I suppose I think that love doesn't ever die once you've felt it. Maybe it only changes shape. Or maybe that's just a fantasy too."

Joey was quiet for a long time. "I wish more than anything that I could make it different, what happened to you."

"Joey, you asked me about my past the other day, and I was too cowardly to give you answers."

"You don't have to explain it. I—"

"I *do* need to explain because I'm afraid I've done you a disservice all these years, keeping it inside. Every year on Passover, at the Seder, I dip my celery into the salt water. We all do. Do you know why we do that?"

Joey grasped for an answer, but nothing. What she remembered of once-a-week Hebrew school was the sprinkle cookies they served during break. "Not really."

"We do it to remember the tears of our ancestors. So every year, I dip my celery into salt water, and I remember them. The only family I knew, before there was all of you. It's not fair to say it's restricted to Passover. My cells remember them, in every moment." G bit her lip. "But herein lies the business of living."

It felt an overwhelming amount for Joey to assimilate, like the entire ocean queuing up to funnel through a very thin hose. "I wish there was something I could say to make things better, G, but there isn't, is there?"

"No," said her grandmother. "No, there isn't. But there's one thing you can do for me."

"Anything, G."

"Will you hold my hand?"

Her grandmother lifted her hand from beneath her pillow, and Joey reached for it. It was veiny and fragile and soft, and Joey sat there in the dark for a very long time, holding her grandmother's hand.

Joey met an unusually restrained Bea in G's kitchen. Bea wore fitness leggings and a black T-shirt. Her face was scrubbed bare. They sat at the table with a half-eaten bowl of cherries, the pits sprinkled among the whole cherries—a melancholy indicator of solo living.

"I thought you should see it," said Joey. "She's not doing well."

"Yes. I can imagine." Bea tapped her nails one at a time on the glass table. "Do you think she'll want to see me?"

"Of course she'll want to see you. You're her favorite person on earth."

At that, Bea winced. "She called you, though, not me. Did you see the part in the messages? I met Milos all that time ago."

"Yeah, what was that about?"

"His daughter was translating, remember? At that re-union? He said he loved my mother. He said to give her his information. I got the gist then. Here was her ex-lover, not Jewish, and she'd sabotaged my relationship with Rand. Or so I thought. I found it to be the ultimate act of hypocrisy. I was just so…angry at her. So incredibly angry."

"So when Grandfather died—"

"I didn't tell her I met Milos." Her mother shut her eyes. "I suppose I just loved my father so much, and once I met Milos, I realized that maybe my father was always my mother's second choice. It felt disloyal to pass on the message from Milos. I guess I was punishing her. It was terrible, I see that now. *I* was terrible."

Joey didn't quite have a response for that.

"You know, Joey." Her mother sighed. "There's this quote by Diane von Furstenberg. I read it once in Oprah's magazine. Oprah asked Diane who her hero was, and Diane said, *Most people, because most people are just doing their best.*"

Joey didn't know what to say. She wanted to say something kind. She really did want to. But instead she said, "So you're saying you're a hero?"

"I know I can't win with you, Joey," said her mother quietly. "You've made that clear. I'm just saying I'm human. I've made mistakes."

"You've made *a lot* of mistakes."

"Indeed, I have." Her mother took a cherry from the bowl. She swirled the stem around in her fingertips. "But I'm hoping it's not too late to make some of them right."

Joey's head was going to combust. It felt like a thousand years since she'd slept. She said, "Take care of G, please. I need to head home."

She was halfway to the door when her mother said, "Joey, do you hate me?"

Joey stopped before the entry to the foyer. "Oh." She closed her eyes. When she opened them, the only sound was that of her mother tapping her nails on the table. "I don't hate you, Mom. No. But what hurts the most is feeling a little bit like you loved Lily more than me."

"What…Joey, what in the world are you talking about?"

"You know what I'm talking about." Joey chewed on her lip. "You knew that Leo had found out about your affair. And Leo's condition for keeping your secret was that you and Rand couldn't be together anymore, but no…still you went to Taverna Salto like a couple! And then Leo ended it with me, and you *knew* why. For so many years after, I was broken, and you knew it. You could have protected me."

"Jo—"

"No! You could have done something to prioritize me. Tried to figure it out. Tried to help me. It just feels like…it just feels like maybe you didn't love me enough to do that."

Her mother stared out the window onto the lawn. "Joey, I regret so many things, but trust me, sweetheart, not loving you enough isn't one of them. Fifteen years ago, well, I was just trying to do the right thing."

"Okay." Joey put a hand on the door handle, but something stopped her from turning it. "Maybe it's not fair," she finally whispered. "To put my happiness on you."

"Joey, I—"

Joey put up her hand. She was utterly spent. "Look, you asked me the question."

"You're right. I did."

"Well, you know what they say?" Joey opened the door to a gust of heat through G's igloo.

"No. What?"

"They say that the opposite of love isn't hate. It's indifference. And I think you can tell that I'm not indifferent at all."

chapter forty-three
Sarah

florida

2019

The foyer was dim. Outside, sunlight glittered atop the Technicolor lawn; Sarah swept the curtains across to shroud the windows. Now she watched the shadows play together on the wall—even the shadows were too happy.

As Sarah padded into the kitchen, she caught her reflection in the mirror by the picture of Sam as a boy. Her white hair shot from her head in fifty directions. She looked like Albert Einstein. She registered it and kept moving. Cherries. She would finish the cherries. And have a glass of water.

The last person she expected to see sitting at her breakfast table was her daughter. Bea looked up, and Sarah's body didn't react in its usual way—reaching for Bea, always reaching. She almost didn't recognize her daughter. Maybe it was Bea's face devoid of its typical irritation or opinion. Or maybe it was that it had no makeup enhancing it.

Her daughter looked older; that's what Sarah really thought. Maybe the way a person looked changed when you started to resent them.

"I didn't invite you to come." Sarah reached for a glass and filled it from the fridge dispenser.

Bea opened her mouth and then closed it. So unlike her to grasp for words. Usually they streamed out like a fire hydrant unleashed on a street corner, dousing innocent passersby.

Sarah drank her water and thought what a foreign thing it was to resent the person whom she loved the most, whom she'd given life, whom for years and years she'd longed for. Previously, Sarah had only experienced negative emotions toward the amorphous Nazis. Toward the boy soldier who'd imprisoned her family. Toward Milos. Toward herself. Toward Sam, even. Oh, Sam. But to feel resentful toward Bea? Well, until today that would have seemed inconceivable.

And yet.

"So Joey filled you in?" Sarah's feet were cold on the tile, but there was something very alive about the cold, and something very alive about the anger churning in her. "You know that I know. That you kept Milos from me. That he wanted to find me and you...you..."

"I'm sorry, but I thought you kept Rand from me!" A horrible silence thundered between them.

"Yes, *Rand*." Sarah lingered evilly on his name, like some sort of movie villain. "I know it all. The man you cheated with, had Lily with. The man you put your entire family in jeopardy and pain for. That Rand, correct?"

"I know. I'm so sorry, Mom. I'm so sorry. I'm sorry." Bea set her head on the table in the cradle of her forearms. "I thought you kept his letters from me, and mine from him. I was so wrong."

Sarah stopped a foot from Bea's trembling back. Her instinct from years of motherly love—maybe motherly conditioning—was to comfort her, and yet she felt incapable of doing so.

"You should go," Sarah finally said.

"But doesn't it matter how sorry I am? How sad I am about what happened to your family?" Bea glanced up. She was crying, yes, but now something like defiance had slipped over her. "It's what happened to my family too! You should have told me."

"Perhaps I should have." Sarah was zapped of it all; the reservoir of strength from which she'd fed all these years now ran dry. "Bea, I am telling you to go."

Her daughter stumbled to her feet, and for a moment, it pained Sarah—the face a spitting image of Sam's, now exiled from the home to which they'd brought her from the hospital in a precious pink cap and with enough love that it could have filled oceans.

"You're mad, I understand it. Mother, I do. But please tell me you won't stop loving me. Mom…" Bea's voice broke. "I really can't have you disappear on me too."

A part of Sarah swelled and wanted to take her daughter in her arms. She thought about her own mother, and the last time she'd seen her, and the time before that too. But sometimes one had to be a mother, and sometimes one had to be a person. And so Sarah walked to the front door and thrust it open. Today she was a person. She was not a mother. Maybe she'd never be a mother again.

That thought nearly undid her. It occurred to Sarah this was anger talking, this was the pain of losing Milos, of losing her family—of losing Bea too, in some measure. But that was all analytical, and what Sarah felt at her core was an inability to pass one more moment in the presence of her daughter.

"For now, I need some distance, Bea," she said, her lips trembling. "Please go."

∽

It was the middle of the night, and Sarah hadn't yet drifted into sleep. Her mind was on Milos and holding hands on the ferry over the sea, their future an unblighted stretch, and then her mind was on Bea and the bunch of daisies she'd picked *Just for you, Mom!* at the park when she was five. Sarah sat up in bed, drenched in sweat. Her longing for her daughter was sudden and consuming.

If only Sarah were a person who could stay angry longer. Bea deserved it. Or did she? She was abrasive, her daughter, self-centered, surely, but she did love. She showed her love in odd ways—the vagina painting for Joey, a true oddity. The articles she sent to Sarah ad nauseam about the queen and her wellness regime. And the surprise Bea had been toiling on for months for the wedding. It was going to be magnificent. Sarah dialed her daughter's cell phone.

Bea answered on the first ring. "Mom?"

"Yes."

"You're still my mom?" said Bea, and Sarah could make out the quiet weeping. Sarah was crying herself now, and something in her chest had unclenched. That's what it was to be a mother. Your child could do a terrible thing, even to you, and still love beat in your heart whether you wanted it to or not. You didn't get to choose whom you loved in this life. Sarah had learned that lesson long ago, and now she was being reminded of it. Knocked over the head with it, perhaps.

"I'm always your mom," said Sarah, and found it to ring

true. Maybe she'd never fully get over what Bea had done, or maybe she would, but earlier when she'd tried to separate being a mother and being a person—well, it wasn't possible to do that for long. Both identities were woven like a tapestry, inextricably bound within her, and that was that.

"I'm really sorry." Bea went off on a fresh spate of tears. "I wish you'd gotten to speak with Milos. He loved you. That was clear."

Sarah could only say, "I know he did." And then because she was a mother and her daughter was crying, she whispered, "It will be okay."

And Sarah surprised herself for a moment by thinking maybe it would be.

chapter forty-four
Joey

florida
2019

Grant tossed the keys to the valet. He wore citrus-green shorts, a white button-down, and boat shoes—his chosen attire when encountering his three sisters, whom Joey internally referred to as the Lilly Pulitzer Fan Club. As Joey exited the car, Grant's eyes darted to her feet like a cartoon character with a neck capable of executing a full swivel. "Flip-flops?" He laughed and kissed her cheek.

"See how I save us money? A lot of brides buy exorbitantly priced shoes. Instead it's these old Havaianas for me, and I'm taking them off the moment we hit the yard." Joey grabbed Grant's hand, and with her other one dug for the evil eye charm inside the right pocket of her seventies-esque emerald-green silk jumpsuit.

"For richer and for barefoot." Grant broke their hand-clasp to drape his arm over her shoulder.

"To love and to frolic in your parents' grass."

"Get a room," said Lily.

They wove around the property, Lily trailing behind

them. They passed the tennis court and the library loggia. They brushed by the life-size stone chess set that Joey suspected had never been played in its multiple decades of existence. They cut through the garden whose centerpiece was the majestic fountain with tiles sourced in Morocco. And at last they landed on the upper lawn of the mansion belonging to the illustrious Dot and Lawrence Newman— the Atlantic Ocean a sapphire stretch beyond. Waiters in white tails traced figure eights among tables overflowing with pink peonies. An eight-piece band played Adele beside the pool bordered in jasmine-blanketed trelliswork.

When Joey had first visited Newman Manor, Dot had delivered a ten-minute explanation about the pool's limestone coping. Joey hadn't known what limestone coping was, let alone that ten minutes could be expended discussing it. But she'd found Grant's floral-adorned, design buff of a mother endearing. Dot could go on endlessly about such subjects as the blanket in the guest room that once belonged to a Navajo chief and the ottoman upholstered in Lee Jofa chintz that was on back order for four years. *Waiting for that, my dear—that's the definition of stamina.*

"Emergency!" shouted a figure in hot pink darting toward Joey. It was Dot.

Joey said to Grant, "Palm Beach is literally the only place on the planet where a gathering of Jews involves more pink than black."

She and Dot did the triple cheek kiss. Dot had a Swiss ancestor, Grant once explained.

"You look beautiful, darling. Not bridal, but I know. You're *alternative.* Now I have the emergency calligrapher here." Dot gestured to a woman in a skintight black tuxedo pantsuit. "Grant only gave me a few hours' warning about the new guests. A…" Dot consulted a Smythson notebook. "Mr. Rand and Mr. Leo?"

"Ah, yes." As if on cue, Joey watched Lily scan the lawn. Her little sister wore an ethereal champagne slip dress, her hair in loose pigtails, the combination of which gave her a rare delicate vibe.

After Joey had spelled the Winns' names for the emergency calligrapher and Grant had wandered off deep in conversation with his brother, Joey found herself alone in the sea of guests. In her periphery, she spied people who made her smile and others she'd never before seen, but she felt content on her own, in a column of quiet. She slipped off her flip-flops and stored them behind a hedge. Then she mushed her feet into the grass and sipped her champagne, until someone stole up to her side.

"Boo!" It was Siya—thank God.

"Ah!" They shared a squeeze. "Where's Aadesh?" asked Joey, at the same time Siya said, "You look gorg, Jo, but what's been happening since that crazy dinner? You've been avoiding my calls."

"I know, I'm sorry. But really, where's Aadesh? I haven't seen him in forev—"

"Josephine Abrams." Siya's eyes narrowed. "Aadesh isn't going to save you from me. Too bad for you that you can't send me to voicemail. I want to know about the Leo situation."

"There's no more Leo situation."

Siya's eyebrow raised. "Look, I remember in college when you and Leo were over. After that summer, you changed. You said you were going to law school. I thought I heard wrong."

"I got a one-seventy on the LSATs," Joey said quietly,

watching all the guests—her guests—talking and laughing. "How could I not go?"

"That's when I knew it wasn't just a funk. That wasn't my Joey talking."

"My dad was thrilled. The day I got into Columbia, he basically printed up my business cards."

"Law wasn't the only way you changed though. I predicted you'd play the field post-breakup and instead, nada. Remember?"

"Even my vagina remembers." Joey stared out at the ocean so that eventually she didn't see people—just a haze of blue. "Three years and I didn't so much as kiss a guy. If he tried to hold my hand, I pulled back like he was some sexual deviant. God. It took me until law school to feel normal again."

"I think it took you until Bali to feel normal again."

"Maybe that's true. I wasted a lot of time. But I'm finally really happy." She was, wasn't she? She was pursuing her passion at last. Living by the sea, with a man who loved her deeply, whom she loved in return.

"Are you?" asked Siya, her face in deep study. "Are you sure you are, Jo?"

"I'm sure." Just as Siya was opening her mouth to respond, Joey let out a little gasp. "Oh, I can't believe it. He actually came."

She watched two men she'd recognize anywhere cross the lawn, neither of whom sported any element of pastel. Rand, with his hair now more salt than pepper, his hands shoved into trousers, that nonchalant stroll. Leo with his back to Joey, striding toward the pool.

Siya turned. "Is that…?"

"Yep." Joey watched the worlds before they collided. Bea

in an elaborate flower crown, flirting with the bartender. Lily perched on the Newmans' limestone coping, taking a selfie. Just then, a woman in a sheath dress with impressive biceps tapped Joey's shoulder—she was Dot's Pilates instructor, did Joey remember her?

The evening began to blur. It could have been the lingering sadness from the catastrophic family dinner, followed by G's horrific revelations. It could have been Joey's three glasses of champagne, which she didn't usually love or throw back, but the stuff they were serving was gooooood. Or it could have been her eyes darting from Lily and Rand to Lily and Leo to Bea and Rand, the latter of whom chatted animatedly at a high-top table for at least an hour. Then there was the cordial reunion of Rand and Scott, which Joey watched while half participating in a conversation about monograms with the entire Lilly Pulitzer Fan Club. That there existed such polarizing opinions about monograms surprised her. Sisters #1 and #2 had nearly brawled.

"So." Lily sidled up to Joey, and the sisters clinked their glasses together. "I met Rand, Jo. It was weird."

"I can imagine."

"He's going to stay the week after your wedding. He wants to get to know me."

"Good. He should. How do you feel about it, Lil?"

Lily fiddled with her dress strap. "I dunno. Maybe two dads will be even cooler than one?"

"Yeah. Totally. Twice as much annoying commentary on your life choices."

"Twice as many comments about my spending habits."

"Twice the betrayals."

"Twice the birthday presents!"

They laughed together.

"You know, we have the same laugh, Joey. Everyone says. Even Rand said."

"Well, we're sisters," said Joey. "You're not getting rid of me."

"Of course I'm not," said Lily. "I live with you now."

"Right," said Joey. "Right."

"Hey, Joey, can I say something sisterly? I saw the painting at Edith's party last night."

"Oh?" Joey had completely forgotten Lily would be there. She grabbed a seared ahi tuna crostini from a waiter scurrying by.

"Joey, you still love Leo, don't you?"

Joey froze. She watched Grant hug G. She felt the presence of Leo somewhere behind her, closer to the house. "Of course I don't. That's ridiculous. I painted a painting I started a long time ago. I had such little time, I had to make do."

"Joey, it's me. Real talk. Sister-to-sister. You don't paint that face, those eyes, if you're not in—"

"Lil, I love you, but I need you to stop talking!"

Lily's eyes widened. "I don't want to upset you."

"Well, you're upsetting me!"

"Okay, Jo."

"Thank you," she said, just as the bandleader announced, "Now the bride and groom would like to say a few words."

It took a long moment for Joey to realize she was that bride. Grant was that groom. Shit. They'd divvied up speech responsibilities weeks ago. Rehearsal dinner to Joey: quick and dirty. Wedding generously assumed by Grant: long and duly praising of everyone who needed to be praised. This was her getting off easily. If only she'd composed something like she'd fully intended.

"Ready, bride?" said a reappearing Grant, a tumbler of scotch in one hand and a pink drink in the other. "Watermelon martini." He handed it to her and kissed her hard. She tasted scotch and happiness. The crowd began to cheer.

"…and obviously we want to thank Dot and Lawrence for being super hosts. What a spectacular evening! From the canapés to the calligraphy, no detail has gone unnoticed, and that's courtesy of my impeccable future mother-in-law. And to my groom—" There was a smattering of applause. "To my groom." Joey wove their fingers together. "I just want to say how lucky…you are to get to marry me!" Now the applause got louder. "I'm kidding. I'm the lucky one. I really am."

"Your parents," whispered Grant, his smile not faltering.

"Fuck," she whispered back. "Now there are two other people we'd like to thank. They've welcomed Grant into our family. Most of all they keep things very…interesting. I'm talking about my parents." Joey saw Scott by the ice sculpture and Bea not far behind, at a table by herself, holding up her margarita for the toast.

"I'm talking about my dad and…my mom, who in particular has spent so much time and effort planning us a beautiful wedding. I can't believe it's tomorrow."

Joey's throat choked with unexpected emotion. "Thanks, Mom."

chapter forty-five
Joey

florida

2019

Tables were being dismantled. Lily had changed into a bikini and was floating on twin swans in the pool with Sister #3. Grant's groomsmen stood in a circle, doing some fraternity ritual that involved shots and a handshake.

"Hey, stranger," said Leo. He wore a light-gray sweater rolled up to his elbows with darker gray skinny jeans.

"Hey," she said. Then, "You know how kids are really happy when they run outside, and we think, like, that's just because they're kids?"

Leo cocked his head. "Yeah?"

"Well, I think everyone can be that happy if they run around barefoot outside. The happy isn't because of being a kid, it's because of being barefoot."

"They got the wrong hypothesis, eh?" Leo slipped off his high-tops and peeled off his socks. "You could be onto something."

"Noooo! Leo Winn, after all these years—barefoot. Can someone call the photographer?"

"If I trust anyone to keep their grass clean, it's your future in-laws."

"They probably had it power washed."

Leo smiled but didn't banter back.

Joey felt the world widen again around them. "Anyway, hey, thanks for coming."

"Wouldn't miss it. Grant's parents know how to throw a party, huh?"

"That they do." Joey took a sip from her glass. Grant had switched her to water, reminding her that tomorrow they'd take pictures that would live in infamy.

She was getting married tomorrow. Despite all the hoopla, somehow she kept forgetting it. "So, where's Rand?"

"He went back to the hotel. I think this was a lot for him. But he's surprised me with Lily, to be honest. I kind of figured that, since he'd known this whole time she was his daughter, he must not have minded to stay on the sidelines. But we talked about it this week. Did you know Bea used to send him pictures and updates?"

"Really?"

"Every few months, apparently."

"Huh. This was so much bigger than us."

"This was always so much bigger than us, Jonesey."

"And what about my mom and Rand?"

"They talked for a while, but I don't know more than that. I asked my dad if he still loves her."

"You did?"

"He acted like I'd asked him the dumbest question in the world. He said, *Son, I loved her a lot. More than I ever loved anyone, I suppose. But sometimes I wonder if I'm just not that good at loving.*"

"Well…I can see that." Joey drank her water but only got a drip before the glass emptied.

"Late-stage self-awareness."

Joey smiled. "I do wonder if they'll go back to their old ways. Because how good is my mother at loving either? Maybe everyone should just be with who they want."

"Let the chips fall where they may?"

"There's no one left to hurt. They've already done it all. So maybe now they get to be happy. Their version of it."

"That's generous, Jonesey."

"I'm just over my life hinging on their lives. I'm so over that."

"Amen." Leo rubbed his scruffy chin.

She wanted to tell him that she liked his adult scruff. And more than that—she liked the adult he'd become. But that seemed like a thing she wasn't allowed to say.

"You seem happy, Jonesey."

"Well…I am."

"That makes me happy." Leo kissed her cheek, and his scruff tickled her chin. "I'm gonna head out. Good luck tomorrow. I'll see you down the aisle."

Joey felt his imprint on her cheek. "Don't let the groom overhear you. He'll think you're making inroads."

"Oh, Jonesey." Leo gave her a sheepish smile. "You don't have to worry about that. You set me straight. Friends, right?"

She smiled faintly. "Friends."

"Get some sleep, huh?" he said.

And Joey watched him fade from her sight one more time.

"All right, babe. I need sleep." Grant held the Navajo chief's blanket in his arms.

"Why do you have that? Your mom will kill you if you get it dirty."

"My mom *gave* it to us. Apparently it will protect our union. She got the chief to bless it or something."

Lily took it from him. "This will be great for a photo shoot. Can I keep it in my room?"

"Lil," said Joey. "About *your* room."

"Eh. We'll talk about it after the wedding," said Grant. "Let's get outta here."

"But it's bad luck for the bride to see the groom before the wedding," said Scott, materializing from inside.

Joey hadn't spoken to him since, when? The dinner of insanity? She realized now he'd been hovering all evening. He'd bobbed his pale head as she'd rubbed the assembly line of bellies belonging to all her pregnant New York girlfriends. He'd lingered in the backdrop as she and G had hugged for ages.

"I'm not superstitious." Joey gave her father a brief hug.

"Wait, he's right, babe," said Grant. "You're not supposed to sleep at our place tonight."

"Great," said Joey. "Where do you suggest I sleep?"

"At home, of course," said her father. "In your bedroom one last time."

"We watched *Father of the Bride* again a few weeks ago," said Bea, walking up, swatting at a fat bee buzzing around her floral crown. "Your dad thinks he's Steve Martin."

"I *don't* think I'm Steve Martin."

Joey's eyelids fluttered. "I'll sleep wherever. Someone just give me a bed."

"You have a bed," said her father. "You always have a bed at home."

"Well, I'm off to my home," said Bea.

"Where's that?" asked Grant.

"A friend is spending the summer in Tuscany. She's a potter. She has a cute little house on Jog. I've been painting up a storm. Rediscovering myself."

"Well, why don't you try discovering yourself quickly?" said Lily. "I think I speak for all of us when I say we'd like our parents to check out of Lost and Found." She strutted off. "Come on, Grant!"

"Lil," said Scott.

Lily glanced over her shoulder. She shook her head. She kept walking.

"That's my cue." Grant kissed Joey—quick and firm. She tried to hold on to him longer, tighter, but he was like quicksand. "See you when—"

"See you when," she said.

"See you tomorrow, JoJo," said her mother. "Well, actually…" She checked her watch. "It's today. You're getting married today."

"See you," said Joey.

Her father was quiet in the car. A Post-it in his script was adhered to the dashboard. It read, *Keep the faith. The most amazing things happen right when you're about to give up all hope.* Tina Turner played on Sirius.

"I'm sorry, JoJo," her father finally said.

"I know."

"I really am. I'm not perfect. I think kids like to think their parents are perfect."

Joey pulled at the suffocating seat belt. When it snapped back, it was like being strangled. She unfastened the buckle. "Maybe. But your version of not perfect affected us all."

"I know." Her father turned down Tina. "I have so many regrets."

Joey jangled her evil eye charm around in her pocket. "I really don't get one thing though. Why did you stay with Mom? It almost seems like you had zero..." She didn't say what she wanted to say to her father.

"You can say it. Self-respect."

A beeping noise blasted through the car. Her father didn't demand that Joey refasten her belt.

"Self-respect. Yeah, Dad."

"Here's the thing, Joey. We were taught that love is perfect. Love comes in this neat little box. It's wrapped in this perfect bow. It's fairy tales and fireworks, right?"

"I don't know."

"Well, that's not my experience with love, Joey. My experience is that love has all these ugly little lumps in it. True love is when you acknowledge the lumps and love someone anyway. It's when you love someone to the end even if it's not the way they love you. I will love your mother until the end. And if she can't forgive me, I'll have to live with it. But I have hope I can keep on having lumpy love with your mother."

Her father turned off the ignition. The beeping stopped. Into the quiet, Joey whispered, "What am I supposed to do, Dad?"

Her father opened the car door, careful not to swipe the Total Gym that had been collecting cobwebs in the garage since the eighties. He patted her hand. "Sweetheart, the thing about lumps is that you never get to plan for them."

chapter forty-six
Joey

florida

2019

It went so fast. Everyone said it would.

There was the fawning over her. The commentary. *Doesn't she look stunning? Daphne, the rose petals are for the ceremony. You don't get to scatter them now! Okay, let's fix the eyelashes. Close your eyes. When you open them, you're going to see a bride in the mirror!*

There were Joey and G appraising their makeup in the mirror. Joey felt the prettiest version of herself, which had been the goal: her makeup a natural glow, with a few fake lashes for just a bit of drama; her hair in a deep side part and relaxed waves she'd done herself; her flowy boho dress with its unusual bell sleeves in Chantilly lace and its neckline a twinge more plunging than she usually veered, with a hand-beaded, zigzag cutout design.

"You're so beautiful, Joey," said G.

"Thanks, G," said Joey. "You're looking gorgeous yourself!"

Bea joined them at the mirror. "You're a radiant bride, JoJo. We've got it going on, Bezas ladies."

And they all smiled at their reflections, the three of them in a line.

There was the first look in the atrium. It was pouring outside. The wedding planner said it might let up for the ceremony. They would wait another hour, but then they had to set up the chairs. The library was a beautiful place for a ceremony. Just last week even, a couple chose the library over the garden, despite the good weather!

Joey walked to Grant, whose back was to her. She tapped him on the shoulder. Oh God, those Baby Bear Eyes. He said he loved her so much. He said she looked resplendent. He actually used that word. *Resplendent.* Perhaps he'd taken a spin through the thesaurus that morning to give her something more meaningful than *amazing.* He said sun was overrated. He made her twirl.

There were fifty glasses of water. Perhaps that was an exaggeration, but water was thrust at her from all directions. From Bea, from the event planner, from G, from various aunts of Grant's, from all the pregnant New York girls. There was Grant's cousin Alexia—the one who never smiled and decided she didn't want to walk down the aisle after all. The event planner made all the changes. She communicated the changes to all the players. Then she communicated the communication of the changes to Joey. A few minutes later, a scowling Alexia told Joey that she would indeed walk down the aisle.

There were one hundred million pictures. There were pictures with Grant's hands on her face, with his hands circling her waist, with Lily's arm on her shoulder, with her parents' hands slung across her back from either side.

Hands and arms. Touch. Far too much touch. There was, *Get closer* and *Touch your cheek to his* and *Now throw your arms up in a silly pose* and *That's not so silly, try to be actually silly.* There was the event planner who crept up as the photographer swapped lenses. *I'm sorry, but we'll have to do it indoors. You'll see, it will be beautiful.*

There was the ketubah signing with Grant's childhood rabbi, who kept calling them the Abrewmans. There was the marriage contract with a giant tree in watercolors that bled over the signature lines. There was Joey's hand moving. Signing her name to it. There was the clatter of a pen. There was Siya scrawling her signature. There was applause. There was Grant checking to see it was her before putting down her veil. *Just making sure it's not Lily I'm marrying!*

To the laughter that followed, Joey felt the veil bind her face. She couldn't breathe. Where was the oxygen in this building?

There was a wave of people into the library. The library she'd never been inside because it never rained long in Florida. But yes, she got it—it was a spectacular place to get married. There was her father at her side, her mother at her other. Her father said, *I can't believe it's time.* Her mother said, *I'm so happy for you, JoJo.*

There was Alexia, complaining loudly to the event planner that her bouquet wasn't as robust as the other ones. There was the event planner pushing Alexia down the aisle anyway. There was Siya lifting her foot clad in a Manolo up in a ta-da before starting her walk. Joey waved, feeling like she was sending off a child to her first day at school instead of sending her best friend down her aisle. Next came Lily in her feathered gown, fluffing her train behind her as she began to strut.

There was the music, the soulful Hebrew song of which Joey didn't understand a word but always made her emotional at other people's weddings. The cue. *That's you*, said the event planner. Her father said, *Congratulations, my darling*. Her mother said, *Congratulations to you too, dear*.

Joey was heading down the aisle now. There was a chuppah draped in bougainvillea. She loved bougainvillea. How had her mother known?

There was Grant at the end of the aisle. There was G waving from her seat. There was the Lilly Pulitzer Fan Club—a schizophrenic lineup of pastel beside Siya's vivid-yellow gown and Lily's cobalt one. There was Rand sitting stiffly in a middle row.

Joey kept walking. She was afraid she wasn't smiling. But it was the most unnatural feeling to walk down this aisle. Everyone said, *You won't notice a thing besides Grant*. But they were wrong. She was noticing everything, and what she noticed was that Leo wasn't there.

The realization smacked her the moment the aisle ran out.

Grant reached out his arm. There was a moment where no one moved. Then she realized, this was her cue to perform. She had to circle Grant seven times. Why? She had no clue. Something biblical, maybe. She began to circle him. One. Where was Leo? Two. Did he decide he couldn't come? Three. But why? Four. Why did she care? Five. Maybe he got lost. Six. But Rand was here. Seven. She was going to faint.

Grant gripped Joey's arm. Her parents filed in to her side. Lily took her bouquet.

Wait. She wasn't ready yet. She needed a minute. But the rabbi was already welcoming the friends and family of the Abrewmans. He was talking about Bali and true love. Joey wondered what she was supposed to say when it came down to it. Maybe they should have done the rehearsal. Was it *Yes*, or *I do*?

Then it began to speed up. She was on a treadmill, and some manic personal trainer was pressing the *faster* button. Faster, faster, faster. There were the seven blessings read by Grant's seven sets of aunts and uncles. It was so perfect, they'd said when doling out the roles. So fitting.

She was fidgeting. She wasn't paying attention to her own wedding ceremony. She took one hand from Grant's and sank it into the pocket she'd had added to her gown. She felt for her evil eye charm. Her lungs sucked in air.

There was Grant's friend Evan coming forward with the rings. They didn't have nephews to take on the ring bearer role, so Evan was the anointed ring bearer. There had been a lot of inappropriately old ring bearer jokes. The rings meant the ceremony was almost over, didn't it?

With this ring, you are consecrated unto me.

The metal was cold as it slid onto her finger. What did *consecrated unto me* even mean?

As my husband.

Grant's hand flashed with his new bling. The bling that was because of her.

May the Lord lift up his countenance upon you, and grant you peace.

Peace. Joey felt like crying at the word *peace*.

Amen.

There was rain pummeling the stained-glass windows. There was the glass on the ground wrapped in a linen napkin. Oh God, there was the glass, and when it broke—

Grant stomped his foot onto the napkin. There was an unmistakable crunch.

Mazel Tov!
Grant reached over to kiss her.
They were husband and wife.

Joey was struggling to get up when she heard a man's voice. Which was strange, because what she was struggling to get up from was a toilet in the women's bathroom. "Jonesey!"

"Leo! Wha…Leo?" The door to the stall flew open. Instinctively, Joey crossed her arms over her chest. "Leo! I'm on the toilet."

"Well, are you going?"

"No, I'm not going. I'm just trying to get all the pieces pulled back into place. You can't imagine how many contraptions and buttons there are."

He seemed to focus on her and her getup. "You look so beautiful, Jonesey."

"I'm on a toilet, Leo."

"You're the most beautiful girl on a toilet I've ever seen."

"How many girls on toilets have you seen?" Joey's head was buzzing.

"Jonesey, can we talk? Before you get married, like, can we really talk?" Leo was wearing a suit, yes, but it was all crinkled, like he'd pulled it out of a suitcase without time for a steam. His hair was damp and rumpled to one side with a cowlick sticking up. He looked like a man who'd just gotten laid while wearing this suit. Maybe he *had* just gotten laid.

Why was Leo in the women's bathroom?

Why did Leo think she wasn't already married?

"Leo, I'm—"

"No, Jonesey, seriously! You need to let me say what I came here to say."

Joey kept her arms crossed across her chest to minimize exposure of the cleavage courtesy of her gravity-defying corset meant to smooth out all lumps, bumps, and organs. "Okay, but Leo, what if someone comes in?"

"No one will come in, Jonesey. I put the janitor's sign out there."

"Where will people go to the bathroom?"

"They can go to the bathroom in the lobby for all I care! This is important."

"Okay." Joey tried to sit as normally as possible on the toilet seat. She had to get out to finish cocktail hour. Grant would be looking for her. They were supposed to be announced to Michael Bublé, whom they'd seen three times in concert.

"Jonesey, I went to that house. I saw it."

"You went to what house? Can you speak in English?"

"Jonesey!" Leo stomped a foot. "Lily told me to. I went to the house with your painting. Whatshername?"

"Edith?" Joey was still. "You went to Edith's?"

"Yes! Yes! I saw your painting."

"Okay." Joey slumped over again. Her arms dropped to her sides. Sitting on a toilet in her wedding dress was like balancing on a medicine ball. "So you saw it. It doesn't mean—"

"It means everything, Jonesey."

Joey felt her entire world unravel in that sentence.

"You know why I came back to Florida, J. I came to find Lily, of course. I came so I could let go of this toxic secret once and for all, yes. But why did I really come? For you, Jonesey. Like I told you that day on the beach, in the stupidest, most selfish way. Damn it, I didn't want to do this again. I wanted to let you live your happy life. More than anything, I want you to be happy, Jonesey. I didn't want to ruin your life by telling you that I've thought about you every day for fifteen years."

Joey was watching a car crash, only it was her in the crash. She was crashing. Now Leo came into the stall. He came right up to her, smelling so heartbreakingly much like himself. "Jonesey, I've always loved you. I never stopped. I mean, I told you at the beach, but I don't know if you believed me. I could say that, when we were kids, I didn't know what we had, but that would be a lie. I knew what we had. I just knew it was impossible. I hoped I would move on. I hoped for fifteen years I would move on, but I couldn't. I never really did."

"You had Arthur," whispered Joey.

"Well, I wasn't celibate. But us, what we had—and it wasn't because we were young and I'm idealizing it."

"I know," she whispered.

"Look, I obviously knew you were engaged when I came back here. But I hoped Grant would be this asshole or something. And you know what? I like Grant. He's a cool guy. And I saw immediately that you loved him. That you were happy. It was one of the hardest days of my life when I saw you at the pier—"

"Leo—"

"It was the hardest day because I got to see you again, and I couldn't even hug you. Not fully. Not when you were standing there, with all your same Joey-ness, that I like just as much as when we were kids. I really want to tell you, I like the person you've become, Jones. I like her so much."

"I like the person you've become too," Joey whispered. "But—"

"But that day I saw you again at the pier was also the hardest day of my life because that's the day I had to let you go again. That's the day I really lost hope. Until now. Until today—"

"Leo—"

"No, Jonesey. I saw the painting. You painted my face. Not Grant's. Mine. It's like the painting you started on Corfu."

"Yes, but—"

"You can't say a *but* about that painting. You captured me. That painting says love, Jonesey. You painted me and not him. Period. You once told me—"

This was the tidal wave. Joey steeled herself for it.

"You once told me you could only paint the face of the man you loved. So this is my plea, Jonesey. You and Arthur, you're all that are important to me in the world. The logistics may seem insane, but I know we can figure them out. Our life together will be so happy, if you just give us a chance. Please don't marry Grant, Jonesey. You can still back out. Please don't. Please don't. Please don't."

Leo put his hands to his knees and bent his head, panting.

"I don't know what to say." Joey crunched down on her lip, feeling tears collecting in the corners of her eyes. She just had to finish this with him before the dam broke. "You have to know something."

Leo lifted his head. "Yeah?"

Slowly, Joey held up her left hand. The hand with her new wedding band. She studied the swirls on the gray marble floor. "I'm already married."

Leo grabbed her hand. He twisted her ring. "How is that possible?"

"The wedding started forty-five minutes ago. It just ended."

"But weddings never start on time!" Leo's face shaded with the beginnings of panic. "Lily only told me, like, an hour and a half ago that I needed to go see your painting. But I figured weddings are always at least an hour late."

"Jewish weddings start on time," she said quietly. "Jewish weddings always start on time."

The sound that came out of Leo was a sound she would not forget for the rest of her life. Joey went somewhere else for the duration of that sound. The scent of thickly diffused tuberose nearly choked her.

Eventually, Leo rose. He walked backward to the door, tearing his collar from his neck with such vigor that a button clanged to the tile. "I'm glad you chose the bigger stall, Jonesey. I would have been right on top of you in one of the smaller ones."

She tried to smile, but her mouth refused to cooperate.

"I don't take any of it back, Jonesey. I love you even if you don't love me."

Then Leo—her Leo who actually still loved her—turned and walked away. He looked back. He said, "Jonesey, you remember I said I had a first yacht?"

"What?"

"Before I got this new yacht, I mean. I bought my first one five years ago."

"Oh?" she managed.

"I named it *Jonesey*." His eyes fixed on a point over her head. "I named my first boat *Jonesey*. I have no idea why I'm telling you that now."

Leo shook his head and walked away very fast. Joey watched his back slip out of sight.

Then the door closed without a thud, without so much as a squeak. Like it hadn't even happened at all.

chapter forty-seven
Joey

florida

2019

Joey was sniffling into a wad of toilet paper when she heard footsteps. She tried to stop crying and be normal. The footsteps paused at her door. Sweet little G materialized through the thicket of her tears.

"How did you get here?" managed Joey. "Isn't there a…sign?"

"I've been here since before Leo came in, darling. My bladder isn't as young as yours." G reached under Joey's arms. "Come on. Let's get you to the couch."

Joey had enough control of her faculties to realize that ninety-three-year-old G lifting her off the toilet was not a good idea. She flexed her legs, but the toilet was a suction gripping her butt. With some effort, she wiggled free. As she tussled with her undergarments to return them to their proper places, she shuddered with a fresh sob. G walked her to the little sitting area with a soft yellow couch. G clicked the lock on the bathroom door.

When G returned to the couch, she said, "You love him."

"You heard?" Joey coughed into her wad of toilet paper. "You heard…everything?"

"I heard everything, and one thing is clear. You love him."

"I love him," Joey heard herself say. "Yes, I love him. I really love him. I didn't even get to tell him that. I was in such shock. What's wrong with me, G?"

"Nothing is wrong with you, my darling. But now you have a choice to make. Now you have to decide, who do you love more?"

"That's apples to oranges, really."

"It's not apples to oranges. You like one better. You either like apples better or you like oranges better. It's the stupidest saying I've ever heard."

"I love them both. Like you loved Grandfather and Milos both. Anyway…it's too late."

"Didn't you read my messages? You probably don't want to hear this, Joey, but I loved Milos more. I always loved Milos more, but to appease my parents' last wishes, I married your grandfather. But seventy-plus years of hindsight has shown me that life could have taken a different turn."

Joey thought about her sweet grandfather, who deserved to be loved the most. She stared at her finger with its new gleaming wedding band. "I don't know, G."

G folded Joey's hands in hers. "Now Leo and Grant. They are both wonderful men. Grant is Jewish, but let's end this right here."

"End this? Grant's going to be looking for me. Oh God, my *husband* is going to be looking for me."

"Forget about that for a second. It's going to be okay." Her grandmother patted her hair, but it was still fluffed to the heavens. "What I was starting to say is I think my mother is in heaven shaking her head. She's figured out the rule they only tell you when you meet the Big Man. That it doesn't matter if a man's Jewish, if he's the counterpart to your soul. I think my mother's up there telling us to stand up for our lives. You get to do what you want to do. You're not pleasing me. You're not pleasing these two men. You just go with the one you love the most."

Joey heard voices at the door. Grant?

"Hold on." Her grandmother peeked her head out the door. Joey heard her say, "We're having an emergency with the dress."

G sat back on the couch. "You don't get to choose, darling."

"Was that Grant?"

"Listen to me. You don't get to say, *God, I choose to love that one more.* You just ask the question. God gives the answer. So now here's what we're going to do—we're going to flip a coin." G pulled a quarter from her purse.

"We're going to flip a coin? That's how we're going to decide my life?"

"It's as sane an avenue as any. Okay, heads it's Grant, tails it's Leo. God will make the choice. You ready?" She didn't wait for Joey's approval. Quickly, her grandmother tossed the coin in the air, caught it, and flipped it to rest on her palm. "Well, there we have it. Grant it is."

"But I don't want it to be Grant!"

For a long time, she and G just stared at each other. In the mirror, Joey glimpsed her face streaked in mascara.

"Good," her grandmother finally said. "There we have it then."

"There we have it?" Snot trickled toward Joey's lip. Every inch of her toilet paper had been saturated. She grabbed a tissue from the box G had placed in her lap. "But it was heads."

"The coin toss." G laughed. "Just a silly thing to get the answer out of you. You see, if it had been Leo, you'd have felt relieved. We're not actually picking a man from a coin toss, my darling. That's insane. So here it is. Settled."

"Here it is, G? *Settled*? I just married the wrong one."

"But you still have a choice, my darling. That's the lucky thing. We don't always have choices, Joey. My parents and Benjamin did not. Sometimes life chooses for you. So when you are presented with a choice in life, you thank God, because it's an opportunity to be happy. And you don't squander it."

"I don't know, G. I don't want to be like my mother, but look at me. I'm exactly like her."

"Your mother has her faults, to be sure. So do we all. Even you who has tried so hard to be perfect. You know, Joey, I think perfect is overrated."

Joey remembered how Leo had said something similar. "But how am I supposed to be with Leo? He has a son on the other side of the world. He lives on boats in the middle of oceans. If I'm with Leo, I'll have to travel a lot. I won't be able to be here in Florida as much with you."

G poured them glasses of water from a carafe on a side table. "You love to travel, Joey. You were always counting down to vacations from that awful firm. Climbing mountains, handstands on beaches, tightroping…"

"Ziplining," Joey corrected, an unexpected laugh gurgling out of her.

G frowned. "I did worry, you know, but that's not the point. And then you went to Bali, and I was so happy for you, my darling, to have that freedom and sunshine you'd longed for. But you only stayed a few months before returning to Florida for me, when I had my heart surgery. And then you ran into Grant. So who knows what you might have otherwise chosen, or where. Now your world is wide open again. And I think it will suit you." G nodded. "Yes, I truly think it will suit you."

"I don't know, G."

"I do. And this is what it is to follow your heart."

Thunder crackled beyond the window. "But that's just it. My heart might say Leo—it does say Leo—but it said Leo before. And then he broke it."

"It's *follow* your heart though, Joey. The follow is the important part."

"I don't know what you mean."

"It means, you don't get to know how it turns out. But you have to follow where it leads. You have to trust that wherever and to whomever it takes you, is where you're supposed to go."

"It's so much more complicated than that, G."

Her grandmother's eyes leaked rivulets through her rouge. "It's not. We make it more complicated. We say we can't undo mistakes. We say we have to live up to standards our parents set. We get too scared to try, and our whole life passes that way. You see? Now no more tears, my darling. Now we have an answer. Marriages can be undone. Things can be made right. You haven't had children and decades with Grant. Leo didn't just die in a coma. This is some money. This is some embarrassment. This is a heartbroken groom, who anyhow deserves someone who will love him in the top slot.

"Rise and shine, my sweet girl. You have the rest of your life to live." Her grandmother cupped Joey's chin. "And what a life it's going to be."

⌒

"There's my wife!" Grant pulled her to him and kissed her. "I was beginning to think you were having second thoughts. You were holed up in the bathroom practically all of cocktail hour."

"Grant, we—"

"Okay, you two, it's time," said the event planner, whose superpower was surely that she appeared everywhere.

As if on cue, Michael Bublé began to croon. The DJ announced, "And now let's welcome Mr. and Mrs. Grant Newman!"

The event planner flung open the doors to the ballroom Joey had yet to see. She took a few steps toward the closest table, a B-list table with a host of clapping, smiling people Joey had never seen before. The table had almost an old apothecary vibe. There were pressed botanical artworks in glass frames announcing table numbers, black-painted candlesticks, hunter-green vases with twisted vines. Antique meets the tropics. It was just…beyond.

But then Joey halted as the ballroom walls came into focus. They were adorned with black and white paper flowers, meticulous and layered, waxy green vines weaving throughout. It was maybe the most beautiful thing she had ever seen. Joey tugged Grant back. She put her hand atop a flower on the wall beside the door. It was black with pearl beads lining it. Joey had seen flower walls before, small ones for Instagram purposes, maybe—but never the entire room. It had the effect of a wild, sexy garden. Bali, at night.

Grant squeezed Joey's hand. She needed to tell him. Her sweet husband. How could she tell him?

As he wove her toward the dance floor, people kept

reaching out to touch her, like somehow she belonged to them all. But she didn't want to be Mrs. Grant Newman. She wanted to be Joey Abrams. She wanted to be Joey Abrams with the freedom to be with the one she loved the most.

She wished she loved Grant the most. She wished love could take into account who you wanted the object to be. As Grant kissed her and transmitted with that kiss everything he was, she wished it were enough.

She waited for the song to end before she said, "Grant."

He looked at her. His face crumpled. "No."

～

Grant kept saying, "No."

He inspected a matte-gold fork as she told him she really hadn't known until today. Until after they'd married. She should have known, she said. She wished so hard she could turn back the clock and spare him this pain. She was so unbelievably sorry.

Grant sat motionless while Joey asked Lily to tell the DJ they were postponing the hora. As a cheery waiter served him his fillet and mashed potatoes—mashed potatoes of which he'd eaten a plateful at their tasting and proclaimed the best he'd ever had—Grant finally pushed away the plate and shook his head vigorously, like regaining his life force. "Joey, we're married. I just…I can't believe this. I want to be married to you! Please don't do this! I love you so much."

Tears spilled out her eyes.

"What about our plans together? What about our life together?"

"I can't possibly explain how sorry I am," Joey said softly. "For the rest of my life, I'll be sorry for hurting you."

Grant swished his scotch. He put a finger atop the baby cactus from which a mini banner was strung that read NEWLYWEDS. He pressed his finger down hard. When he pulled it up, a drop of blood sprang from his skin. "You should go," he finally said, in a new toneless voice.

"Go?"

"Go. Stay. Actually I don't care what you do. But I'm going."

"We'll just go? But all these people—"

"I don't care." He walked toward the door without looking back.

The event planner popped up, brandishing her tablet. "I'm not sure why you guys want to save the hora for later, but we'll do the father-daughter dance instead now."

Joey caught sight of her parents at their table beside the dance floor. Joey watched her father's hand migrate atop her mother's. It rested there. They didn't speak. With her other hand, Bea pursed her lips at a pocket mirror. With his other hand, her father drank a margarita. Her mother retracted her hand first. She stood. She strode toward the DJ booth.

"Jo." Joey felt a hand at her waist.

"Lil." As she turned, she glimpsed a huddle of the Lilly Pulitzer Fan Club. Joey dove her head into her sister's shoulder—part salve, part shield.

"It's okay, Jo." Lily awkwardly patted her shoulder.

"It's so not okay, Lil. I'm terrible. I'm just like Mom. I've ruined Grant's life."

"You didn't ruin Grant's life. You've been married for two seconds. You'll get it annulled. You're being a drama queen. Do you know how lucky you are? Leo loves you, and you love him. I *knew* you loved him. That's why I had to tell him to go to Edith's."

Joey lifted her head from Lily's shoulder. "You couldn't have told him to go yesterday though? Or this morning? You had to wait until right before my wedding?"

Lily had the grace to blush. "Look, Jo, at first I wasn't sure I should tell Leo. I mean, I like Grant. He's always been so nice to me. And by the time I decided I had to tell Leo, I was so crazed with the party for the Sri Lankan jewelry, and it slipped my mind to call him after, and then I totally meant to tell him at the rehearsal dinner, but you can't imagine my to-do list. My head was crammed with—"

Joey put up a hand. "Okay. It doesn't matter. But Lil, what if I got engaged to Grant just to try to prove something to myself?"

"Then you did it, Joey. Seriously, why do you love beating yourself up? So you made a mistake, and now we'll fix it. It will be fine, Jo. I'll deal with everything here."

"Lil, that's—"

"I'm your sister." Lily shrugged. "I got it."

Joey watched a couple she didn't recognize pose by one of the flower walls.

"Jo, you know Mom did the flower walls."

"What do you mean?" Joey saw her mother talking to the DJ across the gray marble dance floor.

"I mean, Mom made them. She's been working on them in the basement for... I don't know, months."

"Mom made like... everything?" Joey did a spin around to absorb it. "All of the paper flowers? But... there are thousands."

"Thousands," confirmed Lily. "She wanted to do something special for you. But, like... don't go feeling guilty about this too. Get it together, sis. Seriously."

The event planner inserted her face between them. Her mouthpiece nearly took out Joey's eye. "It's go time, Joey."

Joey saw her father shuffling on the edge of the floor. His face fell when they locked eyes. He looked like a gangly middle school boy whose crush turned him down when he asked her to Snowball.

Lily said quietly, "Joey, I'll dance with Dad."

"Really?"

"Yeah. He's my dad too."

"But that's not how it works!" said the event planner. "It's a dance for the father and the daughter who got married."

But Lily was already striding toward Scott. Joey watched Lily give their father a hug and then whisper something. Joey walked very fast to the door before she'd have to witness the look on her father's face.

She floated through the remains of the cocktail hour she barely even saw. Past the bathroom where Leo stood in her stall, telling her he loved her. She took off her one-inch block heels that nonetheless she couldn't believe she was still wearing. She needed fresh air. Fuck the rain.

She remembered an outside door by the room where she got ready. The makeup artist had gone through it for a smoke between layers of airbrush foundation spray. Joey burst into the night. A canopy shielded her head from the rain, but the ground was a muddy flood. Her lovely dress swished in the muck, and she didn't care. She reached to the back of her dress and unzipped it as far down as she could force it. She sighed as the first sip of unrestricted oxygen hit her lungs.

That's when she saw the figure hunched over in the rain. That's when she saw the back.

Joey sat on the curb beside him. Leo lifted his face, all red and wet.

"You don't have to console me on your wedding day, Jonesey."

"It's not my wedding day anymore."

The hope that flushed Leo's face was heartbreaking in its infancy—like a first press of grapes, their sweetest production. "What are you—?"

By the thread of her hand through his, he quieted. She looked at their hands woven together. If hands could be a home, she knew that hers was here. They were both sweating, or one of them was, or else it was the rain filling in all the cracks. She'd lived so long avoiding the rain that she'd forgotten how good it felt when it met her in the dark places of herself. In punctuation, the rain turned torrential, like God kicking up the dial.

You can take it, the sky was saying. *Let's fall apart together.*

Joey's whole body was humming with aliveness. Every molecule inside her felt cozy and in its right place.

Leo looked into her eyes, and she met him there. So many questions sprouting, morphing, waiting. The answers in hers, insufficient.

She could say: I'm terrified, Leo. You consumed me once, and the greatest void I've ever known was the absence of myself when I no longer had you.

She could say: I love five hundred million things about you, but most of all, I love how you let me be lost. That you don't try to hurry me up to get to the found. Today, Leo, today I think I'm lost and found, both at the same time.

And: Maybe it will be the two of us when we're eighty,

drinking our coffees in the morning in some place I can't imagine now. But maybe it will be just me, drinking my coffee alone, and honestly, truly, that will be okay too.

The rain ebbed a bit, and Joey opened her mouth to try to lend it all shape, but nothing came out.

Instead she felt her hand give Leo's hand a squeeze. As if in punctuation, the clouds unleashed more—first in fuzzy sheets, like static on an old TV set, and then the lashing. More. More. More.

Because of the rain, Joey could no longer make out Leo's eyes, but she felt him squeeze back. Hard. But then his grip softened, giving her space to air herself out, like one of those sheets on a line, coming back to life in the Corfu sun.

And then she squeezed him again, and he did too in return. Again. Again. Again. Until Joey wasn't sure when her squeezes ended and Leo's began. Just that somehow, he knew that she knew that he knew everything there was to say.

READING GROUP GUIDE

Dear Reader:

The first sparks of my idea for this novel came on a trip to Jamaica in 2015. On the beach one day, I watched two kids from different families and places playing happily together. I thought about the magic of vacation friends and romances. There is something different and special about exiting your everyday life that alters the relationships developed with people you meet on your travels. And so Joey and Leo were born.

If you ask me to vote for the beach or the mountains, I, like Joey, would choose the beach a thousand times over. I feel happiest when next to or in water. I grew up on a lake in Michigan and now live in Tel Aviv, mere steps from the Mediterranean Sea. And so, in choosing the novel's setting, the island aspect of Corfu appealed to me immensely, from Corfu Town's pebbled city beaches nestled in tiny coves to the western coast's endless, spectacular caramel sand beaches leading to an impossibly turquoise sea.

Continuing on the beach motif, I decided to set the remainder of the book in South Florida. Aside from its sunny ambience, I've spent a lot of time there, so it is like a second home. My maternal grandmother, with whom I share a closeness like that between Joey and Sarah, lives in Delray Beach.

And finally, I mined my own experience for Joey's unlikely career transition. Like Joey, I was a lawyer at a large law firm, and I quit my job the year I'd go up for partnership to travel and work on creative pursuits. (Although, unlike Joey, the firm I worked at was wonderful and the people I worked with even more so.)

Joey isn't me, of course, but so much of me is in this book. As a writer, the delight I find in fiction is in collecting the truest things I know and shapeshifting them into a story. I feel privileged you chose to read mine.

Jaclyn Goldis

DISCUSSION QUESTIONS

1. One of the inspirations for the novel was the author seeing two kids meet and become friends on vacation. Have you ever connected with someone on vacation, or outside your everyday life, as friends or romantic partners? How do you think that experience went differently than it would have had it originated amid your everyday life?

2. A theme in the novel is the trauma of "postmemory," that is, how later generations bear the personal, collective, and cultural trauma of those generations who came before. How does this theme play out in the novel? How are both Bea and Jocy affected by what Sarah and Sam endured?

3. Even years after the fact, Joey struggles to find closure to her relationship with Leo. Was it selfish for her to agree to meet with Leo eleven days before her wedding? How have you experienced closure in a relationship? Did the time it took or way it happened surprise you?

4. Why do you think Joey switched from art to law after Leo broke up with her? Have you ever given up on a passion? What would it take for you to revisit it?

5. Sarah must live her entire life with regrets that were impossible to make right. Why was it easier for Sarah to marry a man she didn't love than the man she did? Do you think that even after communicating with Milos, she will ever fully forgive herself?

6. Many characters in the novel are holding on to secrets they eventually reveal. Are secrets in a relationship ever justified?

7. Bea is in many ways an unlikable character. On page 162, she says, "Maybe sometimes you have to risk hurting people you love in order to be happy." Do you agree with her? In what circumstances would you find the statement valid? How does your view of Bea change as the book progresses? Do you think that Joey ultimately finds more compassion for her mother after she leaves Grant for Leo?

8. On page 43, Joey says that with Leo love felt like falling, but with Grant she learned to love on solid ground. Do you think that love can be divided into these two categories? Which have you experienced in your life? Do you think it is possible for Joey to love on solid ground with Leo too?

9. Neither Bea nor Joey was born on Corfu, but nonetheless the island becomes a central facet of their lives. How does the way each of Joey, Bea, and Sarah feels about Corfu change with the events of their lives and the events of the novel? Do you think that any or all of

the women would choose to return to Corfu for a visit after the events of the novel? Have you ever considered a place not your birthplace or home as nonetheless important in your life? Perhaps it is a vacation spot or a place where a family member lives or lived. How did that place become important to you? Have your feelings toward that place changed with time or events?

10. Family history plays a critical role in the plot. How is Joey affected by her mother's and grandmother's paths? Do you know your family history? How does it affect your life? Does it cause you to try to follow your ancestors' lead or take a different path?

11. The concept of forgiveness percolates throughout the novel. Do Bea and Scott deserve Joey's forgiveness? Do you think she has truly forgiven them? Does Bea deserve Sarah's forgiveness for not passing along the message from Milos? Do you think Sarah has truly forgiven her daughter? Is it easier for a parent to forgive a child or for a child to forgive a parent? Why?

12. Were you glad Joey chose Leo? Do you think Grant would have been the better choice? Why or why not?

13. Where do you see Joey five years in the future?

HISTORICAL NOTE

I knew I wanted to write a novel with multiple generations harboring secrets. My father is a Soviet emigrant, and when I was growing up, he never really spoke about his first twenty-eight years before he immigrated to the US. But in my early thirties, my family traveled to my dad's hometown in Ukraine, his first time back since he'd left, and he finally told us his stories. I wanted the protagonist—Joey—to transform, as I did, as she understands the history of her ancestors.

My paternal grandmother escaped Ukraine when the Germans invaded the Soviet Union in 1941. But her parents and some other family members did not manage to escape, and were murdered by the Nazis and buried in mass graves in the rural outskirts of Zhitomir, a small city a few hours from Kiev. I am named after this paternal grandmother, and I feel very connected to her, despite never meeting her as she died shortly before I was born. I wanted to write a grandmother character loosely inspired by her, someone who narrowly escaped the Holocaust but was greatly impacted by it.

I chose to partially set the novel on Corfu because of its lesser-known Holocaust history, and also its island and European appeal. Initially, I spent a few weeks in Greece doing research, including on Corfu, and I met with an expert in Athens on Greek Jewish history. And then over the course of a few years, I read everything I could get my hands on regarding the Corfiot Jews, and I met with and spoke to many people with personal Greek Jewish stories, as well as further experts on Greek Jewish history. Many of them told me, "The world doesn't even know what happened to the Greek Jews during the Holocaust. Our stories have largely been ignored."

I am so grateful to the kind and generous people who shared insights and stories, often painfully tragic. All of it was invaluable to an accurate portrayal of what life was like for the Corfiot Jews in the forties, prior to, during, and after Nazi rule.

The story of Sarah and her family is fictional, but it is interwoven with many real stories and events of the time. For instance, Rabbi Iakov Nechama was once the rabbi of Corfu, and how the Nazis dehumanized him during their rule is historically accurate.

And Costas, who is Sarah's customer on the island of Lefkada, is a fictionalized character based upon Costas Stagiannos, a member of Lefkada Resistance, who courageously aided the escape of some Corfiot Jews imprisoned on Lefkada.

The scene where the Jews of Corfu are imprisoned on Lefkada is rooted in fact. Many of the Corfiot Jews did indeed pass through Lefkada on their deportation to Auschwitz, and many of the townspeople of Lefkada, putting their own lives at risk, bravely tried to help the Corfiot Jews. Pope

Dimitris Thomatzidis attempted to give a cigarette across the fence to a Jew named Daniel Johanna, for which the pope was injured by a Nazi soldier. Daniel, the Jew who accepted the cigarette, was then murdered by a Nazi soldier. And subsequently, a Nazi soldier also injured (and possibly even murdered, according to differing sources) two or three more Jews standing nearby. All of these events are depicted as accurately as possible in the backdrop of the scene in which Sarah sees her family for the very last time.

Before the war, there were about two thousand Jews of Corfu. During the Nazi rule, two hundred Corfiot Jews managed to escape and/or find refuge with Christian families. On June 14, 1944, the other eighteen hundred Corfiot Jews were deported to Auschwitz, where all but about a hundred perished.

It has been an honor to pay tribute to the Jews of Corfu, whose stories have thus far been little told.

ACKNOWLEDGMENTS

I am brimming with gratitude for the many people with their imprints on this book.

My heartfelt thanks to my amazing agent, Rachel Ekstrom Courage, for how much you believe in me and my writing and for finding this novel its perfect home. I absolutely love working together. And thank you to Maggie Auffarth at Folio, for your always insightful edits.

I am enormously grateful to the wonderful people at Grand Central. To my editor, Alex Logan, my deepest thanks for your extraordinary vision of what this book could be and for helping me to make it shine. It is a pinch-me feeling at having landed in your capable hands. And a special thanks to the talented art department, who gave me such a stunningly beautiful cover.

Thank you to Linda Sivertsen, for your mentorship, friendship, and the transformative cocoon of your magical Carmel writing retreats. Thank you to my critique partner, Nicole Hackett, for your always spot-on critiques and for sharing the ups and downs of this writing life. Thank you to Laura Yorke and Alisia Leavitt, for your astute early feedback. And thanks to Zo Flamenbaum, my writing partner-in-shine, for your creative inspiration, always. There are so many other people who have been instrumental to my writing life, but I especially want to thank Natalie Blenford, Alison Hammer, Alexandra Rochman, and Ellen Neuborne. And of course, Jaclyn Mishal and your fabulous Pink Pangea writing retreats. Thank you for being such wonderful friends and for providing me with a vibrant writing community. And thank you to the Women's Fiction Writing Association for invaluable resources and fellowship.

My deepest thanks to the talented Dimitrios Antonitsis, who gave me an unforgettable art lesson on the Greek island of Hydra. Any wisdom imparted by the fictional art teacher, Demetris, I learned from you. Also, thank you to Ron Neuman, who taught me sketching techniques. And a big thanks to my cousin Jeff Pearlman, who answered all my yachting questions.

This book would not be possible without the knowledge and generosity of Daniel Ischakis. From your tailored Jewish Heritage Tour in Athens to years' worth of answering my most minute historical questions, you helped me to tell the story of the Jews of Corfu with integrity and authenticity. And my sincerest thanks to Isaak Dostis for his moving documentaries about Greek and Corfiot Jewry, and for sharing invaluable insights. Thank you to the many other kind people who contributed to my understanding of Greek and Corfiot Jewry, including Angelo Raphael, Daisy Doron, Marcia Haddad Ikonomopolus, Irene Kokodis, and Nino Nachshon through his poignant YouTube testimonies.

Thank you to my friends, spread out across the globe. I cherish you all. Special thanks to Lauren Klitofsky and Jill Salama Handman, for reading early drafts and always believing in me. And thank you to Jim Doyle and Maxine Isaacs, who were both there from day one of this journey. I'm extraordinarily grateful for both of you and the important work you do.

I have the best family in the world. Period, end of story. Thank you to my uncle David Newman, my uncle Jeff Adler, and Renee Potvin, who have always nurtured my dreams, and special thanks to my aunt Nancy Newman Adler, who has read every book I have ever written going back to age seventeen, with unending encouragement. Thank you to my cousins who are also among my closest friends, Mitchell, Eden, and Jesse Adler, and Lexy and Tori Grant. You guys are the absolute best.

Thank you to my brother, Jason Goldis, for reading the first (not great) draft of this book, despite being plainly outside my target female demographic. Thank you for believing in me so much; I adore you. Thank you to my sister-in-law, Arica Goldis, and my brother-in-law, Nadav Goren, for their unwavering support and making me feel so celebrated in the publishing process. And thanks to my nephews, Liad Goren and Griffin Goldis, and my niece, Reagan Goldis, for smiles and cuteness that always make my day.

Thank you to my grandparents whom I never got to meet, Khana Vinarskaya and Shimon Goldis. You and your families faced extreme evil and adversity during World War II and the Holocaust, and your bravery has forever inspired me and my characters. And to my grandparents whom I had the great fortune to see nearly every day of my childhood, my Zadie, Larry Newman, and my Bubbie, Libby

Newman, thank you for your love that I have always felt in my every molecule. Being your grandchild has been one of the greatest blessings of my life.

Thank you to my dad, Alex Goldis, who has inspired and changed me by telling me his Soviet stories. Your support has been a constant, as you've made the transition from telling people about "my daughter, the lawyer" to "my daughter, the writer" with ease. Thank you to my mom, Cheryl Goldis, my earliest and biggest cheerleader. You have read about one thousand drafts of this book, yet always want to read the next. For the record, you are warm, selfless, and immensely loving—the exact opposite of Bea.

Thank you to my dear sister, Susan Goldis Goren, whose incisive critique of multiple drafts of this book made it immeasurably better. Everything good about this book has your fingerprints all over it. And of course, thank you for lending me your childhood secret language for Joey and Leo to use. Zed you so much, Flower!

Finally, as anti-Semitism surges across the world, it is more important than ever to say: Never Again. To the Jews of Corfu, I hope I have done even a small measure of justice to your story. You have forever impacted mine.

ABOUT THE AUTHOR

Jaclyn Goldis is a graduate of University of Michigan, Ann Arbor, and NYU Law. She practiced trust and estate law at a large Chicago law firm for seven years before leaving her job to travel the world and write novels. After culling her possessions into only what would fit into a backpack, she traveled for over a year until settling in Tel Aviv, where she can often be found writing from cafés near the beach. She loves to hear from readers. Please visit jaclyngoldis.com to learn more.